Piñata Belly

And Other Tales of Later Love

Piñata Belly
And Other Tales of Later Love

by

Joe Novara

Gypsy Shadow Publishing

Piñata Belly
And Other Tales of Later Love

by
Joe Novara

Gypsy Shadow Publishing, LLC.
Lockhart, TX
www.gypsyshadow.com

Library of Congress Control Number: 2021940762

Print Book ISBN: 978-1-61950-650-3

Published in the United States of America

First Print Edition: June 14, 2021

Contents

I'm Here

by

Joe Novara

Gypsy Shadow Publishing

I'm Here

by
Joe Novara

Gypsy Shadow Publishing, LLC.
Lockhart, TX
www.gypsyshadow.com

ISBN: 978-1-61950-337-3

Published in the United States of America

First eBook Edition: October 25, 2018

Acknowledgements

Thanks for all the help from my writing group: Cheryl Peck, Barb Vortman, Jim Taborn, Carol Lacey and Thom Jones. Also, the encouragement and support from Maris Soule, David Isaacson, Vi Murphy and my wife/editor Rosalie.

Chapter One; Tre

Sal's lip quivers as he chews his vegetable soup, like he might be ready to cry. He stabs at his mouth with his embossed napkin trying to staunch the overrun. "Purging," he mumbles at the risk of dribbling more soup. "My daughter and son-in-law want to throw out all my stuff. They kept telling me to purge. To basically dump my whole life on the curb."

Funny thing. We grew up in the same neighborhood. Lived across the street from each other for years and now we're stuck in the same retirement home in a maze of endless, carpeted corridors with varnished handrails leading to elevator coves and the occasional outside door. As if we could get very far even if we left. It's a prison basically. And they call it Shelden Ponds.

Turns out, Sal got sentenced because he took too much time trying to decide what to keep and what to throw out. So, by now they probably got a dumpster on the front lawn and are shoveling out his place, so they can sell it and pay for him to live in his cream-colored apartment. I feel sorry for the poor bastard.

Now, me, I ended up in here when my hip got shattered in a car accident. When they got ready to release me from the hospital I couldn't just go back home where my bed and bathroom are upstairs, not to mention the titanium plates, rehab and a lingering infection.

So, my daughters, Carrie and Lisa, decided to ease their consciences by getting me into this place where I could navigate with an electric cart like some old lady in the supermarket. They don't realize I still got game. And as soon as I get on my pins again, I'm outta here.

I mean, look past Sal, poking at his broccoli casserole... by the way, did you ever notice that these senior places all smell like overcooked broccoli? Where was I? Oh yeah. Look

1

past Sal and you think of Lake Michigan with white caps. There's a sea of white hair bobbing up and down all around me. I'm drowning in senility here. I'm not as old or as frail as these folks. I'm not in the target demographic for this place. They can't sentence a juvenile to life. I'm only seventy-three, for crying out loud, surrounded by eighty-five-year-olds... mostly.

That lady at 2:00-high appears a little more my age. Now she's eyeing me. *You go ahead, sweetheart. Don't let me stop you from staring. Do we know each other?* She looks familiar. But then, if you've lived in this town for thirty years and taught at the university, a lot of people can look familiar.

She's not turning away. In fact, she's giving me a little smile. Damn. And now the woman next to her is following her gaze, checking me out. They whisper and giggle. Are we back in third grade lunchroom? Or maybe a better analogy—are the alpha mares scoping the new stud in the pasture? Dream on, doofus. The hallways aren't wide enough to drive our carts side-by-side as we ride into the sunset. But that's going to change. For me. Just wait.

"Sal, who're those women in the table off your left shoulder?" He puts down his spoon and napkin, straightens his shoulders, hands bracing the table for a creaky turn. "No, don't look," I say.

He sighs, lifts his chin in the general direction. "Them?"

"Yeah."

"The 'Yah-yahs, that's what we call them."

"We? There's only like ten guys and two hundred women here."

"And the five of us who aren't married stick together. You make six."

Why doesn't that excite me? One more newbie and we could be the Magnificent Seven. Until I get out of Dodge.

"Why Yah-yahs?" I ask.

"How do I know? That's who they are. They're always together, on all the committees. Decorations. Flower shows. All that..."

The woman with the dark eyes and eyebrows under a well-coiffed pewter helmet... I've come to fancy that look, lately... offers me a head bob. Why do I feel like I'm about to be vetted by the League of Women Voters?

2

"Yeah, they'll be scoping you out. Fresh meat. Ha!" he barks, color rising in his cheeks along with an incipient grin. "Reminds of the story of the new guy in the Catskills hotel... you heard this one?"

"I don't know yet... go on."

"This guy shows up at a hotel in the Catskills. A blue hair lady slides up next to him. 'So, you're new here,' she goes. 'Where're you from?' He goes, 'Prison. Just got out.' The lady says, 'What were you in for?' The guy says, 'Murdered my wife.' The lady goes, 'So, you're single.'"

Sal laughs and laughs. Then he starts to cough. About the time I decide I should hand him my water, 'pewter lady' is standing next to me. No cane. No walker. Nice legs.

"Sal must have sprung one of his groaners on you. Don't encourage him. It's bad for his COPD."

"I see," is all I can think to say.

"You're new here. Welcome to The Ponds. I'm Marjorie. Marjorie Olson, with the welcoming committee."

"Nice to meet you, Marjorie," I reply from my seat in the electric cart. I feel like I'm at the dentist as I look past her imposing bowsprit and up into her nostrils. Wait. They don't do that anymore. Dentists all wear masks and rubber gloves. Well, what my dentist used to look like twenty years ago.

She's waiting. Oh, my turn. I reach my hand out. "Mike Trahan."

Recovering from his joke, Sal adds, "Just call him Tre. That's what we called him growing up."

"Trahan. Might you be the Professor Trahan I had for creative writing at Western?"

"Ah," I said. "That's why you looked familiar to me. Could've been. Could've been," I respond, scrolling my memory bank, trying to morph the woman above me into a younger, dark haired coed.

"I was Marjorie Rawlings back then. You teased me about writing *The Yearling.*"

"Ah! Marjorie Kinnan Rawling. The author." I still couldn't place her. Embarrassing isn't it, the way a professional can make contact at one point in his life and it means so much to the client, student, patient... whatever. But eventually they're just so many raindrops shrinking in a murky puddle.

"That got me reading all her works. I even visited her home in Gainesville."

I nod.

"And I've been writing ever since. Hobby writing, lately. But still. You got me started." She flashes a 'thank you' smile.

Oh man, here it comes—the request to 'look over' her stuff. 'See if it's any good.' A lose-lose proposition. If she really is good, you're feeling jealous or at least one-down. If she isn't good, you're telling a little girl her party dress is ugly.

I hold my breath.

"For years, I did freelance technical writing. It was convenient since I could work from home. Lately, I've decided to try my hand at fiction." She beams like this should please me. "I wonder if you would take a look at a piece or two."

I paste a smile.

"Don't worry. I'm not going to hand in an assignment to my old teacher."

"I'm not that old."

"No, you're not, actually."

"Nor are you," I say, waving a hand to include the entire dining area. "We're like grandkids at a 50th wedding anniversary."

I love her deep-throated laugh.

After a pause, she adds, "I'll tell you my reason for staying here if you tell me yours."

"I'll tell you my reason," Sal chimes in. "My kids want to sell my place and I wouldn't let them throw out my stuff. So, they stuck me here."

Marjorie and I exchange a glance. I say, "I'd like to hear your reasons as long as it doesn't involve an organ recital about every ache and pain we have."

Again, the infectious laugh.

"No. But about my stories... I just want to give you an idea of the level of writing in our critique group. And, who knows, you might want to join us."

I didn't see that coming. I nod my head agreeably.

"So, what's your room number, Dr. Trahan..."

"Tre," I interrupt. Reminds me of my kids when they met their grade school teachers at the country club as adults. Still couldn't call them by their first name. Did it seem impolite? Too familiar? Early imprinting gone amuck?

"Tre," Marjorie says, hunching her shoulders self-consciously.

"302. But, everything's still jumbled. Just moved in and all."

"I understand." Glancing at my conveyance, she adds, "I could give you a hand if you want?"

I close my eyes—this is no Pygmalion moment, the sweet young coed at the feet of her Svengali, purring, 'I'm yours. Mold me into a better me.' I flash back to the early days—pre-sexual harassment and political correctness. Hormones flying faster than misplaced modifiers and split infinitives behind closed office doors. Sure wasn't the same by the time I retired... open doors at all times, both feet on the floor. This is different. This is a mature woman, and she's challenging me— 'show me your stuff and let's see how good you actually are and, by the way, how far I've come over the years since you bled red ink all over my stories.' Okay, lady. You're on. "How about tomorrow after lunch? Make it 2:00." I decide not to add... after my nap. Well, morning PT sessions wring me out something fierce.

"Look forward to it," she says, hand on my shoulder.

I watch Sal watching her walk away. "She never came on to me like that. Maybe I shoulda been a perfessor instead of running a dry cleaner." Then I watch, too. I guess us guys are wired that way. I'm not interested. Not really. I mean, she's attractive and all, but these days I'm like a dog that sees a car going by and has to chase it even if he's not sure what he would do with it if he caught it.

Still, it's fun to watch. You can tell a lot about a person by the way they walk. *C'mon Tre, don't start about 'a person... they.'* Sometimes, I have to sit on the writing instructor in me and ignore number agreement issues. Where was I? It's about their feet—high arched; flat; long and slender; stubby and rounded. And then there's the gait—straight heel to toe, slow schmoozy slide around the side of the foot to the front or sometimes plop and pound. And some folks practically prance like a horse doing dressage. Marjorie's strut says, 'I'm all business and have places to be' as her two-inch pumps tack-tack-tack along the tile cafeteria floor. Nice.

Over lunch the next day, I have to look away as Sal asks around an open mouth of mac and cheese, "Have you heard about some guy who keeps calling the ladies here and breathing heavy on the phone?"

"These ladies?" I ask, scowling around the room. "That's sick."

"Yeah, that's what I think. The old birds are getting all worked up. I hope they catch the bum."

I glance up to catch Marjorie looking my way. She nods. Inviting smile. Holds up two fingers.

That's right, I have to get my nap in before my scheduled 'office hour' with a keen student.

Marjorie wakes me from a deep sleep. "Just a second," I call as I gimp to the bathroom to comb out my pillow-head. With my shaggy mane in place, I'm told I look like Michelangelo's God reaching a finger to Adam. Otherwise, like now, I look like a Sesame Street puppet. Never hurts to appear god-like. So, I groom.

She wears black slacks and a silver-gray sweater—a riff on her eyes and hair. I hobble over to my recliner and point to the couch. She looks at the two boxes on the kitchen counter. "Can I help you unpack?" she asks.

"Oh, no. I can do it later. It's not much." I realize I should be offering something. "Get you something? Soda water? Tea?"

"No," she demurs. "I'm fine." She sets her loose-leaf binder on the sofa seat.

We look at each other for five or six seconds, then both chuckle at once. "You first," I begin.

Marjorie opens her binder and hands me a picture of a dark-haired woman with three school aged children posed around her. "This was taken about the time I went back to school... when you would have taught me."

I look at the picture, then her. I wait in vain for my long-term hard drive to boot up. Nada. "Returning students. It was always good to have one or two in a class." I notice well-worn pleats tighten around her eyes. She knew I didn't recall her. Sorry.

She shifts focus out my window for a long moment. "It's a familiar story." The look she gives me when she reconnects says, you know the scene.

I nod—no husband in the picture, kids in school, delayed career scramble.

"You took me seriously," she says, so simply and directly that I felt something stir in me that I hadn't felt in a long time.

"Well, I'm glad I did," I reply. I stop myself, just in time, from adding, but then I took all my students seriously.

"Your class got me writing," Marjorie announces brightly. "I didn't know I had it in me."

"That was the plan... right? Unleash the creative beast."

"For technical writing?"

"Writing is writing, I suppose."

"It paid the bills," she counters.

"And your children?"

"They're spread across the country. One in Seattle. Another in Atlanta." She pauses to shake her full-bodied hair, finger comb one strand over her right ear. Reminds me of a bird fluffing out its feathers before allowing them to settle back into a molded, sleek outline. "But what about you?" She rolls her hand. "Backstory. Data dump."

"You know, this reminds me of going on a first date where I've often thought folks could save a lot of time by just trading resumes."

"Throw-back technology," she huffs. "That's all done online these days with dating services."

"I suppose," I reply, sweeping an arm to include our whole complex. "Folks in this place would need eight-page resumes—one for each decade."

Another pause. She raises her eyebrows and cants her head. My serve. "Last I heard, Gail, my ex, was living in her family home with her mother and one of our daughters, Carrie. Lisa lives in Denver. I got the house, but it's not handicap friendly," I say patting my sore hip. "So, that's why I'm here. What's your story?"

"I'm glad you asked." Marjorie says, reaching for her binder. "It's about a couple trying to decide..."

"Uhmm," I interrupt, eyes squeezing shut. "That's not what I..." I open to see a corner of her mouth curled. Better and better. A woman with a sense of humor.

"Oh, you meant my life story and how I ended up here?" She clasps her hands on her lap. Short, compact fingers, I notice. Good for sewing and gardening and fluting the crust on cherry pies, Billy Boy, Billy Boy. "I... we... lived on a farm outside Gobles." She raised her shoulders. "It's not a one-person operation, even if you like it. Which I never did. And it's lonely and a long drive into town for concerts and plays and movies and interesting food. Oh, and I hate to cook."

I wait. Her sidelong look says there is more to come. I give her my best dissertation advisor look—go on my child.

She faces me. "Once Harold and the children left, I realized that I had missed something."

I raise inquiring eyebrows.

"Dorm life. This place offers the kind of..."

As she fights for an analogy, I offer, "Beehive activity? Chicken-coop togetherness?"

She levels a parental scowl at me before continuing, "...communal living experience I never had as a returning student."

"Well, I will be glad to look over your writing." I smile, condescendingly, I suddenly realize.

"Our group, the Pen Dragons, meets Wednesdays at 3:00 in the Hamilton Room if you care to join us."

I nod noncommittally.

That evening, I read her two stories. Good, tight prose. She's not a beginner. And if the others in her group are that polished, I wouldn't mind sitting in on their weekly sessions. Keep a hand in the game. Offer some creative advice. If nothing else it would be like joining a serial book club, sharing the next chapter from each story every week.

As I motor up to the door of the Hamilton Room, I hear women discussing annoying phone calls. "He just breathes heavily. Sounds like he has asthma or something."

"I think it's an inside job. Who else would know all our numbers?"

"Well, what can we do about it?"

"I know," one woman giggled. "I would breathe real heavy too."

"Like this lady I heard who flashed a flasher right back. Fixed him."

"I know what I'm going to do if he calls me again," one determined voice announces. BRAAP!

I almost fall out of my electric cart. The group of six women are all laughing when I hobble to the door. One of them, the one who always sits with Marjorie at dinner, holds a portable fog horn. There's a stunned silence for a moment. I feel like a grade school teacher walking in on classroom hi-jinx.

"Dr. Trahan has come to sit in on our group," Marjorie announces. I survey the half-circle and feel like the first day of the semester but with no syllabus to pass or podium to pound. Roll is called for my benefit. Tall, regal Julie tilts her head imperially. Hildy's expressionless sniper eyes zero in between my own. Dolores, hunched in her wheelchair, glows with the keen, open look of a coed eager to learn and impress.

"Dr. Trahan has taught creative writing at Western and has published two books and many articles," Marjorie explains. "He would like to sit-in on our group."

There's a nervous pause as the residents shuffle papers and shift in their seats. "I'm not going to grade you," I try to reassure them. "I just want to share writing. Like 'show and tell' I suppose."

"You first," Hildy says.

I get it. Playground pick-up rules—newbie has to show his stuff, establish his slot in the batting order. "Sure," I say. "Why not." I page through my manuscript of short stories for a suitable sample.

I find the one I'm looking for and grin. "This story is a little graphic, but we've all been around the block a couple times, right? In this segment, an ex-pat..."

"That means an American who lives in another country," Dolores says.

I nod. "This ex-pat runs a posada..."

"That's like a hotel in Latin America," she adds. To my patient smile she adds, "I was a reference librarian."

"Right. So, here's the story.

"Once, some years back, we heard pounding on our front gate late at night, maybe even early morning. It was a neighbor who was helping a midwife with a delivery. Seems the baby was born fine, but the woman was having a problem expelling the placenta. They wanted my wife and me to drive for a doctor. Well, we hurried over a couple of blocks

9

to the house where the midwife was nervously pacing. She ran out to my wife and began making the case for us to get the doctor. I edged toward the front door. The father was hunched over shaking his head. Looking into the room, I could see the mother trying to get her newborn to suck at her breast. Wasn't happening. Something flashed in the back of my mind about postnatal nursing triggering chemicals to make the placenta detach. In two quick strides, I was kneeling next to the woman. I popped her nipple in my mouth and gave five or six strong sucks. The woman's eyes widened in surprise, then she groaned. I quickly stood in a dark corner. The midwife rushed back in, removed the placenta and began massaging the mother's abdomen to stop the bleeding. Problem solved. In middle of all of that, I caught the new mother's eye, winked and held a finger across my lips. She nodded.

Back at the Posada...

"Disgusting," Hildy snarls.

"Oh, I don't think so," Dolores says. "My Sara had a difficult delivery and had to have..."

"We've all got birthing stories," Julie snapped, "but we don't need to write about them... so intimately."

"But, labor and delivery and breast feeding are all so natural and dramatic and important," Dolores explained.

"So is regularity, for crying out loud. But I don't want to read about it."

"Not unless you're a proctologist." Marjorie throws in.

I have to chuckle along with the rest. And after a few more samples of the group's writing I could almost imagine I was in a graduate seminar minus the artistic pretentions. They were actually pretty good.

An hour later, on the way back to my room, Marjorie remarks, "That's the most animated that group has been since I started it. You really got them going."

"Sometimes it's fun to throw a pebble into a pond and watch the ripples spread."

She burns a lowered-brow look at me. I decide to call it admiration and interest. Might just as well.

"So, are you coming back?" she asks.

"Yeah, sure. They're a fun group."

She stops at the corner where we part, clutches her binder to her chest.

"You know, you sound like a tourist enjoying the quaint natives."

"Well this is a nice place to visit. But I wouldn't want to live here... forever."

"Ah, I see."

Is that disappointment I pick up before she turns and sashays down the corridor?

Hunched in the dark between two puddles of patio lights, I make out Sal on his cell phone. I'll chat with him in a minute. For now, it feels good to breathe cool evening air with a hint of lilac from somewhere out of sight. Alone for a minute. Surrounded by so many people all day—waving, smiling. I feel like an airline stewardess saying, 'Bye! Bye-Bye' to a hundred deplaning passengers. Not Marjorie though, she seems to know everyone's name; enjoys taking a moment to chat with each. They ought to pay her to be social director of the place.

BRAAP!

Sal drops his phone. "Damn," he hisses, holding his ear. I scoot over and stare at him.

"Busted," he says. "Don't look at me like that. I got a plan and as long as you're on to it, here's how you're gonna help me."

I just glare.

"No, here's what I need you to do—turn me in."

"Huh?"

"Yeah, see. For all these phone calls, they'll kick me out. But since I been here less than six months, I get my 'buy in' money back and I can go back home before Angeline sells the place. So, blow the whistle on me, buddy. Okay?"

The next day, after my nap, Sal shows up at my door. "Hey. It's cool," he says under a self-satisfied smile. "Just like I planned. I'm outta here. Thanks for your help."

I didn't rat on him. Someone else must have fingered him. But, I feel no compulsion to correct his impression.

"Okay," Sal continues, "I just need to get home. You got your car here, right?"

"Well, yeah, but I can't..."

11

"I know. I know. I'll drive."

"And then... how do I get back?"

Sal thinks for a moment. "Bernice, your next-door neighbor. I get my van running. She drives you in your car. Me and her come back in the van." He cocks his head—it's a plan, right?

"Bernice. Haven't thought about her in a while."

"She's all right," Sal says as he lowers his eyes, hooded and knowing. "Me and her... we always had this... thing... for each other."

"Too bad about her Carmine."

"Yeah. Poor bastard. Went down hard. But at least it was fast," Sal adds with a commiserating frown.

I nod. "We got in a fight in sixth grade, and Sister Stella made us both stare at a picture of Jesus with a crown of thorns on his head for half an hour."

"Yeah, that was him. Always had scabs on his knuckles." Sal gets this faraway look and smarmy smile. "But he musta got religion or somethin' because Bernice and him had this hippie wedding next to a lake. They came out of a white tent and she's wearing a circle of flowers in her hair. Wow. And we all jumped into the lake after." He shakes his head as if to get back to the present. "We'll get my van running. C'mon. It'll be fun. Get you outta this joint for a couple hours."

Chapter Two; Sal

I stare at the Real Estate sign on my lawn, thump the steering wheel. "She said they were 'thinking about' putting it on the market."

Tre eases out of the car and unfolds his walker. Me, I go to the front door and rattle the realtor lock box. "No problem," I shout. "I can get us in from the garage."

By the time Tre finally makes it into the house, I'm turning in a slow circle in the middle of the front room, my face as blank as the walls. The house is naked. "They erased my life," I groan. My face sags and I feel ten years older.

"Your van's still here," Tre says, like that's going to cheer me up.

"Yeah," I finally answer, dragging my finger along the kitchen counter, the pink Formica worn through to the brown underneath.

"Sally! How you doin', hon?" The fireplug of a woman at the back doorway has silver-white hair winched into such a tight ponytail that it looks like a do-it-yourself facelift that starts her lips into an easy smile. A plaid blouse, sleeves hacked off, drapes over cutoff shorts that stop just above her dirty knees. Slapping her clothes, she says, "Been out in the garden... as usual."

"Bernice," I cry, holding out my arms for a long hug. I sob. "My house..."

"Yeah, hon. There. There." Bernice, patting my back, says to Tre. "They really cleaned out his place. First a garage sale. Then a Goodwill truck and finally a dumpster."

"A dumpster?" I go. "They threw all my good stuff in a dumpster?"

"Yeah. It was the big open kind, long as your driveway."

I slam my open hand on the counter.

13

"But, don't worry, I got your bowling trophy."

That makes me smile.

"C'mon over. You both look like you could stand a nice cup of coffee. How're you doing, Tre?"

Now I'm in Bernice's cluttered front room that has the slightly stale, dusty smell of second-hand stores. Makes my eyes itch. I walk to the fireplace where my trophy sits on the mantel between a Hummel figurine and a picture of four presumably stair-stepped grandchildren all saying 'cheese.' Then I look in the mirror. I try to see what Bernice sees. A nice shock of gray hair, thinning, but not bad with my tan face. I do a toothbrush grin. Nice teeth. All mine. Still got a little heft on my bones. Standing tall. Moving good. If I had a gold chain with a cornicchio to hang in a hairy chest, I could pass as a silver-fox lounge-lizard. But my chest is bald. So, instead, I just look like somebody's Italian grampa.

"Don't act like strangers," Bernice calls. "Come in the kitchen, you guys."

We sit at her table and as she turns from the sink with a dish of cookies, I say, "Hold it. Just now, I see the bride you were on your wedding day." She blushes. Looks down. I wink at Tre—never hurts to throw a compliment at a lady.

She plops the cookies down on the table and just the way she says, "Sally, you always were fulla shit," I can tell she liked what I just said.

We're scarfing down her cookies, and she says, "Too bad about your house. But, good thing you're in the retirement place, right?"

Tre. He goes, "Uhmm. Actually..."

Her eyes smile, then her mouth. Then she barks, "Ha! I knew you wouldn't stay there. What? They kicked you out?"

"Something like that."

I can see her wheels turning. "So...? We need to get Tre back with his car... then what?"

I lift my hands—don't know, yet. "You got some blankets and a pillow? I'll sleep in my den. I guess."

Bernice gives me this look. "Don't be silly. We'll come back here. I'll feed you supper. You can spend the night in a bed. I got three bedrooms, for crying out loud."

"Really," I say. "That would be nice."

"Hey," she says, shrugging one shoulder, like no big deal, "I could stand the company." Then she swirls the last sip in her coffee cup and says in a softer voice, "You can stay as long as you need..."

I watch her suck in her lips and widen her eyes like a little girl who has said something she shouldn't. I grin like Christmas.

Chapter Three; Marjorie

A couple nights later, Marjorie joined Tre at supper. "So, your buddy is gone with a dishonorable discharge," she said, twirling spaghetti on her fork.

"Yeah, I guess this place was just not right for him."

She peeked up through lowered brows. "How about you?"

"For me? This is just a temporary deal. Soon as I'm cleared for action, I'm out of here."

"Back to your home... it is a home, not an apartment, right?"

"Yeah, back of Westside Mall." Tre paused, thinking. "Now that we're talking about it, I really should stop by and make sure nothing's drastically wrong. Driving is my only problem."

"Behind Westside? I have a hair appointment there, tomorrow at 4:00. After writing group, I could drop you off and pick you up."

"Would you?"

"Well, sure," she replied, reaching over to his plate for a piece of broccoli he apparently wasn't going to eat. "No big deal."

Tre tapped the heel of his hand to his forehead. "Writing group. I forgot all about it."

"You will be coming, won't you?" Marjorie asked while he averted his eyes, thinking.

"Just trying to decide what to bring," Tre said. "Oh, I know, there's a nice, tight piece of flash fiction I could share."

"It doesn't have to be completed material," Marjorie reminded. "We're not a book club. All of us are working on new stuff every week."

"Uh-huh," Tre replied. "Well, I'm not inclined at this point in my life to begin another writing project. I'm content to rifle my archives until I leave."

Marjorie frowned, offering a flattering view of her high-cheeked profile.

The next day at Pen Dragons, as Tre read his story of an Italian-American girl and her look-alike cousin visiting from Italy, he conveyed a certain relish in the quality of his prose, the rhythm and flow. Finished, he sat back with the condescension of a singer waiting for applause.

Hildy kicked off the critique. "You know, the writing is fine, but both the girls end up being unsympathetic. I don't care what happens to either of them."

"That's a little strong, Hildy," Julie said. "I guess I like the immigrant girl better than the American cousin."

"Well, yeah, I feel sorry for her, but I still think she stabs her cousin in the back during the marathon."

"But she stole her boyfriend."

"See," Dolores began, apparently feeling the need to explain to Tre, "they both are kind of sneaky and snarky and you don't know who to cheer for at the end."

"But not all stories have to have a good guy win," he snapped.

"Of course not," Julie agreed. "All a good story needs is movement from one point to another, and it can be a minor shift."

Next, Marjorie piled on, "Exactly. And these two girls move from barely likable to unlikable."

"And then there's the Point of View shift in two places," Hildy added.

"Yeah, I caught a shift tense in there," Dolores said. "If you give me a copy, I'll find it for you."

Tre, unused to being gang-tackled over his writing, rocked back in his chair. The others, reacting to his shocked expression, took turns scrambling for positive things to say.

"But for all that, I really like the texture and details of the girls' lives while in Italy."

"The States too."

"And the father is such a well-rounded character."

"Not like the Italian boyfriend."

"No. He's a real momma's boy."

17

Hildy concluded the stroking session with, "And your dialogue is very good."

Tre muttered, "Well thanks for throwing me a bone after hitting me with the newspaper."

In the car with Marjorie that afternoon, Tre stared out the window for the first few minutes. At a light, he huffed, then crabbed, "Those ladies sure think they know a lot about writing."

Marjorie cut him a quick glance. "Well they should. They're all professional writers of one kind or another."

"How so?"

"Julie edited a medical journal for eighteen years and also wrote speeches for a state representative. Hildy did technical writing for a pharmaceutical company and was contributing editor for a garden magazine. Dolores has written and illustrated four children's books and was a past president of the local chapter of the Society of Children Book Writers and Illustrators."

Marjorie let Tre stew in his silent pique, while fighting to keep the corners of her mouth from breaking into a smirk. "But, you ought to know," she said, "these ladies really like you and find you challenging."

"Be still my heart," he grumbled.

Marjorie snorted. He grinned.

Chapter Four; Tre

We pull in my drive and take in the overgrown lawn leading to cement stairs, shaded porch and a two-story brick front. Not fancy. Funny how when you've been away for a while you see the familiar with new eyes. And as I slowly ease my way out of the car I find myself counting the front steps.

"Are you sure you can handle this?" Marjorie asks.

I straighten my shoulders. "Sure. It's fine. See you in an hour or so."

Inside, nothing's changed, but seems different. It's like putting down a manuscript for a couple of weeks then picking it up again. Fresh eyes. There's some dust around the edges. The air is a little stale, shut up. My easy chair is frayed and ripping on the seams. I open the fridge. Empty. I check the back door. The knob is loose. I head to the basement for a screwdriver. The steps suddenly look like the Grand Canyon to me. I take a deep breath, grab the railing and slowly make my way down. I have to sit on my workbench stool to let the throbbing in my hip subside.

Screwdriver in hand, I face the cliff of stairs. Three steps up, I have to turn and sit. I guess I sit there longer than I realize when I hear Marjorie call, "Tre. Where are you?"

She soon is facing me. "You look terrible."

"I'd like a second opinion," I reply.

She gives me her quirky grin and reaches her arms to help, "Well, you can't stay here."

"I was just thinking that."

She steps back, trying to read me. "You mean you can't stay here... here?" she says pointing to the steps. "Or," spreading her arms to include the whole house, "here?"

"Both."

"Yeah, well," she says as she pulls me to my feet. "Let's get you upstairs first."

Slumped in my easy chair, I can hear her opening and closing drawers and cabinets in the kitchen. "I found coffee, or do you prefer tea?" she called.

"Just water would be fine."

Marjorie hands me the water and perches on the edge of the sagging sofa. "Is your bathroom upstairs?" she asks. I watch her scale the steps as I would have done without a thought, a month ago. Now I have to go, too. *Not up all those stairs,* I think. I hobble to the back door and pee off the porch. Damn, this place is an obstacle course.

I hear Marjorie coming back down and quickly busy myself with the door knob. Damn, I brought a standard screwdriver. Needed a Phillip's head. When I turn she is leaning against the kitchen sink giving me a thoughtful— and am I kidding myself—compassionate look.

We are locked in our own thoughts all the way back to The Ponds. I like that in a person—comfortable with quiet. Back in my room, while my pain meds kick in, Marjorie makes herself at home on the couch. "It's easier here," she begins. "What a dreadful experience to suddenly find your comfortable home a dangerous pain-trap. So sad. So powerful."

I don't need her pity. Don't want it. Before I can gather my thoughts, she eagerly leans forward, forearms on her knees. "You know, that would make a good story. Or at least a good scene in a story."

So, now she's making me feel like a victim on the 6:00 News being interviewed by the frenetic reporter. My life as story.

I want to shout Art is not photography. It's a step or two back from reality. But she is so sincere, I hold my tongue. After all, we writers are constantly sifting our own and other's lives for scenes and descriptions and crises. What did that T-shirt say? DON'T TELL ME ANYTHING YOU DON'T WANT TO SEE IN MY NOVEL.

I study her eager face. What does she want from me? This feels like my ophthalmologist talking to a hidden dictation machine while he's still examining me. Am I like that— an object of interest to her?

Licking her lips, she continues, "And since it appears you need to be here a while longer, perhaps we could co-write the story."

I'm torn between shouting her out of my room and wishing she would stick around for a long time. "I write very slowly," I finally manage to say.

Marjorie's smile says, 'I've got a lot of time.'

After she leaves, between the meds and the taxing afternoon, I slide into that waking-up-in-the-morning dozy zone when some of my best ideas come together. As often as not, I end up jumping out of bed and onto my keyboard before my half-dreams float away. In this case, however, my stream of conscious rambling is decidedly not leading to a story. And I'm not booting-up my computer. Co-writing indeed. I mean. And with her? I'm not some bloviated politician who needs a speechwriter. Writing is solitary. There's no room in the kitchen for more than one chef. And she wants to use me as the central character. All right, to be fair, she's a good enough writer not to simply replay that scene in my home. She would set it in another time and place, with another person. But good readers always wonder how much of the author is exposed in a tale. That's the alchemy of writing, after all—mining our experiences for a nugget of lead to be turned into a golden story arc. Eww, that's a good line. I think I used it in a lecture once... where was that? And even if I'm a co-writer, people will wonder if that was really me... and now I'm blurring out.

A week later, Sal sits across from me at Panera's. As usual, I catch a disgusting glimpse of his tuna on rye when he opens his mouth to kvetch. "She's got these statues and holy cards and rosaries in a corner of the bedroom. Like a shrine or something."

"So, you're in her bedroom?" I tease.

"You're surprised? We've known each other a long while. Hey, at our age, there's no point in wasting time. Know what I mean?"

"Next thing you know, you're going to say she eats crackers in bed. C'mon Sal."

He's shaking his head. Sucks on his iced tea. God, his face looks like an old hunting boot. I'm sure I look younger than him. I hope. "Naw," he says, "it just feels like I'm back in Catholic school and all the nuns and mortal sins..."

"Sal," I say, "I'm just not there anymore... all that religious stuff. You know?"

"Exactly. Neither am I. But I can feel it coming. She'll have me saying rosaries, making novenas, going to Sunday Mass. Aargh!"

"Hey, Sally, tomato seeds come with the tomato."

"That's Woody Allen, man. Bada-boom. But so, how're you doin' with your...?"

"Marjorie is fine, thanks for asking." I take a bite of my turkey on rye and give Sal some of his own medicine by talking around it. "She wants us to co-write a story."

Sal gives me the eye. He always could read me. "And you don't do duets," he says, nodding to himself. Then he barks a laugh and gets into one of his coughing fits. It takes some water and three napkins before he settles back down and then half-wheezes and half-chuckles, "You're like that John Travolta line in Saturday Night Fever, 'Just because I let her sleep with me, she thinks I'll let her dance with me.'"

I have to grin. He nailed me. Just because I taught her to write. Doesn't mean she can write with me. "Well, here's the deal with Marjorie, and for that matter, most of the folks in that place, she's in the 'here and now' and not dragging me all the way back to the good old days all the time."

"So, that makes me, what, a drag?"

"Well, sometimes it's easier to have a cut-off, you know? People at The Ponds only want to know... maybe the last five years. They say, 'How're you doing today?' Never mind fifty years ago and who your uncle's brother was, back in the day. It's all about making friends here and now."

"Us being friends in the old neighborhood doesn't matter to you?"

"Of course it does. But put it in perspective, Sal. We ran around together, how long? Fourth grade to eighth grade? Five years? Hell, you and I have lived those five years almost fifteen times over."

He circled his glass in a puddle of condensation. "You're sayin' just because we knew each other as kids doesn't count that much. Like maybe we met on a bus tour to Yellowstone Park a long time ago and now we're just a name to each other."

"That's an apt metaphor."

His face clouds. "Don't give me that perfessor shit, Tre. I knew you when nobody would pick you for their baseball team, and I did."

"Look. I'm not trying to discount our relationship from an impressionable time in our lives..."

"Impressionable time," Sal mocks.

I continue. "Here, think of this. You're a guy just back from a hitch in the Marines..."

"Army, man."

"Just imagine, okay? You walk in the door in your uniform, all buff and looking tough. You're a man now. And right in the middle of all that, your older brother shouts, 'Hey, fuzznuts, how's it going?'"

"What brother? I got no brothers."

"I'm just saying... or trying to say... sometimes it's hard to go back home."

Sal stares at me for a long time. He's working on something. "Don't kid yourself, Tre. I ain't just pissin' and moanin' about Bernice, here. I'm letting you know that unless you're looking for more than a friggin' shuffle board partner for more than an hour, you're gonna deal with what got 'em to where they are. Maybe not right away. But who we been is part of who we are. And don't you forget it."

I pick up the tab, which allows me the last word. "You could always tell her you converted to Unitarian."

Wednesday at Pen Dragons, Marjorie reads this piece.

Jose pulled into his driveway, cut the engine, put both hands on the steering wheel and stared at his condo. He hadn't counted the steps to the door before. But now he does. Twelve. How come he never noticed earlier? And inside, more steps to the bedroom and more yet to the rooftop deck. Thinking of all that climbing made his ankle throb inside the rigid walking boot. He closed his eyes, playing back the hit to shortstop and his furious pounding up the baseline to first base. He wanted to beat the throw, to be safe and not be the third out, and allow his teammate to score. The first baseman had to jump to catch the ball that was too high. When he came down his foot was on the base. Jose stepped on it. High ankle sprain, they said. He wouldn't be able to play for four weeks, minimum.

He leaned his head on the steering wheel, letting a wave of self-pity wash over him. All that hope and promise, leaving Puerto Rico at seventeen. Two years in the minor leagues and he finally made it up to the big leagues. They let him start in right field. For three games, he was hitting so well.

And now that he had his own place, his fiancée, Camila, was coming from home and moving in with him. And his parents were going to watch him play. And all his friends back home. And he could barely gimp around with a crutch.

He finally eased out of the car. Grabbed a cane and half-hopped to the front steps. I wonder if old people feel like this? A few steps look like climbing Machu Pichu.

"That's as far as I got," Marjorie says.

"Oh, I like it," Julie says. "How do you know so much about baseball?"

"And you've got the girlfriend to bring into the story. Nice start."

"I can relate to the handicap issues," Dolores adds. "But I wonder if it isn't just a little too abrupt. That's an unlikely leap of empathy from a twenty-year old. Maybe if someone in his family had challenges..."

"Good catch. Let me think about that," Marjorie replies.

Now four pairs of eyes bore down on me as if to say, 'Your turn professor. What do you have to say?'

I tap my pen for a moment. "It's a good start. But I can see room for improvement."

"Like what?" Hildy demands.

I hesitate. Marjorie jumps in. "We've been at it for an hour and a half. I could use a bathroom break." As she slides her manuscript toward me, she says, "While we're gone, perhaps you could show us how you think it could be better."

What can I say? It's time to put your writing where your mouth is, Tre.

I'm in my driveway. Cut the engine. I look at my condo like I've never seen it before. All the steps to the porch. Three floors of steps inside. And my ankle hurts like hell. I

24

bang the steering wheel. Damn. All those years playing ball. People pounding me on the back when I get drafted. 'Jose, do us proud, bue. Be another Roberto Clemente and Willie Hernandez.' And then two years in the minors—instructional league, double A, triple A. Now the show. Starter in right field and I'm swinging the bat real good. Four for nine in three games. I pay for Camila to come see me play, stay at my condo. I made it to the bigs, man.

So, here's me at bat. Bottom of the ninth. Two outs... I get a hit... the man on third scores... walk-off win.

I swing. Top a slow-roller to the right side. The first baseman dives. Comes up throwing from his knees. The pitcher is slow. Gets to the bag just ahead of me. I do like you're supposed to... step on the front edge of the base. The peg is wide, the pitcher lunges. I get his foot instead of the bag. I'm down. High ankle sprain. Four weeks on DL. Damn. And now I'm like some abuela that can't climb stairs. Damn.

The women troop back in. There's an expectant pause after they settle in as my acceptance committee waits to hear my dissertation. When I finish reading, Dolores is nodding approval. Hildy cants her head in a kind of acceptance. Julie raises an eyebrow. Marjorie looks off with a Mona Lisa smile. Ha! She's got me co-writing her story.

"I like the first person, present," Julie says. "It sounds so sportscaster."

I'm impressed that she caught that.

"Yes," Hildy follows, "And now we get to hear what the girlfriend has to say about all this."

So, now we're writing by committee as well.

I'm back in my house. Marjorie is at the stylist. God, it's quiet. I used to look forward to the silence when the girls were gone. In fact, when they went to gramma's for a week, the empty house was an aphrodisiac. Gail wasn't necessarily onboard. But I could feel it, the throb of silence, no one to see us, to disturb us. That's all long gone now.

I look around. The place is a handicap test track. Stairs everywhere. High shelves. Low cupboards. Deep soft sofas. The state could qualify people for disability by watching them negotiate this place for a couple of hours. And it's boring. And the furnace is old, and the rug is matted where it isn't worn, and the curtains need to be washed. Ha, try replaced. Pretty drab overall. Remind me, why do I want to move back here?

The phone rings. I jump as much from surprise as from the piercing sound in an empty house. It's Carrie.

"Hi, Dad."

"Well, hello. Haven't heard from you in a while. What's up?"

"Not much. I was just wondering how you were doing at the retirement home."

What does she want now? I wonder. She's a forty two-year old woman living with her mother and grandmother. What could she possibly need from me?

"Um, Daddy. I'm thinking I would like to live away from Mom and Gramma for a while."

I bite my tongue to keep from saying, 'you think?'

She continues, "So, since you're in a good place, I was wondering if I could move into the house. I'd pay utilities and taxes and all that."

I like the idea. But I say, "Let me think about it for a bit."

"Great. Love you Daddy," she says. "Bye."

They can be so sweet when they want something. But she's a good kid and shouldn't have to live with her mother. I wonder if I should charge her rent as well. Or better yet, rent-to-own. Now there's an idea. Maybe a land contract so she can build up some equity.

Once again, I'm struck by the pervasive silence. I hobble over to the fireplace and the family pictures on the mantel. Cute little girls hugged by a beaming mom. Man, she drove me nuts in that sundress and sandals. And she knew it. Teasing all through long Sunday afternoons in the park, at her mother's. Keeping just out of reach until evening when the dress slid down with the sun.

I hear Marjorie pull up. Car door slams. I look up in the mirror, finger comb my stainless-steel hair. Can't do anything with the forelock that dangles, no matter what—a fetching rumpled-boy look that contrasts with the high, taut cheekbones and firm chin of a U-boat commander. Achtung! I make myself stand straight to my full six-two frame. This aching hip is making me slouch a bit. Get past the gimpy hip and I cut a pretty trim figure with a few miles left on the odometer.

Marjorie walks into the front room and joins me at the fireplace. "Your daughters and wife?"

"Uh-huh." I pause dramatically. "Those were good times."

Marjorie squeezes my hand. I turn to face her. My, she's really very attractive. "Carrie, the younger one on the left, just called," I say. "She wants to move in here... by herself. I don't know if I'm ready to commit to staying at The Ponds."

"I'm sure many of us would like that." With a warm smile, she adds, "I know I would."

Wow. Okay. My move. I lift my hand to stroke her cheek with the back of my fingers.

She jolts away, coloring, frowning. "Oh. I... I didn't mean it like that."

"I... um, thought maybe we were getting closer... another level..."

Marjorie shakes her head, her hair fluffing free then settling back into place. She really has a good stylist. "I was... am, simply being friendly with someone who helped me at a difficult time in my life. Tre. Professor Trahan."

I start for the door.

"Nothing personal."

I turn. "Really? It couldn't be more personal."

She drops her chin, says softly, "Give it... me... time."

The ride back is cool and silent. Time to step back and... what's that thing you do when you reset your computer to the way it was the day before it crashed... like that. I guess I just got ahead of her signals. Still, it never hurts to ask.

I spend the next few days thinking about my future. I run the financials. Consider how little appeal my house now holds for me. I'll be helping my daughter. I have discovered the wood shop on the premises here, use the pool daily and remember how much I dislike cooking for myself. Besides, the house is too quiet.

With Sal gone and now Marjorie avoiding me, I'm often sitting alone for meals. Dolores has taken it upon herself to join me. One day we start talking about grandkids. Turns out we both have a grandson around seven-years old.

"Jeff's got a birthday coming up and I can't, for the life of me, think of anything to get him. Lisa, that's my daughter in Denver, gets that kid every book, toy and game he could ever want. Anything I bought him, he would probably already have."

"Yeah, I know what you mean," Dolores commiserates. "But I tried something recently that my Chad really liked."

"What's that?"

"I used the computer to make him a book out of family pictures my daughter sends me. I tell a little story to tie them together and he really likes it. Makes him feel important."

"That sounds interesting. But I'm not up on graphic programs."

"It's not that hard. Tell you what, how about you come to my place and I'll show you one of the books and how to make it."

I go to the next Pen Dragons. When it's Marjorie's turn to present, she picks up our story with Camila arriving at Nick's condo to find him wallowing in a puddle of self-pity. When she finishes, Hildy and Julie exclaim over it until they run out of comments and then they all turn to me. I simply say, "Good start." After all, there is a limit to cooperative writing with someone who only sees you as her old mentor. "Where's Dolores?" I ask, only now noticing her absence.

"She had to go to the Health Center," Hildy replies, patting her chest which could mean lungs or heart or both. "So, what did you bring to read?"

"Wait. I want to know more about Dolores. Well, not so much the medical details. But this all seems so abrupt. And you seem so matter-of-fact about it."

Julie tilts her head and all but audibly sighs at the need to explain the obvious. "You get used to that around here. Timelines are compressed at our age, aren't they?"

I want to object, at your age maybe, not mine... yet. But Hildy speaks up.

"Oh, Julie, don't be so dramatic. Look at it this way, Doctor Trahan. At your university, faculty are constantly being hired, promoted, recruited. And on your block, if your neighbor suddenly has a moving van in his driveway... 'it's been nice knowing you. All the best.' That's what it's like around here."

Sounds so cold. I look past their heads to the courtyard beyond. Then I reconsider. Actually, they're only facing the reality of staged decline. What's the point pretending they're twenty-year-olds with a lifetime ahead of them?

I make a note to visit Dolores later.

I then pull out my piece, a kind of fairytale/parable I wrote long ago. "I call this Rupuze. It's Lithuanian for frog or toad. It's a derogatory term for someone you don't much like. Here's how it goes...

Once there was a boy who lived high in the mountains next to a sky-blue lake. Every single day, starting with the first day the ice melted in the spring until the last leaf fell in the fall, he swam and splashed and dove in the cold, clear water.

One day, while playing hide and seek with a fish, he bumped his head on a log. Late that night, his head hurt so much that he couldn't sleep. As he paced back and forth, he froze with fear—for there in the mirror was a rupuze.

The boy ran and ran and ran until the sun came up and he could see that he was himself again. "But what if it happens again?" he wondered. "What if I turn into a rupuze every night?"

Sure enough, that night, it happened again. So, he ran all night and slept all day. Ran. Slept. Night. Day. Night. Day. Night.

Until he woke one evening on the beach of a sky-blue lake so much like the one he loved. He sighed deeply.

A beautiful girl came out of the water. "I felt your sigh across the waves. Why are you so sad? Where do you come from?"

The boy jumped up and began to run.

"Don't go," the girl called after him. "Please come back tomorrow. I promise not to ask questions or talk."

He came back the next night and the next night and for many nights after that. They never said a word. The boy always left just as it got dark.

One night the girl said, "I love the water."

The boy looked straight ahead and slowly nodded.

Then he talked.

29

And she talked.

And they talked, into the night.

When the moon came out, the boy stopped talking. It had happened again. He wanted to cry. He jumped up to run. And that's when he saw, in the black water mirror, another rupuze next to him.

She smiled.

After a moment, he sat back down.

They quietly waited for the dawn."

Hildy was the first to respond. "You make the girl the stereotypical female compulsive talker. The initiator."

"That didn't bother me so much," Julie says. "It's just a little too adult for kids to be a fairytale. All that self-loathing..."

"But then self-acceptance," Hildy adds.

"Maybe it's not about kids," I say.

I look across the table at Marjorie. She's assessing me with a penetrating stare I haven't seen before.

Late the next afternoon I look in on Dolores. She's sleeping. Green oxygen tubes, like parentheses, bracket her sleep-flaccid cheeks. She's pale, her hair flattened on one side. I step back in the hall. She wouldn't want me to see her looking like this. As I try to recall the Dolores I saw a few days ago, an aide approaches. "She's sleeping," I explain. "I'll come back later."

"Oh, no," the woman says. "It's time to wake her for dinner anyway." She pats me on the arm like a next-door neighbor chatting over the fence. "I'm Rhonda. Give me a minute with her. I'm sure she'll appreciate the company." Shortly, she beckons me into the room. Dolores is in her wheelchair, fresh yellow blouse, hair brushed, still pale, but eyes smiling. I walk over and reach for her hand. Instead, she leans forward for a kiss on the cheek.

"I'm bored," she says. "I miss the writing group."

"I missed you," I say, without adding... eventually.

"Did you and Marjorie work on another section?"

"No. I think she's on her own for the remainder of that project."

"It's not always easy to work with someone else. When I wrote my children's books I often had to wrangle with the artists. It's so hard to have the same vision."

"I bet."

"So, what did you read?"

"Oh, an old piece I wrote as an undergrad. A sort of fairytale."

"I'd love to read it. That's my favorite genre. I produced two fairytale books, you know."

"I can bring it around after supper."

"7:30?"

Dolores is in the common room. She and two other residents, a man and a woman, are absorbed watching Jeopardy. I never could figure the appeal of taking quizzes. I hated them as a student and I hated creating them and I hated grading them. And yet some people treat it as a game. Go figure. At the commercial break, Dolores spots me. "Oh, Tre!" she calls. The other two look over. Or I should say, look me over. "Dr. Trahan has brought me a story. How about if he reads it to us?" Dolores nods vigorously at me, then them. "Wouldn't that be great?"

"After Final Jeopardy," the man says.

When we've determined the name of the vice president for the third president after the Civil War, my threesome audience turns their undivided attention to me. I read Rupuze to general approval. The discussion quickly shifts from the story and its meaning to memories of favorite lakes and family vacations and the gastronomic delight of frog legs in Baton Rouge. Apparently, it doesn't take much around here—a word, a story—to jump the void between what folks just had for lunch and their first bike as a child. And my stories could do that—help them watch home movies on the back of their eyelids. Ha! Creative writing as geriatric long-term memory therapy. Well, I've got enough first draft sketches and polished tales to keep at it for quite a while.

When I'm asked to return the next night with more stories from my dusty hard drive, I'm pleased to agree.

This time there are seven residents in a semi-circle facing a chair. My reputation precedes me. Where was this kind of word-of-mouth promotion when my books were published? One of the women looks up. It's my ex mother-in-law. "Priscilla," I say as I approach her chair. "I heard you were here. Carrie told me. Are you comfortable?"

She glowers her answer while working her mouth around to a long list of complaints. I hastily retreat toward the central chair, "Look, everyone is waiting for me. Perhaps we can talk after..."

I sit, cross my legs. Marjorie walks in and settles on a sofa near the door. She dips her chin. Of course she would have heard about this. Dolores follows my eyes and twists in her wheelchair to smile a welcome to Marjorie.

"Well," I begin. "Thank you for inviting me here. I'd like to read you a story set in the highlands of Guatemala. It's called, Wholehearted Prayer."

The chicken bus rocks to the right as we swoop through a curve, fighting the pull of Lake Atitlan. Below. Way below. My hip weighs against a Mayan woman. She looks up. Beautiful black eyes. Like Sandra's asking approval for her web design. Back in Chicago. So far away. So close. All the time.

I look up for audience contact and notice that Gail has entered and is sitting next to Marjorie. She must be here to check on Priscilla. Probably has a slightly guilty conscience for putting her mother 'in a home.' And with Carrie gone she'll be alone. I wonder how that will sort out. Strange how I can multi-task—read or lecture and still carry on another stream of thought at the same time. Years of classroom experience, I guess.

The bus, swinging through the bottom of the S curve, tilts me against my wife. She smiles, inviting me to enjoy the adventure, the trek to a cueva sagrada—a Mayan ritual site, a sacred cave. But Sandra keeps popping up, spamming a week of woven colors, insistent vendors and growling tuk-tuks. Sandra. Alessandra—my stowaway.

Oops. I picked the wrong story for Gail and me—a guy infatuated with a work colleague. Marjorie is leaning forward, rapt. Gail glances at her, shakes her head. She's seen that look before. Too many times. Enough times to want a divorce. I messed up. What can I say? Now she looks bored. She knows this story. She should. She proof-read several iterations. She was good at line editing from her PR job.

I'm on autopilot, find myself farther along in the story...

The little guy grins, then takes a bite from an apple he apparently liberated from a sacrificial altar.

For some reason, I suddenly want to apologize to the gods for this blasphemy. He's only a kid. Probably stunted from malnutrition. Hungry. He needs the food more than you do. And help me to be wholehearted. Help me forget Sandra. Focus on my wife alone. Where did that come from? I wonder as I stagger away from the fetid smoke-filled air to the cave mouth and fresh breezes. I'm not religious, not even superstitious. No church. No religion. What was that all about?

Gail rises and walks behind her mother, whispers something in her ear, then leaves.

When we catch up to the kid, he grins and points to a hollow below. A man faces a small smoldering fire, chanting, sprinkling water around the ashes causing tarry smoke to add a fresh coat to the blackened boulder behind it. Another man stands with his palms touching in the universal gesture for prayer. After circling and chanting several more times, the shaman takes a handful of notes from the man—petitions, concerns? and stuffs them in a clay pot along with a red packet with a string hanging out. He sets the pots in the fire. The string sizzles. The pot explodes with a stunning BANG! A cloud of confetti flutters to the ground.

Something lets go inside me.

I take my wife's hand and walk back up the path. At the clearing on the top of the outcrop, we see the kid. He stands on a rock flying a handmade kite in the updraft from the lake so far below. We both pause to watch the kite dip and dance at the end of its invisible tether.

After a reflective pause, the residents launch into a one-upmanship contest of who went where in Latin America when. It's fun to see the juices flowing.

I look at Priscilla who pins me with an accusing eye. I tried, I want to tell her mother. 'Gail and I tried to make us work. Could even try again.' Nah. The ball of yarn is too knotted. More work than it's worth to untangle it all. Maybe it would be better to start over. Fresh. At least there's no history in this train station place.

Two days later, I'm scooting toward the hallway where the resident's 'art' is regularly hung. My cell chirps.

"Tre?"

"Gail. I was surprised to see you the other night. Nice surprise."

"My mother wasn't enchanted."

"I guess. Well, she can't be very happy, shoe-horned out of her home and all."

"Such colorful metaphors. Did you take a creative writing course?" I clench my fist. Pull over. "Yes, mother is unhappy," she continues, "and so am I, especially with Carrie planning to move out as well."

"I'm sure that's difficult for you."

"But you seem to be enjoying yourself. A whole new adoring audience to enthrall with your stunning prose."

"I think they're more interested in memory jolts than fine writing."

"Well, that one woman sitting next to me was interested in more than your syntax."

"Really? And you know this how?"

"Duh!"

I take a long breath. "You called to pick at old wounds...?"

Dropping pitch from whine to serious, Gail says, "This plan of Carrie's makes problems for me."

I try to sound empathic. "I'm sure it does. Can I help?" Marjorie walks by pushing a cart piled with picture frames. I watch her set the stack against the wall and begin hanging them. She steps back to reconsider. Takes one down. Tries another.

Gail's tone is softer. "I'm not sure what would help. When Carrie goes, I'll be all alone in this shabby old house."

"Have you considered an apartment?"

34

"Yeah. That's where I'm leaning. I have power of attorney. I could sell the place. But should I fix it up or sell 'as is?'"

"Uh-huh. Uh-huh." I watch Marjorie place a spirit level on one of the pictures—wouldn't have thought she needed one, she's so level headed. I smile at my own joke. Marjorie catches me watching. No reaction. "Actually, I'm beginning to think I might stay here longer than I first planned. So, Gail, if you need to use my house while you look, for however long, you're welcome to it. What Carrie wants and needs is between you two."

After a long pause and audible swallow, I hear, "Thanks, Tre. That's a nice offer."

"You're welcome. I got to run. Maybe I'll see you next time you visit Priscilla."

Marjorie hangs her last print and steps back to assess the overall effect. I pull up beside her and scan the fifteen matted and framed color prints. A sunset over a lake. Some butterflies. Flowers. A portrait of Dolores—the gamin in her peeking out of her furrowed face. "You took these?" I ask. She nods. "Writer, photographer, you're a woman of many talents."

"Talk about writing," she says, "what did you mean by 'good start' when you heard the next installment in our story?"

"First of all, this is not our story. It's your story. Period. If you are asking me what I would do to make it better, I'd need to see the manuscript."

"Follow me," she says and briskly marches down the hallway.

I park outside her apartment and hobble in on my arm-brace crutch. I'm immediately struck by the mess: piles of paper on what should be a desk, a laptop and printer on the kitchen counter next to a coffee pot, a stack of photographic prints on a window ledge, picture frames, matting and mounting wire jumbled under her window. "Don't mind the mess," Marjorie says as she rummages, head down, through another collection. Before I can reply she points to a poster over the sink:

ORGANIZATIONALLY CHALLENGED
EXISTENTIALLY FOCUSED

I chuckle, take her proffered manuscript and shove magazines to clear a spot on her couch. "Coffee?" she calls from the sink.

"Yeah, okay," I mutter, absorbed in her text. By the time she arrives with a mug of coffee, I've finished Camila's visit to Nick. I take a sip, set the mug down and watch Marjorie fidget, nervously arranging books and mail on the coffee table. "This is pretty ironic, don't you think?" I ask, as I do a deliberate scan of the surroundings. "You've got Nick's girlfriend appalled by the state of his apartment."

Marjorie waves a dismissive gesture—not worthy of comment. Okay. So I continue, "You have her raising hell with Nick. Bawling him out for sloppy, slobby habits until he shouts back, trying to get sympathy and understanding for his career predicament. When they finally wind down and it's time to make up, Camila wants to process the whole experience, arrive at some constructive standards for moving forward and then possibly head to the bedroom. Nick wants to have sex in order to make up, first."

"Your point being?"

"Camila doesn't understand male psychology. That's how guys are wired. Sex makes everything okay."

"Says, you. And besides, it's my story."

"Exactly, that's what I've been trying to tell you. Your story. Not ours." I triumphantly reply.

Marjorie frowns. "I'm not looking for advice on the psychosexual habits of the male species. I'm interested in writing."

"So, use that bit of conflict as the structure of your story. Nick starts by speaking in first-person, baseball-present. Now have Camila tell her side in first person. Dueling banjos to the end."

Marjorie sits back, face slack, pondering. I finish my coffee. On my way out, I stop to admire a photograph of a Monarch on a butterfly bush. "This is a good time of the year for nature pictures."

"Huh? Yeah, it is," Marjorie mutters as she scribbles notes on her copy.

At lunch with Sal, I say, "Nice haircut, Sally." He really does have a nice silver thatch.

"Huh?"

His mouth hangs open. Of the two views, I prefer the Reuben on his plate. "Your haircut," I explain.

He swallows. "Yeah, I went to Vern's last week."

"Is he still working?"

"Uh-huh. Only three days a week, and you gotta make an appointment."

Feeling the hair tickling my collar, I say, "I should go see him. I'm getting a little shaggy."

Sal carefully places the half-eaten sandwich on his plate, looks off in the distance and I know I'm in for a nostalgic, ain't-it-awful screed. "It ain't just the place. The knotty pine walls. The chrome chairs with vinyl seats. The sports and hunting magazines. It's like going to..." He waggles his fingers fighting for the concept. "... a guy's TV in the basement and his sport stuff all over the walls?"

"Man cave?"

"Yeah, that's what Vern's is like. A man cave. Or like a tree house we used to make when we were kids."

"No girls allowed."

"You got it. And if someone's in the chair you can listen or join in... whatever. Vern tells you the latest joke. You lay one on him."

"There's not many places like that left."

"Tell me about it. Last month I went to one of those sports barber shops. TVs big as movie screens, pictures of jocks all over the walls next to pretty boys with weird spiky hair." He's rolling now. I know better than to stop him. He won't finish his food till he's vented his spleen. "And the barbers are all girls. Young girls. Six of them."

I can see where he's going.

"You ever been to a whorehouse?" he asks.

I grin. "No. You?

"Me neither." He sucks a tooth. "Never had to. But I can just imagine."

Now he leans forward, licks his lips. "And they got this back room where after they cut your hair, you go back there. Dim lights. You can see in the doorway, the girl brings a hot towel, puts it on your face and then she massages your head. Whoa!"

"Hey, but, Sally. Wasn't there a time, for a while back then, when Vern used to put a vibrator on his hand and massage your scalp as part of the haircut."

"Not the same thing, Tre. You kiddin'?" Done for the moment, Sal resumes eating. "I'm just sayin', sometimes it's good to get away from women for a while. Know what I mean? Like when we used to go to Vinnie's cabin in the woods."

"Has he still got it?"

"Far as I know. He always says, anytime you want to use it, just go ahead. No need to ask."

"Might be nice to go sometime."

At the next Pen Dragon, Marjorie presents her revised segment of first-person-Camila to the glowing praise of the other ladies. I read my Wholehearted Prayer piece to stunned silence from Hildy and Julie which I choose to interpret as admiration. At least they don't go on about a Caribbean cruise they took twenty years ago.

After the session, as Marjorie gathers her papers, I mention, "Thinking of your photos, I got a buddy with a cabin on a lake. Ten acres. Undeveloped."

"You sound like a real estate agent."

"More like a promoter of the arts." Face turned, she cuts a sidelong glance at me. She likes that last bit and surprises me with her response.

"When do you want to go?"

I shrug. "Tomorrow. 2:30. I'll meet you at the back entrance. You drive."

She raises her chin. Decisive, no nonsense, do-it woman. I like.

I'm at the back door. 2:30. 2:45. At 3:00 I grab my crutch, get in my wheel chair and roll to Marjorie's room. I knock. No answer. Knock again. Is that a moan? Now I'm concerned. I see Rhonda at the end of the hall and convince her to open the door.

It's dark inside, blinds drawn, Marjorie is sprawled on the couch, arm across her eyes. When I wheel next to her, she peeks at me. "Migraine," she whispers. Oh boy. I know the drill. Gail used to get them.

"Where do you keep your Imitrex?" I ask.

"Bedroom," she manages.

I turn to Rhonda. "I need to give her a shot in the thigh as soon as I find her medicine."

"Got it."

I leave her tugging at Marjorie's jeans as I wheel to the bedroom.

No tidier than the rest of the apartment. I don't know where to start looking. I hesitate, feeling like a cross between a cat burglar and voyeur until my ambulance driver persona kicks in. Bedside table—no luck. Dresser. Top drawer. Nada. Second drawer. Bingo. There it was, tucked in with her... what do they call them in Victorian novels... 'unmentionables.'

Rhonda has modestly exposed a patch of thigh for a quick alcohol wipe. I unwrap the set-dose syringe, arm, then trigger it. I look up at Rhonda, nod toward the door. She doesn't move. Marjorie flicks a you-can-go gesture and leaves me to make my way around the arm of the couch. I grasp her head in both hands and begin to apply pressure points to her temple, then the base of her skull and finally slowly squeeze her eyebrows together before massaging her forehead. Ten minutes later, she says, "Better. Thanks," and seems to drift off.

"You should be okay, now," I say, on my way out the door.

Lunch the next day, Marjorie, several tables over, is talking to Julie. Obviously, she is feeling better. I attend to my minestrone, sopping up the last of the soup with a hunk of crispy roll. When I glance over, I catch Marjorie looking at me, then quickly away.

Is she embarrassed that I invaded her privacy so thoroughly, saw her so helpless and needy? I could go over and ask how she's doing. No. I'll let her take the initiative. I've, literally, poked into her life enough as it is. She gets up to leave and as she passes my table she says, "2:30?"

Okay, I'm thinking. Rain check.

We're silent in the car. No profuse expressions of gratitude from her. No detailed explanations of my years of helping Gail through similar episodes. That's all fine with me. We're two wordsmiths saving our words for the printed page. How calm and relaxing.

The two-track road to Vinnie's reminds me of a car wash. Weeds scrub the underside. Branches and shrubs rub the doors and windows. Seeds, leaves and startled insects spray the windshield. We suddenly burst into the clearing beside the cabin. There's some moss on the roof, and the front steps on the north side have green mold in spots. Otherwise it looks in good shape.

I find the key in the usual spot under the top step and open up while Marjorie gathers her equipment. I'm inside raising windows when Marjorie leans in to say she's off. She's not wasting any time. Which is exactly what I don't mind doing on a deck chair on the porch. Some people get energized by the outdoors. I tend to hunker down. More earthworm than robin.

I must have really needed it because I sleep for two hours. Inside I find a six pack in the fridge and pop a cold one. Poking around, I see Vinnie has a couple cans of soup. Some crackers. Back on the porch I start reading a 1982 Reader's Digest short story collection. Hey, that's what you do when you're in a cabin in the woods.

Around 5:30, I start to wonder what's keeping Marjorie. Could she be lost or just lost track of time? We'd have to leave pretty soon to get back in time for supper. When she hasn't shown up by 6:30, I grab Vinnie's fly rod with a mini-popper on the floating line. I tease a few tiny bluegills until Marjorie steps on the dock. There's a sheen of sweat around her temples and her usual hair-helmet is tussled with a couple burrs and embedded twigs. The high color in her cheeks and pleased smile reminds me of Carrie after she won a cross-country meet. Again, not much is said.

I make my slow way back to the porch. The uneven ground aggravates my hip. But when Marjorie joins me on the porch with beers, I get past the pain. Interesting that she's making no mention of returning to The Ponds. Hmm.

Feet up on the railing, she sighs deeply. "You know what I realized today? I don't miss our farm. But I do miss the out of doors. We kind of lose that at the residence, don't you think?"

"Gain some. Lose some."

"Uhmm."

"Did you find much to shoot?"

"Tons. There's a marvelous field of milkweed toward the lake. And birds. I got a pileated woodpecker and a hawk. Here let me show you."

Forty minutes later we finish reviewing the shots in her digital camera. Now it's starting to cloud up. Rain coming. It wouldn't be a bad idea to head out. Maybe stop somewhere for supper. When I suggest that, she says, "Do we have to? This is so nice out here."

I wouldn't have expected that. But now that she mentions it, why not? There's food. One bedroom. I always liked Vinnie's couch. Although I wonder how my hip will like it. It's raining.

"Let me start supper," I say, dragging out soup cans and crackers.

"Give me ten minutes for a quick nap," Marjorie requests from the door to the bedroom.

Thirty minutes later, I peek in to find her open-mouthed, catatonic. She's what you would call a quiet sleeper. No thrashing and turning. That's good to know... how someone is in bed. Meant something else when I was younger.

I warm up some tomato soup, eat my share and read my book. Before long, I'm sleepy as well. Must be the fresh air. I stretch out on the couch and sleep for a few hours.

Around 2:00 a.m. my hip is throbbing, either from the walking on uneven ground or the sagging couch or both. I get up and hobble around in search of pain relief. I must have made enough noise to wake Marjorie, who staggers into the kitchen, yawning. "Wow, I really passed out," she says, turning on the gas under the remaining tomato soup.

In the middle of her second helping, she gives me a long look. "You're hurting," she remarks, then scrabbles in her purse for a bottle of Tylenol. I take three and join her at the table. She eats slowly. I nibble on a cracker. We'll need to stop for a good breakfast in the morning.

While she goes to the sink with her bowl, I head for the couch. Marjorie grabs my hand saying, "No. That couch can't be good for your hip," and leads me to the bedroom.

We sleep together. Meant something else when I was younger.

The next evening, reading to Dolores' group, I come to realize that I actually like living in this retirement community and would like to stay for the duration. When I tell this to Dolores afterwards, she is pleased. "I'm so glad. And as long as you're planning to stay, you could request to move into my former apartment."

"How convenient." I reply sarcastically. "Doesn't Marjorie live next door?"

Eyes twinkling, she adds, "And it's so much larger than your little one bedroom."

I kiss her on the cheek and say, "I'll think about it."

Two weeks later, maintenance men are helping me move into the larger apartment. With furniture roughly positioned throughout the living room, and TV and other appliances in place, I finally plop down in my recliner to rest for a moment. Straight ahead of me, across the room, is a solid panel door painted the same color as the walls. I hadn't noticed it before. I'm thinking closet, maybe storage cabinet, when the handle turns and the door opens. Marjorie. Cluttered apartment and all. She bestows a regal nod and pointedly leaves the door open before going about her business inside. I can live with that.

The next morning, I fill the coffee pot. Two cups of water. Or should I make it four? I glance at the door between our apartments. No. Last night was... just right. She brought popcorn. I supplied my favorite movie—Zorba the Greek and we enjoyed each other's company. Nice. There's no rush. No need to barge in on her. She has her space. I have mine. Let's just let this whole thing happen as it will.

Chapter Five; Marjorie

Marjorie hummed tunelessly as she chopped two mushrooms and dropped them into a pan sizzling with butter. Next, she cracked two eggs from the cheery carton named, Happy Eggs. She smiled to herself, remembering the label from... what milk was it... from contented cows. Nobody who ever had a farm would anthropomorphize like that, she mused. As she snipped a few strands of rosemary growing in a windowsill pot, she wondered if Tre would appreciate her idea of a tasty breakfast. Maybe he was just a crust-of-toast-and-mug-of-coffee kind of guy. Well, she reminded herself, there was no need to rush. She would answer that and many other questions about Tre, in good time.

Mid-morning, sorting through her photos, she heard Tre's doorbell, door opening and closing, a woman's voice. She couldn't help it if her desk was right next to the door between their apartments. She swung her chair around and could actually hear the conversation if she sat still.

"Mother is in PT. I thought I'd stop by and tell you how Carrie and I are getting along."

It had to be Tre's ex, Marjorie surmised. She dredged her memory for a name till Gail came to the surface. Now she could follow the dialogue.

Tre: Would you like some coffee?

Gail: No, thanks. You always make it stronger than I like.

Tre: Well, I'll just grab a mug. What's Carrie up to?

Gail: Work, Busy as ever with her second graders. She has a boyfriend, you know.

Tre: No. No, I didn't know. Tell me about him.

Gail: I've never met him. I just answer the odd call from a man named Kirk and pass it along. Sometimes I feel like a college roommate with Carrie. Only she never talks about who she's seeing.

43

Tre: She learned well from both of us.

Gail: You more than me.

Tre: Maybe.

Gail: What's that supposed to mean?

Tre: How do I know what you were up to...

Gail: All the time you were chasing around?

Tre: Can't we just let all of that go? I mean, after all that time and where we are now?

Gail: That's easy for you to say.

Tre: Oh, c'mon. You weren't faithful Penelope knitting at home, either.

Gail: You started it. And that really hurt.

Tre: Look, can't we agree that infidelity makes too much and too little of sex at the same time?

Gail: That sounds like a line from a bad play, or maybe even from one of your stories.

Marjorie waited through a silent lull. Finally, she heard footsteps and a door slamming. After another minute, she gently knocked on the door, and stuck her head in. "Hi, Tre," she said, brightly. "I was planning to make quesadillas for lunch. Care to join me?"

Before he could answer, the bathroom door opened, and Gail walked out. All three players froze. Tre, mouth open, looked from one to the other.

Gail raised her chin and one eyebrow in an appraising stare. Marjorie squared her shoulders, tugged her Western sweatshirt down over her pilled black slacks and took in Gail's russet business suit. Wouldn't you know it, she thought. Get comfortable and suddenly you're in a faculty meeting. Well, she does have a certain commanding presence for someone our age—good cheekbones set off by a flattering haircut. The chestnut tint works with the whole ensemble. And here's me in my pink mules. Oh, well. Might as well laugh it off. "I feel as though we're in a bedroom farce... doors slamming, people entering and exiting."

"Agreed," Gail remarked, "and this is my exit cue." Grabbing her purse and heading for the main door, she paused for her parting line. "I've played this role before."

Marjorie looked at Tre as if to say 'Well, is that so? Am I just the latest of many to you?' He simply hunched his shoulders, hands at his side, palms up, speechless. "Forget lunch," she said, leaving Tre to hear two doors slam in quick succession.

Plopped in her easy chair, drumming her fingers on the armrest, Marjorie replayed the past few minutes. Poor woman. I know what I felt when I saw Mark with his lady. Like... like seeing someone wearing the sweater you dropped off at Goodwill. You didn't want it anymore, but you didn't like to see someone else enjoying it. But who knows what Gail and Tre did to each other, and when? Who stepped out first? Probably him. He sure looked good when I had him in class. Had him. Isn't that a strange expression? As if I 'had' him to myself on a cruise ship for a semester and he was there seducing me with facts and skills and feelings I never knew I had. And then I get to port and can start a whole new term, to be 'had' by yet another. Gail Trahan. It must be hard to be the wife of an engaging professor.

Marjorie got out the soft tortillas, manchego cheese, leftover chicken breast and a jar of salsa. While the tortillas crisped and browned in the pan, she chuckled to herself, picturing Tre flummoxed. The man-of-words at a loss for words. He might be able to write great dialogue, but he doesn't do improv worth a damn. Maybe in a couple days' time this scene will appear in a story and his male character will have a witty reply. She flipped the tortilla, snatching a hot fragment of chicken that escaped the cheese glue. All right, so maybe he's not what I imagined, back then. Who is? Infatuations end. I think I'm going to treat him as if he were a classmate I ran into at a reunion. That was then, let's see who you... we... are now.

Marjorie looked for Tre in the dining room that evening and was surprised when he didn't show. The next afternoon he was missing at Pen Dragons as well. After her hair appointment, she decided to swing by his house.

Marjorie knocked on the front door. When no one came, she peeked in the front room window. All was still.

"No one's home," a woman's voice announced from an overgrown clematis vine climbing a neighboring fence.

Marjorie stood abruptly—discovered. "Uhm," she began in a high-pitched voice, "I know Tre from The Ponds. It's a retirement..."

"I know who you are," the woman said, her tanned, smiling face rising above the profusion of purple flowers. "I'm Bernice. Come get a cup of coffee."

"Well," Marjorie began.

"Sal told me all about you guys and I saw you bringing him home once."

"Well, in that case," Marjorie acquiesced, "why not? We're practically family."

The kitchen felt comfortable and familiar: Formica table with chrome legs, red vinyl chair seats, multi-painted cabinets and a percolator on the stove adding Maxwell House fumes to stale cigarette smoke and soaked-in whiff of old-house. Bernice set two steaming mugs on the table with a resounding thunk, loud in the surrounding silence. Marjorie glanced at the sugar bowl in the center of the table. An ashtray with two stale butts rested in front of an empty chair. "Sal." Bernice apologized as she whisked it away and dumped the contents into the garbage under the sink. She grabbed a Christmas decorated cookie tin and brought it to the table.

"How's he doing?" Marjorie inquired.

"Oh, Sal's fine," Bernice replied as she nimbly perched in her chair, loaded two scoops of sugar, stirred and took a delicate sip. Prying her fingernails along the edge of the tin, she popped the lid. "Sorry, these are all I've got to share, just now. Eyes twinkling, she added, "Special treats." She pursed her lips and raised her eyebrows like a naughty child.

Marjorie declined when Bernice pointed to the brownies. "So, where is your guy? I kind of miss him."

"Not sure, Hon. He took off for a couple days." Bernice studied one of her homemade confections before taking a not-so-delicate chomp. "Not that I mind. A little space never hurts."

"Kahlil Gibran says, 'Eat bread together but not from the same loaf.'"

"Smart man... whoever the hell he is. Bet he'd like one of my medicinal brownies."

Marjorie's eyes widened, cut a look to the back yard. It took a moment to recognize a row of palmate plants shyly tucked between the garage and a jumble of zucchini vines, tomato plants and corn stalks. Back to Bernice and a tilt of her head toward the cookie tin, Marjorie said, "Don't mind if I do."

A second cup of coffee and brownie later, Marjorie said, "I was just trying to track down Tre. Haven't seen him for a couple of days. And his bad hip and all..."

Bernice blinked slowly. "I bet Sal and him took off. Probably went to Vinnie's cabin."

"I've been there. Nice place."

"Can't stand the spider webs. Gives me the creeps." Bernice said.

Marjorie mumbled, "He never said anything..."

"They don't need to. Yeah, well, it's snakes and snails and puppy dog tails."

"Huh?"

"That old nursery rhyme... What are little boys made of? They need to get away once in a while. Dig some worms. Yank out some fish guts." She tapped her temple. "The reality show in their heads."

Marjorie giggled. "Leave them alone and they will come home, wagging their tails behind them."

"Never hurts to leave a trail of bread crumbs," Bernice said as she wrapped four brownies in a napkin.

"I don't plan to go to the cabin."

Bernice cocked her head, "Sure, Hon."

Two days later Marjorie drove out to the cabin, telling herself it was for photo ops with the osprey nest next to the lake. The cabin was locked, empty, so she helped herself to the key and the use of the facilities before climbing a hill that offered a clean shot with her long lens of the two fledglings.

Chapter Six; Tre

Sal calls. "Eh!" he goes, "let's get outta town for a while. You know, before winter socks us in."

"Nah. I'm okay, right here."

"You don't sound like it. C'mon man, you gotta scuffle a little or you're gonna start sinkin' roots in that place."

I pause for a second and Sal takes that for assent. So, he pours it on all the more.

"I'm thinkin' up north, Traverse... Boyne Country like that. See some colors. Sleep in my van. Wadda ya say?"

"I can see the leaves out my window."

"What? You got a thing goin' with that Marjorie lady? Don't want to leave her..."

I'm silent again.

"Oh, I get it... just the opposite. Troubles, eh? Best way to fix that is to get away. A little space never hurts."

That's what I need—Sal, the volunteer marriage counselor, giving me advice. "Sal," I say, "if I wanted to go up north I'd drive myself and wouldn't have to sleep with you in the bargain."

"Oh, yeah? You can't drive a car more than an hour or so. And this way, I'll drive and if you get sore you can crawl in the back and lay down."

That's not all that bad an idea. Maybe I could stand a change of scenery. The more I think about it the better it sounds. Sal once more takes my silence for agreement.

"So, bring your sleeping bag and a warm jacket. I got all the rest. I'll see you at the back door... say 1:30. You can get your afternoon nap in the van and that way we can beat the rush hour traffic in Grand Rapids. Awright?"

I don't need to answer. Why bother.

The next day we find an access road to a beach. Secluded. Indian Summer warm. Sleeping Bear Dunes, to the north, slides down to Lake Michigan. I love it. Strange contrasts: the overwhelming presence of people, people, people at The Ponds versus the one-on-one quiet with Sal. Well, not so quiet, come to think of it. He's constantly on about something or other, especially the need for personal space. And somehow, he has this perverse habit of trying to see how close he can come to running out of gas before filling up. It's nerve racking. He says the drama keeps him awake on long drives. Thank God he's off looking for Petoskey stones at the moment. I can barely see him a mile down the shoreline. He's right about too much togetherness, though, especially after spending the night with him in close quarters.

I sigh and take in the big lake. I didn't realize how much I needed this. Sometimes you just have to stop shaking the snow globe and let it all settle.

I do this thing where I look at the lake with two eyes open and it rolls on and on, to the horizon and beyond, like the opening to the first Star Wars movie. Then I close one eye and it turns into a two-dimensional seascape, a constantly moving mural—beach on the bottom, blue water two-thirds of the way up, sky at the top. Either way, the big water opens me up. Calls to me. A buddy left for New Mexico and I asked how he could stand not having the big lake. "It's the sky out here," he said. "The endless sky." I guess that could work. But the lake is still the lake.

I notice a woman, bent over, slowly patrolling the waterline—for what? Beach glass? Driftwood? She looks up, sees me watching and offers a shy wave. Primitive wiring and ingrained habits kick in—observe, assess, evaluate. She's around my age. Slender. Tall. Outdoor-catalog boots, jacket and hat. Inviting smile. Intelligent face. Falls right in my demographic. What's not to like? It wouldn't take much to engage, to connect, to pursue... but to what end? If I wanted a companion, eHarmony would be more efficient—online instead of mall shopping. Sounds so un-romantic coming from a romance writer. But really, after a certain point, the pheromone buzz for man-the-hunter tapers off. Isn't that the wisdom behind arranged marriages—get past turbulent romance to comfortable companionship like Charlotte and Mr. Collins in Pride and Prejudice? What happens when

Miss Bennet moves into Pemberley with Mr. Darcy for the 'happily ever after'? Or me at The Ponds, and Marjorie?

I close my eyes, take in a deep draft of wave-wash aroma, then drag myself to the van to wait for Sal. I suppose we should head downstate. And then? Who knows? I'll decide when we get there.

"Sal," I nag when we're back on I-75, "you're down to a quarter tank."

"Yeah, I'm looking for a Shell station. We'll fill up when we stop for lunch."

A few miles on, a State Police car pulls us over. The trooper, a 30-ish woman, stands just behind the driver window. After the usual scrabble for license and insurance, Sal finally gets a look at the woman. "Hey, you look familiar to me."

"Yes, sir," she says. "Your license plate is missing the current yellow tag."

Sal hand-bonks his forehead. "Wait. Wait. I know it's in here somewhere," he moans. The trooper heads back to her vehicle. He bends under the steering wheel and into the floorboard around my feet. "Aha!" he finally exclaims holding up the Secretary of State envelope. "I knew it was here."

When the officer returns with his documents, he holds out the sticker. "I'll put it on right now." His face curls in a knot. "Sandy. Allesandra," he shouts with the joy of the prodigal son's father. "This is Sandy." he tells me. "She used to play with my Angeline." Turning to the now embarrassed trooper, "You did a sleepover for Angeline's fifth birthday and played soccer with her." He jumps out of the car and fronts the woman who nervously backs up a step or two. "My God, look at you. All grown up and working as an officer of the law." The trooper raises her hands to chest level, palms out, as Sal opens his arms and advances for a family hug.

"Uhm, Mr. Palladino," she mutters, looking around at cars zooming by and backing up steadily. "This is not the appropriate time or place..."

"Aww... Sandy. Alls we ever hear about is police community relations. Let's give folks a good example of it." He lunges at her and she does an arm-length pat-pat on his shoulder to avoid a two cheek, Italian kiss-kiss alongside the freeway.

Back in the car, grinning from ear to ear, "Wait till I tell Angeline," Sal says. "Makes you feel old, doesn't it, when kids you used to know, now run the world? Doctors. Priests." He pulls into traffic and doesn't stop chuckling and smiling to himself. "And on top of it all, I got off without a ticket," he says as we limp into a Shell station on fumes for the second time this day. Sal goes, "Seein' that kid made me think of old times. And then I'm thinking, as long as we're going through Detroit anyway, why don't we check out the old neighborhood?"

I'll agree with anything as long as he fills up this gas-guzzler.

Did you ever have a dream where you're someplace familiar but parts of it aren't quite right? That's what it was like driving in our neighborhood. The street signs were the same, but many of the landmarks were gone—the New York Carpet World store, The Van Dyke movie theatre, the Gulf gas station on the corner of my block. And space. Spaces where houses used to be. Green squares like a live GPS map where uncles and cousins and friends used to live. I can see a street corner four blocks away. Never could have seen it back then for all the houses in between.

I check out Sal. He's shares my open-mouthed surprise as we try to reconstruct the Armageddon scene. Like special effects in a movie, Spada's cheese and Wajo's grocery and Sweety's corner store morph from now empty lots. Missing teeth in the face of our memories.

"Let's get back on the road, Sal."

"Yeah. No. It's just I can't get over how the place has changed. Like a bomb landed here. You see places but there's nothin' there anymore. Somebody oughta remember it the way it was, or it won't matter anymore."

For once, Sal is quiet for the next couple hours as we tool along I-94. I guess we both feel as though someone has broken into our memory bank and stolen our past. But no one has the right to expect his neighborhood to be maintained like a drive-through museum. A Greenfield Village for the generations. We just resented the slow fade in our absence.

And I wonder if he's thinking what I'm thinking—that you can't really go back. That even if the whole area was exactly the same, like some Italian hill town—rock-built homes and walls and towers growing out of the mountain, you still couldn't capture or recreate your own moment in time, in that place. Never step in the same river twice. Need to keep moving. Making new neighborhoods and friends.

I spot a billboard—Shell gas station five miles ahead. "Sal" I say, pointing to the sign.

"Nyah, we got a good quarter of a tank. We'll catch the next one." And so it goes, all the way back to Vinnie's cabin for one last night out. This time in a real bed for me. The couch for Sal. I'm not spending another night sleeping next to him and his volcanic eruptions and random exclamations amid a symphony of snores and snorts.

Marjorie's car is parked at the cabin when we pull up, but she is nowhere to be found. Since I have a taste for fresh fish after a couple days of oatmeal, hot dogs and fast food, I grab Vinnie's fly rod. The lily pads accessible from the dock hold promise for a mess of hand-sized bluegills. The pendulum rhythm of casting gets me thinking. Marjorie's car is here. Why? Does she miss me? Is she chasing after me? Dream on, lover. But then, her camera bag is on the hood. It's not always about you, Tre.

About the time I have six on the stringer, I hear Marjorie and Sal talking.

"Hey, Marjorie," Sal says. "Nice seein' ya."

"You too. I came to take some pictures."

"Knock yourself out. Just don't take any of me."

"Don't worry. I'm looking for wildlife, not still life."

Sal starts a wheezing chuckle that progresses to a rattling cough. "Damn allergies," he gasps between hacks.

"It's better in the city," Marjorie suggests.

"Uh-huh," Sal mumbles through the handkerchief muffling his mouth.

"Bernice would kind of appreciate knowing how you're doing."

"Is that right? And I'm thinkin' you'd appreciate knowing how Tre's doin.' Is that why you're here?"

A two-pound smallmouth smashes my popper and I don't hear her answer. After I land him, I decide I have enough fish for supper and cross to the cabin. The door bangs open and Marjorie is staring at me. We both freeze. My mind races. All my recent thoughts about genteel companionship evaporate. Damn. This lady is special, and there is something very special going on with us. You'd think I could say it better, writer that I am. But I just plain like her and want to be with her—not anyone else.

She makes the first move—nods like the Queen of England. She and I together. Yes. Golden wedding anniversary announcements are fine. A long history together is sweet and satisfying. I smile and nod back. But sometimes history is when you decide to start making it. Like now.

Sal sticks his head in the doorframe, eyes the fish. "Ehh, looks like you got enough for supper."

"For two of us," I say, eyes on Marjorie.

Sal scrunches his mouth, checks out Marjorie's smiling eyes for me. "I can take a hint. I'm outta here."

"Nice trip, Sal," I call as he climbs into the van. "Great idea. I needed to get away." He waves dismissively and drives off.

The next morning, we drive back to The Ponds. I haven't felt the urge to write in a long while. So, I'm at my computer before coffee smells drift from Marjorie's suite. This is one of those rare occasions when a story comes to me whole and I have to write it before it slips away. Nice feeling. Creativity. Losing yourself in creation. Is that what God is like—the total absorption in making something from nothing. Beauty from words. Gold from straw. Marjorie must recognize the zone because she simply sets a mug of coffee next to me, runs a finger along my neck and leaves me to it.

Chapter Seven; Marjorie

Marjorie peeked in on Tre. *He can eat later,* she told herself and went about eating breakfast while culling her osprey photos. The phone rang. It was Bernice wondering if Tre and Sal were back.

"Tre is here. I saw Sal yesterday evening," Marjorie said. "He drove off from Vinnie's in his van. He hasn't been home?"

"No. And I was just wondering..."

"Let me ask Tre."

"Tre, it's Bernice," Marjorie shouted into his apartment. "Sal never got home."

"What do you want from me?" he answered, the tone of unwelcome annoyance loud and clear. After a moment and an audible sigh, he came to the doorway and held out his hand for the receiver.

Leaning on the doorframe, he grumbled, "Bernice, who knows where he went? How does anybody know where Sal goes when he decides to take off?"

Marjorie punched the speaker button on the phone.

"Well, I was just wondering." Bernice's voice quavered for a moment. "Do you think he's okay... and all?"

"Don't worry about him. We just spent a couple days up north. He can take care of himself." Tre paused, raised his eyebrows and pointed his chin at the coffee maker on the counter. Marjorie poured him a cup. After a noisy slurp he added, "You know... we were just in the old neighborhood."

"Where's that?'

"Detroit. Near Eastside. Maybe he went back there."

"Don't know it," she snapped, an edge in her voice. "And even if I did, I wouldn't go chasing after the jerk like a jealous housewife out to drag him home by the ear."

"That's the right way to treat him."

"Treat him? I don't need to treat him. He's the one getting the good deal here. If he doesn't realize that, he can go jump in the lake for all I care. It's not like I need to be fulfilled by washing some old fart's underwear."

Tre held the phone away from his ear and mouthed a 'wow' to Marjorie.

"You tell him, Bernice," Marjorie shouted toward the phone.

"I just wondered if you knew he was okay," Bernice said. "Sounds like you don't give a damn."

Tre puffed his cheeks, looked up at the ceiling and blew out. His voice took on a professorial tone—the instructor at his lectern. "Bernice, what we're looking at here, is a classic example of man on a journey, man the wanderer. It's a familiar trope in literature over the ages from Homer in the Odyssey to Lancelot in the Middle Ages to the Lone Ranger in our times."

"For crying out loud, Tre. Who asked you for a lecture?" Bernice said.

Marjorie snorted. Tre blanched.

"Naw, man," Bernice continued, "what we got here is a little boy running away... the cowboy who loves his horse more than a woman. Love 'em and leave 'em. Clint Eastwood and John Wayne got a lot to answer for."

"Wow, that's a very perceptive insight. I never put all of that together, Bernice. Hmm. Most of us are wired to be nomads and some have more of those genes than others... an evolutionary imperative, as it were."

"Save all that BS for your college students, Tre. Sal is scared of me, and him getting too close is what this is all about."

Tre huffed through his nose, his voice back to conversational register, "Bernice, Sal got bit by a nostalgia bug. He's probably just ghosting around our old stomping grounds reliving the good old days. Which, now that I remember them, were more old than good."

"Yada, yada, yada. You're one to talk. Gail always complained about you taking off for conferences and workshops every chance you got. Evolution, ha!" A loud smack was followed by a dial tone.

Tre handed Marjorie the phone and retreated toward his room, shaking his head dismissively.

"You could just call him, you know," Marjorie suggested.

"Sal?" Tre stopped, wrinkled his nose in disgust. "That's not us. We don't hover."

"Look, he's your buddy, right? Bernice is good for him. They're right together."

"Hey, Sal's Sal. A grown man. He's got to figure this out for himself."

"A friend can help. Talk it out."

Tre tossed his head—forget it.

Marjorie held the phone to her ear. "What's his number?"

Tre lingered in the doorway while she dialed, then hit speaker phone.

"Sal," she began after a moment. "Yeah, it's Marjorie."

"Hey, how you doin' Marjorie? Wassup?"

"Well, we were just wondering... where you are..."

"We? We is what, you and Tre? Tre doesn't give a rip about where I go."

"Well, Bernice, actually, called us to see if we knew where you might be."

"Ah, now I get it. You're bird dogging me."

After a three-count pause, Marjorie persisted, "So, where are you exactly?"

"Where am I exactly? I'm at the corner of Georgia and Isham, parked in the driveway where my Uncle Leo used to live. Only there's no house here and there's only weedy lots for blocks and blocks. Oh, yeah, way over there is a set of cement steps going up to nothin.' Get the picture?"

A smile in her voice, Marjorie said, "So, you're camping in your van like a cowboy and his wagon in the middle of the prairie cooking beans over an open fire."

"Something like that. Except, I found a fried chicken place up Gratiot a ways. I hate to cook."

Marjorie frowned and got to the point, "Sal, we're calling because Bernice is upset and worried about you. And I... we... think you ought to at least call her."

"What good is it to get away if you have to leave a note, get permission and check in every twenty minutes? Huh? I ask you?"

Tre leaned in toward the phone. "Sal," he barked. "Give Bernice a call, for crying out loud."

"For crissake a guy can't even get lost in the middle of nowhere, anymore."

In the dining room that evening, Tre jokingly inquired, "What can we learn from this Sal thing?"

"You tell me," Marjorie said.

"Umm. You like to be aware of the whereabouts of people in your life."

"Well, not the GPS coordinates, but a general approximation would be appreciated. And besides, Bernice is my friend."

"I see," Tre said as he squeezed a wedge of lemon over his tilapia fillet.

"So, tell me," Marjorie asked, "what was it like living in that neighborhood, which would have been when, exactly?"

"Right after the Second World War. Our school bags were army surplus backpacks. And instead of baseball cards, we collected war cards. During recess, we would pitch them against the wall and trade for the best ones. It's only recently that I can stand to wear anything olive-drab."

"So, you knew Sal from back then?"

"I think we met in second grade, in the public school. Do you remember how in those days we used stamps as money?"

"Nuh-uh."

"They would say on an advertisement 'send stamps or money orders to...' I recall Sal standing in line with me to pay for our week's lunch milk holding a sheet of stamps. I started to count them one by one. He showed me how to count along opposite edges and multiply. I was really impressed. He always was good with figures."

"Were you in the same class?"

"Yeah. We were. One day the teacher asked how many of us had a radio. We all raised our hands. Then she asked how many had a TV. No hands. She said, 'Someday, as many of you who have radios will have TVs.' We all sat there like some social prophet had just pronounced a man would go to the moon. Sal shouts, 'No shit!' and gets sent to the principal's office."

"That was back a ways, wasn't it?"

"Yep. And then I went to the Catholic school—St. Joe's for third grade and convinced Sal to go there too. I was really proud of myself... righteous, like a missionary who saved a godless native. But I'm not sure it took. I always had my suspicions that he was the one who wrote a nun's name in the urinal, that time."

"What was it like living around there?"

"It was a blue-collar neighborhood. Lots of Italians. Hell, Sal must have had family on every block for a square mile. He was welcome any time to snag a cookie and a glass of milk, especially if it was raining or snowing. Me too, if I was with him. Made you feel safe." Tre helped himself to a lonely French fry on Marjorie's plate.

"So, what did you guys do for fun?"

"Simple things. We played marbles on any bare patch of dirt we could find. We hit grounders to each other on the cinder playground until the cover wore off the baseball and then the friction tape on top of that. No Little League. No coaches. We taught ourselves... for better or worse."

"Sounds like a good place to grow up."

"I suppose. More like a good place to be from... pardon the ending preposition. I think it meant more to Sal than to me."

"So, how did Sal end up living across the street from you?"

Tre folded his napkin. "Angie, their daughter, went to Western. Took my class. Small world and all that. Sal and I reconnected when he came to see her. After his wife Pia died, he sold the dry-cleaning business. Must have liked it here."

"How did she die?"

"I forget. It was ten years ago."

Chapter Eight; Tre

The next evening after supper, I visit Dolores. She seems reduced. Ropey blue veins stand out on her emaciated arms. But her eyes are still bright, even if her face is fighting a losing battle with the tug of gravity. "Have you brought something to read to us?" she asks.

"Yes, actually I just finished it. Yours will be the premier reading."

"Great! I'll tell Rhonda to gather us in the common room. And in the meantime, you can tell me all about your trip with Sal."

"How did you know?"

"Bush telegraph," she says smiling coyly.

"More like nosy biddies seeing Sal pick me up in back."

"Well, you must know what they say about teachers... 'Them that can't... teach.' Well, those of us who can't get out can only fantasize about those who can."

I gently squeeze her hand.

"Talking about doing things. Have you ever noticed how important a couple years can be in a child's development? A one-year old is light years ahead of a newborn and so far behind a four-year old. It all evens out eventually. What's a couple years difference in your fifties? But when you're older it's just the reverse. Something you could do six months ago, you can no longer do. Can do. Can do. Can't do." She sighs. "If I was younger, I would love to play with this concept and come up with a children's book."

I watch her mull over the idea, eyes looking off my shoulder. "Yes," she finally says, as if picturing the final product. "A grandmother reading to a child in bed. A child reading to a grandmother in bed."

"What's your title?" I ask.

She closes her eyes. "I have to think about it."

I hesitate to ask her. But damn it, why shouldn't I? "Dolores, how do you feel about...?"

"Dying?" she supplies, eyes popping open.

I nod.

"No one ever asks, and yet it's the most obvious thing, as obvious as the tubes going in and out of me. I'm ready to go. Been ready for some time. Actually, I'm kind of excited, like sitting in an airport waiting to go on a mystery trip."

She surprises me by hunching up in the bed and screwing her face into the earnest frown of a pig-tailed girl, "I want to find out if all this was worth it."

"You mean... afterlife... heaven."

Dolores rolls her hands to indicate—all of that. Rhonda sticks her head in the doorway. "Everyone who can make it is in the common room, professor."

Professor, I muse, as I take my seat at the top of a circle of couches and chairs. Lecturer, Concert Master, we both conduct a symphony of sounds in lambent phrases and syncopated rhythms. I notice Marjorie in the back row, her intelligent, no-nonsense gaze, stops me short. Cut the poetic crap, I tell myself, and just share a nice piece of clean, lean prose.

"Well, I've come to understand that some of you know about my recent trip with Sal Palladino, of recent ill repute in these quarters. We had a fine trip up north and were thrilled with the marvelous fall colors around Boyne Country. My only regret is that we didn't take Marjorie and her camera along with us, so we could share our trip with you. But some of you who knew Sal would understand how that threesome might not have worked."

I can't help it. I feel a lecture coming on and find myself tightening my diaphragm in order to project more fully. "In any case, a writer creates pictures with words and I wrote a story... not exactly about this trip because if it were an exact recounting of everything we saw, it would be a photograph, right? But, as in all my writing, I try to fold my real-life experiences into a story the way a baker folds yeast into a batch of bread." At this point I note Marjorie's rolling eyes. I immediately shift register and conclude with, "So, for what it's worth here's something rising from our trip

North. By the way, the names of any characters have been changed to protect the innocent."

Just Enough to Make It Home

"Hey! I found a bulldozer on the Internet!" I exclaim to my buddy Cal. "And it's free! We just have to go pick it up in Nebraska."

"What you mean, we?" Cal mumbles.

To someone who doesn't know him, Cal's reply would seem to imply a certain reluctance to drive across four states with his truck and trailer. But I know better. I just need to pay some dues before he'll go along with the gig—philosophize, jaw about this and that, drop some compliments on his old truck. Like that.

It worked. So, here's us on the way back from Lincoln. There's a World War II surplus bulldozer, drab green and rusty, trailing behind us. Cal is driving. That's a condition of his involvement—only he can drive his International Harvester truck. That leaves me with the task of navigating and keeping him awake during the long tedium of wheat fields waving.

"You know we're down to half a tank of gas," I thoughtfully remind him. "We might as well top her off at that gas station coming up," I helpfully point out.

"It's not a Shell station," he replies.

I start in on another thirty minutes of non-stop chatter followed by a glance at the fuel gauge—a quarter tank to empty.

Next, I start in on how I could use the dozer to scoop out my little seep-pond and line it with clay. Then I could stock it with bluegills so me and my boys could trot down there in the evening, catch a few fish for supper and watch the sheep come down to drink.

"What sheep? You don't have any sheep."

"Not now. Wait till I get that dozer going and I clear out my road frontage property and sell off a couple or three lots. Then I'm gonna go buy me a flock of Merinos for their wool. And then I'll get my wife to make yarn, and sew up fleece slippers and hats and such. Then we're going to get a web site and sell our sheep products over the Internet. How's that sound?"

"Sounds like you want a whole lot of things."

"I'll tell you what I want... a tank full of gas," I say. "I'm thinking that we've been riding on empty for the last five or ten miles and I haven't seen a Shell gas station sign. Why are you doing this?"

"To keep me awake," he says as he scratches the gray stubble on his chin that looks like a spring cornfield waiting for the plow.

Twenty minutes later, the truck wheezes, stutters and dies. I'm mad.

"Damn, Cal. Now look. We're stuck without a farm house in sight and nothing but a long road sloping down to the horizon."

"The operative word, here, is down. If the road slopes, let's put the truck in neutral and see what we find."

So, we slowly trundle down the long, curving road until it rounds into a small town with a Shell gas station on the corner.

Cal is grinning so hard I'm afraid he can't see the road.

"Now, what did that prove?" I scold over hamburgers and blueberry pie.

"That you only need enough to make it home. No more."

Chapter Nine; Sal

At first it was nice to hear from those guys. Now, I'm getting pissed. What the hell? I don't need anyone to check up on me. And Bernice... well, they'll tell her I'm okay, soon enough. I don't need to check in with mommy. Damn. Besides, I just want to wander around for a while. First, I get kicked out of my house. It's empty, waiting for another family. Then I come here, where I grew up, it's empty too. That's a lot to get used to.

There, across the street is Carmine's old house... or where it used to be. Man, I had the hots for his sister. What was her name? Rose. That was it. Rose. She used to fondle my safety boy belt when I stood on the corner. And over there, that's the shortcut alley I used to take till Pete Valvano and Mike Presti jumped me and took my lunch money and I had to go to school all dirty with a bloody nose. I went the long way around after that.

At the corner of McClellan and Harper, I stop. Kick a rock. Who cares what I remember? They say you know you're old when you spend more time remembering what you did than what you're going to do. Well, godammit, I am old. So, I remember. What's wrong with that? Besides, I don't know what I want to do next.

That weedy field is where we used to live. I was so glad to get home after 'Nam. Musta been a month, me moping around the house, trying to get back on track. Sure wasn't ready to jump into the dry cleaner store. My dad, he decides this is a good excuse for him to visit the relatives in Sicily and for me to do a roots trip. He was right, I needed something to get me off my ass.

See? That's the way I feel now. Like I'm stuck. Italy was good once. Why not again?

Now, I'm excited. I'm in my van, charging the phone, looking for flights to Italy. I got my passport, $135.00 in my wallet, credit cards. What more do I need?

Chapter Ten; Bernice

Bernice, pulling on the latest ragweed intruders in her vegetable garden, spotted Gail carrying a bag of trash toward the garbage cans. "Gail," she called, "haven't seen you in forever."

Gail detoured, a welcoming smile lighting her face. "I just moved back to our old homestead."

"Yeah, I heard Carrie is there. Tre is at the home…"

"The 'home'… that's funny. Yeah, he's there—under the same roof with my mother, of all things." Gail plopped her bag next to the fence, propped her arms on the top rail opposite Bernice's shoulders, ready for a nice natter with her old neighbor. "We put her there last month." Bernice nodded like a person who has heard a joke before but wants to hear this teller's version of the tale. "Had to do it. She was getting to be too much to handle."

"Hmm," Bernice affirmed, sweeping her loose silver hair out of her face to spread over her shoulders. "How's she like it?"

"Oh, you know, the usual crabbing about this and that. But down deep, she's really happier. With me and Carrie working every day, she was lonely. Now she's got round-the-clock company and attention."

"For sure it's got to make you feel better. But, isn't it strange to think of Tre and your mom in the same place?"

"Yeah. Sure is," Gail said, looking up and off, pondering the idea. "He's like a fifth grader in high school."

"But his friend Marjorie is the same…" Bernice clenched her lips, "oops maybe I shouldn't have…"

"No, don't worry," Gail said with a longsuffering expression and tilt of her chin, "I know all about her and their adjoining apartments. Same old Tre. Let someone have a turn trying to live with him." Pointing to the garden, she asked, "But how are you doing? This is a lot to keep up."

"Yeah, you know. I been thinking I could stop any time now," Bernice replied, patting her knees just above the top of her cracked and muddied Frye boots that used to go so well with her mini-skirts and bra-less tank tops, "arthritis... and energy too. I just can't go as long as I used to. These days it feels like the garden is going to grow right over me."

"The house too," Gail said. "It's a lot for one person."

"Well, yeah. And it's falling apart, just like me. I should get rid of the place and move into something smaller. But, first I got to go somewhere fun. Been living here most of my life."

"Where to?"

"I don't care. Name a place. As long as it's far away and different."

"I can relate," Gail replied.

"You're still working, I take it," Bernice enquired. "I see you leaving in the morning... all dressed up."

"All dressed up... funny how that has changed. It used to be work was an excuse to wear certain clothes, look professional. These days the hospital has gone to business casual." Gail waved her hands down her body indicating her pullover and jeans, "Now every day looks like 'Casual Friday.' I mean, hospital employees need to look professional. Don't you agree?"

Bernice tried not to glance down at her soiled cut-offs and tie-dyed T while she nodded in agreement. "Tre always looked sharp when I saw him coming or going to work."

"I'll grant you that. His choice of suits and ties was what attracted me in the first place... and probably the other women, as well. But, you know Bernice, you can't hug a suit on a hanger when the guy isn't around." Her eyes went soft focus. "Leaves you with an empty feeling."

Thinking of her deceased husband, Bernice reached a calloused hand to squeeze Gail's arm. "I know."

Chapter Eleven; Sal

Next morning I'm on Alitalia 1257 to Rome and I'm thinking how it was the first time I went. All the cousins. Lots of kissing and hugging. Getting used to the language. My dad's family could hardly understand his Sicilian it had been so Americanized over the years. I got a good ear and understood more than I needed to say. Which was just as well. Because, one long afternoon, here's us sitting in high-back chairs in a huge marble-floor room, all the aunts and uncles in a big circle going 'how is so-and-so?' and 'who died?' and 'who is on the way to dyin'?' That's when I notice my Pia sitting across from me. All the old-timers go on and on, but we don't need words, me and Pia. You remember that scene in the Godfather where Michael Corleone gives his fiancée a gold necklace and she fingers it and gives him a coy look? Like that. That's how Pia looked at me, off and on, all afternoon. Every once in a while, I would catch her nonna giving me the eye. This girl was her social security. If she hooked up with me and left for the States, gramma would be left high and dry with only her son's wife to look after her old age. Didn't matter. Me and Pia, we hit it off just fine. Pop stuck around for the wedding.

You heard about war brides? Well, this was sort of like that. It took me a while to get the picture. Basically, I had dragged this beautiful girl/woman out of her home and away from her mother and family and shoved her in with my parents, my mother. No English. Strange food, strange city and right away pregnant. No wonder I would find her crying sometimes. I mean, I got it. This was hard for her, and I had caused it.

Once we got our own place, and she had Angeline, things got better. But she still got mopey every time we called long distance to Sicily. And now here's me on my way back to all that. I get the jitters. Is this a good idea, after all? I mean, all that's left of her family is maybe an old aunt or two. And if I show up at their door they're gonna feel obliged... what's the word? *dovere... e il mio dovere.* They have to show hospitality or be shamed. Hell of a thing to do... drop in on them. Especially since the last time they saw me I was kidnapping their favorite niece.

When I land in Rome, I get a connecting flight to Palermo and rent a car. Just for old time sake I get a Fiat Cinquecento—cute little bug of a car. As I tool along the semi-arid countryside—reminds me of Southern California, San Diego, like that—the dry air-like fingers in my hair, a smell I can't describe—maybe hot cactus and baking rocks, and all at once I'm thinking of Pia. Pia and me that first month together. And pretty soon we're floating around fountains and parks with palm trees—lovers holding hands in a mushy fog like in the movies where you swear they put Vaseline on the camera lens. Holding hands. That's all we could do on those evening strolls on the boardwalk next to the ocean. Actually, you got a nasty whiff of rotten seaweeds along there. And one time some yahoos from the country opened their car door and a snake crawled out. The stampede got the whole boardwalk rattling.

So, every night, after supper, there we were, slow walking, smiling, nodding. *'Buona sera,'* and all that. Pia showing me off to her girlfriends. Her mother stalking behind to make sure we didn't do anything to ruin the family name—as if we could try anything in the middle of that crowd. But, in some ways I liked that. That traditional stuff. It made for a special time. Like, did you ever notice how much feeling you can charge into your hand, or even just your fingertip caressing a palm?

Driving along the west coast, I see a sign for Segesta. The Greek temple at Segesta. It's a ruin actually. No roof. Just parts of pillars. But I remember me and Pia going there on our honeymoon. I take the cut off for the historic site.

A parking lot is filled with tour buses, engines dieseling to a low rumble. There are more buildings, concession stands, than I remember. Yellow ropes corral traffic. Some guy whose face looks like Ty Cobb's baseball glove with an unlit—when are they ever lit—Parodi cigar that looks like a tree root growing out of the corner of his mouth, waves me into his farm field and holds out his hand for two euro.

"*Grazie Dottore,*" he says, like I look like a doctor, and like flattery will get him a tip. I'm losing my feelings for this place. I try to focus, to ignore the swarm of school kids pushing and shoving and shouting around me. At the base of the hill to the temple, I let them run ahead. I close my eyes and picture Pia and me starting that climb, holding out our hands to help each other over the ruts and around the boulders. Then finally we get to the top to the temple. And we walk into the middle of it... some pillars like broken oak stumps, others straight and tall all the way to the top and then you look up and there's nothing but solid blue sky. It's like you're at the bottom of this invisible tube, like a silo, maybe, that keeps going and going forever. Swear to God, I never felt anything like the vibrations I felt in that place. It felt holy. I tell you, I never felt anything like it in any church, not even St. Peter's in Rome. This space marked-off with stones, broken stones... it hummed. Yeah, that's it. That's what I'm tryin' to say, it hummed. Gave me goose bumps. Now, maybe you can say, it was just because I was there with Pia. No that wasn't it. This was bigger than us.

So, I need to get to the top of the hill, to the middle of the old temple. I take a deep breath and start to climb. I'm breathing hard. Damn lungs. I'm sweating. But I got this grin plastered on my chops. I'm looking for that vibration, that buzz from a holy place.

I finally walk to the center of the sanctuary. Look up. I'm waiting. Nothin.' No nothin.' Three kids come racing by, playing tag, shouting. I wait for them to disappear. Still no vibes.

As I lurch back down the hill, I picture *Mazara del Vallo*. Do I really want to go there? See some familiar landmarks? Yeah. Sure. Could be fun. I wonder if they still have that raft on the river where everyone crowds on and some guy pulls on a rope to get them across. Or that fish market where the fishermen fling their morning catch of pink and silver and blue fish across the cement floor and people crowd around grabbing that night's supper and arguing prices. Yeah, that would be fun to see. But what if they built a bridge over the river? Or they have tables and trays for each kind of fish and take credit cards at the market? And what about all the new buildings, the McDonald's, the super markets and brand-new high rises? Maybe, Pia and me, that was our time and it's gone—no more Vaseline on the lens. Maybe I could honor her by not trying to relive it, to be disappointed. Maybe I could just remember it as it was.

I get in my car and go back to the airport. *Arrivederci.*

Chapter Twelve; Tre

All that dwelling in the past gets me remembering an autobiographical piece I wrote long ago and used in my classes as an illustration of a narrative essay. I always thought it was a good example of how to make a point with a story. So, I look it up on my hard drive and take it to Pen Dragons.

Turns out it takes me longer to get to our meeting room walking with a cane than with my wheelchair. As I near the room, I hear sharp tones, abrupt pauses. Insulted silences. When I open the door, all conversation stops. It reminds of walking in on my girls when they were talking about something they shouldn't have been. I notice the straight-ahead stares, the self-conscious shuffling of paper, throat clearings. Something's going down or has been. But I'm not about to inquire.

You know, I don't like sports analogies in literature, let alone the boardroom, but after I sit, I do a slow scan of the defense. I'm facing some squint-eyed linemen intent upon sacking me.

You go first," Holly insists. "Last one in, first one up."

"Oh, okay," I agree. "Ladies, as you may know, I've recently been visiting my boyhood haunts and..." I pause picking up sloe eyes, clenched lips. I continue, "I'd like to read a snippet from that trove of learned lessons called childhood."

Wrens, Turkeys and Rabbits

The fat wren tipped over. Fluttered its wings. Rolled off the roof and fell to the ground. I was stunned. I hadn't thought I would ever hit one, let alone kill it. I knelt next to the little bird. I felt bad, started to tell myself or God or someone that I didn't mean it. That it was an accident. I hadn't realized that this would happen. Why did I feel so bad?

When you live on the east side of Detroit, you don't see much wildlife. And yet, years later, when I saw a movie about a Bushman of the Kalahari praying to an animal he had just killed, I knew what he was feeling when he apologized to his victim for taking its life. Only I didn't have any good reason for killing that bird, and I felt terrible. Strangely, I couldn't bring myself to touch the bird. It was part of another world. The world of wild things. I got a shovel. Dug a small hole. Lifted the bird with the shovel and buried it. Then I put the shovel away. Then I put the gun away.

Killing the bird wasn't the same as shooting at Mr. Jack's cats. His cats were fun to shoot at. They were as grouchy as he was and just wanted to be left alone to sun themselves on the black tar roof just across the alley from my upstairs attic window. Invariably, it would take a few shots to get the range since the B-Bs had a curved trajectory over that distance. Eventually a shot would land on the roof next to a cat—just enough to get it to raise its head and look around for the source of the disturbance. The next shot would score, and the cat would leap from the roof in one bound, gone for the rest of the day.

See, that's what I was trying to do with the birds. Tweak them. Not kill them.

It wasn't that I had never seen animals killed. Like the time when the Irish-American club had a Thanksgiving Day raffle. The big wheel with nails stuck around the outer edge clicked slower and slower until it landed, with a breath-jarring tick on my number. People shouted for my Grampa, who was playing cards in the back room. He was proud of me that night. He told me that he had never won anything in his life and now I had won something for him. I can still see him walking ahead of me on the way home, his tweed suit collar turned up against the cold, his floppy golf hat slouched over one ear and the turkey tucked under his arm looking back at me. The turkey stayed in the coal bin for a week until, in a matter of fact way, Grampa twisted its neck. Gramma dunked the carcass in boiling water and pulled off all the feathers singeing the tiny small ones over the gas stove, leaving the smell of burnt hair in the cellar. The turkey, my turkey, looked so beautiful and golden brown for Thanksgiving dinner, and I had made it all possible.

And when my uncles took me hunting, it was always my job to skin and dress the rabbits after a long day in the field. I didn't mind handling them. So, why was I so squeamish about touching that tiny wren? Why did I feel so bad about killing it? Then it hit me, the difference was, on gramma's back porch, skinning rabbits and putting parts in her special tomato-garlic sauce, I was helping us eat. That was the difference.

There is the usual pause after a reading and then comes a pile-on.

"So simplistic."

"Trying to be Hemingway without the rain."

"Gross. How could you be so blood-thirsty? A poor little wren."

"How could your family support hunting and guns?"

I want to defend myself, to say I was only 11-years old, for crying out loud. And as the story should indicate I learned a redeeming lesson from it. But I don't say a thing. I can tell when I'm not wanted. So, I get up, leave, go to my apartment and close the door to Marjorie's.

An hour later I hear a soft knock. Marjorie sticks her head in, "May I?"

I nod. "Coffee?"

"No. I'm good."

I begin, "Seems as though I just whacked a hornet's nest. What's up with those ladies?"

"It's not about you. Or rather it is... but me too... both of us."

"Us? We aren't anything." Noticing Marjorie jerk back as if slapped, I hastily add, "Yet." A dropped-chin glare induces another walk-back. "I mean, officially, as yet."

"I will have some coffee," Marjorie snaps on the way to my sink. She bangs a cup on the counter, shoves it in the microwave, slams the door and gives it two minutes to simmer while she does the same.

Back on my couch, she takes a careful sip then a deep breath before forcibly composing herself. "They're mad at me, mostly, and took it out on you."

"What have you done?"

"I've been seeing you."

I look out the window at nothing in particular. Returning to Marjorie, annoyed, I demand, "What is this? Seventh grade Best Friends Forever? You got a boyfriend and now you don't have time for us anymore? That kind of thing."

Marjorie waggles her head—sort of. "You have to understand. This is serious. Men are a supply-and-demand problem around here."

"So, next you're going to tell me I better not visit Dolores, or I'll get your friends in a dither."

"It's about attention, Tre. I've spent a great deal of time on projects with these women. We connect. We share. And lately I've more or less dropped out. How would that make you feel?"

I frown, trying make that shoe fit.

"Look. How do you feel about Sal, your old buddy, when he goes missing in action?"

"Does not compute. Sal and I are like passing ships in the night... toot-toot. Catch you later." I watch Marjorie swirl her cup before I push on. "Okay, so your friends find it hard to share. They miss you. I can get that. Where does that leave us?"

"Well, it doesn't have to be them or us," Marjorie almost pleads, "does it?"

"No. But if they really are upset, it certainly doesn't help for us to be living together right under their noses."

Marjorie cants her head, glimpsing the direction this conversation is heading. "You're thinking of moving out?"

"Well, my hip is definitely on the mend, and it would be cheaper to find some one-floor condo." I watch her eyes widen. I raise my eyebrows and nod invitingly. "Just sayin.'"

Marjorie gives me a long hard stare, then, "And I'm just sayin'... yes."

We grinned at each other for a long moment.

Marjorie moaned, "But what about my friends?"

"We can always drop in... check on them. I'll want to see Dolores."

"So, you're saying this is a nice place to visit but...

"We don't need to live here... just now."

Chapter Thirteen; Bernice

Bernice was just finishing her pot roast dinner, gathering energy to scoop a serving of peach cobbler, when she heard a car door slam. She got up from the table and peeked out the front room window to see Sal's van in the driveway. "I'll be damned," she muttered.

She hurried back to the table, finger combed her hair over her shoulders, while conflicting feelings fought for attention like a classroom of kids raising their hands. Before she could decide between resentment and joy and sensible caution, there was a click, a door closing, then a tired, gravelly voice, "Helen, I'm home."

Bernice thumped the table with a closed fist. As Sal eased into the kitchen, obviously trying to read her mood, Bernice turned her head toward him, lips sucked in, and decided to let him make the first move.

Sal pulled out a chair, turned it around so his arms rested on the back. "So..."

"What the hell does 'Helen I'm home,' mean?" Bernice demanded.

Sal waved his hand dismissively, "Something my dad used to say."

"Your mother was named Helen?"

Sal shook his head. "It was something he heard on the radio... way back."

Bernice cocked a questioning eyebrow.

Sal took his time to respond in a soft voice, "He meant what I mean... I'm here."

"And you can be anywhere, anytime... just as you please?"

"I'm here."

Bernice stormed away from the table. At the sink, she ran hot water to do the dishes, then whirled around. "Yeah, well, where were you anyway?"

"Trying to figure out where I want to be."

She slammed the faucet shut. Turned, her angry face softening. "And exactly where did you go... to find all this out?"

"Italy."

"Your wife was from Italy."

Sal got up, walked to the sink and looked Bernice in the eye. "It's a nice place to visit."

"But... you don't want to live there?"

Sal shook his head and reached for her hand. "Did you ever notice," he began in a low, serious voice, "how much energy you can pass to someone else, just with your hand?" Caressing her palm with his fingertip, he added, "And how much caring with your fingertip."

Chapter Fourteen; Tre

Sal grabs a chicken quarter with a set of tongs and then liberally sloshes it with a leaf of lettuce loaded with his Sicilian garlic, tomato and who-knows-what-else sauce. Gently laying it back on the grill, his deep sigh floats like a cartoon thought-bubble in the brisk March air, then blends with the smoke from Bernice's Weber grill, perched in a dirty snow bank. We're pushing summer... a bit. And it's not just Michigan winter blahs. It's like we're celebrating our jailbreak from retirement village a while back.

"Sal," I had said on the phone this morning, "they got watermelon here at Harding's." I could almost hear his smile.

"Grab some chicken and beers. Bell's. Get some Bell's. Two-Hearted, if they got it." His voice is muffled, but I can hear him talking to Bernice. "Oh, yeah, and Tre. Get a bag of those yellow potatoes and some fresh oregano, if they got any. Otherwise dry. Come by around 3:00 and I'll have the grill going."

So, here we are hunched in our coats like guys on the corner around a burn barrel. Man the hunter burning meat, mesmerized by the flickering flames. Man of words that I am, silence feels like a vacuum. Marjorie and Bernice are inside. And this is the first chance I've had to be alone with Sal since he got back from his Italy junket. So, I break the spell. "Haven't had a chance to ask you yet. What was that Italy trip all about?"

Sal takes his time. Rolls a slightly scorched breast in the bowl of sauce. Gently places it just off the center of the grid. He gives his Robert DeNiro 'you tawkin' to me?' shrug and squinch.

I push a little. "Just wondering, is all."

He nods. Talks to the chicken. "I'm like the guy jumped naked into a cactus, says, 'seemed like a good idea at the time.'" He catches my half-smirk. "Naw. You know, I just needed to get some shit worked out. An' I did. Me and Bernice. Here. Together. It's good. How you guys doin'? Like your new place?"

"Yeah. We like being right downtown. Second floor. Balcony over the mall. We watched all the Christmas and New Year's stuff. Everything's close... bakery, lunch, movies."

"Got enough room?"

"Well, she gets her own work space—the second bedroom. I don't go in there and she closes the door on her 'stuff.' The rest... we simplified. But yeah, it's okay."

There's that pause where your database is whirring through 1s and 0s looking for connections—what to talk about next? Sal snaps a hit on his beer. I savor a longer swallow. We hadn't seen each other for a while. Much had changed, I would imagine. There's always an awkward transition back to intimate sharing after a break—like a basketball player coming back to his team off injured reserve. It takes a while to re-establish timing and rapport.

Finally, Sal says, "She wants to go on a cruise."

Funny how some men refer to their significant others as 'her' or 'she,' pronouns with an implied antecedent. Perhaps it's the parallel of women referring to their spouses by their first names, "John always says..." listeners obviously aware, or expected to be, of who John is.

"That sounds like fun. Where're you thinking?"

"I'm not thinkin.' She is."

"Ah," I nod, absorbing the implications, bracing for the rest of the story.

"It's not just one cruise to, like, the Caribbean. She wants to go cruising. Like living on a cruise boat, one after another."

"Really? Serial cruise ships?"

Sal slams his longneck on the picnic table. "Yeah, she read some article about a woman comparing the cost of living in a retirement home to living on a cruise ship and it's supposed to come out cheaper. Go figure."

"But you don't live in a retirement home. You don't have that cost to offset."

"I told her that. Know what she said? 'It's still cost effective. We could rent out the house like an Airbnb and pay for the cruise.' And on top of that, she says we might be able to actually get paid for being on the cruise by doing something like she does with handwriting analysis. You know, study the customer's handwriting, as like entertainment or something. And if I wanted, she goes, I could maybe even work in the ship's dry cleaner room." He raises his eyebrows, "Nice, huh?"

"Sounds like she's serious about this idea." I take a long swallow. "Good luck with that."

"Yeah, well, you don't get off that easy, bud. What do you think she's talking to Marjorie about, right this minute? You're next."

"No."

"Think about it. What would you have to offer, Marjorie too, for that matter, to entertain folks after dinner for a few nights."

I suddenly picture a brochure with educationally redeeming opportunities for bored cruisers: Memoir Writing for Family and Friends; The Poet in You; Your Novel... The First Chapter. Oh, God. I shake my head in denial. "No way."

"Yeah, way," Sal says, plucking chicken parts onto a platter. "And the worst part isn't my seasickness." He turns pleading, desperate eyes on me. "I don't want to go anywhere. That last trip to Italy reminded me of that. I just want to stay at home. Hunker down. *Basta.*"

I close my eyes. Both our women have lived constrained, limited lives. The allure to see the wide wonders of the world must be intensely seductive. And once they've clasped that cruise ship idea to their bosoms, we're going to be cast as the villains trying to drag that sweet babe from their arms. Damn. And that chicken smelled so good just a minute ago.

"What's our plan?" Sal whispers as we climb the back stairs.

"I'll think of something," I mutter, "follow my lead."

Chapter Fifteen; Bernice

"I wouldn't mind going on a cruise," Marjorie allowed. She looked up from the stack of vacation brochures she and Bernice had been exploring. "But don't you think serial cruising is a bit over the top?"

Bernice shrugged and flipped a Vikings folder on the coffee table. "Yeah, but it never hurts to aim high. It may end up just you and me settling for a cruise to the Virgin Islands." Waiting for a reaction, she added, "Not all bad, huh?"

They both looked up when the back door thumped shut and watched Sal heel off his loafers and pad barefoot into the kitchen. Tre, they noticed, stomped in with muddy shoes, oblivious to his buddy's newly acquired domestic habit.

Marjorie shot a raised, go for it eyebrow at Bernice, grabbed a handful of silverware out of the drawer and called over her shoulder to Sal, "Chicken smells great."

Tre sliced the watermelon at the sink while Bernice pulled the parmesan-crusted potato wedges out of the oven. "We may be rushing the picnic season but we're not having cold potato salad today." Bernice said.

For the next five minutes the only sounds were forks stabbing and knives clacking on china and the occasional 'Pass the chicken' or 'Nice barbecue sauce.'

When they all came up for air after diving into the first serving, Tre exchanged a look with Sal and asked, "That pile of brochures on the coffee table... are you ladies working on some travel plans?"

Marjorie canted her head toward Bernice who delicately spit a melon pip onto her plate and took a measured pause, like a featured speaker using a moment of silence to focus attention, then launched into her pitch about the advantages of living on cruise ships rather than houses: ten meals a day, free pool, workout facilities, washer/dryers, free utilities, TV, daily clean sheets, towels and housekeeping, doctor on board, nightly live entertainment and new people to meet every seven to ten days. Then she catalogued the potential locations: Europe, the Caribbean, Alaska, river cruises, Galapagos Islands and Greece. When she ducked her chin to conclude the presentation, Tre asked, "Do you get seasick?"

"I know, I do," Sal volunteered.

"That's why God made Dramamine," Bernice countered with eyelids at half-mast.

"Why do you need to go anywhere?" Sal whined. "What's wrong with right here? Your garden. Nice neighborhood and," adding a self-deprecating shrug, "me."

"You?" Bernice shrilled, clanging her fork on the plate— like a bell for the first round of a drag-out fight. "This, from the man who took off for Little Italy without a word. Then zooms off for real Italy, again by himself. He's gonna tell me to be happy at home? Me, who has been stuck in the same house all my life, growing zucchini and tomatoes and kids. And now, just for a change, when I would like to see the bigger world while I can still walk, he wants me to hunker down. Huh!" As a final exclamation point she added, "At least I thought to invite you along."

After a breeze of icy silence blew through the room, Tre cleared his throat and asked, "You're interested as well, Marjorie?" When she nodded, he glanced at Sal, who was intently focused on slicing his chicken breast. No help there. In his role as chairman of the English department, he had regularly encountered conflicting interests between opposing factions. Creating a committee to report back later often proved a helpful strategy to defuse tensions. "If both of you want to go on a cruise," he said, "why not do it? See what it's like. See if you like it. See if you think Sal and I would like it and report back to us. And while you're away, Sal and I can hang out at Vinnie's cabin." He wondered at the self-satisfied curl at the corner of Bernice's mouth.

Over dishes in the soap-filled sink, Bernice said, "I never thought Sal would want to go on a cruise anyhow. So, where do you want to go?"

"I don't care just so it's warm and sunny. Ten days... two weeks would be nice."

"Me too."

Marjorie grinned and shook her head. After a pause to slide into other subjects, she said, "Vinnie. I've heard about him but never met him."

"You've slept in his cabin," Bernice said, "that should tell you something about him."

"He's got nice taste in bedspreads?"

"The construction. He made it all himself. He's a carpenter. Works on the maintenance staff at a hospital."

"Which one?"

"Mercy."

"Doesn't Gail work there?"

"Used to. She just retired."

"Poor Gail," Marjorie said. "I feel kind of bad for her... single, living with her daughter. And here's me with her ex and us partying right next door."

"Don't feel sorry for her. Gail's okay. Since she put her mom in that place where Sal and Tre used to stay. I see her, all the time trotting around like when her and Tre were neighbors back when. Except now you don't see her in panty hose and business suits. She was always one to dress professional."

"Yeah, well. I still don't know how to act around her. You know... how she would feel about me and Tre."

"Gail? She's past Tre. Been past for years. Let someone else try to live with him, is what she would say."

"I guess. It's just... I've seen her peeved at him, and I don't want to step in the middle of all that."

Bernice waved her hand dismissively, "Nah, just be cool with her. Don't try to be bestest friends or anything and you'll be all right."

"Hmm. So, tell me more about Vinnie," Marjorie asked. "What's he like?"

"To see him, you'd never picture him being a carpenter. He's tall. Perfectly combed hair. Trim mustache. Mostly gray now, I'd imagine. Haven't seen him in a while. Quiet man. Talks slow and deliberate. He cuts and polishes jewels for a hobby."

"Sounds solid."

"Yeah. But, you know those movies where people crowd around a ballroom in old fashioned clothes... bustles and tuxedoes and all that?"

"A period piece?"

"Yeah, I guess you'd call it that. Well, Vinnie could be one of the extras. There he'd be, standing tall with a red sash with medals across his chest. Chin up taking champagne from a waiter."

"But he grew up with Tre and Sal?"

"Uh-huh. Go figure."

"I wonder if Gail knows him?"

"I bet Tre brought him around, sometime, or like at their wedding or something. But I never saw him next door. Maybe Gail's seen him around... in the cafeteria and that. Could you picture her and Vinnie together? Him, all tall in his three-piece suit and her in one of her boardroom matching outfits."

Finished drying, Marjorie hung the damp towel on the edge of the counter. "Is he married?"

"No. Never been."

Chapter Sixteen; Tre

I'm sitting in Vinnie's boat with Sal, shivering. That's what happens when you try to go fishing in April, in Michigan. It's not bass season yet. The bluegills aren't anywhere near on their beds yet, so fishing is slow. We're about to spend three days drowning worms, playing cribbage and staring at each other over hotdog suppers.

"Boring. Cold," Sal booms like an airport announcement in the early-morning still of the steaming lake. "They couldn't book a cruise they liked, so they went to Chicago for a long weekend. Just as well."

"Not all bad," I mumble as I check my now limp worm then cast next to some lily pads. My bobber dances. The red and white float scoots sideways. I take up the slack and tug. We're both surprised. It's a slabby 'gill.' "A couple three more of these and we'll have enough for a good lunch," I say. While I unhook the fish and re-bait, Sal plops his line right in my spot. A little bit of Sal goes a long way.

An hour later, heading up for breakfast, there's a tan KIA Sorrento between our cars. "Vinnie," Sal says. "Wonder what he wants."

Turns out, Vinnie is planning to replace the punky boards on his north-facing deck. We find this out after a brunch of buttermilk pancakes and scrambled eggs. Sal and I decide to help him with the project... can't exactly bail at this point. So, while Sal pries off splintered and rotted 2x6s with a crowbar, Vinnie and I unload the fresh lumber and set up the sawhorses and chop saw.

I strap on a spare tool belt with a drill and pouch full of stainless-steel screws. Sal gives me the eye. "Gimme those," he orders, "before you hurt yourself... or me." I huff in indignation as Sal explains to Vinnie, "He hardly knows which end of the screw goes into the wood. Helpless. Here," he says, handing me an old deck board, "take the nails out of these puppies. Where do you want them stacked, Vin?"

"Just next to the fire pit would be good," he says pointing to a ring of rocks filled with gray ash.

I prop the first plank on a stump, back-pound a rusty nail and flip the board to claw it out. I'm annoyed. Sal has no reason to throw shade on me... nice phrase, that. Heard a football player complain about a teammate... "Why's he throwin' shade on me?" See, that's what I am—a wordsmith not a wood worker. I listen for turns of phrase and then look for ways to use them. That's when the board jumps off the stump and whacks me in the shin. "Damn!"

Sal piles on. "Told you he was a klutz. I bet he hasn't picked up a tool or a paint brush in what—fifty years?"

I look up. My face furrowed in hurt pride.

"Don't gimme that look. When's the last time you painted a wall or fixed a leaking faucet? See, Vinnie, that's what happens when all your life you got the maintenance department to..." he pauses to flap his wrist dismissively, "take care of that piddly-shit stuff."

"That's okay. Folks like him kept me working," Vinnie allows.

"You still at it?" I ask, glad to change the subject.

"Nah. Yeah, I'm retired, but all the widows five blocks around keep me hopping. Loose hinges. Railings. All that."

"He could probably earn more than his social security if he ever got started on your old house," Sal chortled before grunting to lever out another tread. "See this," he said holding out the rotted plank. "That's what guys do. We see what has to be done to make something safe, to make it work. But not ladies. They gotta change things because it's boring, been there too long. Move the furniture. Get new drapes."

"Who wound him up?" Vinnie asks.

I shrug, grab a plank and walk away.

"Take this shirt," Sal continues plucking at his plaid flannel shirt. "It's old. You can tell because you can see the white poking through the collar and on the cuffs." Rubbing his sleeve, he goes on, "But feel the cloth. It's like silk. So soft. I know clothes. When you been in the cleaning business like me, you know clothes. It takes a long time to get a shirt to feel like this. Or jeans. Take jeans. There's nothing softer than an old pair of jeans..."

"Just before they fall apart," I call from the stump.

"Like a good wine... just before you drink it. Ha?"

There's a pause while Sal scoots to the far end of the next twelve-foot plank. "But no. Ladies want to get rid of a nice old shirt." In falsetto he says, "Aren't you sick of wearing that rag?" He stands to stretch his back. "Remember Donovan and his song about a shirt?" He croaks a few bars, "I love my shirt, I love my shirt, I love my shirt and my shirt loves me." He nods in agreement with himself. "Yeah, guys can relate to that song,"

"What do you think, Vinnie?" I prompt.

"I think I like to work without people singing and talking."

"Sorry," Sal says, "but there's no free lunch. Us volunteers talk. It's in our contract."

"Not all women are like that," I say, "or not to that degree, anyway."

"Perfesser, this ain't no classroom... this distinction, that difference. So maybe I'm talking broad about broads. But tell you what. You better notice that kind of shit, and work with it, or you're gonna end up divorced."

Catching a look at my startled face, Sal mutters, "Oops." Pauses. "Well, hell if the flu shits wear it."

"I never stopped Gail from buying stuff," I protest.

"Glad I missed all that grief," Vinnie says, shaking his head.

Sal pops loose another plank. "It's just part of the deal, Vin."

I carry a fresh board to Vinnie to fill the slot left by Sal's work. I help him center it on the joists. "What do you think, Vin, would you be willing to stop by my place and see what needs to be done? Carrie and Gail live there now and keep bugging me to fix a bunch of things."

"You don't live there anymore?"

"No. We divorced a while back. I'm with someone else now. But really, the house could stand some attention. I'll pay whatever you charge."

"Oh, no. Just materials. I enjoy keeping busy. How about I come by tomorrow morning?"

I glance at Sal. It will be good to get away.

Chapter Seventeen; Gail

Gail eased down the stairs, yawning. At the sound of voices in the kitchen, she stopped, massaging the morning ache in her lower back. Tre and Carrie were talking to someone else. A quick peek around the doorway revealed the back of a tall man with white hair.

Well, excuse me for living in my own house, she groused to herself on the way up the stairs. In front of her closet she studied her wardrobe, trying to decide what to wear. Don't have to wear jeans just because it's Saturday. Saturday. That's why Carrie's not at work. Nice slacks and a blouse would be fine. In the bathroom, she ran a brush through her hair. Paused at the mirror, tilting her head to one side and the other. No more need to keep it business prim, she thought. Shoulder length would be good... and auburn rinse this time.

Coming down the stairs she called, "Carrie, what's for breakfast?" as if unaware of company and swung into the kitchen, smiling broadly like a movie star making an entrance. Tre barely looked up from the back door where he was crouched, rattling the loose knob for the stranger. The man turned slowly and gave her an appreciative look, followed by a *Downton Abbey* gentleman's bow. *Well now,* she thought. Isn't he a nice vision before breakfast. But wait, he's familiar. Why do I recognize him?

"This is Vinnie Di Palma," Tre said, "He ran with Sal and me when we were kids."

"I'm sure that's not his only claim to fame," Gail said, enjoying the amused response in Vinnie's eyes.

"You met him once when we were first married," Tre supplied.

Gail studied the guest, trying to morph him back forty-five years, adding black hair, smoothing out his laugh-line crevices. "Yeah, I guess. Maybe. But somewhere else,"

Gail muttered, "recently." She liked the way the man held his counsel, eyes steady, amused, waiting for her to make a connection.

Tre stood and took a sip of coffee from his mug. "He worked at Mercy. Maintenance."

Gail placed him now, sitting in the corner of the cafeteria with the hospital electricians and plumbers and carpenters. Blue uniforms versus lab coats and business suits—another version of high school cliques. Had she really bought into that? She and her business office colleagues never sat with those guys. But then, none of them broke ranks either. And now, here she was standing in front of this man she had worked with for years but never really met. "I didn't recognize you out of uniform," she half-apologized.

Vinnie paused for a two-count before answering. "Well, I'm retired now." Another pause. "And you're out of uniform too."

"I guess it's Casual Friday... every day, these days," Gail said, tugging on her untucked blouse with the vague embarrassment of friends seeing each other in bathing suits after a long winter.

Vinnie nodded and broke eye contact as well.

"Dad was just showing Mr. Di Palma some things that need to be fixed," Carrie explained.

"And then I gotta run," Tre said.

"No problem. I can take over from here," Gail offered. "In fact, we could be at it all morning. Let me freshen that," she said, reaching for Vinnie's mug. He's so tall, she realized, and I love his bearing, his dignity. How could I have not noticed it before? "Have you had breakfast Mr. Di Palma?"

"Ah, no. Not yet."

Gail gestured to a seat at the table. "Scrambled eggs? Carrie? You too?"

Vinnie's work-curled hands rested on the table, like the iconic picture of the solitary old man silently praying over his daily bread, before he finally said, "Sure. But you can just call me Vinnie. Everyone does."

"How about Vincent? May I call you Vincent?" Gail asked.

"That would be fine," he replied, a bemused grin twitching his precisely trimmed mustache as if trying out the sound of 'Vincent' in his mind.

As Tre headed out the front he could hear Gail asking, "What do you think about these cupboards? And, you know, I have always liked the idea of a butcher-block island in the middle of a kitchen."

"Vincent!" Tre muttered to himself. "Poor bastard doesn't know what he's in for."

Chapter Eighteen; Tre

Marjorie flops onto our couch, feet on the ottoman, and rubs her eyes.

"Tired," she moans.

"Coffee?" I ask.

"Uhm, yeah," she says.

After she's had a couple sips, I ask, "So, how was it?"

"Great time. We saw a play. Went to the Field Museum. Shopping. Bars on Rush street."

"Checking out the local talent?"

"Bernice sure did. Think 'flower child' at seventy. Saturday night she didn't get in till way late... got back to the hotel after I was asleep." Marjorie yawned and stretched before continuing. "There's more to that lady than meets the eye. Bernice."

I squint a question.

"Oh, I don't know. Everything is beautiful. Peace. Love. And shouting requests to the balding folk-singer with a wispy goatee and applauding after every song."

"We talking Burl Ives?"

"No. More like Bob Dylan without the harmonica and Nobel Prize."

"Oh-oh. Poor Sal."

"Yeah. Well, he hasn't given her a ring, has he?"

I decide to live dangerously. Into the pregnant pause, I ask, "So, how about you? Did you chat-up anyone interesting?"

Marjorie forced her sleepy eyes half-open. "What would you think if I did?"

I suppose we had to have the 'us' talk one of these days. I just wasn't quite sure what to say next. I fumbled, "We certainly are more than compatible roommates."

She opens one eye fully. "You think?"

"Well, if you want, we could..." I begin.

She raises one hand, mutters, "I'm happy with a committed relationship."

I whistle silently. Before I think to add, 'Same here,' she's zoned out, breathing regularly under a sweet smile.

I sit at my computer across the room. Studying her, I feel the need for words. To spell out where we're at. Or more importantly where I'm at. Bad grammar. Good questions. I asked her if she was looking around. How about me? Granted, I'm not some crinkled creep thinking there's a trophy waiting for the guy with the most dyed hair, orange tan and busty babe on his arm. So, okay, I'm more sophisticated. Selective. But when I run into an attractive, available woman how come I need to engage?

Let me play this out in a sketch. I finger the keyboard. Picture a character. He's a writer. A fifty-something hobby writer. Gets stuff in magazines, the odd anthology. He goes to a Book Expo in Chicago. Makes the rounds looking for gigs.

Cerulean Blue

It takes till mid-morning and traversing half of Mc-Cormack Place before I find the section with my kind of publishers. Adams Media. Maybe I can convince them to include another of my stories in one of their chicken-soup-for-the-soul collections. Or Bathroom Reader's Institute. I saw their latest anthology called Flush Fiction. Any pot in a storm. What about outdoor magazines? I've done okay in that market. Hey, it's all exposure and work. I've just got to find it.

I drop off a couple of cards, get some leads, names to call back. Over a plastic ham and cheese, I notice a woman, what? Maybe late fifties, sitting a couple tables over, scanning a catalogue. Nice, intelligent-looking, streaked blond hair, well-cut. Her taupe business suit is set off by a cerulean blue blouse and matching shoes. No wedding ring. I could easily start up a conversation, tap dance a little... like this, like that. Find out where she lives. Talk about her children or grandkids, or if she's single, her nieces and nephews. I could. But why?

Sipping my Coke, I watch the woman reach in her purse for a tissue. Is she a honker or a barely discernible puffer? You don't know any of these things right away. It takes time, being together. She discreetly dabs her nostrils. So, there's the first thing—she's a puffer. There's so much more to find out: what her Saturday morning routine is like, 'No, Honey, I'll have coffee in a minute, with my toast.' Or that she reads bodice rippers in bed or maybe biographies of Civil War generals and takes forever picking out her clothes but is a terror zooming around in traffic. Finding all that out, getting used to it, takes time. Like where I'm at with Carol. I know how she likes her scrambled eggs. And I found that secret spot on the back of her neck, just below the hairline... makes her purr. We're easy. Getting along. 'In relationship,' she calls it. Whatever that means.

So, why do I feel compelled to play Wal-Mart greeter with every woman I meet? Maybe it's time to lay down in my yard and stop chasing every car that goes by. Maybe it's time to stop mixing metaphors...

I save the file. Draw a throw over her. It feels good to have Marjorie here. 'Committed relationship.' Yeah, I like that.

It's Easter Sunday, a couple weeks after the Chicago trip. We're in Bernice's backyard admiring the thin row of hyacinths and daffodils marching around her freshly spaded vegetable garden like a Planned Parenthood protest... all about reproduction, fertile ground. I tell myself to stifle the metaphor-making, save it for the printed page. Besides, it's forced. Needs work.

Sal calls me over to hummus and pita snacks. "Your house must be looking pretty good these days," he remarks once we're seated and sipping wine on the patio.

"How's that?"

Sal pauses to purse his lips and blow out a couple times. "Damn lungs," he moans, continues, "Vinnie's been there every day for the past ten days."

"Place needs a lot of work."

"And his truck's been there all night for the past four."

"Ahh," I say. How can I respond? An old buddy has now moved into my house. Is remodeling it. Is sleeping in my bed with my wife... okay my ex. Why should I feel anything but happy for both of them? Damn him.

The women join us. Sal's got enough breath to step right in it. "So, now after a nice girl's weekend, we can all concentrate on sticking around here, right? Nothing wrong with a 'get away' once in a while..."

Bernice cuts him off, "Actually, I got another idea, Sally. Better than a cruise. We ran into a couple who described their trip to Tanzania. You tell them Marjorie."

I exchange looks with Sal—damn.

Before she can begin, we hear, "Hey, you guys." It's Gail. "Vincent!" she shouts, "come see who's next door."

We all stare at the back porch, waiting.

"Vincent?" Sal grimaces. I lift my hand—don't go there.

As usual, Vinnie takes his time responding to demands. Could it be all those years working on the clock? Take your time. There will always be more to do. No rush. When he does step out, he's not dressed for carpentry. He's wearing tan linen slacks and a Madras shirt. A new Vinnie. Gail must be getting to him. He answers our stare with an apologetic hunch of his shoulders. He flashes a palm at his waist. "Hi."

"C'mon over," Bernice invites.

I go to the gate while Sal gets more glasses. Vinnie touches my arm as Gail joins the women. "Look, Tre," he begins, coughs, vaguely waves his arm to include Gail and the house. "I didn't plan on this." I wait for his usual manual-typewriter double space between sentences. "She just landed on me like a ton of bricks. I'm not trying to..."

I flash to the Aesop's fable about the dog in the manger keeping cattle from their hay. Why should I begrudge my buddy all that I loved in Gail?

"It's okay, Vin. You deserve a break." I watch his face relax.

"It's a miracle, man. I never thought it would happen to me."

I fist bump his arm. "Go for it." He grins as if I've just given him a blessing.

Soon we're all listening to Marjorie describing a tour for seniors that involves a safari to the Serengeti plains and Olduvai Gorge and nights in tent camps and days in land cruisers disturbing animal tranquility.

I watch Sal smacking his lips as if readying a reply. I shake my head. He clenches his jaw. He reads me—not yet, not now.

"I've always been fascinated by Africa," Vin says. "I watch every nature channel show about African animals."

Gail perks up, "Really? Me too." Bernice and Marjorie add their enthusiasm to the mix.

"I've never traveled," Vin says, "never had anyone to go with." Bernice and Marjorie look at us at the same time. They must be good at reading faces because they exchange glances and Bernice immediately offers, "As long as you want company, Vinnie, maybe you could go with us three women and we'll just leave these stick-in-the-muds at home."

Marjorie shoots a meaningful look at Gail who stares back at her, chin up, face askance for a moment, then shrugs as if to say, 'Yeah, we're okay.'

I can feel centrifugal force pushing Sal and me to the outer limits of this newly formed constellation. Meanwhile, Vinnie looks like the kid who just got elected homecoming King. It's a great honor, but he's not so sure he wants it. That doesn't stop the women. They're on a high roll when Sal and I go inside to watch the Tigers.

Marjorie is pumped on the ride home. No sooner are we in the door than she's online comparing tour packages, safari clothes and nature sites. Before I can find the Tiger's game on TV, she calls out, "Did you know there were crocodiles in Tanzania?"

Turns out, I do, actually. Some of us at a conference in Johannesburg went on a one-day tour. I know. I don't want to start sounding like the world-weary globetrotter—been there, done that. But... What's that story I wrote a while back? I pull it up on the computer. Read it.

Turn, Turn, Turn

I climbed out of my seat and crossed the aisle to get my first glimpse of Mt. Kilimanjaro. I'd never been to Tanzania before, but I was as excited as when I went to Guatemala with the Peace Corps, some fifty years ago. Of course, it wouldn't be the same, but I was getting back to a third, or was it second-world, country? Whatever. I was getting out of my comfort zone at last. Noreen never understood my longing to revisit that life-expanding experience. Fort Wayne was as much of the world as she needed. Well, with her gone, I was free to explore and could hardly wipe the grin of anticipation off my face as we started our descent.

From my hotel room on the third floor I looked down on the swarming busyness of downtown Arusha—women draped head to toe in kitenges of shrieking colors, dolla-dolla buses crammed with people, stringers of fish and baskets of fruit on top, cutting in and around and through pedestrians and traffic. I used to love riding chicken buses and tuk-tuks around Panajachel—literally in touch with the locals. I felt different riding in from Kili airport. Maybe riding in a cab isolates you in a detached bubble. Squeezing a fourth person onto a two-man bus seat integrates you the way lighting up a cigarette blends you into a smoke-filled room.

And the confusion. At one point my driver had to hit the brakes to let another car cut in front of him, which had to stop to let a pedestrian slide by in front of another car waiting to proceed. Somehow, what used to feel like a fun computer game of dodgeball traffic now just seemed chaotic and unnerving. My plastered grin was beginning to droop. Had I forgotten how it really was? Or had things changed? Or had I turned into a testy old fart?

Zanzibar offered more of the same. Vendors waved from the beach, unfurling gaudy shawls. I used to like haggling for souvenirs. How much for one bracelet? How about for three? Not anymore. I found that I resented beggars and street vendors—people making me say no, making me feel stingy or rude or somehow beholden.

I began counting the days until it was time to go home.

Nostalgia trip over, I was on Qatar Airlines flight 357 direct to Chicago, stuck in the middle seat of the middle row, facing fifteen hours in a straitjacket. How come I never seemed to remark the length of a flight when I was younger? Maybe I was geeked back then and didn't have to pee every hour and a half. Instead I compared my situation to post surgery bed confinement, to a jail sentence, to slave ship quarters, to a woman in labor with no way out until it was over. I had a long talk with myself about centering, living in the moment as the teenaged boy next to me knocked my elbow off the arm rest for the third time, and we hadn't even taken off yet.

I watched the GPS read-out on my TV screen. We were going from Doha to Chicago by way of Moscow and Helsinki and Sault Ste. Marie, Michigan. Fifteen hours. I noticed the young African woman on my left. She sat primly with her hands in her lap and the self-satisfied smile of a righteous doer-of-good on a mission. It takes one to know one. With some gentle prodding, I found she was on her way to Chicago. For the next half hour she explained that she had trained as a nurse technician in Kenya under a program that required two years' service in return. She would be working in a clinic in Chicago's south side.

After she pumped me for details of life in the big city, I wished her well, pushed my seat back, closed my eyes and gave myself over to the steady throb of the jet engines... more power to you, young lady. Ride the wave of optimism and energy. It's your time. Your season. Turn, turn, turn.

How do I begin to explain all those feelings to Marjorie?

Chapter Nineteen; Vinnie

Vinnie called Tre. "I gotta talk to you." Paused.

Tre said, "You're talking to me. So..."

"Gimme a chance to finish what I'm trying to say before butting in. Okay?" After Tre's audible sigh, Vin continued. "Can you come out to the cabin tomorrow?"

"Uhm. Okay. What's it about? Oh, let me guess... what's new in your life?"

"Early. Say 7:30?"

They were in the boat next to Vinnie's favorite weed bed. No wind. The sun poking shafts through the morning mist. Vinnie hated to break the spell. Tre didn't mind. "I guess you want some help with Gail... right?"

"Well, yeah. Sort of. That and... the whole Africa thing."

Tre cast into a pocket between the lily pads. "First of all, let me just say, I'm not a marriage counselor."

"And I'm not married."

"Let me finish," he snapped, giving Vin a dose of his own medicine.

"Second, my track record with Gail isn't so hot. So, I wouldn't be the one to give advice in dealing with her. And third, even if I did want to, she deserves a clean shot with you, without my input. And fourth, living with a woman is not like making a house from a blueprint. This is more like hiking the woods with no GPS. You've got to find your way, just like the rest of us jerks."

"You done?"

"Yeah," Tre answered reeling in a stunted sunfish.

"Can you just be my friend and listen." Vin took a deep breath. "You know more than I do about women."

Tre shrugged. "Fire away."

Vinnie came across self-conscious. He had been awake half the night thinking about all the things he wanted to say, but now he couldn't get started. He was happy to catch a nine-inch perch. It gave him time to drop it in the live well, re-bait with a fresh wax worm and cast. "I feel crowded. I'm not used to having someone around me all the time. And especially not someone so... interesting."

Tre nodded. "It takes a while to adjust. I even had to ease into life with Marjorie after being alone for a few years. Give yourself space," he said, waving his arm over the lake.

They went quiet for the next twenty minutes, busy hauling in a half-dozen 'keepers.' During a lull in the action, Vinnie said, "She wants me to do things different. To change."

Tre barked a laugh that got a crow flapping and cawing from a tall spruce along the shoreline. "Change... thy name is marriage."

"I'm not married."

"Yet."

"But she doesn't like to change. I tried to show her how to prime some wallboard and she just..."

"Don't do projects together. And it's not just her. I read that wallpapering together breaks up more marriages than infidelity."

"Okay, I get it, Vinnie said. "But what about this trip? For sure Sal doesn't want to go."

"Neither do I. For one thing, it would cost too much for Bernice."

"How's that?"

"If I went with Marjorie and you went with Gail, Bernice would have to go as a single and the prices are typically based on double occupancy. She'd have to pay more."

"Hmm."

"Also, I have no desire to travel. I've done a lot of it, starting with Europe on Five Dollars a Day in college and then symposia and conferences and sabbaticals over forty years."

"You're not even interested in Africa?"

"Been there... hell of a long flight."

"What about Gail? Did she ever go with you?"

"Once to Norway. But most of the time she was either watching the kids or working and besides, the university would never cover her expenses."

"Huh. Well, she sure acts like she's traveled a lot. She's making sure I got a passport and shots and malaria medicine and..."

"That's Gail. When she gets..."

Cutting off Tre in turn, Vin carried on, "There's books and maps and forms to fill out." He stopped for two quick breaths. "And she found the best flights and signed us all up." He shook his head in disbelief. "I never spent so much money for so many different things. And special clothes. Turns out we have to fit ten days of clothes in, like, a jock bag to fit in the jeep for the safari."

"Nylon and UV..."

"Yeah, and flimsy and weird with pockets all over and pant legs that zip off and even a jungle hat. Like I'd ever wear that stuff anywhere else."

"Fishing out here?" Tre snuck in quickly.

"Maybe. At least no one will see me."

Tre huffed a half-laugh. "You could always go to Anna Maria Island. You've already got the wardrobe."

"Do folks there... where is it exactly... dress like they're hunters in a Tarzan movie?"

"Florida."

"Oh. Well, don't count on it. I've never gone anywhere before." He paused, thinking. "Not on a trip like this. Not with a woman." Another pause. "Not with three women."

"And not to Africa," Tre piled on. "Better you than me."

"Hey!"

"Nah, look. It's the same thing as here. If things get too confining, take off for the afternoon. Go get a beer."

"In the middle of the Serengeti Plain?"

"Well, yeah, that could be a problem."

Vinnie's bobber twitched. He jerked his line. Missed. "You guys owe me."

Chapter Twenty; Tre

Marjorie comes out of her office and sits on the couch near my computer. Just the way she plops herself down makes me realize she has something on her mind.

"Yesss?" I enquire.

She holds her counsel for another moment before beginning. "We need to talk about... some things."

I save my document and swing my chair around.

"I know we generally keep our finances separate and independent, but for me to go on this trip..."

"I'll pitch in," I offer. "How much do you need?"

She smiles graciously. I love the way her hair slides across her forehead when she ducks her chin that way. "Thank you, but that's not what I need. What I'm thinking is, since we live downtown and are within walking distance of most everything, maybe I could sell my car. That would more than cover the trip. And I could buy an iPad." When I don't immediately respond, she rattles on. "And later we could use some of the extra for a trip to... wherever. Your choice. I know it might make for some inconvenience from time to time, but there are buses and cabs. And like I said, we can walk..."

"That's a good idea," I concur. "I'd been thinking of suggesting it myself." I get up for my second cup of coffee, call from the kitchen, "So, tell me why you need an iPad."

"Well, for pictures."

"But you have such a wonderful camera and lenses." I turn and register her blank stare. Her foot is waggling at the end of her crossed knees. I'm missing something, by a lot. What is she looking for? What am I missing? Then I get it. Sharing. She's trying to share the trip with me. Maybe feels a little guilty to be going without me. Or at least wants me to enjoy it with her. I should act interested. Let me back up and around. "You're thinking mini iPad?"

She nods.

"And you're thinking there will be internet available at the various safari camps. And you'll be able send me daily reports."

Her face says—Duh!

I sit next to her. "Uhm, Marjorie. I'll look forward to your emails about how you're doing, but we can enjoy your nature shots, like last summer... the butterflies at the lake... when you get back."

She uncrosses her legs. "Uh-huh," she says. "But in the meantime, I could send the odd record shot to help you visualize... you know, the tent camps and people and places as we go along."

"Ah, I see."

"Not to mention keeping up with the news."

"Yeah," I agree, "there's no TV and newspapers in the bush."

Marjorie flashes me a 'you got it' smile and retreats to her room.

Good. I dodged that bullet. Newspapers and online news reminds me of a story I wrote. I print it out for her—a little follow-through on a theme, for later, to make up for being so slow on the uptake.

eNewspapers?

I was just trying to enjoy my raisin bran muffin and dark roast breakfast blend, but the guy next to me kept flapping and snapping the Saturday morning Gazette. I normally wouldn't have noticed that level of noise, but I had just started wearing my new hearing aids and it sounded like microphone static right inside my cranium. That, and stools lined up along the front window put us elbow-to-elbow, so not only the noise but also the newsprint cutting in and out of my peripheral vision had me flinching and ducking, and scalding my lips on the fresh coffee.

The shaker-and-rumbler on my left looked like he wouldn't hurt an old man. In fact, he looked like a professor. What could he do? Threaten to fail me? So, I pulled out my iPad and opened my NY Times app. After two harrumphs and enough breeze from opening the sports section to cool my coffee, I said, "Don't you wish more people could read their newspapers online?"

"Huh?"

"Digital newspapers," I said, holding out my eReader.

"Not the same," he grumped. "Besides, I like the feel of a newspaper."

"I guess I can see where you're coming from." I replied, nodding to myself. "I miss the feel of unrolling a fresh parchment scroll on a Sunday morning in the Forum."

After a sidelong appraisal, complete with raised eyebrow from the space invader, I added, "Or, for that matter, the heft of a good set of stone tablets. Can't beat that."

"Very ironic—lecturing a cultural anthropologist on throwback technology. Well, allow me to paraphrase Mark Twain, 'The reports of the demise of daily newspapers are greatly exaggerated.'"

"No one's arguing that they're still around. We still have horses in the age of the automobile, after all. I just wish we could get through the current generation's information-on-crushed-trees fix."

Sporting a smarmy, patronizing smile, the professor-guy allowed, "I bet you would do well as a guest presenter in my 312 course. You could lead a debate on the historic implications of conditioned communication patterns and the assimilation of new technology."

See? I was right about him being a professor. I half expected him to quote himself, ibid, page 227. After a pause to stare out the window, and a shake of the head, he muttered, almost in defeat, "Who can keep up with all the buttons and nets and 4Gs and WIFIs? Too much. It's all too complicated."

I grabbed a section of paper and began reading a column. "Wait," I exclaimed, "where did this story start?" I thrashed open all the sections scattering them, pretending to look for the lead. "Hold on, this says, 'continued from A1.' Maybe there's an alpha sequence at play here. So now I just have to find a part A. Oh, and the pages are numbered," I announced as I further separated the sections page by page.

"All right, you can stop," the professor conceded. "You've made your point. There's learned behavior in something as simple as reading a newspaper."

"It's not really simple. It's just familiar."

The resulting cold glare put the final chill on my coffee. Tugging his beret onto his head, then donning his coat and scarf, my man gave me a long stare, rolled his tongue around his mouth, sucked at something between his teeth and swallowed. "You could have just moved."

Chapter Twenty-One; Vinnie

Gail obviously knew her way around airports as she guided Vinnie, Marjorie and Bernice from the check-in machines and baggage checks to the security line and finally the boarding gate. "We have forty-five minutes till boarding starts," Gail announced to the trio sitting in front of her. "So, relax, get some coffee. We're in Group 4 so it will be a little longer than that. Still, it would good if we were all here at the same time."

Vinnie looked up at the new person in his life. Tall, chin high, her reddish-brown hair framed the face of a woman in charge. The power-dressed department head he used to see at the hospital showed through black linen slacks, magenta silk top and matching sandals. He had mixed feelings. In part, he was flattered that a management type could and would relate to him. In a certain sense, it was like a boss still telling him what to do. He was used to that. But then, this was different. They were away from the job. A new set of rules were in play—man/woman; what I know/what you know. For the moment, she knew more about traveling than he. He could defer to her judgment. No problem.

He stood. There was so much to see and learn. A freeway streaming people. A wall of monitors scrolling arrivals and departures. Announcements about unattended bags. He wandered into a bookshop. More stimuli. Modern Woodworker jumped out at him from the magazine display—something familiar for the long flight ahead. A coffee and pit stop later, he was back in his seat next to Gail.

She patted his thigh and smiled. God, he was lucky to have her. If, for the moment, she made him feel like a kid with his teacher on a field trip, he could handle it. He was learning so many new things. After so many years of making all the decisions for himself, he was letting someone else take charge. *Let's see how that works.*

"Boarding Passengers in Group Four," the attendant announced.

"That's us," Gail said. "Get your boarding pass out."

Vinnie waited for Marjorie and Bernice to follow Gail before he grabbed his backpack and fell into line.

First Day and a half—the long flite

Gail Trahan
to Carrie

Whew. We're finally in Africa. Shuttle from the motel in Chicago at 6 am to Toronto. Our flite to Ethiopia delayed 4 hrs. Missed our connection. Overnight in Addis. Had to pay $200 extra for a ride to catch up with our tour at the first stop. But I got us through it... with Vincent's help. At the very end of the trip we were hot, crowded into a small custom's room, everyone on the flite trying to get out and away, we have to fill out some kind of entry visa form and pay $100. We knew about it in advance and each of us had our money ready. I had made sure we all had crisp hundred-dollar bills. Wouldn't you know it, the rubber stamp guy got mixed up, or acted like he was, and said we were short a bill. I started to argue with him. He wasn't buying it. But then Vincent put his hand my shoulder and just stared at the guy. Then he pointed to a stray Benjamin on the side. The guy acted like he just now saw it. Problem solved. I felt like a woman buying a new car... they don't take you seriously unless you got a guy along. Aargh!

Mom
I hope the rest isn't as bad

Marjorie
to Tre

You would have hated it. Delayed before we even got started on the main leg of the trip. Sitting around killing time. Hours and hours in the air. Vinnie was cool. At one point when Gail was losing it over more delays and waiting, he told her to think of it like a double shift (except he was hourly, and she was salaried). Don't fight it. Don't think ahead. Just take it one minute at a time... right now. He's a rock. But I sat next to him and more than once I saw his knuckles go white on the armrest when we ran into some turbulence. Does he usually go to the bathroom every hour or so?

He was cool when we landed... some trouble with customs. I hate to sound sexist, but the official was giving us grief until Vin stepped up. He didn't have to say a thing. I'm glad he's with us.

Well, we're at the hotel now.

And we just met our tour guide, Matthew, who lives here in Arusha and is part Masai. He was educated in England at some point and seems very competent. Our remaining two tour-passengers are men. No rings. Gail thinks they may be gay. I'm reserving judgment. Can't two buddies just travel together without raising weird questions? Allan and Stanley are very articulate. Allan is a magazine publisher. I suspect we'll have a lot to talk about in the coming days. Stanley is an actuarial... whatever that is.

I'm exhausted and just now feeling the last of the jet vibrations leaving my body. So good to be still at last.

Mar

Chapter Twenty-Two; Bernice

Bernice leaned on the door frame of the hotel computer room, her second gin tonic in hand, watching Gail and Marjorie punching away on keyboards like old-time newspaper reporters sending in their breathless scoops. She could wait to tell Sal, or anyone who was interested, about her exciting trip. Actually, there weren't any folks she could show her pictures to, now that she thought about it. And those that might be interested were on the trip with her. Well, maybe Tre. Forget Sal. So, anyway, she should just enjoy what's happening while it's happening, she decided. Like how delicious it had felt to baste herself in sunscreen, stretch out flight-cramped muscles and bake in the African sun beside the pool. Was it her imagination, or was the air silk-sheet smooth and perfumed? Just drink it all in, she reminded herself, you're never coming this way again.

"Hey, you guys," she called, "Matthew says dinner is in ten minutes."

"Almost done," Marjorie answered. Gail nodded.

After dinner, Matthew gathered the group in a corner of the lounge and ran through the safari drill. Bernice, sprawled in a cloud-soft sofa, facing Stanley, one of the two men joining their tour. She scoped Stanley the whole time Matthew explained that each day passengers would rotate one row forward in the van to give all a chance to sit close to the front, that they must drink lots of water, call out stops for photos and say, 'Sawa, Sawa' in Swahili to let the driver know when to move on. Stan, she called him in her mind, was short and rounded. Maybe a little younger than her. What's ten years when you're of a certain age? She liked his muscled forearms shown to good effect by the turned-up cuffs of his khaki hunter's shirt. The pockets. So many all over the shirt. She loved pockets. Secret places to stash things, to be prepared for anything. He had a high hairline

of fading blond on a biggish head. A ready grin went agreeably with his strong chin. The next ten days could be fun,
she thought... the animals too.

Chapter Twenty-Three; Vinnie

The first day bouncing and cruising the Tarangire game reserve was exciting for Vin. Despite all the nature channel shows, it was still surprising to see the animals in the wild. Yet he somehow felt like a voyeur peeping out the cruiser window to watch a giraffe nibble on an acacia tree and then awkwardly bend to drink from a recently formed puddle. Baboons, impalas, warthogs, gazelles, elephants, zebras were all getting on just fine without zookeepers and large animal veterinarians. Well, he knew that, but somehow their backdrop was larger than his 42" television screen, as though he had only known them through a limited viewfinder. That was it. The landscape was immense, flat, as far as he could see. He hadn't been able to gauge the scale of the habitat that seemed so barren with only sporadic trees and meager grasses to sustain so much life. But, of course, he reminded himself, not all of Africa was dense, steaming jungle. If he had lived in Nebraska or Montana instead of Michigan with its tangled woodlands, home to deer and moose, he might have had a better sense of the life-sustaining possibilities of open plains. *Think of bison herds,* he told himself as he viewed thousands of wildebeests, slowly grazing, while on their constant cycle of migration.

Watching the animals was almost as much fun as helping Gail take pictures of them. All the safari members took pictures, especially Marjorie with her variety of lenses. But Gail sat next to him and when they stopped with the roof up for a photo op, he had the pleasure of steadying Gail's hips as she stood on the seat for a shot or two.

Matthew regularly slowed and stopped along the two-track to chat with another guide passing on his right. One time, as they pulled away, Vinnie could see him grinning in the rear-view mirror. "We are almost to our camp for the night," he announced, "but first I have a surprise for you."

109

He had often connected with other guides during the day. It seems they all helped each other with information about sightings.

Vinnie tapped Stan's shoulder. "You know, this reminds of charter fishing on Lake Michigan where all the charter boat captains cross-chat about pockets of feeding salmon and trout."

"Yeah," Stan agreed. "Same on the Wisconsin side of the Lake. You fish?"

Before long the whole group joined the discussion.

"You ever been to Yellowstone or Yosemite?" Bernice enquired. "Same thing. Everyone stops... big traffic jam, campers and cars all stopped to watch a moose or bear."

Ironically, that exact phenomenon brought the discussion to a sudden halt. A dozen land cruisers in a semicircle bristled with camera lenses aimed at a male and female lion—a mating pair, apparently, when the male lazily raised on all fours and trundled over to the female who obligingly rolled onto her stomach to endure a ten second encounter. Fifteen minutes later when the tour group had put away their cameras and were ready to get on to camp and dinner, the male got up to tend to business once more. "This goes on for three days," Matthew informed his clients. "Incredible," Gail said "How can she stand it. Sometimes less is more, you know."

Everyone chuckled. Amen, Vinnie sighed with relief.

Chapter Twenty-Four; Bernice

For the second time the next morning as they cruised the Ngorogoro Crater, Bernice called out to Matthew, "Golden opportunity, please."

"Can you hold it a little?" Matthew answered as he swerved and bounced over flooded ruts from the previous night's rain. "I need to find a safe spot."

"Safe?" Bernice asked. "What, you're afraid there might be a horny lion behind a bush gonna jump me when I moon him?"

"From what we saw last night," Stan said, "at least it wouldn't take very long."

"Like some guys I've known," Bernice replied.

"Well, you haven't known me," Stan said.

"Really," Bernice purred.

Five minutes later, Matthew pulled into a clear cove of bare earth, trees and scrub some twenty yards away. "Stay close," he advised.

Stan puffed his lips and rolled his eyes at Allan before elaborately making room to let Bernice out the side door to his right. "Hey, I caught that," Bernice said. "Tomorrow, I won't have a second cup of coffee at breakfast. Okay?"

A short while later, Stan twisted in his seat and stood abruptly to peer out the raised roof. "Bernice," he stage-whispered, "walk faster... but don't run."

"You were watching, weren't you? Pervert," she called.

Matthew, glancing in the side-view mirror, shouted, "Get in, now!"

"Huh?" Bernice began before she caught Stan's wide-eyes staring behind her. A quick peek over her shoulder, and three quick steps landed her in a pile in front of Stan who slammed the door shut and called out, "Sawa, Sawa!"

By the time she got on her knees, she and all the others were looking out the back window at the tawny-maned

111

beast, raised-nose sniffing, as he disdainfully scratched the ground with his hind paws and sprayed a bush to re-mark his invaded territory.

Late that afternoon, Bernice was enjoying a cold Tangawizi ginger beer in the tent camp lounge when she noticed Stan was missing. "Wonder where Stan is," she remarked.

"Oh, he was fussing about something or other when I left," Allan replied, "he'll probably be right along."

Bernice grabbed a handful of peanuts and strolled to Stan and Allan's tent. Outside the zippered screen door flap, she could make him out on his hands and knees muttering to himself. "Looking for something?" she called unzipping one side of the screen and entering the semi-gloom of the interior swept by a flashlight beam along the floorboards. Stan pointed toward his camera with a telephoto lens.

"Screw fell out."

"So, you're looking for a little screw," Bernice said. The flashlight stopped in mid-arc. "Thought you'd never ask."

Stan rolled back onto his heels, stared at Bernice for a moment, then roared a deep throated laugh.

Bernice frowned. "It wasn't that hilarious."

Stan leaned his hand on the floor to rise but yelled, "Ow!" Embedded in the heel of his hand was the missing part. "There it is," he said, "my little screw."

"You're quite easily satisfied," Bernice huffed.

Stan laughed again. This time Bernice joined in.

Gail looked in at the door. "What's so funny? And what are you two doing in here... on the floor?"

Stan shook his head, chuckled. "This lady is a hoot. Reminds me of my sister... she always made me laugh."

Bernice scrambled to her feet. "Sister!" she hissed, before slapping the flap aside on her way out.

Like a little kid on a trip

Gail
to Carrie

Our next-door neighbor should have stayed there. That Bernice is a piece of work. When she isn't making us stop every twenty minutes for a potty break she's wandering off making us wait while we search to find her or drag her away from some crocodile infested river or hippo pool. And today she had a lion following her back to the van. Gave us a heart attack because she didn't even realize it till the last second. Sweet Bernice... who knew? Or as Stan would say, 'Who Gnu?' Ever since Matthew reminded us that a Wildebeest is also called Gnu, he has been pelting us with sorry puns like—what do you call a baby wildebeest? A gnu born. Then he laughs at his own joke and Bernice laughs like crazy with him... think schoolgirl crush. Oh, and when we got to our tent camp I saw her go in Stan's tent and caught a glimpse of them on the floor laughing. Poor Sal should be here to protect his interests. I think there's more than giggles in the works.

Interesting man

Marjorie
to Tre

You would like Allan. He's a little younger than us. Publishes a magazine... *Our World*. Do you know it? I've seen it from time to time. He was interested to hear that I write and photograph. After watching a pair of lions mating he liked my photos of them and wondered if I could write an article about it. He laughed when I told him it would be flash fiction. But then he told me about a book he had read called *White Masai* about a European woman who marries a Masai warrior. Seems their sex was as perfunctory as lions mating, and when combined with polygamy, could be a rather in-depth piece comparing lions and Masai culture. What do you think?

Also, we got into a great discussion about high and low context societies. Matthew, our guide, frequently stops to chat with fellow guides, seems to know every park ranger and their kid's names... nothing like our computer driven automatons crunching numbers in honeycombed cubicles. It's refreshing to see such a different culture, but it can be annoying as well. Like when we hired a cab and the driver picked up his cousin to go along for the ride... on our nickel. Makes us tourists feel like we're so much cattle to be herded here and there, but not really part of their lives.

Oh, and Bernice mooned a lion on one of her frequent pit stops... had to go again shortly after barely diving into the van ahead of the annoyed feline. Speaking of her, she and Stan are really hitting it off.

Mar

Chapter Twenty-Five; Tre

I'm bored. As a man of words, I should probably pen a sonnet to my love across the seas. But I'm not that kind of romantic. I guess I miss Marjorie. But it's not like I can't exist without her. It's just more interesting when she's around. God, I sound like a guy who needs a dog to have something live to talk at. Well, it's not just her absence. I've hit a flat spot in my writing. No juice. I decide to call Sal.

Over beers at Bell's we look at all the younger folks preening and posing in a fog of pheromones, pairing off for the night. Sal is wheezing pretty bad. Says his COPD is acting up. Cramps our conversation. "Did you hear about our gals watching a pair of mating lions?" I ask.

Sal sips his pint of Two-Hearted Ale then does that bad-lung thing where he puffs his cheeks and blows out through pursed lips. "Yeah, Carrie passes along the stuff Gail emails her."

I'm not one to gossip or create problems for friends, and I imagine my daughter is censoring Gail's messages about Bernice and that guy Stan. I wonder if I should give Sal a heads-up. Or maybe no news is good news. The way I would rather not hear all about Marjorie and the magazine guy and them discussing the marital habits of African men.

I decide to speak up. "There are two guys in their group whose company our ladies seem to be enjoying."

"Yeah, I heard about them." Sal finishes his beer in two long swallows. Belches. "You can't wrap 'em in cellophane and keep them on a shelf just for yourself," Sal pronounces. I get up to order another round and a basket of fries. When I come back to the table, Sal picks up the thread as if I hadn't been away for five minutes. "Space. You gotta give 'em space."

See, that's what infuriates me about Sal... he reads me, finds a sore spot and pounds his point home. Aiming a French fry at me like a teacher with a piece of chalk, he carries on. "Remember when the nuns used to tell us about detachment?"

"That was about things... material possessions," I interject.

"Your pecker's not a material thing?"

"What? How did we get...?"

"You can't lock up a woman like you're some sheik with a harem. Not smart. Doesn't work."

I don't know where to go from here. So, I take a long slug and bang my mug on the table.

Sal gives me his guru on-the-mountain-top look. "We're not gettin' any younger, you and me. Can't do everything we used to. So, punt once in a while."

Amazed that I'm tracking his ramblings, I want to respond, but he suddenly breaks into an impish grin. "Remember this story? A couple goes to a marriage counselor. The wife unloads for forty-five minutes, 'he never notices this, he never says that, he never... blah, blah, blah.' Finally, the therapist jumps up, grabs the woman, sweeps her over and plants a long deep kiss on her. 'See,' he goes after he catches his breath, 'this is what she needs once a week.' The guy goes, 'Okay. I can bring her here on Tuesdays or Thursdays, but Wednesdays I golf.'"

I level a blank stare. He shrugs and mutters, "We can't be everything for them, all the time

Chapter Twenty-Six; Vinnie

After two more days of African massage—bumping and bouncing over ruts carved by hundreds, perhaps thousands of land cruisers—Vin was less than enthused by yet another five thousand wildebeests milling along the horizon. At one point, while Bernice exclaimed over a baby zebra, Stan glanced back at Vin and rolled his eyes. Vin nodded. It felt good to find a kindred spirit reaching the same point of wildlife-spotting overkill. He liked animals. But after he'd seen one elephant herd and one giraffe or even sixteen of each, how many more could he possibly want to see and photograph?

Gail was starting to get on his nerves as well. He appreciated an organized person who made lists and made sure everyone was ready for the next day's activities. Someone had to do it. Like the way he used to set up projects at work from plans, to materials, to sequenced construction for his team. But he was retired now, he told himself, and could just let things happen. That's what tour guides were for. Let them do their job.

One afternoon, the land cruiser came to a thumping halt due to a flat tire. Gail frothed about missed animal-sighting opportunities, not to mention supper at the next tent camp. While she was carrying on, Vinnie, falling back on his supervisory ways, got out to watch Matthew and two passing tour guide buddies change the tire. They got a jack in place under the frame, but when they pushed on the makeshift wooden handle, it broke. He couldn't understand Swahili, but it was clear they were upset and confused about what to do next. When you have a cabin like I do, Vinnie thought, you learn to improvise instead of driving all the way into town for just the right tool. So, he studied the situation, found a large rock and wedged it under the axle. Next, he grabbed a trench shovel and dug a hole under the tire. After replacing the tire, he filled the hole and invited the troops to push the van off the rock. The Africans looked at him in a way he had not seen before. It was like they saw him for the first time, that he was not just another helpless tourist. And not just them. After they were again under way, Gail gave him a look he hadn't seen before—a mix of surprise and appreciation. At least he thought it was.

That night at the Lake Manyara camp, Vinnie decided to fix the hinge on the van's lift-up roof that Matthew had jerry-rigged with a nylon strap. After unwinding the strap, he walked around to the cook tent and asked Lucas, one of the staff, if he could locate a ¼ 20 nut and bolt. While Lucas was searching in the maintenance shed, Vin noticed a strange barrier of cyclone fence, ropes and poles outside a section of the cook tent. Lucas explained in his rather surprisingly good command of English that an elephant had tried and succeeded in crushing the tent and raiding their rack of fresh produce housed inside. That was a new thought. At first it seemed that all they had to do was cruise around and stare at the wonderful animals in their home turf, watching them graze or laze in the shade. But here was a new wrinkle. You also had to think about protecting yourself from them when you camped in their backyard. Figures.

The following morning, Vinnie lay under the covers waiting for Gail to finish her shower. He had been up two times during the night fumbling first for, then with, a flashlight as he shuffled to the bathroom. The second time, in the silence following his sigh of relief, he heard a low rumbling outside the tent not unlike a diesel truck starting up. He turned off the flashlight and, after a moment to allow the return of his night vision, peered out the small screened window. In the clouded moonlight he made out a long, low form, dark mane, long tail, gracefully gliding away to grunts and a deep cough not unlike his grandfather's before morning coffee.

Back in bed, Gail sleepily muttered, "You okay? Heard you grumbling." Vinnie smiled to himself. Maybe he would explain in the morning.

But now that it was morning and Gail was so brisk and determined as she emptied her bag and carefully re-arranged socks, underwear and toiletries he couldn't bring himself to break her concentration. Through narrow eye-slits he saw her reach for his bag and had to stifle an urge to call her off, to claim boundaries to his privacy. But Gail glanced at her watch, dropped his bag and called, "Vincent, breakfast in five minutes." After rolling up the tent flap she reached for the screen zipper and yelped, "Aach!"

Ten feet in front of the tent stood a cape buffalo content-edly grazing. Gail scampered back to the bed, jumped in, shoes and all, and snuggled under him. Uhm, he thought, I guess we all have our gifts.

Chapter Twenty-Seven; Tre

Marjorie sent me an email with attachment last night. Woke up at two in the morning thinking about it. Seems this magazine publisher guy liked her lion photos and pitched her a story concept—basically an illustrated compare and contrast essay. Interesting idea, I have to admit.

Marjorie is no Margaret Mead, but she could work up a Sunday Supplement level, cultural anthropology piece, okay enough. Good for her. But it's the next part that bothers me. She wants me to review her outline like I'm her live-in thesis adviser. We're not in a writer's critique group where there is an implied *quid pro quo*. I don't do this kind of thing for nothing. Beta readers get paid by the page for editing and review... for crying out loud.

Besides I sleep with the woman. And one of the first rules of writing is not to ask a spouse... okay, significant other in our case... to critique your stuff. Like one woman in a group I was in tearfully reported, "My husband says my writing sounds just like me." We had to reassure her that that was her voice. Helpful critique demands fresh-eyed objectivity.

And, what if I find serious faults? It's like the time we engaged a family friend as our real estate agent. He walked through the house pointing out dirty windows, chipped woodwork, smudged walls, stained carpet. Gail had a fit after he left. 'Is that what he noticed when he came to visit us in the past?' See, you can't mix professional and personal. That's why you don't invite your proctologist to your cocktail party.

And then there's the thought of this Allan guy head-banging with Marjorie as they bounce and lurch through endless bush and exotic animal sightings—shipboard romance potential. No fair. Almost as bad as prof-student relationship. Svengali territory.

See how your mind can work in the bowels of the night?

The next morning, in the bright sunshine, over coffee and eggs I admit my curiosity is tweaked. After all, writing is writing, and I'm challenged to get back into harness. So, I print out her outline.

Lionized Living
(pictures of male lions mating, fighting, eating kill)

Intro: Masai warriors live among lions and seem to have adopted some of their traits into their own lives: mating, fighting, territoriality

A. Mating:

Lions—functional, quick, unromantic, multiple partners

Masai—much the same

(cf White Masai European woman who marries into Masai culture)

polygamy

B. Dominance:

Lions—First to eat after females bring down a kill... 'lion's share'

Masai—Wives cook, and sons bring food to 'man'

C. Territoriality:

Lions—Define/mark territory. Fight intruders to the death over mating rights

Masai—Tribal conflicts, killing a lion to prove manhood

Conclusion:

Quotes from tour guide Matthew as part Masai.

Deep-seated primitive instincts hard to erase or control on both sides (lion tamers/civilized mores)

I think for a while. I know she could write it well and I will likely have to proof more than one draft. Basically, it's an interesting premise. So, I offer some gentle feedback:

1. Your territoriality section is a little vague and needs work. Idea: the only real rivals to 'king of the beasts' is human wannabe kings (trophy hunters, circus lion tamers)

2. Beware of implying African men are animals. Refer to other cultures evolving around the animals in their environment: American Indians/Bison; Laplanders/Reindeer

3. End with a connection to larger society: Masai as throwback to primitive male dominance, a symbol of what many men also deeply, and not so secretly cling to? e.g. (feminist tease) men expect the women in their lives to provide meals.

Chapter Twenty-Eight; Vinnie

Back home, finally, Vinnie and Gail are surprised to find a pair of size 13 running shoes draped with a pair of smelly socks in front of the living room couch. Upstairs in the bathroom, Gail found a razor on the sink and a wet towel on the floor. Carrie's bed was unmade. All unusual. Gail stomped down the stairs to find Vinnie at the kitchen sink examining a half-eaten slice of pizza. Five empty beer cans surrounded a grease-stained Hungry Howie's box. "Someone's been sleeping in my house," Gail said.

"Technically, it's Tre's house," Vinnie replied.

Gail flung the box across the room like a Frisbee. Vinnie swallowed and calmly said, "Maybe this would be a good time to make other arrangements... for us."

"What, and move into your jail-cell apartment?"

Hurt look on his face, Vinnie said, "There's nothing wrong with my place."

"For you. But not for two. Not for me."

Vinnie opened the fridge for the remaining beer, popped the tab and said, "Let's go sit on the porch for a minute."

Gail glowered, but when she realized that they might be at an important juncture in their relationship, she grabbed a cold can of cola and followed him out.

"We could always move out to my cabin," Vinnie began once they were both settled on the porch swing.

"It's a nice place to visit for a day or two. But I wouldn't want to live there. Too primitive... like a boy's tree house."

Vinnie digested that, took a long breath then added, "And I wouldn't want you to hang curtains in it, either."

Noticing his pinched lips, Gail hastened to add, "Vincent, honey, it's like a safari tent. Nice enough, but not a place to really live in." Then with a curt look, added, "Besides, I don't sew. Curtains, or anything else."

Vinnie propped his feet on the porch railing and got them gently swinging.

That rail needs a coat of paint, Gail noticed. *Matter of fact, the whole place could be spruced up. One more project,* she groused to herself as she focused on the rhythmic squeak of the rusty chain hooks. *And oil the chain.* She sighed, then realized that Vinnie wasn't simply dawdling between sentences. On the verge of saying something, anything, to fill the gradually lengthening pause, she recalled a hard-won take-away from marital counseling with Tre and decided not to preempt the next move, to let Vinnie serve.

"But you do like it... out there... at the lake," he probed, "don't you?"

"Oh, yeah," Gail agreed. "It's beautiful. I love it."

More silence. Finally, Vinnie said, "Maybe I could build us a house on the ridge. And we could live in the cabin till it's done."

Gail focused on the 'us'... 'build us a house.' She swung around to face Vinnie. "That's a pretty serious offer." Vinnie dropped his feet to the deck, met her gaze. "I hope you really mean it," she said.

He nodded. "Yep. I do."

She jumped up, sat in his lap and gave him a long kiss.

A car pulled into their drive. Carrie and her boyfriend got out and stared. "Geez, you guys. Get a room."

After a considered pause, Vinnie replied, "We're working on it."

Chapter Twenty-Nine; Tre

I'm looking over Marjorie's first draft of her piece on lions. Over the top of the page I can watch her pretending to be nonchalantly folding laundry. But she glances up, every once in a while, to catch my reactions, to see if I'm frowning or nodding in approval, wondering what I'm scribbling in the margins like a first-time mother anxiously fretting while a pediatrician examines her baby.

I finally set her manuscript down and pretend to cough to get her pretend attention. "It's good. You might want to tighten the conclusion... just a bit wordy here and there. The rest are just minor line edits. Nice job."

She smiles. It feels good to please her. Then she breaks the spell by announcing that Allan will be giving the keynote address at a publisher's conference in Chicago in two weeks. Damn. Now she's going to want me to go. Probably to show me off to her Out of Africa buddy. But I don't want to meet the guy. Bad enough to know he exists. Besides, I don't relish playing adoring student listening to a lecture by a successful publisher. I'm just some wordsmith mentor of the craft that he's using to earn more in five years than I ever did in my whole career. And I'm sure he wouldn't particularly appreciate having someone like me in the audience critiquing his style, vocabulary, and content word by word... presuming he even remembers my former profession. Thinking misery loves company, I say, "I know. I bet Bernice and Sal would like to go, too. And hey, maybe Allan's buddy Stan will be there too. Bernice would enjoy that."

"Naw," Marjorie replies. "I already mentioned that, and she said, 'screw Stanley. I already got a brother.' I guess something happened between them when I wasn't looking." She looks up at me, waiting for my response.

You know, I'm not above learning from my mistakes. Lord knows, I made a few with Gail. And one of them was putting profession and career ahead of family... and her. I guess I learned that I was pretty intent on making my bones professionally back then and now that I'm retired, perhaps I can push reset rather than default setting. So, I grit my teeth and mutter, "Sure. Let's plan on it." Marjorie is pleased.

The morning we're supposed to leave for Chicago and the grand presentation by Allan, Marjorie gets a migraine... a bad one. While I administer shots and try all my tricks and massages, she still is prostrated with pain by the time we should have left. "I can't go like this, Tre," she moans, "I know you really aren't that excited about the whole thing, but I still appreciate your willingness to go with me."

"I really want to be with you," I say, "to be there for you."

She smiles at me... man, she's lovely... before diving back into her all enveloping pain.

Chapter Thirty; Sal

Bernice has a stack of Post-It Notes and is busily paging through a river cruise catalog sticking yellow flags every other page. I don't know where that leaves me now that I got these goddam oxygen tubes stuck up my nose. I feel like a snorkel diver, only out of the water. She seemed happy to see me when she got back last week. And she was sad to see my breathing got worse while she was gone. But now she's looking for ways to get out of here, again. Well, for sure it won't include me. Makes me kind of sad. *Brutta vecchiaia,* my grandfather used to say. Yeah, I can finally say it myself... old age is a bitch.

I watch her concentrating, marking pages. She flicks her ponytail back over her shoulder. The way she did when we were first neighbors. I'm on the front porch or doing something with the lawn and she is walking by with her dog. God, she looks good. Short-shorts, hiking boots with rolled down red socks at the end of her little big legs and her backpack popping out her chest. She would let her dog sniff around my tree, flick that ponytail over her shoulder and pretend she had just noticed me. Smile. 'Hi, Sally.'

Now she stops flipping through the brochure like she just noticed I was watching her. She goes to flick her hair, but it's already over her shoulder. When she looks up we lock eyes. I don't blink or look away. It's her move in more ways than one. She says, "What?"

"I was just remembering the Bernice that used to cruise by my house with her dog."

She shakes her head. I'm not sure how to take it. Is she thinking that was so long ago that I'm silly to hang onto the memory and she's so changed that I'm just playing her. She keeps looking at me. Why do I feel like I'm in the dugout and the coach is trying to decide to let me pinch-hit? Well, as my dad used to say, 'shit or get off the pot,' Bernice. Are you with me or not? I may not be as exciting as some guy on a safari, but I'm not chopped liver. And I like you a lot. But, truth be told, she really doesn't owe me anything. Like I told Tre, you gotta be detached.

She takes a deep breath. Man, I wish I could still do that. Then she sighs. "Sal, honey, you ever see that movie, As Good as it Gets?"

I hunch my shoulders. Never seen it.

"It's about this couple that finally realize you can't live in a dream world. Be glad for what you got, for who you got."

Is she sayin' she's gonna have to settle for me? Is that what she's sayin'? That's not very romantic. But, I can't say that. I go, "You ever watch Sonny and Cher on TV? See them singing, 'I Got You Babe.' That's us."

She gets this soupy look on her face. Nice. Maybe I said the right thing for once. Then she cracks up.

"But they broke up."

I laugh, too. But, then I start to wheeze and cough. She slaps the brochure on the table and walks over to me on the couch. She pats me on the back. I'm still not sure what she's thinking. I guess I can always go live at Vinnie's cabin. I grab tissues and wipe and snuff. All the time I'm thinking, maybe I should say the things I'm feeling for her, like I never did with Pia. Like I wish I could now. So, I finally face her and take her hand, "I still see the you I liked back then. You're still the woman that might have been."

I watch something soften around her eyes and then they tighten like when you make up your mind. She stands up, walks in front of me.

"Sal, honey. Know what? Africa was enough. I don't really need to go anywhere else."

Okay. So far, so good.

"I watch you struggling with your breathing. Maybe it's time to get you somewhere... where you don't have to climb stairs... where if you get worse they can take care of you."

Next thing you know, she's gonna be selling me a casket and a burial plot. I stare at my slippers.

"I'm thinking it's time we got you to that home you were in... what was the name of it?"

"The Ponds," I go, givin' her slant eyes. "I won't be welcome there."

"But I will. I'll sign up for a two-bedroom unit and slide you in with me."

"Why do you want to go there? And why two bedrooms?"

"One for us and one for my office. So I can get away from you when I need to," she gives me this look, "and to remind you that you're not the only game in town."

"You'd do that?"

"Well, yeah. You didn't think I'd leave you there alone, did you?"

Now, I'm sucking oxygen real fast. I don't know what to think. She really must like me. Great. But, how do we pay for it? What about her and that Africa guy? Is she gonna be chasing the old farts in the home, too? Will they let me back in? Will she like it there any better than I did? Will I like it now? Do I have a choice?

Bernice breaks into my thoughts, "I got a hold of my friend Sandy, the realtor, and she's gonna put this dump on the market. She's coming by tomorrow to see what we should ask for it."

Some people, you just don't deserve.

After 25,000 Masses

by

Joe Novara

Gypsy Shadow Publishing

After 25,000 Masses

by
Joe Novara

Gypsy Shadow Publishing, LLC.
Lockhart, TX
www.gypsyshadow.com

ISBN: 978-1-61950-353-3

Published in the United States of America

First eBook Edition: Monday, September 23, 2019

Chapter One

The tour guide paused in the middle of the church and raised his chin, revealing a prominent Adam's apple bobbing above a red bow-tie and purple plaid shirt. Tim recognized the man as someone who reveled in his task, savoring the attention that came with his carefully memorized speech for this stop in the tour. This was a man who liked to play the expert, if only on the history of Amelia Island.

"Who can tell what parable is being portrayed in this stained-glass window?" the guide asked. Before anyone could respond, he continued, "It's the parable of the Prodigal Son."

Tim knew it wasn't. It was the story of the Good Samaritan, but he wasn't going to tip his hand or upstage the poor fellow. He had held forth enough times over the years to let someone else have a turn. He decided to simply tune him out the same way dozy parishioners had endured his homilies.

How many sermons had he given? How many masses? On average, ten a week, counting weddings and funerals, for fifty years. That was over 25,000 masses. God, that was a lot. No more. He was done with all that. Retired. Honorably discharged. It was time to be just plain old Tim McRae, retiree on a senior tour. A chance to make new friends who wouldn't be calling him *Father*. Maybe even a lady friend. Whoa!

"Let's get back on the bus, folks," the tour guide announced. "Next, we'll be heading to the house where the *Pippi Longstocking* movie was filmed."

Tim smiled to himself as he played peek-a-boo with the Atlantic Ocean glinting between shoreline condos. Mention of the red-haired storybook girl with pigtails reminded him of a woman he had met in Aspen years ago—she too a redhead, but with mini-ponytails sticking out between her ski hat and goggles strap. Could a woman have two ponytails, one on each side? The woman kept glancing at him as they rode the chairlift to Big Burn. She finally said, "You remind me of a priest back in Grand Rapids."

He hated when that happened—getting dragged back into his role in the middle of a get-away vacation. Maybe she was a parishioner, one of 18,000, at St. Cyril's. But then, maybe not, and he would never see her again. So, he deflected, and asked her what the odds were of running into another good-looking guy like him. She cut him slant-eyes before popping her goggles down and hopping off the chairlift. Of course, she came up to receive communion from him the next Sunday, glowering from furrowed brows as she stuck out her hand for the host. He was caught red-handed and red-faced from sunburn on the glaring slopes.

During the bus ride, Bernice tuned out the tour guide babbling into the PA system about the local excitement of a *real Hollywood film crew* and studied Tim across the aisle and one row up. Ha, she huffed to herself... the only single guy on the tour. And him short as me. Said he was a counselor at the group introduction. Looks more like a priest to me. Guess you could call a priest a counselor. But how many counselors wear black pants, black shoes and black socks? Guy needs a wardrobe consultant. She shook her head. Nah, he's a priest. Look at the way he sits—like he's got a candle up his butt, and he tilts his head with this *I'm all interested* look. Bet he throws in a *dearly beloved* or two before he's done. Yeah, he's a priest.

Wait a minute, she thought as Tim offered his profile, something about him rings a bell. She snapped her fingers twice, waking her long-term memory. The priest we had at St. Cyril's. Senior year. It was his first parish. Me and Cindy had a priest-crush on him. Can you believe? But, it really could be him, just older, like when they age someone on a computer.

As the group filed off the bus, Tim stopped at the edge of his seat and motioned Bernice forward, pausing to check her name tag. He smiled. She caught his hazel eyes, smiled back. For crying out loud, it's him, she realized. Father Tim. She tried to remember his last name. Mc... something. McRae. Fr. Timothy McRae. Yeah, but he was so determined to be cool back then, he insisted we call him just plain Tim, which only made him more a priest to us. He wore his hair long, sideburns and a mustache. And the night Martin Luther King Junior was killed he gathered us all at the rectory to share, to absorb. He was cool then. I wonder what he's like now. Might be fun to find out. Not much else going on since he's the only unattached guy on the tour.

That evening, Bernice looked across the supper buffet to spot Tim sitting alone. As she scooped a serving of vegetable lasagna, she weighed opening gambits in her mind. If she pounced on him with the priest tag, he might flinch. After all, there was so much flak about bad priests these days, he might just want to duck into his shell. Or then again, he might not even be a priest anymore. There was a lot of that going around. She nodded to herself as she sprinkled parmesan over her entrée. She would respect his privacy, she decided, just play it light and see where it led.

Tim looked up to see Bernice bearing down on him. She knows me, he realized. It's the smile of recognition around the eyes. And she's going to expect me to know her. Could she be another past parishioner? He couldn't remember them all. There had to be thousands. But she could easily remember him. He closed his eyes, sighed and braced himself for '*Father* this' and '*Father* that' over the next half-hour.

"Can I join you?" Bernice asked.

"Of course," Tim replied.

Noticing that he had begun on his lasagna, she asked how it was.

"Oh, fine. Like all the food on this program."

"Yeah, great all around," Bernice said. "Well, maybe not today's tour guide."

Tim looked up from his plate, past raised eyebrows, utilizing the one-second delay of broadcasters, priests and politicians to assess their audience before responding with a conspiratorial chuckle. "A bit taken with his own importance, you might say."

"Uh-huh," Bernice concurred. "And how about that stained-glass window bit? I mean, anybody who's ever flipped through the Bible knows the difference between the Prodigal Son parable and Lazarus and Dives. You don't need to be a Bible scholar..." then pointedly added, "or a priest."

Oh, no you don't, Tim thought. She was not going to get him to correct her, tell her it was really the Good Samaritan. Clever lady, trying to draw him out. But, he wasn't going to bite, not just yet. "I wonder why you would mention priests. You wouldn't be a Catholic, would you?"

"Why do you ask?"

"Well, you could have said *minister*. Ministers of any Christian denomination would be familiar with the Bible. Maybe even more so than priests. My guess... you come out of the Catholic tradition."

Bernice shrugged. "You're right. I went to a Catholic high school—St. Cyril's, in Grand Rapids—and there was a Father Tim who taught us religion. He knew his Bible."

Tim sighed deeply. She had him pegged for sure. But just for the fun of it, he decided to play-it-out a bit more. "So, tell me Bernice, if you knew a Father Tim, what 45... 50 years ago, what he would be like now?"

Bernice posed a Mona Lisa tease. "Oh, I don't know. I would guess he might look like the other old-timers on the tour. Might even wear black shoes and socks."

"Is that so?" Tim considered. "Maybe it's easier to match socks if they're all black. What else?"

"Other things... not so obvious."

"Like what?"

Bernice's eyes drifted off, focused on the middle distance. "Well, you'd have to get to know him some. But I bet he would be a little clumsy... dealing with women."

"You don't think Father Tim would know a lot about women from hearing confessions and counseling for years and years?"

Bernice arched an eyebrow. "No more than a bachelor gynecologist would know how to live with a woman."

"Oh!" Tim said, flinching.

In a softer tone, Bernice asked, "Okay, try this. You ever seen the movie, *Moonstruck?*"

Tim shook his head.

"Well, there's a scene where the Olivia Dukakis character tells a womanizer guy, 'What you don't know about women, is a lot.' This priest we're talking about... you couldn't expect him to be *real* with a woman. Not when, for all his life, women either washed his socks or tempted him to sin."

Tim didn't answer, pursed his lips and went to the dessert table.

While unconsciously diagnosing Tim's stiff left-legged gait as an old knee injury or arthritis, she admonished herself to go a little easier on the guy. On second thought, if he couldn't take the heat, she didn't have time for a make-over project with him or any other man.

When he finally returned with a slice of Key Lime pie, Tim began, "That theoretical priest may not be very smooth with a woman. Such as knowing how to be romantic or how to dance and things like that..."

"Dancing? That's what you think relationship is all about? How about thinking of the other person? Like asking if she might want dessert?"

Tim opened his mouth, stunned. "Oh," he said, sliding his plate toward her.

Bernice raised her palm to stop it. "That's not the point. The point is he's not used to thinking ahead—asking himself what this person would need. His whole life he waited to be asked: 'Father forgive my sins,' 'Father listen to my problems.' Our 'Father Tim' wouldn't be used to looking for, to asking, 'what do you need now, honey?' Being a mother teaches that."

"Huh!" Tim grunted, nodding, before adding, "So, if your hypothetical mother is so tuned to the needs of others, would she notice I need coffee... I mean, when she goes to get her own dessert?"

Sliding into testy-mother mode, Bernice snapped, "She'd say, 'You've got two good legs. Go get it yourself.'" Then she clenched her lips as she remembered his bad knee.

Tim's voice dropped. "Maybe that's the kind of response he deserves. That he needs. Maybe he would be looking for it. Longing for it, for a change... to have a woman challenge him, correct him." He was dabbing at his pie when he added, "To make him feel not-so-special and for all that... cherished."

"Doesn't he have a sister?" Bernice taunted.

Tim laughed out loud. Bernice did too, then got up to get her own dessert. On the way there, she paused and turned, "Cream and sugar?"

"No. Just black."

Tim found it easy to watch Bernice stroll across the room, her sturdy, rolling gait. She would be hard to knock off her pins. He smiled. Grounded. That's what she was. A massage therapist, she had told the group. He liked her hands... so expressive, but strong and used to probing and working a body. No, don't go there. he told himself. Keep it simple. See her. Look for the person inside. Celibacy taught him that at least.

When she sat back down with her apple crisp and his coffee, Bernice took a deep breath before saying, "All right, enough beating around the bush, Tim... Father McRae. Is you is, or is you ain't?"

Tim took a long moment, to stare over the lip of his cup before slowly putting it back on the saucer. "I'm trying not to think of myself as a priest anymore. I'm leaving all that behind."

"You can't do that."

"Once a priest always a priest, is that what you're thinking?"

"Well, yeah. Or, more like being a mother. You can't walk away from that."

"Do you have children?

"Yes, two grown daughters."

"Do they still live at home with you?"

"No. One lives in Boulder. The other in Cleveland."

"You say you can't walk away from mothering. It appears they walked away from you. And now you're free to go on trips, explore, make new friends... maybe meet an interesting man." Tim held out his open hands. "So, after fifty years of 'fathering' why can't I..." Tim fumbling for words pleaded for understanding with outstretched hands.

Bernice drummed her fingers on the table. "That's not the whole story. Priests don't just leave...for no reason." Her eyes flashed, "And anyhow, what about your vow of celibacy?"

Tim locked eyes. "Technically, celibacy is about getting married. I'm not looking to marry."

Raising her chin, Bernice added, "Yeah, well, what makes you think every unattached woman is looking for a man?"

"We all look for friendship. Don't we?" Tim hunched his shoulders in a silent appeal. "I've never had a woman friend..."

"Ha!" Bernice snapped. "You think some sweet, caring woman is going to drop all her years of religion... everything she tried to teach her children and just run off with a man of God... even if he's decided he didn't want to be that anymore."

Tim paused before speaking slowly and sincerely. "I'm trying to get to know a sweet, caring woman, as you describe her, who can take me as I am. I'm tired of trying to love the whole world. I just want to love one person and be loved by one person. I've never been allowed to do that and so, never did. As for what happens after that..."

Chapter Two

The tour guide with his red bowtie spoke in a loud voice to the diners. "Just to remind y'all," he announced, "breakfast at 7:30. Bus leaves at 8:15 for a morning of dolphin watching."

Bernice stood abruptly, considered Tim with a searching glare and said, "See you at the dolphin watch," before heading up to her room.

Timothy nodded.

The tour boat rolled in the gentle chop off Black Hammock Island. Tim and Bernice hadn't spoken to each other at breakfast or the ride out and now sat on opposite sides of the craft. The captain, a little less enthusiastic than the previous day's guide, delivered a laconic history of local shrimping until a sharp-eyed tourist called attention to breaching dolphins swimming alongside. Tim elbowed into a spot next to Bernice. "Ooh! Ah!" he mocked, as if watching fireworks.

Bernice poked him. "It's what we came for... right? Dolphins, manatees, local history."

"I suppose," Tim replied. "The brochure just made it seem so exciting. Come to find out, I'd rather be catching fish than watching them. If I just wanted to see fish, I could go to an aquarium."

"You're a fisherman?"

"Uh-huh. Often as I can. And every summer, a bunch of us priest buddies would go to a fishing camp in Canada for two weeks."

"A little male bonding?" Bernice teased.

"Well, it wouldn't be female bonding, now would it?"

"Did you bring a designated housekeeper along to cook?"

"Are you kidding, that was the only chance I got to cook all year... bouillabaisse, paella, almond crusted walleye, trout almandine..."

"Stop. You're making me hungry and all we got is a soggy sack lunch."

Tim leaned back on the railing, a grin of anticipation creasing his face. "Are you a 'foodie?'"

"Well, yeah. I guess so. I mostly like food I don't have to cook. But I can certainly get into ..."

"More dolphins on the other side!" someone shouted. "Looks like they're feeding."

Bernice and Tim were left alone on the starboard rail. "What else do you cook?" she asked.

"Like I said, all my efforts were based on fish camp. Trying to cook in a rectory is like insisting on carrying your own bags at a hotel. The help thinks you're depriving them of a job. Consequently, I'm top heavy in fish dishes. What about you? Any favorites?"

"My ex-mother-in-law taught me how to make chicken paprikash. And my friend Sal taught me a great recipe for eggplant parmesan."

"That sounds good. Anything else?"

"The usual. Roast. Spaghetti. Mac and cheese."

"Do you like fish?"

"Uh-huh."

"Well, I should have you over some time... maybe serve salmon on a plank."

Bernice deflected. "Where do you live?"

"In our family home. A hundred-year old cottage on Lake Michigan. How about you?"

"Kalamazoo. I got the house in the divorce."

Ignoring the dangling thread of Bernice's marital status, Tim absently stared at the wake purling off the bow as they headed back to the marina. "You know," he began, "I'm not used to doing this kind of thing."

"What? Chatting up a woman?" Bernice said with a wry smile.

"Is that what you'd call it? Sounds like something a guy would do in a bar."

Bernice gave him a level glance.

Tim blanched. "Well, that's not what I'm trying to do... come on to you... like that. And if I come across clumsy, well, all my dealings with women have always been professional—counseling, the parish council, the altar society. So, bear with me, okay? I can't recall a woman ever asking me, 'How are *you* doing? How are *you* feeling?' They called me father. What kid asks her dad how his life is going?" Bernice focused intently on Tim, waiting for him to continue. "I need practice being a friend with a woman, and you and I have a history. Right?" He stared at Bernice, scouring his memory bank. "I still can't say I recognize you from St. Cyril's. Sorry." He frowned, continued. "But anyway, would you humor me, please? Okay?" Tim ducked his chin and said, "End of speech."

Bernice stared out at the water, rubbing her fingers along the rail. When she turned back her eyes were soft. "I saw a documentary the other day where seniors did speed dating, moving from table to table to share a short resume before chatting with a potential partner. Want to try a version of that, even if there's only the two of us and there's no timer running?"

"Huh! So, a quick verbal resume for the basic facts like family and school and work so we can move on to more important stuff."

"Maybe the basic facts are the important stuff," Bernice countered.

"But it's the blanks around those landmarks that are most interesting. And besides, we don't have time. Today is our last day."

The grinding crunch of the gang plank hitting the dock paused the conversation until both settled at a picnic table. Bernice unwrapped her sandwich, and said, "You first."

They both chewed in silence, swallowed, before Tim began. "I grew up in Grand Rapids... an only child... and went to the seminary when I was fourteen."

"So young? How could you know?"

"That's the way it was, back then." Tim shrugged. "Twelve years later, I was ordained and sent to your parish."

"I know. Cindy and I were your fan club."

With a smile warm with memories, Tim asked, "Do I remember a birthday cake? Small. Chocolate frosting. Was that you?"

Bernice clenched her eyes in embarrassment, rolled her hand—keep going.

"After two years in your parish, I got sent to the seminary to teach for the next ten years. And then I was pastor of St. Theresa's in Rockford, 'til a month ago when I retired. Your turn."

"I grew up in Grand Rapids, too. An only child. I married Pete and we had two girls. Moved to Kalamazoo. Five years later, we got a divorce and I single-parented the girls. Worked for a physical therapy practice. And now I'm retired and that's my whole story."

"Not at all. C'mon, dig deep."

"Sometimes I can't trust my memory."

"Like which high school girls made you a birthday cake?"

"You got it."

There were no scheduled activities for the remainder of the afternoon. Bernice went to the hotel workout room with her cell phone. Tim hitched a ride to a nearby mall.

"Marjorie, it's me," Bernice announced while pumping on the elliptical machine.

"Hey, how's the tour going?"

"It's okay. I'm flying back tomorrow. Oh, you wouldn't believe who's in the group. A priest I knew from high school."

"And?"

"We all thought he was so cool, for a priest."

"But now he'd be around Tre and Vinnie and Sal's age... Sal. I keep forgetting he's gone. Miss that old fart."

"Yeah. Me too. A lot."

"So, what's this priest-guy like?"

"Actually, he's kinda okay. You know. No more hippie hair. But still just a little shaggy. Makes you want to run your fingers through it. But good. He looks good. And he's kinda glommed onto me."

"Like finding your uncle is on the same cruise with you. Any other interesting talent?"

"No, he's the only single guy."

"Boo."

"No, but you gotta hear this. He says he's retired, done with being a priest and is over celibacy."

"Uhmm. How would that work? And what? He's 'getting out there' like after a divorce?"

"Seems like. But I don't know..."

143

"Girl, grab onto that man. It's like getting a guy fresh out of prison but without the criminal record. Where's he live?"

"On the beach north of South Haven."

"Possibilities?"

"I guess. But he's got a lot of baggage. He's so needy. So much to learn. So much house-training."

"Are you kidding me? Would you prefer some three-times divorced guy from an online dating site? Get your head right, Bernie. And if you don't want him, I know some women who would."

"Uh-huh. See you on the weekend."

"Play it out. See where it goes. Okay? Bye."

Chapter Three

That evening at supper Bernice didn't immediately spot Tim. Having filled her plate with fish tacos, avocado and bean salad, she was scanning for a free table when she finally noticed Tim sitting with a couple from Ohio. She hadn't recognized him at first in hiking shoes, khakis and Madras shirt.

She joined a couple from Kansas for the meal and when she went for dessert, Tim showed up beside her. "Nice outfit," she remarked, "looks good on you."

"Yeah. J Crew—the new black," Tim replied. "Want to join me for coffee in the lobby after?"

"Okay."

Once they were settled in a quiet corner and had watched the last of their tour partners head to a conference room for the wrap-up session, Tim asked, "Where should we start?"

"My kids?" Bernice asked.

"Well, I certainly would like to know all about them... at some point. Right now, I'd prefer to know about you. How it felt to be their mother, to single parent. Maybe even what the experience of birthing them was like for you. What you thought and felt before, during and after."

Bernice set her cup down. "Excuse me? That's very personal and no man has ever asked me about any of that."

Tim arched his shoulders as if to say, 'well I'm asking.' "The way I see it, we only have this evening to talk together. No promises for more. And sure, we could talk about your children's personalities and careers and about your house and your job and... and. I'd like to know all about you. Who you are... But I bet something like carrying a child and birthing her would get close to who you really are."

Bernice searched Tim's face for an uncomfortably long time as if trying to decide if she should trust him. As he said, they might never see each other again. This could be a shipboard encounter heading for port. Then the corners of her mouth began to quiver. "Outside," she rasped.

They walked around the grounds, stopping by the pool. "You're poking at the most beautiful and most painful times of my life, and you better be careful with it," Bernice admonished. For the next twenty minutes, she described the joy of her first pregnancy. The excitement and anticipation. All the careful attention to nutrition and exercise and pre-natal classes. Her husband not quite so enthusiastic. But she had enough for both. When she got to labor, Bernice got intense.

"First births can be extra-long. Mine had been going on from 4:00 in the morning 'til 6:00 that night. Cindy was with me the whole time. Pete, the live-in sperm bank, was MIA. My contractions were two minutes apart and had been for two hours. I kept calling for my doctor, but when he finally checked me, he said to give it another hour. I was freaking out. Like I was in one of those sci-fi movies where a monster is trying to chew his head out of your belly. And I was sure my baby was going to die if she didn't get out soon. After one really long contraction, Cindy saw my legs shaking and she ran out to the nurse's desk and grabbed a different doctor and practically dragged him in. He took one look at me and hooked a probe on the baby's head. Said it was fetal distress and hauled us to the delivery room for a C section. About the time we got there, things started moving and I delivered just fine. Julie was perfect. But I was a mess. Nightmares and nerves and depression for weeks."

Bernice took several deep breaths before describing how life normalized and they coasted into their third year of marriage before things started unraveling with her husband. By the end of that year, she got pregnant in the hope of saving the marriage. Eventually they separated and divorced. As a single parent, she learned much about herself, about children, about surviving on her own.

Finished, she pushed off the pool railing and swung in front of Tim. She felt naked, exposed and not a little upset with the man who had encouraged her to drag through those long-buried feelings. "I bet you're used to having women unzip their souls to you. Just another day in the rectory."

Tim raised his head slowly, shook it and with a soft break to his voice said, "Not like this. Not like a gift."

Bernice looked away. She didn't know what to make of this man. His response. The way he drew her out. She walked a few steps. Spun around and returned. "Your turn. And it better be something important. Something you try not to think about... or talk about."

"Teaching in the seminary," Tim said, casting his voice intentionally low. "That was a strange time."

"How old would you have been?"

Tim paused, searching his memory files. "Early thirties." He paused again before describing how the Church had gone through confusing times as it implemented changes from the Second Vatican Council. Priests, especially, were disillusioned, confused about their role. At a time so many of his classmates had left the priesthood, he was assigned to grooming the next generation.

"Get to the good stuff. Get real," Bernice challenged.

Tim slapped a mosquito nipping his neck. "Yeah, okay. Let's go back inside. The lobby should be empty by now."

After a trip to the lounge for a glass of wine for Bernice and an Old Fashioned for himself, Tim slouched into a sofa across from her. "There was this one student, Ramon... Ray. What was his last name? Doesn't matter. He grew up in Fennville, near our cottage. I had him in freshman English class. Torres, that was his name. Ray Torres. A simple, sincere kid, a little slow on the uptake. But you had to like him. And he would, as other students did, come around to our rooms after and between classes to talk about himself. Like the time he fought back tears because he wasn't picked for an intramural basketball team and he thought he was better than the guy who was chosen. I would listen and nod and play coach and father and friend—and watch him grow. After his sophomore year he couldn't stop talking about the thrill of working at a church camp up north—the fresh air, the chance to ride horses, to spend the summer with other seminarian camp-counselors. And he looked so healthy and tanned. His voice was changing and he was filling out his skinny frame. It was like watching my own kid grow. And one summer after his first year in college..."

"Where did he go to college?"

Tim was puzzled. "Why, right there. We had the high school and college on the same campus and I taught in both."

"I see."

"So, this one summer he worked at a country club, on the grounds crew, and got to be friends with a girl in the clubhouse. I spent the next three months talking him back onto the celibate vocation track only to have his academic record start dragging him down. We had these faculty meetings where we'd all compare notes on our students. If you happened to be a mentor... spiritual director, we called it... to a particular student, you had more to say. Well, Ray just wasn't cutting it at the early college level and was facing yet more of a challenge for his upcoming major in philosophy. I tried to explain that he was basically a very caring individual and maybe the Church didn't require all our priests to be academic whizzes. But the consensus was—he had to go. As the Dean of Men, I was the one who had to tell him."

Bernice set her glass on the table. "I bet that was painful."

Tim took a deep breath, exhaled slowly, then whispered in a shaken voice, "I had to disown my kid. Kick him out of the house." He drained the last of his drink, plunked the glass on the table, slowly rotated it in the water mark. "He just walked out of my room. Never said another word to me." Tim looked up, past Bernice, pain in his eyes, his voice. "Never heard from him again. He could have gone to another diocese that had less demanding vocational standards and have been happily serving as a parish priest. Never heard." He locked eyes with Bernice. Was he asking for understanding? For forgiveness? "And so many of his classmates we had judged 'intellectually superior' had long since dropped out of the priesthood."

"Ouch," Bernice commiserated.

Tim noticed the desk clerk's head bobbing between yawns. "C'mon, let's take a walk on the beach," he said, pointing his chin toward reception, "and give that poor guy a chance to put his head down."

Outside, a lone car approached the blinking red light for the T-stop at the beach and made a lazy right turn. They both took off their shoes and enjoyed the granular foot-massage on the way to the shoreline where a gentle slough of waves was the only hint that the solid black ocean lay before them.

As they strolled along, the encroaching tide edged up the waterline, pulsing waves of sadness through her. The openness and candor of the evening had brought fresh, painful memories of her marriage to mind. She was feeling warm and close to Tim. But she had felt that way about Pete, too, so long ago, and Sal more recently. Could she really trust Tim, or any man for that matter, who could walk away from a lifelong commitment?

She kept walking until she noticed that Tim was no longer beside her. She stopped. Turned. Called softly, "Tim?" Nothing. She felt her eyes fill. Alone again. Panic. Anger. Then she mentally slapped herself. You've been alone before. You can take care of yourself. You don't need... and she wasn't going to get lost, she just had to keep the ocean on her left until she could see the traffic light. What kind of game is that jerk playing, she wondered.

She walked briskly back the way she had come, for a while, until she heard, "Hey."

"What, the hell!" she yelled. "You scared the shit out of me."

"Sorry," Tim replied, voice soft and settling. "I turned my ankle and you kept going. I could tell you needed some space. So, I decided to wait for you... to decide..."

She rolled her head back, closed her eyes and took a deep breath; let the cross-chop of feelings subside. One answer stood out. Yes. Yes, she would give him her number.

Chapter Four

It was the kind of foggy morning that sometimes happens on Lake Michigan when an inversion of super-chill water from the thermocline comes to the surface and meets muggy warm air. Tim didn't need to stick his bare foot in. He knew it would ache from the cold. He smiled to himself at the way West Michiganders asked each other the deciding question before taking a plunge: 'Does it hurt?'

The flatulent foghorn off the South Haven pier cut through the sea-level cloud as Tim trudged along pondering his encounter with Bernice. She was fascinating. Exciting. Disorienting. His only romantic experiences with women in the past had been fragmentary and self-conscious.

He replayed a breakout session at a conference on racism, him in civvies—ten men and one woman eight months pregnant. At the end of the day, participants milled about, waiting for someone to suggest plans for the evening. The woman pulled him aside. Short, her cheeks ripe, her smile pleading gently, she asked if he would have dinner with her. Glancing at the other men, her puffy fingers massaging her purse, she added, "You seem so safe." He had wanted to shout back, 'So do you.' But chivalry prevailed.

Safe. He chewed on that word all evening. Was that how he came across? Safe? Even without the collar? It was one thing to promise to be celibate. It was something else to feel like a Father's Day card.

That's where his head was the next evening when the woman sitting next to him at the wrap-up session had leaned over and whispered in his ear, "Your smile reminds me of Alan Alda." For once in his life, his first thought was not, 'What would Jesus do?' but 'What would Hawkeye do?' Five minutes later they were up in his room.

That's where he clutched, Tim recalled, picking up a flat stone and counting the splashes as it skipped into the mist. He and the petite brunette had chatted for a bit, looking down on nighttime D.C. After a while, he realized that he was falling into his default professional response to an attractive woman—drowning temptation in empathy and advice. But that woman didn't have any problems, just then, that needed to be solved by talking to him. After some half-hearted snuggling, she smiled graciously and took her leave. That's what happens when you're conflicted, Tim realized as he jumped the shallow creek emptying into the lake. No more.

A woman about his age suddenly appeared out of the fog. She smiled as they passed. Funny, he thought, how beach walkers feel safe. Maybe it's because we're practically naked and defenseless—where could we possibly hide a weapon? Clothes can make such a difference, he mused, flashing back to a particular nun at a summer session on Vatican II liturgical reform at Notre Dame. So many overwrought nuns and priests. A paraphrase of Gerard Manly Hopkins poem popped into his mind—the world was charged with the grandeur of ecclesial makeover and anti-war protest and civil rights and feminism. The frisson of revolution and openness to change left many religious questioning their vocations, examining options, checking biological clocks. Sister Clair Jean and Fr. Tim McRae hit it off. The long, handholding walks and measured kisses left an empty longing far into the fall semester for Tim. Clair Jean's letters expressed much the same sentiments as she slowly arrived at her decision to leave the convent. They were two novices at romance pushing the optimal age for marriage and family.

A day after Christmas, Tim was jangling with excitement as he knocked on Clair's apartment door. She opened with a flourish to show off her new look: styled hair, bright red holiday dress and matching pumps. She was lovely indeed. But Tim had to work hard to suppress his disappointment. Clair was no longer Sister Clair Jean. She was just... *ordinary* Clair. The Cinderella magic was gone and before the evening was over they both realized there was no glass slipper to bring it back.

Tim flung a driftwood stick over the water. I wonder if Bernice thinks of me that way—some kind of carry-over mystique for a man of the cloth. Ha! Do I really care one way or the other? As long as she wants to spend time with me, whether it's just going out, or sleeping in, or even moving in, I want to go for it. It's all about loving and caring. Clair and I should have seen it through. Maybe things would have been different.

Chapter Five

Bernice dug neat furrows in her raised garden bed dropping carrot, radish, Bibb lettuce and cucumber seeds four inches apart. Tomato, sweet pepper and zucchini sets waited in black plastic trays. It felt good to get her hands in the soil after a long winter of clean fingernails and tasteless salad bars. Digging also set her mind free in a way no other activity could. Tim. Father Tim, actually. Did she want to get involved with him? Pete had soured her on marriage... marriage, not men. But she had not looked for serious love since. Her neighbor, Sal, thank God, had been around for years, nibbling at the edge of her... what?... belief in love? He would stop by and give her a hand in her garden or fix something in her house. And just the way he looked at her, never anything more, let her know he appreciated her. A little of that kind of attention could go a long way. Then, when Pia passed, it just seemed natural to let him move in with her. It felt like he belonged there... had been there a long time. Sally. Her Sal. He was a man who would be there. The way he would say, "I'm here," made her feel secure, cared for. He was her rock. And if the Catholic Church didn't want her to receive the sacraments because she was divorced, well hell, she didn't need to be married to live with widowed Sal, good man that he was.

When she was first excommunicated, she felt very isolated from her religion, from her scolding parents and sister. So, she clung to her two girls and took what she needed, what she could get, from the Church even if she couldn't receive communion. Vigil lights and palm branches, holy cards and prayer books provided familiar, predictable ritual the same as washing on Mondays and spaghetti on Thursdays and a rinse every month. If an occasional man happened along, especially once the girls were out of the house, well, that would be all right too. So what if she wasn't consistent or logical? Sal used to tease her about how she could fall asleep next to him saying the rosary. "Pick one," he used to say, "me or religion."

"Why," she used to answer, "when I can have both?" Sal used to laugh and squeeze her behind. God, she missed him.

After carefully tugging the tomato plant from its pot, she gently set it in the shallow hole and backfilled the well-tilled soil. As she walked to the spigot and watering can, she tried to imagine being in bed with Tim. It wasn't an awful thought. Actually, she bet he would be fun and what he didn't know she would sure enjoy showing him. But that was the easy part. It was letting a man back into her life that was hard. All the stages to go through. The fuzzy, warm 'aren't we something' phase. Then the irritation phase—'You always... Yeah but you always...'. And then finally getting it together for the long haul. He wouldn't know what he was in for. She would. Was she up for another go-round? Well, it was a moot question since he hadn't called since they got home from the tour. Damn him.

A week later, Bernice walked into her apartment at Shelden Pond. She yawned. She had eaten too much tuna casserole for lunch. Not that she much liked the dish, but the company at table was so boring she had to do something... didn't she? She had friends among the residents. But every once in a while, she got stuck with some particularly tedious folks. All they talked about was aches and pains. If not their own, then those of others... near and far. She hated detailed organ recitals and the inevitable food coma and long naps they occasioned. Snuggling in for a snooze, she reminded herself that she was almost a generation younger than most of the residents and had only come here to be with Sal. Maybe she should move out.

Ten minutes later, her cell phone jangled her awake. Disoriented for a moment, she sat up in her recliner, looked out the window and finally punched the accept button. "Uhm, hello."

"You sound sleepy. Did I disturb you?"

"Huh? Who is this?"

"Tim. Tim McRae." After a pause with no response, he added. "From the Florida tour. Tim." With still no response, he continued, "Look, maybe this is a bad time. Why don't I call back..."

"Tim. Yes. Oh, hi. Excuse me. I was sound asleep. Too much casserole..." Bernice yawned, "Uhm, yeah. So, what's up?"

"Apparently you are, now. Sorry to wake you."

"No, that's okay. I had to answer the phone anyhow."

"Bodda-boom."

"Yeah, that was Sal's favorite line."

"Your ex?"

"No... well." Bernice glanced at the photo of Sal and her on the coffee table. He had taken off the oxygen tubes for the picture and was holding her hand, the way he did... stroking her palm with one finger. She sighed. "No, Sal and I weren't married. Just good friends. Together for a few months till he passed."

"I see."

"I don't think so. It's a long story."

"If you got the time I got the... Ha!" Tim barked. "That reminds me of the story about the guy who goes to confession and says, 'Bless me father, I stole some lumber.'

The priest asks, 'How much did you steal?'

'A lot.'

'Like enough to build a doghouse?'

'More than that.'

'A garage, then?'

'More than that.'

'Never mind. For your penance, do you know how to make a novena?'

'No, but if you got the plans, I got the lumber.'" Tim laughed. Bernice didn't.

"Do you do this a lot?" she asked. "Blurt out jokes?"

"Yeah. I suffer from anecdotal Tourette's. Sorry."

This time Bernice chuckled. "Never heard of that." She cleared her throat. "Just FYI. I make novenas and say the rosary and I don't joke about any of that. Just sayin'."

They both felt the pause, like the moment a car stops backing up before it goes forward.

Tim spoke first. "Oookay. I hear you." After a beat, he added, "Moving along... I wonder if you'd like to do something together."

Bernice broached a self-satisfied smile. "What did you have in mind?"

"I don't know. I could come into town and maybe we could go to dinner. Where are you, actually?"

"Shelden Pond."

"Oh, I know the place. I used to visit some of my parishioners there."

"Then I better meet you at the curb. It would curl some of these ladies' blue hair tighter than it already is if they saw me heading out with a priest."

"I'm pretty sure there's no danger of that. Last time I was there was at least five years ago and the ones I visited were about to kick off."

"Whoa! That's a cold way to talk about..."

"Is there some other euphemism you'd prefer?" Tim said, voice on edge.

"What I'd prefer," she quickly pivoted, "is a solid meal that didn't feature boiled broccoli. The food around here gets pretty predictable."

"Any suggestions?"

"There's a ton of breweries and good restaurants we can try."

"Just one will do. For now."

Bernice bit her lower lip, reminding herself to slow down, not to get too far ahead of herself, or him. "I would like that, Tim. What time would you be by?"

"How about 6:30?"

"Okay. Let's decide where to go when you get here."

On the phone to Marjorie:

"Marjorie, the priest guy, is taking me to dinner tonight."

"Surprised?"

"Well, I was beginning to wonder if he would ever call."

"Where're you going?"

"I don't know. He wants me to choose. What do you think?"

"Someplace nice but not too formal. How about the Black Swan? Wait, it changed its name. Doesn't matter. It's the same place. Mario's would be good."

"Yeah, either one, I guess."

"What? You sound unsure. That's not you."

"When I was a kid I had a crush on him. Like he was Paul McCartney or something. And now we're both old, and it's so real, and there's so much to find out, to work out, if it's going to go anywhere."

"Don't overthink it, Bernie. Either he likes you the way you are and you like him... or not. Either way you're not going to be crushed or heart broken. Not at our age. What have you got to lose?"

"Ha, nothing but my hopes to blow this joint and shack up with a 75-year old virgin."

"Bernice!"

"See ya."

Chapter Six

"You marking anything?" Tim asked his ex-priest class-mate as they trolled in ninety feet of water out of South Haven.

"Nah. Nothing yet," Marv replied as he toggled through the depth and temperature readings. "Thermocline's at 60 feet. Raise that port side downrigger, would you?"

Marv and Tim had been ordained together. Marv left the priesthood after three years, married, and now had three sons and five grandkids. He kept a boat on the Black River and frequently asked Tim to fish Lake Michigan for Coho, King and Steelhead. The boat slogged along at trolling speed and both men relaxed with a cup of steaming coffee.

"How's Marianne doing?" Tim asked.

"So-so. That knee surgery has been harder on her than we expected. It's still swollen and she has to use a walker after three months."

"I gotta have you two over to my place... maybe serve that salmon we're about to catch."

"Your place. Yeah, how do you like living in a real house instead of a rectory?"

"It's okay. A little lonely. But I feel more like a normal person—fixing doorknobs, mowing the lawn, putting up screens. Only thing missing is a lady of the house."

"Little late for all of that, isn't it?"

"Oh, I don't know. You seem to be doing okay... at our age. Hey, if you could leave and get married, why can't I?"

"But you're late to the game, man."

"I'm still breathing, ain't I? And so far, it's kind of exciting."

"You've met someone?" Marv asked, his face a cross between pleased and incredulous.

"More like, she met me," Tim replied, pushing away from the console and tossing the last sip of coffee over the gunwale. "On this tour in Florida, turns out one of the women knew me from St. Cyril's." He lowered the starboard downrigger a couple of feet before adding, "She and a girl-friend had a kind of *thing* for me."

"God," Marv groaned. "Must have been your long hair and beard and anti-war protests and civil-rights sermons. And you played folk guitar back then, too. Right?"

"I didn't mind the attention, and you're just jealous you didn't have a fan club in your parish."

"Spare me."

A pole released, springing free of its tortured arc and pulsing with the weight of a good-sized fish. "Fish on!" Tim called out.

Marv raised the other lines to avoid tangling, cut the motor and reached for the net. A silver torpedo broke the surface, rolled, then dove for a sustained run. "Nice King," Marv shouted.

Before long Tim had the fish next to the boat in that delicate moment when its gray back looks translucent, still part of the mystery deep. And then it was in the net, thrash-ing, helpless on the hard, white deck. Five minutes later, salmon in the box and the rods reset, Tim leaned against the rail. "So, this lady—Bernice—she spotted me first. And we kind of hit it off. And to tell you the truth, it's kind of fun."

"What's she like?"

"Oh, I don't know. My height. Kind of low slung..."

"No, I'm not asking for a scouting report... 6' 2", 230. I mean what's she like," Marv asked, rolling his hand for more, "personality wise."

"She's pretty direct. Tells you what she thinks." Tim paused, posed a worried frown. "And she's churchy."

"How so?"

"Like when we went back to her apartment after din-ner..."

"Wow, that was fast. Back to her place after the first date?" Marv grinned salaciously.

"Look, man," Tim began, eyes narrowed, "if you're gon-na jerk me around about all this, we can just concentrate on fishing." He turned his head indignantly to the horizon.

"Okay. Okay," Marv backed down, hands raised in surrender. "So, where were we? You're in her apartment..."

"...on her couch where I could see over her shoulder to an Infant of Prague statue, a votive light, couple of rosaries."

"Uh-huh. And meanwhile you're finding all about her kids and ex... or was it late husband?"

"Ex. And the widow guy she knew from her neighborhood. Turns out he was near terminal and she and him moved into this two-bedroom apartment at the retirement home. And then he died. And now she has an extra bedroom and did I want to spend the night to save a trip back to the Lake."

"All this while the Infant of Prague is staring at you."

Tim laughed. "Right. So, that's what she's like. Coming on and praying hard at the same time. But I like her. She's sassy the way every priest needs a sister to keep him humble."

"How would you know? You never had a sister... or a brother for that matter."

"Your point being?"

"So... you're thinking of her like a sister?" Marv asked.

Tim stared at his friend, face blank. Shook his head slowly.

"Holy shit. She's getting to you, isn't she? Wait till I tell Marianne."

Tim propped the landing net in its holder and said rather softly, "She asked me to spend the night... in the spare bedroom."

"Wow, she moves fast for a holy-card lady."

"It didn't feel that way," Tim said. "In fact, it just seemed... friendly, at the time."

"So, did you? Stay?"

"No. No I didn't. It didn't feel right... just yet."

"Just yet!" Marv poked Tim on the shoulder. "You old fart. Who knew you still had it in you?"

Tim looked at his buddy hurt and perplexed. "I've never had *it* in the first place... if ever."

"Don't make too much of sex."

"Easy for you to say. You and Marianne all these years."

Marv checked the fish-finder. "Marking three at 65 feet." He looked up. "All I'm sayin' is, it's part of a bigger picture." He fiddled with the dials, looked back at the rods. "Any second now..." Tim kept his eyes on his friend waiting for more. "Look," Marv said, "did you ever see one of those guys run naked onto a ball field—remember the streakers? That's not how you get in the dugout... be part of a team. It's a long process." Marv shouted, "Fish on!" and he lunged to the stern for a thrashing rod.

"Buzz kill!" Tim called after him.

Chapter Seven

After dinner at New Delhi the following week, Tim and Bernice went to Cinema 10. Later, McDonald's hot fudge sundaes in hand, they sat in Tim's car discussing the movie about Mister Rogers. When Bernice expressed only moderate enthusiasm for the film, Tim said, "So, you weren't impressed with my choice."

"Well, I could understand how a priest could find the story about another minister interesting..."

"I'm not a priest... anymore."

"If you'd let me finish my sentence," she snapped. "I was gonna say... like a lawyer watching a courtroom story or a cop... or better yet, an ex-cop," she tilted her head, mocking, "...watching a cop movie?"

Tim grinned, despite himself. "So... what? You like romantic movies or fast and furious action?"

"What I like? I'll tell you what I like. I like a movie that tells me something about myself and other people at the same time it keeps me guessing and on the edge of my seat to find out how it ends. I know how Mr. Rogers ended. No surprise there."

Tim chuckled around a mouthful of soft ice cream.

"Hey, don't you go laughing at me, like you're some kind of high and mighty."

Tim waved his hand—no, no. He swallowed, took a deep breath. "I wasn't laughing at you. I was just so pleased at how well you... I was agreeing with you."

Bernice cut wary eyes before adding, "Uh-huh. Are you always this good at backtracking?"

Good Lord, Tim reflected, stunned by the warm blue eyes pleading with him. She's lovely. She wants to trust me. What do I say? Keep it light, fella. "You kill me. I love your attitude."

"Well, thank you," Bernice said, "I guess."

"And, I uhm... I picked this movie because I didn't want to take a chance offending you. I mean... with your devotion to... devotions."

Bernice lowered her chin, blue eyes gone icy, "When I say the rosary, I say the rosary. And when I go to the movies... I go to the movies," punctuating the last with a head jab followed by an indignant glare out the side window. "That goes for a lot of other things too."

"Got it," he said, slipping his cup into the bag hanging from his dashboard. "Let's take turns. Next time, you pick the flick."

Bernice was silent while she scraped and licked the last bits of nuts and fudge, smiling to herself over the promise of next time, before absently stuffing her napkin and spoon into the cup and holding it carefully in her lap.

Something's coming, Tim realized. Another turn of her kaleidoscope. I've never been with anyone so fascinating, so fun.

Bernice hitched her thigh on the seat to face him, eyes smiling, she began in a rush, "I'm thinking you would like my friends Marjorie and Tre... and Vinnie and Gail, too." Her hand with the cup waved erratically. "And Vinnie... he has a cabin on a lake near here." Tim took the cup from her hand and dropped it in the trash. "And you like to fish," she continued, eyes soft-focused, off his shoulder. "We should all get together."

"I'd like to meet your friends," Tim said in a calm, warm voice, without adding, 'but mostly because I'll be with you.'

On the way out to Vinnie's place that weekend, Bernice played social secretary, briefing the visitor on the hosts they would meet. "So, Gail and Vinnie are married... well, might as well be. She was my next-door neighbor before she and Tre divorced. Nice woman. Worked in administration at the hospital. Funny thing about that, turns out Vinnie worked there too as a carpenter. They might have seen each other but never connected until..." Bernice took a breath to gather her thoughts. "See, their daughter... Tre and Gail's... Carrie, she's a schoolteacher, moved back into the house after Tre and Marjorie hooked up. And anyhow, Tre had Vinnie, who he knew from when they were kids, came in to remodel the kitchen."

"And that's who we're going to see out at this lake."

"Yeah. Them and Tre and Marjorie. Tre used to be a professor at Western and Marjorie..."

Tim held up his hand. "Bernice, if these people are your friends, I'm sure I'll like them. But let me be surprised. I'm pretty good at getting to know people."

"So, you're saying I should shut up and skip all the *coming attractions.*"

Tim waggled his head. "You could put it that way."

Bernice lapsed into offended silence, except for directions.

On the drive along the lake, Tim felt his pulse rise, as it used to as a child, at the first glimpse of silver-blue winking between the trees. "Wow, I'd love to wet a line if we get a chance. Got my gear in the trunk."

"I'm sure Vinnie will let you use his boat."

"Well, I hope he'd join me. I've made some of my best friends, fishing."

Vinnie and Tim anchored off a weed bed. "What do think?" Tim asked, "panfish or bass?" After a considered pause, Vinnie said, "Either one. We can cook them later for a choice along with brats."

"I like smallmouths for eating," Tim said.

"Well, then I'll go for the sure thing—bluegills."

Tim nodded and rigged his rod. "I like that house you're building. It's your own design, right?"

"Uh-huh. Me and Gail worked on it. She has some strong ideas."

"Do I understand you and she worked at the hospital?"

Vinnie nodded, "Uh-huh, but in different parts of the building. She was upstairs with the big shots. I was in the basement with the maintenance crew... carpentry."

"You never saw her there?"

"I saw her, but we never met. Not till we both retired."

"I do some woodworking myself," Tim said. "Got a shop out back of the house. You might want to come by some time... give me some tips."

"Don't know about that," Vinnie demurred. "I did mostly remodeling and such."

"Still..." Tim's face brightened. "I know. I've got some beautiful rough-cut walnut planks, that would make a great dining room table for your new place."

Vinnie, mouth open, nodded his head. "Wow! Really? That would be great."

"Sure. Gimme a call." Tim held out a black plastic grub before impaling it on a weighted jig. "A fishing buddy told me to try this new lure. I've been waiting for a chance to use it."

"I'll stick to worms and bobber," Vinnie said.

Tim flipped the lure out and let it drop to vertical before slowly jigging up and down. "So, tell me how you two finally got together."

Vinnie glanced down, a smile inching past his walrus mustache. "Tre asked me to remodel his kitchen and Gail was living there with their daughter." He looked up to explain, "Him and Gail were divorced and he was living with Marjorie, see?" Sweet smile back in place, Vinnie continued, "That's when I got to know Gail. For a bachelor like me... I never had a girlfriend before... it was a miracle."

Tim stopped jigging. "I know the feeling."

It took a moment for Vinnie to recall Tim's past. Nodding slowly, he said, "I guess both of us got a lot to learn."

Tim pointed a fist-bump toward Vinnie, adding, "Here's to learning."

Vinnie barked a sharp laugh and that's when the fish started biting.

Chapter Eight

Back at the cabin, Gail and Bernice were settled in deck chairs with wine and hummus. Gail slid a slender tanned foot across the weathered boards, leaned back and shook her auburn hair, grown shoulder length and full since she retired. She seemed happier, Bernice noticed, perhaps more content and mellowed than her years as Tre's wife and next-door neighbor. "The house is really coming along," she remarked.

"Yeah, Vinnie's a real task master. He had me nailing down the sub-floor in the kitchen this morning. I pounded forty nails!"

"Whoa! Forty huh?" Bernice said. "Uhm, Gail, carpenters don't count the nails."

"Exactly. I'm not a carpenter." Gail mock-grimaced. "Just trying to get with the program."

"You guys doin' okay?"

Gail posed a satisfied grin, nodded vigorously. "Oh, yeah."

Both women focused on Tim in the front of the rowboat, rod bent wrestling with a fish. "Looks like we might have fish tacos along with brats for supper," Gail remarked.

"Maybe fancier than that. Tim considers himself a serious cook when it comes to fish. Made me some great poached salmon couple nights ago."

"He had you to his place?"

"Yeah... a vintage cottage on the beach."

Gail raised an eyebrow and rolled her hand. "And... anything else?"

"And sweet corn and homemade rolls..." Bernice deflected, just as a car pulled up and honked. "Marjorie and Tre."

"That'll be Tre," Vinnie said reacting to the car horn. "I think you'll like him." He pulled up the anchor while Tim lifted the stringer of two bass and six *gills* into the boat. On the way to the dock and a waiting Tre, Vinnie described his friend. "Tre used to teach at Western. We go way back. Grew up in the old neighborhood. Sal too. He passed away last fall."

"He's the man Bernice helped move into Shelden Pond, right?"

"Uh-huh. She's a rock. Bernice. You can count on her."

"I'll remember that."

"Do any good?" Tre asked as they snugged to the dock. Tim held up the stringer which proved to be an ice-breaker when introductions were made. Tre poked at the largest bass. "That one's got to be twenty inches. What were you using?"

Marjorie huddled with Gail and Bernice, watching the two tall men surrounding Tim. "That's your guy, huh?" Marjorie asked. "Kinda short, isn't he."

"He's just right," Bernice said, straightening to her full 5'2".

"And he's a good cook." Gail added.

Marjorie hugged Bernice. "And?"

Bernice looked from friend to friend, deciding how much to share. "We're taking our time getting to know each other."

Supper was delicious. Tim grilled bass fillets in a cornmeal crust with lime juice. Then he fried the blue gill fillets, laid them over a bed of fettucine and poured a lemon, capers and butter sauce over them. Gail tossed a garden salad while Vinnie grilled brats and sweet corn in the husk.

On the porch watching the sun sink over the lake, Tim asked Tre, "What was your subject at Western?"

"Creative writing."

"Fiction? Poetry?"

"Mostly fiction."

"Do you write as well?" Tim asked.

"Mostly short stories," Marjorie answered for him.

"Slowing down a bit, lately," Tre allowed. "Do you write?"

"Depends if you count a tight ten-minute sermon every Sunday for fifty years."

Tre leaned over the chair arm and gave Tim five. "I heard you've left all that behind."

"Yep," Tim said as they both eyed Marjorie and Bernice heading indoors.

"I bet that would make a good story."

Over the sink, Marjorie said, "You know, Bernie. I think you should marry him."

"What? You don't even know him. How can you say that?"

"I don't know. Just a good feeling I get from you and him together. And that quirky corner- of-the-mouth smile of his. I love it."

"I should marry a smile?"

"Or at least move in together," Gail added. "You deserve a good man in your life."

"Give me a break, you guys. I barely met him."

"You knew him way back in high school, didn't you?" Marjorie asked.

"Doesn't count," Bernice protested. "Nobody's responsible for anything that happened more than ten years ago. Not at our age."

"And besides," Gail said, "he's got this shy-little boy look that makes you want to give him something he's missing... but he doesn't know what it is."

"God," Bernice said, "he's not a stray cat. Besides it's not hard to figure out what a man who's been practicing celibacy for fifty years is missing. He's a little shy. We're taking it slow."

Gail ziplocked a final packet of left-overs. "I know. You two ought to take a trip. That's what clinched it for Vinnie and me."

"Could make or break the whole thing," Marjorie warned.

"Yeah, but they met on a trip, didn't they?" Gail replied. "In Florida."

"Not in the same room though."

Bernice grabbed a bag of brats and headed for the door calling over her shoulder, "Thank you, ladies."

Chapter Nine

Over dinner at Shelden Pond a couple days later, Tim and Bernice were joined at table by two women residents. Both Tina and Carol, tall and slender, seemed synchronized to each other in the way of grade school best friends—heads coming together to some unheard cue for a whisper and nod while hyperactive eyes kept constantly moving, noticing. Tim was not surprised to find that they were both elementary school teachers, which further reinforced his otherwise unexplained inclination to raise his hand to speak. Tina's hands quavered, as did her head, while she broke and buttered a roll. Carol spoke in a measured, carefully modulated deep voice. Both were most interested to meet, quiz and assess the new guest of their friend Bernice.

Over the main course of baked ziti, the two friends exchanged excited glances when Tim invited Bernice to 4th of July festivities in South Haven—parade in the morning, art fair in the park and fireworks at night. Tim was sure they squeezed hands under the table at the prospect of their friend's fun day away from the *home.* Bernice was a little more discerning. "What time's the parade?"

"11:00" Tim replied.

"Hmmm," Bernice calculated. "For you to go home tonight. You'd have to turn around and come back tomorrow to pick me up... what? 9:00... 9:30?"

"No problem," Tim said.

"Nah. You'd do better to spend the night here. Besides, I've seen enough clowns in my lifetime. I won't miss one more parade." Looking up brightly she added, "And that way we can take our time getting up in the morning."

Tim, exposed to years of startling revelations in the confessional, kept a straight face. Tina and Carol, however, first offered a full view of half-chewed pasta and then the tops of their blue-permed coifs as they stared at their plates.

Wow, Tim thought. I was hoping she'd invite me to stay the night. I'm ready this time. I just wouldn't have been so *out-there* in front of her ladies. Now look at their sly glances. They love the juicy news. Let's give them more to talk about.

"Well, I would like to stay Bernice, but I didn't bring a toothbrush."

Bernice cut Tim a conniving look. "Oh, that's all right. I kept it from last time."

The ladies promptly got up and scurried to the dessert cart while Bernice and Tim quickly finished and headed for the elevators. Watching the floor numbers descend, Bernice studied Tim's clenched lips; his fixed, straight-ahead stare. She nudged him with her elbow. "Hey, relax," she said, "I invited you to sleep over, not sleep together."

"Damn," Tim said, flashing a disappointed frown. Bernice couldn't hide her surprise and delight. When the doors opened, he pulled her inside. They stood facing each other, fighting grins of anticipation. Sealed shut, Tim felt something he had never allowed himself to feel before—delight in a woman inviting him into her life, her love. He'd seen that look before, that implied offer, more than once over the years. He'd protected his vocation in the past. But not now. Not this time. He was free.

They kissed through the next two floors and only paused when the bell sounded for the fourth. The doors opened to a gentleman hunched over his walker, waiting his turn. Tim and Bernice abruptly stepped apart like guilty teenagers before tripping and scrambling down the hall to her room, suppressing giggles while she fiddled with her keys.

On the car ride out to South Haven the next morning, Tim kept stealing glances at Bernice. "What?" she finally asked before adding, "you're looking very pleased with yourself."

"I'm pleased with you," he replied, reaching over to stroke the graceful arc of her bare calf. He wriggled in his seat. "I feel like shouting to the whole world." A chuckle erupted. "All right. All right. This reminds me of the guy who goes to confession and tells the priest, 'Father, I'm 91-years old and I made love three times last night with a hooker.'

The priest says, 'For your penance say three rosaries.'

'What's a rosary?'

'What kind of Catholic doesn't know what a rosary is?'

'Who says I'm a Catholic?'

'Then what are you doing in the confessional?'

'Hey, I'm telling anyone who'll listen.'"

Tim took his eyes off the road, grinning in anticipation of Bernice's response. He got a blank stare. "Why all the jokes about confession, and rosaries and novenas? What-cha got against all that?"

"Geez, Bernice," Tim replied, "a joke's a joke."

"Uh-huh. More like trying to convince yourself you're past it all."

His smile subsided for a moment, as he swung out to pass a tractor. Just before cutting back into his lane, he added, "Damn, I love your blue eyes." This time when he snuck a peek, he caught a pleased expression flitting across her face.

Hanging on Tim's elbow in the park, Bernice, complained, "This is supposed to be an art fair. All it is, is kitchy crafts. These people give craftiness a bad name."

Couldn't have said it better myself, Tim thought. What a hoot, she is.

Bernice joined the line at a sugared-almond stand while Tim waited under a shady maple, eyes on her. She peeked over her shoulder at him, as if aware of his attention—perhaps expecting it. He felt tugged by a newfound force, an invisible cord, to this woman who made him laugh, and feel whole, and excited all at the same time. He allowed himself a shy hand wave.

"Father McRae, how are you?" a voice called. He took in a young mother... Sandy... Sandy Ackerman he finally recalled, and her daughter, obviously, sharing the same blond hair and matching yellow sundress. "Haven't seen you in forever," Sandy said. "Carrie," she told her seven-ish daughter, "this is Father McRae." The child held his gaze. "He baptized you." Grinning, anticipating her own joke, she added, "And he married Daddy and me. Not in that order, of course." The girl looked overwhelmed and confused. As did

Tim when Bernice snugged next to him and offered a friendly smile to the woman. When Tim failed to make introductions, Sandy introduced herself and offered her hand. Failing cues from Tim, Bernice finally shook hands and said, "Hi, I'm Bernice, Tim's friend."

"Father Tim has so many friends and we all love him," Sandy gushed.

"I can see why you do," Bernice replied, hugging his stiff, unresponsive arm. "He's such a loveable guy."

Sandy's forced smile, finally moved Tim to say in a tight voice, "Nice to see you again Sandy... you too, Carrie," and then to awkwardly raise his right hand between the start of a blessing and an on-your-way gesture.

Bernice munched on a nut while mother-daughter moved out of hearing. "Well, wasn't that special?"

"I thought I could handle it," Tim muttered. "Running into old parishioners. But that little girl..."

"I can tell you've never been divorced. It's always awkward the first couple of times you meet ex in-laws. Some get it. Some don't. Don't beat yourself up."

Tim stopped and stared at Bernice. "How do you know all this?"

She shrugged. "Been there. Done that."

"But it's not the same. Not at all. Priests and parishioners..."

"For crissake, Tim, get over yourself." Bernice paused at the car door. "By the way, what's for supper? I'm getting hungry."

"Uhm, I was planning to pick up some whitefish from Louie's."

"Great. Then I want to put my feet up on your porch and just chill."

After dinner, Tim and Bernice gently rocked the squeaky porch glider to the slowly setting sun along the western horizon. "Soon as it gets good and dark," Tim said, "we can go down to the beach to watch the fireworks out of South Haven."

"I'll get the quilt from the spare bedroom," Bernice said. "Oh, and where do you keep the mosquito spray? I didn't see any in the hall closet."

"In the bathroom cabinet." Tim felt a twinge of annoyance shoot through him, thinking, she's really making herself at home. Not that I really mind... I guess. It's just that... I was here first.

After the pyrotechnic grand finale, Tim helped Bernice to her feet and folded the quilt. "Would you mind taking it in?" he asked.

"What?" Bernice asked.

"I..." Tim mumbled. "I just need some alone time. A lot of things happened in the last two days..."

Bernice could not see Tim's face but she could feel the edge in his voice. A little panicky. Like a claustrophobic person in a small room. "Sure," she said, instead of insisting that he share his feelings. She faked a yawn and said, "I'll leave the porch light on. I'm really tired. I don't know about you but I didn't sleep real well last night."

"Why's that?"

"You were on my side of the bed. The left side." She lightly added, "But don't worry. I got dibs on it tonight and will probably be sound asleep when you get back." She wondered if it was her imagination, but when Tim squeezed her hand, she sensed his relief.

The next morning, over scones and blueberries, she asked about times for mass in the local church.

"There's a 9 and an 11:00 at St. Basil's."

Checking the clock, Bernice said, "We'd have to hurry for the 9:00. Why don't we go to the 11:00?"

Tim grimaced. "I won't be going." To Bernice's surprised expression, he added, "I'll drive you there since you don't know where it is..."

"Oh," was all she said as she nodded her head in acceptance. Take it one thing at a time, she reminded herself.

As Bernice entered the side door of the church, Tim took in the block-square complex of school, rectory, office and gym. Matching red brick throughout. The influence of various architectural trends in evidence from 1940s square school to vaguely Norman style church and 70s aqua blue trim and glass office building. Landlord, he thought. Never had any classes in the seminary on building management

173

and construction financing. Yet that's what I had to do for so many years. Some people make whole careers out of being superintendent of schools, I was expected to learn on the job. God, I'm glad to be out from under all that brick and mortar.

He strolled across the street to a bench on the bluff overlooking South Beach and the lighthouse pier. Used to morning meditation, what he called 'centering himself,' Tim replayed and wondered at the happenings over the past few days.

A man walked over and sat on a second bench a few feet away. Tim glanced at him. Looked again. Could it be? His head was down. Gray at the temples. It was him. Ray Torres. The seminarian he told to leave the seminary.

Thoughts swirled and dove like the flock of seagulls roused by a boy on the beach tossing crackers in the air. Do I want to say anything to him? Ignore him? Act surprised if he recognizes me? That never works. You can always tell when someone is faking it. And anyhow he just checked me out. Made me.

"Father McRae," he said.

"Hi, Ramon."

"No one's called me that in a long time. Not since Mexico."

Tim didn't pick up the dangling thread. Instead he flashed to him and Ray sitting in the sepia-toned light coming through the diamond-shaped windowpanes of his seminary apartment. The student with his quirky smile at the foot of his mentor, his guru.

"Who's the lady got out of your car?" Ray asked.

Tim took a deep breath. It's not the same, he thought. We're equals now. "She's a friend... close friend. I'm retired." He flicked his head toward the church. "And sitting out here, instead of in there, suits me fine."

Ray nodded, concurring. "My wife's inside, too." He pulled a pack of cigarettes from his shirt pocket. "Loving her... some things are bigger than Church."

Amen, Tim thought. And here we kicked him out because we thought he was dumb.

After refusing the offer of a cigarette, Tim watched Ray shake one loose and with the practiced precision of a ritual, tap the filter on the box, pop it into his mouth, light up to a deep draw, raise his chin and exhale a long plume lost against the roiling clouds.

"Your smoking outside church reminds me of the Jesuit who thought to ask his novice master if he could smoke during meditation period. On second thought, he decided to ask if he could pray while he smoked."

"Priest word games." Ray shook his head, walked over and sat next to Tim. "Still telling stale old jokes and stories. You never change."

"I'm trying."

Ray ruffled the gravel underfoot with the toe of his sandal, looked up with a teasing smirk. "So... your friend... better than bacon, huh?"

"How's that?"

"You know, the Rabbi and priest on a plane. The priest goes, 'Just between us. You ever tried bacon?' The rabbi shrugs—yes. After a bit he asks the priest, 'You ever been with a woman?'"

Tim snorted. "Zing. Jokes and parables... short-cuts to the truth."

"I guess, yeah."

He fixed Ray with a searching gaze. "You're happy."

Ray nodded as they watched the four-foot rollers climbing up and across the pier. He stubbed the cigarette and flicked it off the seventy-foot cliff. A snatch of hymn and organ penetrated the steady thrum of waves. Tim spoke in a confessional whisper, "I've always felt terrible about making you leave."

Ray huffed in surprise. "It wasn't your fault. I never blamed you. It was Powell. Father Jim Powell," he said with contempt and barely controlled anger. Tim's puzzled expression drew Ray on. "He wanted me out for what he tried with me."

"No," Tim pleaded and denied at the same time. "I never suspected anything... like that." Reflecting a moment, he continued, "Wait a minute. He did leave abruptly in the middle of the next semester and I had to take over his classes. How did I miss... back then... and all the other abuse stuff coming out now? Not notice... for years?"

Ray hawked and spit over the edge. "Our minds can play tricks on us... I know. Don't let us see and admit... stuff."

"And to think the diocese... the Church... carried him so long. Moving him from assignment to assignment."

Suddenly Ray's mouth drew closed and his eyes tightened. "They won't be moving him around anymore. I blew the whistle on him."

Both men leaned, elbows on knees and stared at the tumbling gray and white tumult before them until two car horns toot-tooted. The guys turned to spot their partners standing in the open doors of the last two cars in the parking lot. They fist-bumped and without a word walked to their waiting women.

On the drive downtown for lunch, Tim seemed preoccupied, shoulders tense. Bernice reached over to massage the base of his neck. Tim absently shrugged her off. Sitting back, unsure how to respond, she finally asked, "Who was that guy? Seemed like you knew each other."

Tim nosed to the curb in front of the Blue Water Café. He turned off the engine, hesitated, and finally replied, "Someone I used to know..." He grimaced, stammered, "Uhm, Bernice, I..."

Bernice stamped her foot on the floorboard. "Dammit, Tim, you're getting on my nerves. Talk to me, mister. Share. Dish. Whatever you want to call it. You're not behind your desk listening to someone else's problem and then offering advice like some kind of guru. You're part of this problem. And I don't like being 'the other woman'... like I'm causing it all." Breathing hard, brow furrowed, demanded, "Well? Say something, dammit."

Tim's hands worked to unspoken thoughts.

Bernice jerked the car door open, climbed out and slammed it shut. She paced to the corner and back. Twice. Then she opened the door, buckled in and said icily, "Take me home."

Silence reigned for the thirty-five-minute ride to Kalamazoo. At the Shelden Pond entrance, Bernice finally spoke in a subdued voice, "Bring my overnight bag back sometime. Leave it at the front desk."

"It will keep at my place... for another time."

"Like hell," Bernice snapped. "In your dreams, buster."

"Please be patient," Tim pleaded. "I'm worth it."

"Aargh!"

176

"And you too… you're worth it too," Tim called after her as she slammed out of the car.

Chapter Ten

Vinnie ran rough-cut walnut through the planer while Tim edged the planks on the jointer. Lost in the smells of wood shavings and the rhythm of the work, Tim replayed the mosaic of the weekend, searching for pattern or purpose. He gave up, finally, and settled on the more tangible task of arranging the wood for lamination. Vinnie had a keen eye for grain and markings as they shuffled and re-aligned one and another plank into a giant tabletop.

With the wood glued and clamped, they took a break on Tim's porch. "Where'd you get that fine walnut?" Vinnie asked over the penetrating squeak of the glider.

"Me and my buddy, Marv... we know the guys at the township. They let us take what we want from their log pile... from storms and construction."

"And then?"

"Well, we load Marv's trailer and go to this sawmill in Gobles where we exchange helping him for getting our stuff sawn."

"Beautiful wood. I really appreciate it. Gail's gonna love this table in our kitchen." Vinnie sipped at his coffee and as he was setting it down, announced, "You and Bernice will be our first guests to sit at it."

"Uhm... yeah. That would be great if we ever do sit down with each other... again."

Vinnie coughed and cleared his throat.

"Look, I don't want to drag you into this," Tim said. "Suffice to say, we're having trouble getting used to each other."

"Uh-huh." Vinnie rose, opened the screen door and hacked a juicy gob. Work-hardened hands idly jostled the screen door, loose in its frame, registering the need for repair.

Tim watched him fill the door frame—tall, wide shouldered, his Prussian soldier impression aided by a raised, square jaw and full white mustache. Vinnie turned and sat back down on the paint-bare glider. Settling into the flattened, mildewed cushions, he took a deep breath before proclaiming, "Us long-time bachelors have a lot to learn... at first."

"Yeah, like I jolt awake every time I roll over in bed," Tim whined. "I'm used to sleeping alone," he explained, then quickly added, "don't get me wrong... not that it isn't exciting, too."

Vinnie furrowed his brow and parted his lips a couple of times before blurting out a practical solution. "In the new house... we got separate offices. Me and Gail. Each got our own room."

"So, you're saying space is important. Psychological and physical."

Vinnie hunched his shoulder, "Yeah... like you say."

"But how much? I mean, should we have separate beds? See each other only so-many days a week? Stay in separate houses? This house?"

Tim glanced over his shoulder at the squat, dark interior of his Beatrix Potter-like hut with vines going up the roof and mold growing down the north side. What made him think Bernice would even want to spend serious time there? Since his parents passed, twenty years ago, he had done nothing to the property. Bernice's visit made him look at the place with fresh eyes, as if he were a realtor with no sentimental attachment to the sagging four poster bed and familiar Africa-shaped stain on the kitchen wall. Suddenly the worn-through scarlet couch spoke shame rather than comfort. And the Formica kitchen table with chrome legs and cracked vinyl-seat chairs forfeited their nostalgic air for second-hand functionality. See what happens, Tim pondered, when you let someone else into your ordered existence?

Having plumbed the depths of his marital insights and patience with another's reflections, Vinnie slugged the last of his coffee and stood. "Let me show you how the legs should go. I'm thinking trestle table."

They trudged back to the re-purposed carriage barn behind and off to one side that served as Tim's workshop.

Wide double doors, allowing easy access for long boards and finished projects, stood open. An interior staircase lead to an upper floor kitchen, bedroom and bath. Tim considered it his tree-house getaway when his parents had filled the cottage. At the moment, however, he simply looked forward to losing himself in the sounds and smells of sawing and sanding.

"I recommend the Italian Wedding soup," Marjorie said to Bernice reading the *Tre Sorelle* menu.

"So, we drove fifteen miles, to Plainwell, just for a bowl of soup?" Bernice crabbed.

Marjorie lowered her chin and glared at her friend. "Get what you want. I don't care." Folding her menu, she continued. "What's eating you anyway? Troubles with Mister Father?"

As soon as the waitress left with their orders, Bernice unloaded, "He doesn't talk. He's got all kinds of things going on in his head but he keeps it in. All right, take this. Saturday we're at the art fair in South Haven."

"How was it this year?"

"Same as ever." Bernice paused for a sip of iced tea. "So, just like you'd expect, we run into one of his ex-parishioners, and dear old *I'm-done-with-the-priesthood* gets tongue tied. Like he hasn't figured this would happen and how he should handle it. He was so sure of himself in Florida. He meets one person from his other life and he shuts down, goes into a shell. So, what am I—the *other woman* home wrecker? Someone he's ashamed of? Someone he doesn't want to be seen in public with? They pause while the waitress serves their steaming bowl of minestrone. Bernice takes a taste and nods her head in silent approval. "So, then, Sunday, we go to church..."

"Wait. You went to church? Where in South Haven?"

"Yeah. What do you think?"

"So, that's where his place is, right? Near there."

"Yeah. It's a cottage. Old. Inside is like a hunter's cabin."

"Bernice," Marjorie cautioned, "you didn't try to arrange his silverware, did you?"

"No, not really. Not that. Besides he's only got three forks and two spoons. Mismatched. He's like a guy in his man cave."

"So, let him have his space."

"Oh, yeah. No problem there." Bernice ripped off a twist of crusty bread and dipped it in the dish of puddled olive oil and parmesan. Around her mouthful, she continued, "So, where was I? At church. Well, I went into church. He stayed outside looking at the lake. After mass I see him talking to this guy. When I ask who it was, he clams up. Like I'm bugging him. Like I'm pounding on his door and he doesn't want to let me in."

"Sounds like he's not good at sharing his feelings. I suppose if you spend your whole life telling people what's right and wrong, and listening to their problems, you're not used to sharing back."

"Quit defending him."

Marjorie looked off, fixated on something off Bernice's right shoulder. After a moment she snapped back in focus. "You remember that movie about a lion... Elsa? People raised it then had to train it to live in the wild? Born Free. That was the movie."

Bernice, eyes twinkling above an amused grin, said, "Uhm. So, Tim has been kept in captivity... is that where you're going? And I'm supposed to Free Willy. Is that it?"

Marjorie shook her head resignedly.

Hunching forward in her chair, Bernice went on, "He doesn't even know how to have a good fight. When I get mad at him, he doesn't get mad back. He doesn't yell or even raise his voice. What fun is that?"

"Hey, c'mon Bernice. He's been in the *soothe and forgive* business. Make love not war. Speaking of..."

"Don't go there. It's fine and all. He's like a kid opening a present."

"Omigod. What's not to like? And at our age."

"But he wants to sleep on my side of the bed and so we both toss and turn all night."

"And now?"

"I've got my own bed all to myself... for the foreseeable future."

"Hmm. I see. Would it help if I arranged a double date... movie... dinner?"

Bernice tapped her glass hard on the table, sloshing iced tea on the white linen. "I don't know what I want. But it's his move, now. He has to figure out what he wants and how to share with me."

"Are you sure you really want to know what he thinks... all that much? You'll find out in good time." Marjorie patted her lips with her napkin. "And sometimes, what a man is thinking is not that much."

"Says Ann Landers."

"Look," Marjorie entreated, "this is a good guy you got here. I like him. Don't blow him off. It's all about adjustments. Give and take. He's good for you, Bernice."

Cocking her head with a sidelong appraisal, Bernice finally nodded, muttered, "I guess..."

Chapter Eleven

The following Saturday, Tim and Marv drove down to the South Beach parking lot to make their own assessment of the small craft advisory on the radio. Before they came to a stop, it was clear there would be no fishing that morning. Sand swirled in rolling heaps against bumper curbs. Rain spit and thrashed against the windshield blurring the red lighthouse and cross-hatched waves beyond.

On the way to the Blue Water Café for a consolation breakfast, Tim suddenly chortled. Marv grimaced. "Joke on the way."

"No, you'll like this. This weather reminds me of the guy who gets up to go fishing. Gets his boat, bait, lunch, gets to the lake and it's blowing like hell. Like today. So, he goes back home. Puts everything away. Sneaks back into bed and rubs his wife's back. She says, 'Can you believe my dumbass husband went fishing in this weather?' Poor guy can't decide if she's teasing or not. But he never goes fishing again. Ha!"

Tim held his grin, waiting for the obligatory groan from Marv. Extended silence drew a puzzled glance at his friend. "That stuff's not a joke, man," Marv said.

"Okay," Tim said, apologetically hunching his shoulders.

"Infidelity can put a real wrinkle in a relationship. Hurts for years."

It wasn't until they were seated, the usual cake and egger ordered, that Marv, focused just past the placemat, began, "It's work, being married. Not like we thought in the seminary." He looked up, reaching for eye contact, linked memories. "Remember Father Bradfield telling us to be careful of girls, not to date because girls would be a threat to our vocation. That if they succeeded in getting us to drop out, that would make them better than God."

"That was in high school, for crissake," Tim replied, as he cut into the over-easy egg layered between his pancakes and waited for the yolk to mingle with syrup and butter before forking a mouthful.

"Yeah, but we soaked it up. Like Jedi Knights listening to Yoda."

"That was all before Star Wars."

"Okay. Then Marines. When the going gets tough... the tough hang in. Whatever. My point is, we were made to feel that marriage was the easy fallback, plan B, for guys who couldn't handle the program."

"Okay. So? We're a hell of a long ways from that."

"I wonder if you are."

Tim offered a questioning frown.

"Early ideas die hard, Tim, and marriage is not easy. It causes pain. Takes constant work."

"You think I don't know that? That I haven't spent hours and hours trying to help folks..."

Marv held up his hands in a stop sign. "I know."

Tim shook his head. "Remind me not to tell you any more marriage jokes."

"Is that a promise?" Marv teased. A couple bites later, he said, "No, really, how's it going with your...?"

"Bernice. Her name's Bernice." Tim looked out at the street thronged with disappointed beach goers. "And she's not my *anything* right now."

Swallowing a gulp of coffee, Marv rolled his hand as if to say, 'so tell me.'

Tim set his fork down carefully, parallel to his plate. "We were at the art fair last Saturday. And this lady I barely remember from the parish, jumps me. Says I baptized her daughter. Who can remember?"

"That happened to me a lot for the first couple of years after I left," Marv shared. "I disappointed some young couples when I didn't remember marrying them. Hell, in my two years I must have married a couple hundred people. One big blur of veiled beauties and shaking hands pushing wedding rings on sweaty fingers."

"Surprisingly, I remembered her name."

"You're gonna keep running into parishioners," Marv said around a sip of coffee, "get used to it."

"Yeah. But then I ran into a guy from my seminary time. Come to find out about Jim Powell and what he did. Bastard. And there's all the news about other guys abusing kids. And the cover-up. I had no idea of any of that was going on."

"Honestly, I didn't either. Back then. Maybe it was 'Hear no evil. See no evil.'"

"You were lucky to get out when you did," Tim said. "I stayed in and now I feel... tarnished, tainted. Like I should have known or somehow prevented it." Waving his hand in disgust, he added, "I want nothing more to do with the Church. Period."

"I hear you, man. Me too."

Tim pushed his plate away, half eaten. "And now I'm all screwed up with Bernice." Marv looked up, eyebrows raised, questioning, supportive. "How do I explain all this stuff to her. I don't know where to begin. I can't just dump on her."

"Yes, you can," Marv said.

"It'll push her away."

"She's away now, right?" Marv asked.

"Yeah. We're apart." Tim thumped his fingers on the table. "I miss her. I think about her a lot." He held his hands out in a silent appeal. "I was happy before... alone. Now it feels like I'm missing something, cheating myself out of... really living. And I want to be with her. Around her. But I'm not sure how much. Because, sometimes I feel crowded and... startled that she's around. Like when someone suddenly walks into the room. And she's there all the time and wants to talk to me. Wants me to listen. Wants me to talk. Know what I'm saying?"

"Hey, don't forget, I've known rectory life," Marv said. "It's regimented, compartmentalized. Counseling by appointment, confessions 4 to 6. It's a bachelor existence—your time is your own unless otherwise scheduled. Relationship is not neat and tidy like that." Marv grinned broadly and reached out his hand for a high five. Tim, puzzled, gave him a reluctant five. "Face it. You've stepped in it, man. You're in love. Welcome to the ride."

Tim flattened his expression to mild scorn. "Who died and made you the doorman to marital bliss?"

Ignoring the jibe, Marv pushed on, "You can't back down from this lady." He narrowed his eyes, leveled his brow. "Now, that would truly be a sin, guy. You're onto the real thing and it takes work. Go to her. Put yourself out."

Tim shook his head, overwhelmed. "Look," Marv counseled, "me and Marianne have been married what... forty-five years? Everything is locked down and in place with a mortgage and pension and seven grandkids and vacations in Mexico." They both paused to drop credit cards into the folder. Tim finished off his coffee. "But you guys," Marv said, eyes sparkling with joy for his buddy, "you've landed on a desert island. You can define your own world. Keep your own place. Hell, keep three places—yours, hers and a love-nest in between. See each other when it feels good. Have separate beds. Go on separate vacations. Go on tours together... that's how you met, right? Help her with her hobbies. Bring her along with us fishing."

"Not her thing," Tim said.

Arm across Tim's shoulder on the way out, Marv finished with, "Just don't run away from love. Not now, man."

Tim sat behind the wheel, chin down. Marv finally broke in, "Just relax, okay? You're used to retreats. Take long walks on the beach. There's a lot to think about. Think. Then stop thinking. Just be open to possibility. Something will come to you. You'll know when and how to move."

The next day, Tim was strolling the beach in front of his place. There were always surprises washed up after a storm: beach glass, driftwood. He studied a shriveled balloon twirling in the shallows, the *Happy Birthday* barely legible on the deflated, crenellated surface, like a tattoo on a 90-year old man. Somehow folks in Milwaukee loosed helium-filled good wishes for graduates and newlyweds while those on the other side of the Lake are left to watch the bedraggled good cheer scrubbing against the hardscrabble shoreline with the push and pull of unrelenting waves. Tim wondered if there was a metaphor here.

A mile along, he spotted a rare Petoskey stone shining from under the wave wash. It was as big as a baseball. A beautiful specimen. He hunkered on a log under the curling bluff to study his find. Round. No flaws. He would take it to the rock shop in town to be polished. It would make a stunning gift for Bernice. Would she appreciate it? he wondered. Would it be given a place of prominence next to the Infant of Prague statue?

After a bit, he sat on a log, stretched out his aching knee and massaged it. Part of a riser and stair-step protruded from the sand, the wood worn and green with mold. Like my front steps he mused. Washed up like my cottage. How could I expect Bernice to like such a moldy old place, to want to stay there? I gotta fix it up.

All the way home, Tim rolled the stone in his hand, planning. He'd ask Vinnie to help him fix the roof... and the screen door... and, while they were at it, the whole porch. Maybe add a ceiling swing. And what about the kitchen? And new tile in the bathroom. And, of course, paint the walls and maybe a new couch and even a rug. Shouldn't cost too much and he could do a lot of the work.

After supper of Tilapia fillet and sweet corn, he called Vinnie.

"Hi, Tim. Hey, you gotta come here and see how great the table looks in our dining room. Gail is going to be so surprised when she sees it."

"She hasn't seen it yet? We finished it Friday."

"Oh, I guess you didn't know. Her and Marjorie and Bernice all went on one of those senior tours out West... Yellowstone, Tetons, Jackson Hole."

"Bernice never mentioned it... before."

"They had it planned for a long time. Bernice told me she wasn't that interested in some old geyser spouting off every few hours, but she wouldn't mind meeting some old geezers. Ha! she makes me laugh."

"Yep. I bet she does. So, Vin, I was thinking I could stand to freshen up this old place of mine and was wondering if you would be willing to help."

"What are you thinking of doing? I know that screen door is loose."

"Lot more than that. Maybe major stuff like roofing and laminated floor and paint. I don't know. It could use a face lift. I could pay... some."

"Naw, not at all. I'm stuck at home alone for two weeks. So is Tre for that matter. I bet he wouldn't mind pitching in."

"Really? That would be great. It would be such a surprise for Bernice when she gets back."

"I'll call Tre and we'll be by in the morning. Or at least, I will. See ya. Oh, and I'll bring my compressor and nail gun and we can decide what you need from Menards."

Two days later, while Tim and Tre primed lapstrake siding on the north side of the cottage, Tre told of his short term stay at Shelden Pond to recover from hip surgery. From three rungs up the step ladder, he slapped primer on the raw lumber while Tim worked just off and below at ground level. "At the time," he recalled, "I wanted to get out of there in the worst way... not quite so much once I met Marjorie. But now, looking back, that place kind of reminded me of dorm living, classes... campus life." He paused, brush dripping, a smarmy smile on his face. "Lots of folks coming and going... just a lot slower."

Vinnie called from the roof, "Hey get me another pack of shingles, would, ya?"

His errand completed, Tre continued, "Actually, I go there every two weeks to conduct a memoir writing class. It's a stitch."

"How so?"

"As soon as one person reads a couple paragraphs, everyone else chimes in with, 'When I was a kid' stories."

"Sounds more like long-term memory therapy," Tim said.

"Well, whatever it is. I enjoy sitting in and poking it along." He stopped to rub his cheek with his shirt cuff, leaving a white smudge on his chin, before continuing. "To tell you the truth. I enjoy it. Look forward to going. I guess I miss the classroom. All those years of holding forth, interacting with students. It's my way to keep a hand in, to gently motor back... pickle ball after tennis."

They worked in silence for the next while, Tim recalling, and missing, the Scripture Study sessions he mentored in the parish. He had been living in the cottage since early spring and had to admit that he was a bit lonely, missed the hubbub of parish living: phone calls and classroom visits and pre-Cana conferences and catechetical instructions and counseling and sick visits and... now the treadmill had stopped.

"Time for lunch," Vinnie announced as he started down the ladder, forcibly moving Tre down as well.

"Got a plastic grocery bag?" Tre asked.

Tim shrugged. "I guess. Let me look."

When he returned a moment later, he was surprised to see Tre wrap the bristles from both their brushes in the bag and twist it shut. To his questioning look, Tre explained. "This will keep them from drying out."

Soon all three were sitting on the fresh-made front steps with ham sandwiches, beer and a bag of potato chips to pass. Between the sounds of chewing, slurping and crunching, Tim mentioned, "We were just talking about Shelden Pond and Tre's memoir writing class."

Vinnie swallowed his mouthful, said, "Memoir. Isn't that a fancy name for a biography?"

"Similar," Tre said. "More like autobiography."

Vinnie barked a laugh. "Reminds me of something Yogi Berra said. Someone asked him if he had read his biography. He goes, 'No. Didn't need to. I lived it.'"

"I wish some of the folks in my class had more sense of humor and less total recall."

"I met a couple of ladies there one night over dinner," Tim said, "Tina and Carol. Bernice's friends. They seemed pretty bright."

"Those two," Tre said. "Tweedle Dum and Tweedle Dee. Like they're attached at the hip. They keep asking me to run a book club. Jane Austen... *please.*"

"I'm a Jane Austen fan," Tim said.

"Hmm. The way you've kept up this palace," Tre replied with a smug smile, "I would have guessed Jane Bronte and *Wuthering Heights.*"

Deliberately ignoring the rib, Tim asked, "So how often do you meet?"

"Bi-weekly. Any longer and they would forget what they said last time."

"Hell, I forget what I said five minutes ago," Vinnie declared. "Did I tell you about Yogi Berra and his biography?"

The next morning, before the others arrived, Tim called the activity director at Shelden Pond and yes, they really would appreciate someone heading up a Jane Austen Book Club. She mentioned Tina and Carol as primary contacts. On his morning beach walk he allowed himself a self-satisfied smile. He could get in a little social contact without all the responsibility and baggage of church and religion. And following Marv's advice, he would be around Bernice and have a chance to slip into her good graces. In the meantime, he would be fixing up his nest to entice her back in.

Chapter Twelve

After lunch, Bernice stopped at the bulletin board outside the cafeteria. She scanned the activities posted there: Current Events Discussion with Brian Denning; Film Follow Up: Loving Vincent with Martha Dunstan; Memoir Writing with Dr. Trahan; Gentle Yoga with Carol Dirks; Jane Austen, the woman and times, with Tim McRae. Before she could read more, Tina and Carol slid next to her, "Bernice," Tina began, "so good to have you back. Did you see that your friend Tim is conducting a book group on Jane Austen?"

"Uh-huh. He seems to have moved right in."

"We love him," Carol said. "There are seven of us in the group, and he knows so much about Jane Austen. We're working on *Pride and Prejudice* right now. Four chapters a week."

"Who knew?" Bernice replied with a forced smile. "Tuesdays at 3:30 in the reception room. I might look in."

"Oh, why don't you join us?" Tina asked.

"Uhm, Jane Austen isn't exactly my cup of tea. My taste runs to Harlan Coban and Sara Paretsky."

Carol flipped her hand as she and Tina walked on. "Your loss."

In her apartment, Bernice leaned back in her armchair, feet propped on the windowsill and stared down at the rolling green grounds of the retirement home, lost in thought. I basically came here to be with Sal in his decline. But I'm ten or fifteen years younger than most of the folks here and while it's nice to have a main meal waiting every day, I don't really need it. And really, I don't want or need all the togetherness and planned activities. Hell, I spent the last twenty years all alone in my own place... except for when Sal moved in. That was sweet while it lasted. But I

191

really don't need all this *busyness,* like I'm at some kind of geriatric summer camp. And it's not cheap to stay here. Not for as long as I might live.

Tuesday afternoon around 4:00, Bernice stopped outside the card room. Tim was at the head of the table, back to the door. The seven ladies offered the rapt attention eager co-eds gave a favorite professor. Tim was speaking. "Let's talk about Mr. Collins, the minister, and cousin to the Bennet family. Obviously, he is portrayed as a self-important prig. But the role of clergymen in those days was very different from now, don't you think?"

Bernice listened for a few minutes to the excited exchange of opinions about Anglican clergy and the place of religion in 18th century England, compared to modern priests and evangelical pastors. She walked away forced to admit to herself that Tim really was at home with a group, quite a good facilitator. He listened and summarized and prodded the discussion when it flagged. She hadn't seen that side of him before. *More power to him,* she allowed.

For the next week, Bernice half-expected to receive a call from him. When Tuesday arrived with no contact, she wandered down to the front lobby around 4:30. Before long she heard the voices of Tina and Carol punctuated with Tim's basso, obviously prolonging the week's discussion as he headed for the parking lot. After 'so longs' and 'see you next week' Bernice buried her head in her book and acted surprised when Tim said, "Oh, hi Bernice. How're you doing?"

"I'm fine. I see you're conducting a book club."

"Yes. It's fun. Your friends Tina and Carol really make it work. They're so enthusiastic and knowledgeable."

The conversation stalled. Tim shuffled his feet. Bernice put her marker in place and closed the book. Tim's face suddenly lit when he thought to ask, "So, how was your trip? Did you get to see any old geysers?"

Bernice flashed slant-eyes. Was he ragging her? She caught the corner of his mouth twitching. "You've been hanging out with Vinnie, haven't you?"

"Yep. And Tre. We've spent the last two weeks fixing up my cottage. You ought to see it now."

She cocked her head at him as if to say... really?

"I have something there. Special. For you."

Bernice lowered her chin, eyes locked on Tim's, "I'd like to see your cottage. Sometime."

"How about right now?"

Not wanting to seem too eager, she said, "I don't know... I..."

Tim shook his head, brooking no demur, and jerked his head toward the cars. "C'mon, let's go. You're gonna like this."

Where did 'mister-take-charge' come from, Bernice wondered. Not that I need it or particularly want it. But no point in blowing out a candle is there?

"And in case dinner runs a little late, you still have your overnight bag out there."

"Don't get ahead of yourself, big fella," Bernice warned.

In the car on the way out, Bernice pulled a rosary out of her purse. "Haven't said my beads today," she explained.

"Be my guest."

"You never say the rosary anymore?" Bernice half questioned, half accused Tim.

Rolling along M43, Tim took a glance at Kubiak's blueberry farm and the pickers working the field, before answering. "Bernice do what makes you feel good. You have no idea how many rosaries I have said in funeral parlors for sad and teary mourners. I've said all the rosaries I'm ever going to say. But don't let me stop you."

Bernice clenched her lips, irritated. "You think I'm silly to pray like this."

"No. No, I don't. I just don't have any use for it, myself."

"How can you do something all your life and then just stop?"

Tim tapped the steering wheel with his right hand then said, "Johnny Carson..."

"This isn't gonna be another joke is it?"

"I guess, yeah. This 91-year old woman was asked why she filed for divorce after being married for 70 years. She said, 'Hey, enough is enough.'"

Bernice waved her hand to one side, flicking away his words.

"I've just plain gone off it," Tim said. "Haven't you ever decided you no longer want something? Like when I was a kid I had Cheerios for breakfast every morning. Then one day I stopped. Finito."

Bernice half turned in the seat, eyes opened wide and brows pulled together. "You can't just shut off religion—prayers, hymns, Holy Week..."

"Look, the way I see it, formal religion, the Church, is like a marathon. It provides a starting line, cheerleaders along the way and a welcome at the finish line. Some folks need all that structure. Others don't. You can run twenty-six miles on your own, any time you want."

"Do you have to mansplain with sports talk?"

Tim sighed, started again. "Okay. How's this? For fifty years I've heard confessions and counseled and preached all in the name of getting people to love themselves... and to love others. Now, I can finally practice what I preached."

"Wait. What?"

"You." To Bernice's blank stare, he responded, "I love you. Okay?"

"Oh," she said softly. "Really?" Then added, "That's sweet. But..."

Tim sighed with exasperation before passing around a police car, bubble lights spinning, behind a car pulled onto the shoulder. "See?" Bernice said. "What if that was an accident? You mean you wouldn't get out to hear the injured person's confession or give him last rites?"

"I'm not some kind of spiritual EMT waiting for a 911 call. People die the way they lived. Live right. Die right. Don't count on magic from me."

"That's cold."

"I'm not cold, Bernice. If I saw an accident I'd pull over to see if I could help with first aid and maybe stay with folks as long as they needed. Or if one of your friends, Tina, say, was ill or dying. I'd visit. Talk to her. Be there for her."

"You wouldn't hear her confession?"

"Not anymore. There are other guys on duty. Look, I'm as compassionate as the next guy. I just don't show it with ritual anymore."

"How can two people be so different?" Bernice mused as she shoved her rosary back into her purse and frowned out the window for the rest of the drive.

She was thoroughly surprised when they pulled up to the cottage freshly painted sunflower yellow with bachelor-button blue trim. "Well, look at that," she exclaimed, "I love the colors."

"They remind me of you," Tim said.

"Do they, now? How so?"

Tim shrugged. "Dunno. Just do."

"And look at the porch. And you got a swing. And new screens and screen door."

"And roof and some new siding. You gotta see inside."

Bernice hugged Tim's arm as they went indoors. She stood in the middle of the front room, stunned by the cerulean blue walls. "I love it. You can sink your teeth into that blue. So rich. Did you pick it out?"

"Uh-huh. And you should see the bedroom if you like rich colors."

Bernice gasped at the raspberry red walls. "Yes," she hissed. Smiling broadly at Tim before looking away and grimacing. "But the orange bed spread... I'm afraid it clashes."

"I've still got the receipt," Tim offered. He went to the fireplace and picked the Petoskey stone off the mantel. and held it out to Bernice. "For you." She fondled it dearly, looking up with brimming eyes.

After a tour of the kitchen featuring new second-hand appliances, painted cupboards and laminated flooring, they sat on the new couch in the front room. "My, my," Bernice said. "Who knew there was an interior decorator hiding inside you."

"It still needs curtains for the front room and kitchen. Maybe you could pick those and new towels..."

"And tableware and dishes," Bernice supplied. "We could go to the outlet mall in Indiana for some good bargains."

Over the next three weeks, Tim and Bernice split days and nights between the Pond and the Lake playing my place... your place. At the Pond, Bernice harvested vegetables from her garden and offered massage therapy two afternoons a week. Tina and Carol were her first clients. At the Lake, Sal's old van, retrieved from Vinnie's yard quickly became their second vehicle. Tim built a hutch to display their new dishes, and Bernice toured the local nurseries for a clematis, Japanese maple, trumpet vine and a pair of hydrangeas to stage around the property.

Munching her marijuana brownies on the porch swing one evening, Tim sighed and said, "Oh, yeah. This is good for my glaucoma."

"You don't have glaucoma."

"See? It's working."

After a loaded pause, Bernice said, "You know, a lot of the time you're fun to be with."

"Mmm."

"But, I've been thinking. I like it out here so much. I'm not sure I want to live at the Pond anymore. I lived by myself for a long time. I don't mind being alone. In fact, I kind of miss it." Tim stiffened, moved away slightly. "Oh, not you, Tim. We're fine. It's just the larger..." Bernice held her hands apart, shaping space, "the larger context. There's so much tail wagging and butt sniffing at the Pond. Here it's quiet. The waves. A walk in the woods. The openness of the big water." She reached for his arm, clutched it. "We could just stay here. Save the money it costs to stay there." Excitedly adding, "And we could use it for trips and tours instead."

"I see," Tim muttered.

"Oh, God," she complained. "You're not going to get all moody and take one of your monk walks on the beach, are you?"

"As a matter of fact, that's exactly what I'm going to do. I've got to think some." With that, he raised his eyebrows— okay?—and headed to the shore.

Bernice called after him, "Why can't you just say, I don't like your ideas Bernice and I'm happy the way things are? Huh? Why can't you say that?"

An hour later, Tim climbed into bed smelling of fresh air and lake. He propped his pillow on the headboard, gently prodded Bernice and said, "I finally figured out what I want... for us." She immediately sat up, confirming his belief that she wasn't really asleep. "Here's the deal: I like living at the Pond. It reminds me of the seminary when I was a student and a teacher... you know, scheduled times for lunch and dinner and classes and activities all day long and lots of people all around. Same thing in a parish. All the bustle and constant activity."

Bernice slapped her hands on the covers and burst into tears. "Can't we ever get this together? Just when it looks like we're cruising along you got more roadblocks."

Tim reached over and pulled Bernice onto his chest. "You didn't let me finish what I was going to say. Here's what I'm thinking. Let's switch places. You live here permanently. I move into the Pond. You officially move to a single apartment... cheaper than your two-bedroom set up. Then we can slide back and forth, like we've been doing, two or three days a week together here or there. Maybe more time in town during hard winter. More time out here in high summer. That way I get what I want. You get what you want. How's that?"

"There's a hole in your plan. We need to be married for me to make you my permanent partner. House rules."

Tim shrugged. "So, we get married. You good with that?"

"That's the worst proposal I've ever heard of."

"Well?"

"Yeah. Okay. Let's try it."

Piñata Belly

by

Joe Novara

Gypsy Shadow Publishing

Piñata Belly

by

Joe Novara

Gypsy Shadow Publishing, LLC.
Lockhart, TX
www.gypsyshadow.com

ISBN: 978-1-61950-646-6

Published in the United States of America

First eBook Edition: April 6, 2021

Chapter One; Harry

It was 4:30 am, Flores, Guatemala, and I was bouncing in a suspension sprung bus with a dozen other tourists on our way to Tikal and the ancient Mayan ruins located there. So far so good, except for the man seated behind me who was talking a couple decibels louder than necessary to Kerstin, his female seatmate. He was carrying on in that droning, aggressively all-knowing, professorial tone of a lecture hall warrior. I should know. I used to be one. And to my surprise Kerstin, the social worker from Minnesota, whom I had just met in the hotel lobby while waiting for our bus, seemed to be encouraging him with softball questions. That didn't seem right. She had seemed smart, her Nordic, open face alert and perceptive while the rest of us huddled under blinking blue fluorescent lights trying to suck color, if not life, into our sleep drawn cheeks. I wondered why she was either flirting or being polite with this obviously obnoxious guy?

I kept wanting to doze off as we hurtled over pock-marked roads in a tunnel of darkness, but the megaphone behind me seemed to be directed at my right ear. I was just about to lambaste his pontificating on everything and anything Guatemalan in a constant data dump that violated every principle of gauging audience interest and patience. I mean, you learn that being a teacher, a coach and a guide. Guide. I suddenly realized he was a brother in the fellowship of tour guides and Kerstin had engaged his services. I sighed. Professional courtesy prevailed. You never disrupt another guide's gig.

Actually, I hadn't always been a guide. I had taught American History in high school until I retired. And I predictably chaperoned yearly senior trips to either our nation's capital or Civil War battle sites. If you think about it, historical tour guides and history teachers have a lot in common. When you've taught in a classroom long enough, you can practically run any given day's lesson on auto pilot: the Constitutional Convention, the battle of Mobile Bay, Gettysburg and Appomattox. Professional tour guides have their spiels as well, including site-related jokes and quips to keep their clients smiling. So, not surprisingly, while teaching, I looked forward to retirement and becoming a guide myself. Which is what I did... have done for the past dozen years. I have my specialties and favorite tours around D.C. But lately, as I span my early seventies, I've been plagued by a restlessness to explore new venues, to guide in new places, like Central America.

Which brings me to the pre-dawn bus ride. I had to chuckle to myself. Have you ever heard of a bus driver taking a bus ride for his vacation—the proverbial *busman's holiday?* That was me—a tour guide on a guided tour. On this trip however, I was doing background research, scoping local talent for patter and style while sizing up the competition in case I decided to join their ranks.

Slowly, slowly as morning sun crept into our bus, I was able to make out a woman my age across the aisle and a girl, probably her granddaughter, sleeping against her shoulder. I noticed an iPad in the aisle under the girl's dangling hand. I reached down and gently placed the screen in her lap. Gramma made squeezed-eye contact. A striking woman, perhaps in her later sixties, she sported outdoorsy clothes and her trim, no-fuss, silver-helmet hair suggested an active lifestyle. Everything but a retractable walking stick... probably had one in her backpack. I took the girl for a junior, maybe a senior. She was tall, taller than her grandmother, reminding me of so many of the kids I had taught, counseled, or coached... volleyball. I was the girls' volleyball coach. All of us teachers had extra-curricular commitments. I didn't mind. I had played setter in college.

Gramma offered a winced smile wrapped in a *thanks, but that's close enough mister* look. You get that a lot when you're black. Down here, in these south-of-the border countries, I found myself blending in a lot better with the dusky-skinned population than up North. Can't say I've missed getting a reminder of my place, Gramma.

Here's the thing. I've always liked working with teenagers. Not everyone does. They are so unformed. Searching so hard for self, for acceptance, for a place of comfort and support outside of their families. And they have such great radar. They can tell immediately if you like them... *get* them. You can't fake it. I *got* them and they knew it. Trouble is, with all the news about priests and coaches and Boy Scouts these days, people might wonder if you're weird or dangerous. Okay, I'm an only child. I never married or had children of my own. And, yeah, I rely on my roles as teacher and tour guide to give me context and access to kids. But I'm okay, normal... whatever. I just plain like teens and enjoy helping them mature. So, don't worry, Gramma... I'm not going to offer your granddaughter candy.

At the ruins, a site-escort, Miguel, took over our group and preempted Kerstin's guy. Being kind of stocky myself, I can't look down on many guys, but I could look down on Miguel. Bandy-legged, twitchy and restless, we teachers could spot a *Miguel* the first five minutes of the first day of class. You're sure they skipped their Ritalin that day as they tic and wriggle as fast as they talk. And in Miguel's case, the talk is vintage, 100-word vocabulary, street patois minus the X-rated words. He must have called us *my friends* at least once in every sentence as he tagged temples, named birds and identified howler monkeys, which if you've ever lived near a freeway, sound like semis grinding up to speed. But he was good. He knew when to talk and when to let us absorb. He would give information as we approached one or another temple or ancient site but then back off and let us take pictures and finger the bas-relief carvings of Mayan gods and mythical figures. And better yet, as we transitioned from one spot to another, he talked to individuals as though he were genuinely interested in us. *Nice work, Miguel.* I gave him a big tip.

Lunch provided opportunity to engage with others in our group who were sleep-fogged on the ride out. I reveled in the opportunity to be just another fellow traveler and not the group leader responsible for herding my flock from place to place. Gramma and girl sat at a picnic table, the girl tossing bits of bread to the sparrows. In full light, I could study her better. She looked bored. Perhaps her phone was out of range... or maybe bars. Her complexion ran to *latte* with an extra shot of milk topped by thick black hair and dark brown eyes. A DNA test would probably identify some ancestors from around the Mediterranean. Gramma, on the other hand, must use a ton of sunscreen to keep from broiling in the Caribbean sun. Huh! And she carried her chin just a touch high—genteel South or Mayflower heritage, maybe.

I wandered toward the Temple of the Masks on the far edge of the Plaza of the Temples.

After climbing the first couple outsized stair-steps, I turned to find the girl trailing behind. "C'mon," I said, "I'll race you to the top." She gave me slant-eyes. "We were on the bus this morning," I said by way of explanation in case she hadn't noticed me in the group yet. "My name is Harry. Harry Benson."

She slowly and pointedly looked away, moved over a few feet and continued her climb. Someone had taught her not to talk to strangers. Although I could hardly be considered a threat in such a wide-open space crawling with tourists and a grandmother sitting nearby. Still. Okay. I've been around enough adolescents to know when to back off.

From the top of the pyramid, I spotted Kerstin talking to a guy from our hotel. He looked around her age. What? Early thirties? Buff. A jock. I could picture him at home on a tennis court or gridiron. But he wasn't comfortable with Kerstin. What was it? Maybe the way he held his shoulders tight and high. The way he nodded too vigorously. Looking off instead of at her, as though afraid her blue eyes would mesmerize him. Trap him. Well, I could relate to that. A long time ago, I had run from a lady who gave me the eye. She wanted me to change: my hair, my car, my apartment. I booked, buried myself in my work, kept things uncomplicated, under control. Standing on top of that temple with the sun at my back, I felt like a Mayan priest in a parrot-feather cape, arms raised, channeling energy on that young couple to come together, to join as one... like I never did. Had I missed a lot?

On the bus ride back to Flores, I was seated directly behind the driver. If you've ever seen a one-man-band-guy with harmonica, drum, and accordion going all at once, our driver was doing a good imitation. After he stopped to pick up some guy who plopped on the engine cowl, he proceeded to alternately chat with him and someone else on a cell phone held to his ear, while shifting with his free hand and steering with his elbow. At first, I was amazed. Then I got annoyed. It seemed like we, the paying customers, were imposing on his convoluted social ties. I happened to glance across the aisle and noticed the girl, of the girl-and-Gramma girl, scowling at the driver. She wasn't happy with him, either. Her eyes flicked at me. *Help?* Time to act. I marshalled my classroom-Spanish vocabulary to let the driver know that his driving was making me and other passengers nervous because it was dangerous and, actually, rather slow. I must have touched a chord because he quickly put the phone away, put both hands on the wheel and added fifteen miles per hour to our speed. I didn't glance back at the girl. Sometimes less is more with teenagers... the way a guy who has just scored a key basket doesn't turn around and wave to the stands.

Back at the hotel, I sat on my tiny balcony looking at the lake across the street, nursing a Dos Equis and watching folks jump off a tall wooden dock into what, to a Michigander would seem like a large woodland pond with turgid, root-stained water and patches of lily pads scatter-rugged across the surface. The tall wooden dock had steps leading down to the water.

I finished my beer and spotted the girl in her bathing suit walking toward the dock with her grandmother in tow. I was taken with Gramma's look, the contained energy in her crisp stride, the self-focused calm—sufficient unto herself. I bet she wouldn't be clingy, could appreciate a guy, but not need to lean on him. And the way she moved, she would make a good back-line specialist on a volleyball team. But, I was getting no signals she wanted me on her team.

The girl screamed. She had slipped on the last step going into the water. Probably it was slick with moss and weeds. After some thrashing and crying, she limped back up clutching her bloody leg. I raced out. People were crowding around shouting in Spanish and English. I took one look at the three-inch cut on her calf and using my lunch-room-monitor voice demanded in Spanish for directions to the nearest ER or clinic. As I sorted directions, I pulled out my pocket knife, tore a strip from the girl's towel, wrapped it tightly around her leg and asked Gramma where they were staying. Turned out, their hotel was on the way to the urgicenter. Thinking they needed a Spanish speaker, I waited in their lobby while the girl got into dry clothes and then accompanied them to the clinic.

After waiting fifteen minutes for the receptionist to return from lunch and log us in, we were ushered into a smallish room with two other people on gurneys in various stages of treatment. By then, I had determined the girl's name was Bryn and the grandmother's, Cobi. The doctor examined Bryn's wound, slathered the area with Betadine and proceeded to lay-in five stitches. I translated after-care instructions to my new friends. Total cost: $30. We stopped at a *farmacia* on the way back for Tylenol, anti-biotic ointment and dressing. After which, I was graciously thanked and summarily dismissed.

That evening, strolling the waterfront for a place to eat, I spotted Kirsten and the American guy from our Tikal visit. They invited me to join them for dinner. Turns out Brian was from Ohio, a CPA, looking to snorkel and dive in the Caribbean. He was eating a local fish from the lake. I took a taste and was not impressed. But my bowl of *pozole rojo* with hominy, pork and shredded lettuce really hit the spot. As we reviewed the day, it became clear that Brian was not a wordsmith as he struggled to keep up his end of the conversation. During awkward pauses, I tried to help the poor guy by throwing in jokes and stories about our driver and Bryn's leg. I wished he could just relax a little. Kerstin sure seemed interested in him.

An after-dinner stroll took me past a restaurant billowing smells of cilantro and salsa, beans and grilled beef. A group of American kids sat at an outdoor table, Bryn in the center, her bandaged leg propped on a chair. She looked up for a moment, noticed me and raised a palm off the table to offer a shy wave. She must have said something because the two boys and three girls all stared at me. I replied with a dignified chin dip.

On my way to my room, I stopped at the front desk to ask about getting to Belize City the next day. One option was a standard tour bus. I chose the other option, a downscale mini-van. I wanted to immerse myself in the culture I might be showcasing as a guide someday. It never hurt to *press the flesh* with the locals.

At 7 am the next morning, I got pressed all right. The van pulled to my curb. An assistant heaved my suitcase on the roof rack and before I barely settled my butt on the three-person seat, two more people jammed in. As we circled the city proper, the guy hung out the open door, welcomed more riders from the curb, grabbed their fare, and unceremoniously shoved them inside. Now there were five people in my seat. Two children stood in front of me, butts in my face. A man with a huge net-bag of avocados wedged himself onto our seat and accepted a half orange sprinkled with pepper from a man crowding the driver up front. Eventually, some people got off which meant we had room to cram-in three American college students stranded at a crossroads. Apparently new, paying customers were more important than the comfort of already paid customers.

After two hours on the open road, we finally came to the Belize border and custom control. Belize City was unremarkable and I was glad to get on the ferry to Caye Caulker as soon as possible. I was barely seated, luxuriating in enough space to relax my elbows when Kerstin plonked down next to me and poked me in the arm. "Harry," she cried, "we meet again."

"And again, and again and again," I replied, squeezing her wrist in greeting. "Did you ever notice how that happens when you're traveling? You keep running into the same people at different places."

"Yeah, right. But it makes sense. All the tourists want to hit the same spots. The rest is timing and schedules." She paused, grinned. "You know, it's like one of those nature movies where you see herds of animals migrating from waterhole to waterhole. They gotta meet someone they know along the way."

"A gnu they knew."

"Huh?"

"Wildebeests in Africa. On the Serengeti. They're called Gnu."

"Okaay." She gave me a forced smile.

I shrugged apologetically. "Bad puns helped in the classroom. A groan is better than blank stares." She nodded. "Uhm. So, how's Brian?" I asked.

Her whole face smiled. "Oh, he's fine. *Fine*," she emphasized. "In fact, he went to Caulker yesterday to get us a cabin."

Did I detect a note of triumph?

"And he's planning to dive the Blue Hole today."

My efforts at matchmaking had paid off. But before I could gloat, she turned the table.

"How are you and Cobi doing?"

"What do you mean... me and Cobi? I don't think we've exchanged a dozen words."

"Words aren't the only way to communicate," Kerstin allowed.

I just shook my head in question.

"You never noticed?" Kerstin teased.

"What?"

"Cobi notices you."

"Oh, c'mon," I pleaded. "We're not playing the girly *so-and-so likes so-and-so* game, are we?"

Kerstin hunched her shoulders. "Just sayin'."

She got up to stand at the starboard rail, leaving me with my tumbling thoughts. It was one thing to fantasize about a woman, but if Cobi was really interested in me... then what? Getting to know someone is a lot of work. What she likes. What I like... don't like. How close to get. God... what about bed, at my age? I mean, what if? And what about money? Would I have to go to church or cook or do my share of the laundry? As we slid against the island pier, I told myself, *all right, calm down, Harry. You'll probably never see her again.*

Onshore, wandering along the main street made of crushed shells, I spotted a rental agency. An hour later I got off their golf cart at a classic island bungalow with a hammock slung from palm trees out front and deck chairs on a veranda. I loved it. Buyer's remorse came an hour later after a sweet nap in the hammock. The bare skin between my shirt and pants was covered with tiny bug bites. At least they didn't itch. A stroll to the end of the street brought me to a small airport and the inviting possibilities for continuing my open-ended odyssey in a few days.

That evening, looking for supper, I stopped at a restaurant that had two tables at street level splayed with fresh lobster, shrimp, oysters and deep-sea fish. I couldn't resist picking out a bright red snapper and watching it cook from my table a couple steps above the smoking grill. What a marvelous meal.

However, I almost choked on my second *piña colada* when Bryn called, "Hey! Hi Harry." She, Cobi, Kerstin and Brian were all staying at the Pink Conch. I seem to have missed the memo about *the* place to stay. Over coconut ice cream and coffee, I felt a little tense, checking out Cobi— looking for wistful glances and subtle smiles. I used to get a lot of that on my tours: the away-from-home flirtation from certain women. This was different. Cobi would catch my eye from time to time when I spoke... naturally. I caught her checking me out once. Nice. But no kind of serious vibes. I was irritated with Kerstin for setting me up for a big nothing.

When the conversation got around to fun tourist attractions, Kerstin talked about an off-shore Marine Reserve and how a boat took you to a shallow spot where nurse sharks and stingrays swam around visitors wading in waist deep water. Bryn got very excited. Cobi not so much. In fact, she professed distinct disinterest in having sharks curl around her ankles like pet cats and further reminded Bryn that her not-yet healed cut had to stay dry for two more days. On our way to the internet café, Bryn snugged up next to me and whispered, "If you take me on this trip, I can keep my stitches dry. Please. I'll work on Gramma."

The following morning Bryn and I sat in an open launch barreling out to the open-water reserve. Bryn reached into her backpack and pulled out a black plastic garbage bag, stuck her leg in and proceeded to seal it at the ankle and just below the knee with waterproof adhesive tape. I had to admire her ingenuity and determination which proved to work in the end. Hours later, onshore, over conch *quesadillas*, the only observation Cobi made was the strange lack of sunburn on her granddaughter's right leg.

Bryn, Kerstin and Brian hung out the next day. I made my way down to the cut—a kind of channel at the north end of the island. I parked myself at an outdoor table with a beer and jerked-chicken wrap, content to watch some locals jump off a square-nosed barge piled high with white sand. A minute or so later, the divers emerged, climbed on board and helped haul a dripping bucket of sea-bottom onboard. I guess that's one way to get sand for pot holes and cement.

"Hello, Harry," Cobi said, surprising me. "Would you mind if I joined you?"

"Sure. Please," I said and watched her request a spare chair from folks at a neighboring table. Her measured motions—gently placing the chair just so, hanging her oversized sun hat on a corner and easing herself down wasn't arthritic slow, I decided. More like the dignified, stately, rhythm of her adagio beat. Fascinating, the way she so easily slid from brisk, on-task striding to *Tai Chi* grace.

"How is your food?" she asked.

"Good," I answered, "It's chicken but I hear the fish is good too."

After she ordered, there was one of those moments when two people, just getting to know each other, simply stop and drink each other in. We had never been alone till then. I took the opportunity to burn a portrait in my mind: Cobi, porcelain white skin, high, wide, almost oriental cheek bones setting off pale jade eyes under black eyebrows capped by a silver bob. All that and a studied calm. I sighed.

I wondered what she saw in me as she ran her thumb and forefinger down the corners of her mouth—considering. Why did I feel exposed, studied? I was no stranger to whole classrooms watching me, to busloads of tourists fixed on me. This was different. New for me. I reverted to form and began spouting facts and dates: English lumber harvesters of local mahogany forests, thousands of African slaves brought to work it, and the 1798 Battle of St. George Caye.

I kept talking while Cobi took a delicate bite of her fish taco, eyes sliding up and over like a child trying a new food, lips tapping, tasting, testing. She nodded as she chewed. I wasn't sure if she was approving my historical data-dump or the flavor of the fare. Either way, at least she didn't tell me to shut up. Hey, we can only be who we are.

While she ate, I motor-mouthed through my resume, adding my current assessment of guiding opportunities in Latin America. By the time she tamped her lips with a napkin and sat back, I had run out of patter. Another lull. *Now what?* I wondered. When you've counseled kids, you learn to pause, let the silence draw them out. Cobi was doing that to me. No way. "And where do you live," I prodded, "when you're not squiring your granddaughter around the Caribbean?"

210

"Guatemala," she replied, "on the shore of Lake Atitlan."

"I've heard of it. It's a huge lake, right? Like in a volcanic crater."

Cobi nodded. "Water taxis go to cities all around the rim. If you are at all interested in Mayan culture, you'd be right in the heart of it."

"Uh-huh. So, what do you do there?"

"I run a B&B. In Panajachel." She offered a gentle smile. "It pays its way and isn't hard." The look she gave me—interested, wary, inviting, lingered in my mind long after we later connected with the *kids* for supper.

In the way of random-met travelers on loose schedules, none of us shared plans for our next stops. And so, early morning, two days later, Brian and I found ourselves at the little airport near my house, waiting to board the four-seater to start a journey to Rio Dulces. We would be heading back into Guatemala by plane and boat.

As we watched our pilot do a pre-flight check on the Cessna 172, Brian allowed as how he was a little unnerved by how much he liked Kerstin. "It could get heavy, man. Her. Me. It's kinda scary."

"I know the feeling."

He shot me an aggravated look. "You're supposed to tell me to go for it."

"So, go for it," I said as we walked to the plane warming up for our first hop.

From behind I got a dismissive, "Ha!"

What did he want from me? As if a bachelor my age should be an expert on women.

Turns out our flight was not unlike my recent van ride in that passengers boarded and left all along the way. First stop was across the channel to Belize City. Two passengers got off. Two more got on. One of them was an English speaker, Carlos. Next, we flew over marvelous expanses of tidewater flats of scarlet scrub and deep green shrubbery to Placencia and then up and on to Punta Gorda. The three of us—me, Brian and Carlos—shared a taxi to the port where a launch at the end of a pier was filling with passengers about to depart for Livingston, Guatemala. One look at the long jetty and the custom house three hundred yards in the opposite direction got us running to pay both the exit tax from Belize and the boat fare.

By the time we got to the boat, the only space left was a bench seat in the bow which meant we were going to be exposed to sea spray. A crew member passed us a plastic tarp for cover up. We were barely settled when a young woman in a Michigan State green and white sweatshirt burrowed her way onto the end of our bench.

"Hi, guys," she said, taking in my Detroit Tiger's hat. "I'm from Lansing. How about you?"

"Originally," I replied. I had noticed how tall and graceful she was as she made her way into the boat and was about to ask what sports she played when Brian broke in. I knew enough to change places with him and let the two of them go at it.

He seemed so much more at ease with this Jenna—the Spartan horticulture major, as we quickly learned—than with Kerstin. Was Kerstin looming as a serious relationship and he needed some space, some freedom? And here I thought he needed my help to hook up. He was doing just fine on his own.

I snuggled under the tarp and chuckled to myself. How is the witness protection program supposed to work if people from your home town can spot you in the middle of... where were we? Punta friggin' Gorda on our way to Livingston. Livingston. I chuckled again. I wonder what the good doctor felt when the only other white man in Africa rolled up to his porch and said, "Dr. Livingston, I presume." We travelers can run but we can't hide.

We docked an hour later at a crowded cement wharf. Before I could say goodbye, I lost Brian and Jenna in the crowds flowing into town. Carlos was at my side. "You going to Rio Dulces?" he asked.

"Yeah, I guess that's my next stop."

"Me too. Maybe we can share a ride. There's a public boat in three hours but we could go right now if we hired our own. Split the cost."

"Okay, but first, I need to get money... exchange dollars for *Quetzales.*"

"Not on a Sunday. Let's ask the guy in this restaurant."

Flush, a short while later, we hired a ride on what was supposed to be a most beautiful river. And it was. Our driv-

er was a wannabe guide, it appeared, as he shouted frag-
ments of information at us as we barreled along the river:
"Rain Forest!"
"Castillo de San Felipe!"
"Jungle!"
"Seven Altars!"
"Cliffs where they filmed Tarzan diving!"

During a lull in the visual attractions, my eye and
imagination snagged on a pole planted offshore with a dugout tethered to it, sidling in the current. I thought of Brian and Jenna, about how we can meet and connect and
disconnect. Over and over. All my life as a teacher, I got
new kids every few months, every four years. And as a tour
guide I was regularly meeting new and interesting people.
Were Cobi and me more of the same? No. She was different.
She meant a new... something... for me. I wanted to be like
that dugout, latched onto that pole. I wanted to stay in one
spot, anchored to some*one* for a change. To put all my focus
on one person... not give pieces of myself to many.

Rio Dulces was a real downer. I had heard it was a good
place to stay by the water. Not. It was shady, but damp-
shady, more outdoor bar and restaurant on the wharf than
comfortable lodging. Okay, maybe I was a little depressed
after that exhilarating plane-boat jaunt and thoughts of
continuity, of mooring, for a change. I slouched up to the
bar, ordered a burrito and cold beer. I sighed, sad, until I
spotted a dinghy putt-putting up to the seawall. It was one
of those inflatable-looking tenders. The man and woman
barely fit in it. But most importantly, it flew a North-Ameri-
can-neighbor Canadian flag. I don't know much about sail-
ing, but that kind of craft goes with sailboats and yachts.
Big boats docked in marinas. So, when the couple sat at the
bar, I wandered over, introduced myself and asked where
they were berthed and if I might be interested in staying
there as well. Turns out they were at the Calypso Marina
around a bend in the river and yes there were accommo-
dations on the island and many fellow Americans on hand.

Anything would be better than where I was. A call
to the island brought a boat. Ten minutes later, I was at
check-in, gawking at the soaring *talapa* roof of the open-air
lobby and the large-screen TVs, like stadium jumbotrons,
carrying the Detroit Lions/Green Bay Packers game. I col-

lapsed on a lounge and was offered salsa and dip to go with my *Cuba Libre*. Well, I told myself, you did go native, sort of, with the minivan trip. Now you could allow yourself a little *gringo* self-indulgence.

At half-time I went to my cabin which was suspended on pilings over the river. I could have fished from my front porch. Inside, you could hear the river purling beneath the floorboards. A twinge of big city paranoia had me wondering how safe it would be to hang over a river where anyone could dock and break in without a sound. But, instead, I hurried back for the second half of the game.

"Hey, Harry!" a familiar voice called. I turned to see Bryn dripping from the pool. She rushed over and stopped just short of hugging me in her wet bathing suit. We paused, deciding how to show affection. Finally, I just grabbed her hand and squeezed. Bryn was pleased to see me. Gratifying, that. But I was casting about for Cobi. "Where's your Gramma?" I finally asked.

"Oh, she went off with some guy on his sailboat. Said she would be back this evening."

Was that a jolt of jealousy that I felt?

"Where are you staying?" Bryn inquired.

"Cabin 12."

"We're in 15. You gonna go swimming?"

"Maybe, when the game's over."

"Well, for sure let's have supper together."

I nodded. "Ask Cobi when she gets here. Let me know, okay?"

When it got to be 7:30 and still no word, I went to the restaurant and had begun on my *ceviche* when Bryn bounced in and bee-lined to my table. "What's that you're eating?" she asked through lips curled in distaste.

"It's a cold seafood salad."

"Eeew, with octopus looking thingies."

"That's squid actually." I speared a curly tentacle and popped it in my mouth with relish. "And shrimp." To Bryn's shudder of disgust, I added, "No sign of Gramma yet?"

"Nope. And I'm hungry."

"I ordered the *paella* special. It should be out shortly. You can try it and see if you like it."

She did like it, to my surprise, and the *flan* for dessert which was followed by a leisurely stroll along the marina to inspect the ranks of luxury sailboats berthed around the perimeter of the island. I saw her to their cabin. No Cobi. About 10:00 I got a knock on my door. With her grandmother still MIA, Bryn was frightened of being alone in a strange place. Deciding not to compound her anxiety about river-access intruders with my own, I simply nodded, grabbed a book, escorted her to their place and burrowed into a front room couch while she slept in the back.

Cobi got in around 2:00 am. "Oh! My god," she cried when she saw me. "You gave me a start. Why...?"

"Bryn was frightened to be alone. I'll leave now." As I got to the door, Cobi grabbed my arm, affectionately, and smiled in a way I hadn't seen before. "Thank you. I appreciate it."

I got a strong whiff of wine. "We have to talk," she muttered, nodding.

The next morning Bryn and I met by chance at the breakfast buffet. The food was great. I usually don't eat much in the morning, but it was hard to pass up the omelets and sweet rolls braced with fresh papaya, mango and excellent coffee. We chatted about her trip and how she had every intention of returning for all of the next summer.

Over my second cup of coffee, I looked past Bryn to see Cobi studying us with a soft, loving smile. She grabbed a sugar bun and joined us. "Sorry I was so late last night." She frowned then went on. "That..." she clenched lips trying for the right word before spitting out, "creep! He tried the old, *Oh-oh, I ran out of gas,* game and *we'll have to stay out here all night.* I said forget it. I would paddle us to shore before I fell for that gag. Then he really couldn't start the engine. So, anyhow..." She looked at Bryn. "Honey, you need to get packed. I'm all ready to go."

Bryn stood, looked at her plate, then up. "Thanks for everything, Harry. It's been nice knowing you." She came behind me, clutched my shoulder. I patted her hand.

"Same here." I said.

After Cobi and I watched her dart away, she began, "Last night... this morning, actually, I said we should talk." She paused, pulled the corners of her mouth down with thumb and forefinger, a familiar gesture, "I owe you some backstory." She frowned. "And maybe some forward story. I hope you're interested." Without waiting for my reply, she plowed ahead, "I'll start with Bryn. My lovely young woman has latched onto you. Her mother has been a single-parent since Bryn was two. You're the father-figure she needs." We locked eyes for a moment. "You give her what she craves."

"I've worked with teens all my life. It's second nature."

"Well, what you've got... maybe it was already there. But I bet you made it better."

Wow, I thought. Strong praise indeed. Don't stop now.

"Maya, Bryn's mother, is my child by a Guatemalan father. I was in the Peace Corps." She paused, eyes unfocused, spanning the years. "I've lived here since."

"Wait. Wait," I demanded, scowling. "You've lived here all your life? And you run a B&B? You must speak Spanish like a native." Cobi rocked her head from side to side—yes. "So why did you let me babble on with my fractured Spanish when we were on the bus and when Bryn got hurt?"

"You were doing fine. And me, I don't need to be in charge. I can step back. Bryn too... let someone else handle things." Cobi fiddled with crumbs on the table. "It's a relief." When she looked up, she nodded slightly and gave me that sidelong look again, the one I had been longing for the past few days—inviting but tentative. *Huh,* I thought. *This could be for real. Me and her. Maybe. My anchor pole.*

All at once, Cobi took a quick breath, firmed her chin— as if she had made up her mind about something. "If you make it to Panajachel," she said, "you could stay at my place. For a while." She paused. Added, "As long as you want." When I didn't react immediately, she hurried on, "I always need someone to fix things. You know how to fix things..." she said, nodding her head as if to validate her presumption. When I didn't respond, she continued, "Don't you? Like leaky faucets and painting and stuff?" When I still didn't react, she huffed, as if exasperated but determined to say it and be done with it. "I like being around you, Harry. Would like you to be around... be buddies?" She stopped then, eyes down at the table—one of my girls waiting to be subbed into a game... *me coach?*

Well, she had been so cool with me. Watching from the sidelines. Sizing me up the past while. She had a little coolness coming her way. Even if my stomach was doing back flips. I took a sip of my coffee, cold by now. Set it down carefully and said, "I'll think about it. Do you have a card for your place?"

A self-satisfied smile snagged at the corner of her mouth as she fumbled in her purse. I don't think she noticed the turmoil clouding my face. Why did I feel like a dog who had been chasing a car and then it suddenly stopped? Now what?

Chapter Two; Cobi

Having seen Bryn off at the airport, I was clawing my way through Guatemala City morning traffic on my way back to Panajachel. There was a time I enjoyed a chance to go to the big city for a fancy meal, some serious shopping and a good haircut. Now, I couldn't wait to escape the fumes, the crowds, the policemen and their shotguns sticking up their backs. Not my Bryn. Last night she was all about the big city experience. She was grinning, peppy for a change, window shopping, all but saying, *see Gramma, that's what I've been missing after three weeks of your sleepy tourist towns and boring monuments.* A kid her age, how can you tell what sinks in? What will register and stay with her? No matter. She was an answer to my prayers. A chance to finally meet her. To get to know her. And all the better, since she was the one who looked me up. It was her idea from the start.

Well, turn-about is fair play. Bryn was now doing to Maya what she had done to me so many years ago. Maya never forgave me for raising her down here as a single mom; keeping her from my parents and the genteel life she was owed in Charleston. Maya, in her turn, kept Bryn to herself all these years and now her child was on a *roots* trip to find the culture and the grandparents hidden from her.

ANTIGUA 15 KM >

I read the sign—divide by 10 multiply by 6. After all these years I still don't think in metrics. I still have to translate liters and meters into pounds and miles. So, nine miles to go for lunch. Good. I was getting hungry. I had a mouth for the green chili at *Gallo Rojo*. I could look forward to ordering without Bryn wrinkling her nose. That child! She practically lived on plain *tortillas* and beans. I could only do so much for her stunted palette in our short time together.

I relaxed in the restaurant, soft focusing on the sidewalk and the passing crowd. I had ordered fifteen minutes earlier. Why was service always so slow? The chili had to be bubbling on the stove, ready to serve. Isn't it funny how, after all these years, I still think like an American teenager? I expect my cheeseburger and fries to be served chop-chop. I mean, that's why they call it fast food, right? And maybe that's why most of my B&B customers are U.S. tourists. Breakfast at my place is *no wait* for mango nectar, pecan pancakes, eggs, sausage and strong coffee all briskly served. They're at my gate, ticking off sites in their guide books before the toothpicks are out of their mouths. I suppose you could blame it on early imprinting since I came to this country right out of college and have never been back. But I still expect and offer the kind of service I grew up with.

Back on the road, I was determined to make it home before dark.

ZARAGOZA 43 KM > tugged at my memory. Zaragoza. My Peace Corps placement... and Mateo. For six months we worked side by side making cement blocks for his village. For six months I watched his strong, beautiful hands and arms and his soft sweet eyes. He didn't have to smile, his eyes did it all by themselves. I never told him I was pregnant... so complicated, confusing. I decided to hide in plain sight, down the road, in Panajachel.

Now, finally, there's Bryn, my granddaughter who's Mateo's too, for that matter. I wonder if he's still alive... and his wife. The last time I saw them was around twenty-five years ago. I forget why I was in their town. They were in the market selling mangoes. I hung back in the crowd, watching. In a break between customers, I caught a look his wife gave him. Good, I sighed, he was loved. A teenage girl came from behind him and nudged up against him. He unconsciously put his hand on her shoulder. What a lovely girl... Maya's half-sister, I realized. Then I noticed his eyes. His eyes were hard. Hard and a little dull. Had I caused that? I quickly turned and left. Too many feelings.

Since then, I've had no interest in reviving that whole drama. Yet Bryn seems on a mission to trace us down. Did she do one of those ancestry searches to get started? If she's anything like her mother, after locating me, she won't stop until she's at Mateo's door. That girl is throwing a big rock into a still pond, stirring up all kinds of muck and waves.

Look how she's already got me digging up long-buried memories, making me replay that dreadful time. There was so much to face. Single parenting in a foreign country. No job. Thank god for Karen and *Posada del Sol.* She was like a mother to me all those years, letting me work there and later buying it from her.

It's been forty some years now. Hundreds of guests have passed through my doors. Many interesting men. Lots of opportunities. Not to mention fine men from around Pana. Good men. But it's like I've been in a fog, a nun abstaining for Lent but Easter never comes. And all at once there's Harry. Why him? Now? He's a little bit nerdy. Teacher nerdy—spouting facts and information for a living. Or maybe he was just nervous around me. Man-splaining about this and that the way he does. I enjoy sitting back, watching him spout. He would probably slow down and quit once I got to know him better. Or not. After all, he was a teacher and a guide. Repetition is their thing. Or just hearing their own voice. Whatever. What really got to me was the way he caught on with Bryn. Like I told him, she needed someone like him. That was sweet, the way he was there for her, but all the while looking over her shoulder at me. There's more to him than meets the eye. I wonder if I made a fool of myself, practically throwing myself at him right before he left? A guy like that, a life-long bachelor, you can scare him off. And here it was the first time in forever that I allowed myself to feel anything for a guy. Easy there, girl. But he's got those football player shoulders. So solid. Like you could lean on them, if you needed to, and he could handle it.

At the last curve down the mountain home, I wondered if the couple from Texas had arrived yet. I left a note on the gate. I sure could use some help. A person needs to take a break once in a while. That's what children are for... to take over family businesses. Right? Not Maya. I can't count on her. No way. She was always such a difficult child and I see so much of her in Bryn: *'Hey, look at me! Oh, poor me. I'm bored.'* History repeats and apples don't fall far from trees. Am I living in a family cliché? Maya ran away to the States and now Bryn is doing the reverse, making her way down here.

I wish Harry were around to... to what? Make sure no one gets hurt? Wow. Where was that coming from? I've never needed a man to lean on. I must be losing it in my old age. Still, it would be great if both Harry and Bryn were here for the summer... next summer. She was so different around him... more sure of herself, maybe. gave her confidence to make choices. That's so important at her age. Sometimes kids need that sort of nudge from a neutral source, from outside the family. I'm so glad he was there and I wish he could be around her more. Around me, too, for that matter.

Chapter Three; Bryn

I snuggled into my own bed. Felt so good. For once, Maya didn't drag me up at 6:00 to cook and serve. I grabbed a bun and coffee like I was one of the guests and sat on the porch facing drowsy old Battery Street and Charleston Harbor. It was my favorite time, around 9:00, when the guests had finished breakfast and left for the day. It was still morning-cool and the city was just getting going.

But it felt different. Maybe because I had just spent three weeks in another country. I was noticing things I hadn't noticed before. Like the air. The ocean breeze felt thick and heavy. Salty. Barely waving the palm trees, tickling my hair. Not like at Panajachel, high in the mountains, with the wind brisk off the freshwater lake. Just think, two days ago I was in one guest house. Today I'm in another. So same, so different. Cars and carriage-rides here. Three wheeled *tuk-tuk* scooters and chicken buses there. Here it was all so familiar, so usual, the way things are supposed to be. Like in the airport, it felt so good to scarf down American food... like French Fries, and to have a burger be $6.00 and not 50 *Quetzales*. You got tired doing the math every time you went to buy something—*how much is that in real money?* Now everything was back to normal... but boring.

I barely got home and I already missed Gramma, Harry, the strange clothes in bright colors, the Spanish making you think before you talk and then sounding like a dumb first grader. And feeling like you don't fit in... like you're a new kid in a new school. But underneath, inside, there was a snug under-the-covers sense that I was in a familiar place. That I belonged there. My home.

I never got that feeling from mom. Maya wants nothing to do with Guatemala or her mother. Ever since she ran off to Charleston, she never said a word to Cobi, not even after she had me. No pictures. Nothing. I wonder what made her so mad. When Nanna passed and Maya got the house she turned it into an Airbnb, maybe it was the only thing she knew how to do from growing up with Cobi. Not me, though. I don't know what I want to be, but I'm sure not going to make beds and serve breakfast to strangers for the rest of my life.

"Hey, lazy bones, don't plan on sleeping-in tomorrow," Maya called from the doorway.

I sipped my coffee and gave her stink-eye. But I could tell she was glad to have me back, even though she had given me all kinds of grief when I told her I was going to see Cobi. She hadn't known I had been emailing Gramma for months. And she hadn't known that I had paid for an ancestry analysis out of my allowance and was basically trying to find all the folks that went into making me. I wonder what she would think about my tracking down her biological father? Whoa. Maybe that's something she always wanted to do, to know, but couldn't. Maybe that's what made her so mad at Cobi.

I got up and followed her into a guest room. As she shook out a fresh bedsheet, I grabbed her from behind and hugged her. "I brought something for you from Cobi." I felt her stiffen. When I came back from my room with the package wrapped in brown paper, Maya was sitting on the porch, her feet close together, hands on her lap, chin down like a child waiting to be served spinach. She stroked the paper as if feeling memories, then carefully untied the twine and slowly unwrapped the bundle. "A *huipil*," she whispered, "Juanna's... from when I was little." She held up the beautifully embroidered square of heavy cloth with a head-hole in the center. The cloth was covered with stamp-sized tropical birds in dazzling colors, no two alike. After a while, she stood and slid her head through the hole, then fastened the sides and turned in front of me, elbows up, modeling the native blouse. I caught a look on her face I had never seen before. Maya, getting misty? Whoa, that was new.

"Did you know Juanna helped birth me?"

"What?" I gasped.

"Uh-huh. She was the *partera* in Panajachel back then." When I wrinkled my face in question, she continued, "She was a midwife working at the same *posada* as Cobi.

People would come for her when they needed her to deliver a baby. Made it convenient when it was Cobi's time."

"So, if she worked with Cobi she knew you growing up?"

"Yeah. No. More than that. She took care of me. Like an aunt or grandmother. Always there. Just there." She stroked the huipil, "Wearing this beautiful blouse." Maya took it off, folded it carefully and partially re-wrapped it. "Until I went up north." She nodded to herself, remembering, "Uh-huh. And there was Karen, the owner. She was there much of the time. And I thought all the people who came to stay for a day or two were coming to see me, like Jesus and the Magi. They all wanted to play with me. A big happy family with lots of friendly people." Her face clouded over, "But never a daddy. I never knew my father. Even though I asked a lot, as I got older."

Later, Maya hung the *huipil* out flat on her bedroom wall like a picture.

I went into town and had a print made of Harry and me at that Marine Reserve off Caye Caulker. It was a shot of us surrounded by sharks and stingrays feeding on the crackers we were tossing. My friend Josh, when he heard I was home, he came by and got all into the picture. And when he asked about the garbage bag around my leg his eyes got real big. I knew his buddies were going to hear all about it when school started. I framed the print and put it on my dresser.

After a while I got back to normal, boring, school for my senior year. Spanish was more interesting now that I knew where you could use it and that people really spoke it, like all the time, unless they were Mayans living in the mountains. They had their own language. And I got a chance to do a Power Point presentation to my class about the trip and all. That was cool. But eventually the excitement wore off and I got back into everyday life and stuff like talking to my counselor about college. Him and me figured out that I'd like to be a doctor and we looked at different places and their programs and sent out applications.

Another cool thing. Harry had told me about being a volleyball coach at his high school. Made me think I ought to try out for our team. Turns out I suck at bumping. So, I had Josh video me doing it the way I do and I emailed it to Harry. He answered:

Hey, Bryn,

How're you doing girl? I know I'm bored. It's hard to get back to everyday stuff after all the excitement we had. I could tell you were grooving on everything on your trip even if you kept trying to look cool and detached. Didn't fool me. So, anyhow, you're playing volleyball. Good. Except for that stumble into the lake at Flores when you cut your leg, you seemed pretty coordinated to me ;). In your video your problem is you're trying to swing your arms up. But the secret to bumping is to create a rigid platform with your arms. Your arms need to stay still, like a board. It's your legs that provide the lift. Check out the video I attached. Also, there are some links to other instruction sites, like for serving and that. Good luck. Let me know how you do.

Oh, and by the way, heard anything from your Gramma?

Harry

Chapter Four; Harry

Back home in D.C. I slid into the familiar routine—three or four tours a week cycling around national monuments and government buildings. It all suddenly seemed so stale. I couldn't find the kind of enthusiasm I used to have and, to be fair, *needed* in order to give my clients their money's worth. Then, one day in early October, it hit me. This is boring and I'm bored. And worse yet, I'm coming across bored. So, while I sat in the tour bus waiting for my party to return, I decided to do something I had been resisting for a month. I emailed Cobi.

Cobi, how are you doing?

I'm sitting here at the Lincoln Memorial waiting for my 27 customers to gawk and stare and slowly walk around taking pictures. I gave my spiel and now only have to wait until they satisfy their curiosity and clamber back onto the bus. Boring. Which reminds me of why I went down your way in the first place. I was looking for some new... what? Places to see I had never seen before? Facts to learn so I could pass them along? I've scoured every history book and guide book for interesting details to share about Washington and I still got nothing new. I never thought I would say that. Me, who loves to hear his own voice, is tired of saying the same things, peppering historical facts with the same old japes and jokes. But, ever since I've come back from your country, it's like someone turned the technicolor movie into black and white. What I'm thinking is, I'd like to take you up on your offer to move to the bright colors and sunshine of Panajachel. (watch, as soon as I get there you'll have monsoon season or something ;).

You asked if I had some handyman skills. Years ago, when I lived in Lansing, I had a small house and did all the minor maintenance stuff. Now that I live in a condo there's a repairman who comes with the place. But, yeah, allowing for metric differences and construction styles, I think I've still got the touch. It would feel good to be useful. Use my hands. Fix things.

But mainly, I would like to learn what you do. In a certain sense we're both in the hospitality industry. You, into bedding them down. Me, into moving them around. We're both used to dealing with high-turnover public. Our skill sets could be a good fit. Anyhow, I was thinking I might come by around Halloween—oops, do they have that down there? Or maybe it's a version of *Día de los Muertos*? Anyway, I'm thinking the end of October. How does that sound? I'm sure I could be useful around your place once you train me... for a coach, I am very coachable.

Talk about coaching, Bryn asked me for volleyball advice and sent me a video of her problems. I sent some instructions. She improved... felt nice to help. You know, I like that girl. Well, I liked all my kids at school. But once in a while you just click with certain ones... the same wavelength, or something. Anyhow, she strikes me as special. Look, here's the thing. I think it would be fun if I were still around your place, if and when she came down for the summer. Huh?

But, I'm getting ahead of myself and here come my people. Basically, I want to know if you've changed your mind about having me around for more than a two-day visit.

Harry Benson
That night back at my apartment, I got online and found this email from Cobi.

Harry,
I haven't changed my mind. And yes, you would be very welcome. I also have a lot of tools you can use. But you are always welcome to bring your own. Any time you can come is fine. And by the way, Bryn and I are in the process of arranging a summer stay for her.

Cobi

Well, she hadn't forgotten me. And while her response was not over the top, I have to say I really liked it. A little understatement goes a long way with me. And concise, clipped communication. That too, I find endearing. I got right on booking flights and subletting my apartment. Who knows how long I might stay?

Chapter Five; Bryn

One night after supper, me and Maya were making biscuits for breakfast and talking like we always do. While I greased a tin, I snuck in about hanging with Cobi for the summer... "to help her out and work on my Spanish."

"I see," Maya hissed through tight lips. "You got plans? All on your own? All worked out?"

I nodded eagerly. "Gramma's paying for it. And guess what? Harry is going to be moving down to *Posada del Sol* at the end of the month."

"Hmm," Maya murmured as she took off her apron, then sat down with her cup of coffee. She patted the table, like inviting me to join her for an *us girls* talk. "I saw you in a picture with this Harry guy. So, tell me about him."

I waggled my head. "I dunno. What can I say? He gets me. He helped me when I was hurt." I lifted my leg to show her my fading scar. "He takes care of me and he tells me things, like how to play volleyball." I stopped, grasping for the feeling. "He's like, maybe an uncle. Or a grampa... if I had one."

Maya pursed her lips, shook her head.

"Well I don't have a real grampa, do I?" When Maya didn't answer, I continued. "How come I don't know your father? Who he is. What he's like."

"How should I know?" Maya snapped. "Cobi would never tell me, no matter how many times I asked. Like she was embarrassed. Didn't want him to know about me and didn't want me to know him." Her face tightened. "That really hurt. You know? But that's Cobi for you." Maya thumped her cup on the table. "As far as I'm concerned, I could have been the result of artificial insemination. Not that they would have had that down there, back then. Nope, I was just an illegitimate bastard come-by the old-fashioned way. Or she might have been raped. She might have loved the guy. He might have run off and left her. She might have run off and left him. Who knows? Cobi wasn't about to tell me any of that and in the meantime, she made me grow up in that dump of a town washing tourist's bed sheets. All the time hiding me away," she swept her hands to include our B&B, "from all this."

I reached over to touch her arm. "Aw, Maya..." I began.

"I'm not Maya to you. I'm your mother," she scolded. "And don't patronize me. I've given up wanting to know who my father was... is. At this point I no longer give a damn." We both noticed the first whiff of burning muffins. She grabbed a towel and yanked the oven door open. "Cobi and her secrets."

"All right. Okay, *Mom*. I'll call you *Mom*. But I learned from you, you know. Calling *your* mother, *Cobi*," I said to her back. Maya clutched the dishtowel and pulled the two trays out and clattered them on top of the range. "And anyhow, you're not the only one. I don't know my dad either... well, besides his name and your wedding picture." I waited a moment before asking, "Are you ever going to tell me about him? So I can learn something? Maybe fill in some blanks?" I watched her shoulders sag. "C'mon, Mom. Can we talk? Huh? About important stuff?"

I heard her sigh as she tucked a loose strand of hair out of her eyes. When she turned, the look she gave me said that we would be talking on another level from now on. Woman to woman. Not mother to kid.

"So, tell me," Maya said, "how's Cob... *my mother*... doing these days?"

"Well, she's fine. Works real hard. She's got those four bedrooms and meals and cleaning."

Maya shut her eyes and shook her head disparagingly. "You don't have to tell me about *Posada del Sol* and how many bedrooms it has and how much work it takes to keep it up. I dusted and mopped every one of those rooms for years and changed the sheets and made the beds."

"How come I can relate to that?" I taunted.

Maya glared through lowered brows and raised an admonishing finger, then lowered it, before asking, "So, the place is doing okay?"

"Far as I could tell."

"Hmm. What's her thing with Harry?"

230

I shrugged. "I dunno. I just got the idea they hit it off. Like she wouldn't mind having him around."

"Around... around? Like a handyman? Or more than that? What?"

"Mom!" I gasped. "That's none of my business. Or yours either."

Maya sniffed and took a swallow of coffee. "There's no one else she's seeing down there?"

I shrugged my shoulders. "Not that I could tell. Or care."

"So, how's the business going? And did she ever get city water?"

"How should I know? Look, maybe you could ask her yourself. She's online, you know. I just emailed her yesterday."

Maya raised her chin and looked away.

Chapter Six; Cobi

In June, I got a shock. A red letter day. Maya called.

"Cobi," she said. Her voice quavered. I hadn't heard her speak in twenty-five years, but I knew she was in trouble. We both held our breath.

"It's good to hear your voice. Maya. Is everything all right. You okay?"

"Now, yeah. I had a bout of pneumonia."

"Oh, no!"

"Well, it isn't too bad. Just when it started to look like the worst was over, I guess I relapsed. Bryn has been a champ taking care of me. I didn't need to be hospitalized. I guess I tried too much too soon. But I'm finally getting back on my feet."

"Sorry to hear that. Good thing Bryn's there. She's a good girl."

"Yeah, she is, but she keeps talking about coming to see you right after graduation. Has tickets and all... of course, you know that..."

"Uh-huh," I muttered. "Harry and I can't wait. Been talking about it all winter. But you need me."

"No. No. Wait. Don't even think about coming here. That's not why I called. I just wanted to let you... I don't know..."

"I'm coming," I insisted. It was a breakthrough, finally. A chance to connect with my daughter after so many years. Another thought quickly followed, clinching my resolve. Bryn had been bugging me so much about her grandfather over the winter... what if she happened to locate Mateo while I was away? That wouldn't be all bad. I quickly added, "Harry and Bryn... will be fine down here. I need to be with you." We both held our breath until I could almost feel her nod over the phone. "I'll be in touch. Let me make arrangements. Okay?"

"'Kay.

As soon as I got off the phone, I found Harry in the sitting room chatting with one of our guests. I hung back in the doorway. There was the man who slid so smoothly into my life. How had I lived without him? My rock. That's what he was.

He was engaged, listening. Such a good listener. His face, his hands, the way he leaned in, nodded. He was all there. He listened to me for the last nine months. I hadn't realized how much I had to say, to tell. How lonely I had been.

He was a big help, too—shopping, cooking, booking guests. Then he expanded. We designed one-day boat tours to the towns around Lake Atitlan: San Marcos, San Pedro, San Antonio. He made brochures, distributed them to hotels and left them for our guests. The tour guide was back in business.

It has felt so good to share my life, for a change. I smiled. Harry. When the guest left, I beckoned him onto the terrace. I held both his hands. "Harry, I need your help."

Head slightly askance, concerned, he muttered, "Uh-huh?"

"Maya, in Charleston, is recovering from pneumonia and needs me there."

"Huh!"

"Bryn's coming here next week, as you know."

"Still?"

"Yes. And I'm getting tickets for the same day. It'll save a trip to the airport." He nodded digesting this, raising an eyebrow—and? "So, I'm hoping I can count on you to take over here. You know how things work..."

"And Bryn. Take care of Bryn for... how long are you planning to stay away?"

"Dunno. I haven't seen Maya or talked to her since she was Bryn's age. We have a lot of catching up to do." I pleaded with my eyes. "I need to do this... please... for as long as it feels right?"

After a moment, he nodded. We hugged. Good man. As I started to walk away, he added, "It's more than just seeing her, isn't it?" I paused, then kept walking.

Harry and I left Pana early. Bryn was due-in at 11:30. My flight was at 2:00. What a treat to have him drive. These days, I get sleepy after the first twenty minutes on the road. With him behind the wheel, I could nod off whenever I felt like it.

I closed my eyes, mulling. The Karma of it all. Three generations of us. Back and forth between Charleston and Pana. Like passing ships in... I almost chuckled out loud. Harry would say, "Like passing sheeps in the night." That's another thing. He makes me laugh. I'm going to miss him. But I have to take care of my girls.

We watched Bryn drag her carry-on bag down the hall. She looked great; grew an inch, lost a couple of pounds, got a great haircut and moved like she was in shape. Harry whispered, "She's been working out."

She ran the last couple of steps. Hugged me hard. Did the same with Harry, burying her chin in his thick shoulder. "Man, I've been looking forward to this," she said. Harry caught my eye, grinned. They were going to be all right.

Over lunch, I asked how Maya was doing. "Mom is busy but not up to full speed. She's gonna miss me not being around. But I got my friend Josh to take my place... sort of... till you get there, Gramma. And I promise to give Harry a hand at your place while you're gone." She chuckled around her bite of *empanada*, adding, "Well, even after you get back."

I smiled vaguely.

Chapter Seven; Harry and Bryn

I watched Cobi wend her way through the security-check maze. At the last turn she waved to us. Patted her heart. I was going to miss her. Miss being with her every day. I never knew what it could be like... living with a woman. The whole thing, together all winter, was a miracle. And now she was leaving me. Damn.

All the way home to Pana, I listened as Bryn nattered about everything that happened to her in her senior year. I might be missing Cobi but I was going to be busy keeping tabs on her granddaughter.

Turns out, I was really surprised when she appeared in the kitchen the next morning and got right to squeezing orange juice and frying sausage. As we chatted about this and that, I remembered Cobi describing how she and Maya did the same work together so long ago. I was being swept right into a family tradition... and it didn't feel bad. In fact, I kind of liked it.

It was one thing for Bryn to cruise the exciting tourist spots in Guatemala as she had last summer, but settling into one region, one town, like Pana, was a whole other thing—going deep rather than wide. That afternoon, I took her with me to the market where I introduced her to the crowds, the colors, the smells and my favorite vendors who knew not to waste time haggling with me about prices. She didn't realize how I was getting a fair price without having to bargain until I stayed back and told her to approach an unknown vendor behind a stack of papayas. To my surprise, she haggled the guy down from his initial asking price and actually smirked at me when she got a great deal. "Ha!" I said, "it's late in the day and he wanted to unload his stock."

"Sure, Harry."

It wasn't long before she settled into our... actually Cobi's... world into which I was only recently introduced. I have to say Bryn really took to it. She enjoyed walking down Calle Santander past the vendors braising skirt steaks and the women roasting ears of corn over charcoal braziers. As chary as she had been about local food last summer, she surprised me one night by buying a roasted *elote* slathered with spicy butter and lime. She took a healthy bite of the corn-on-the-cob and announced that it tasted like popcorn. Go figure.

She was even tolerant of the roving street vendors bombarding her with requests to buy all kinds of souvenirs and gimcracks. Over my long winter stay, most folks got to know me and left me alone. I explained to her that, in third world countries, marketing could be very primitive and almost abusive. Vendors would wave their fare in your face, join you at table as you tried to eat. When with me, of course, she was safe from harassment. However, after a while I observed her in action and could tell she had found the right balance between friendly refusal and no-eye-contact disengagement. She was a quick study.

One day, Bryn and I happened upon a walled-in courtyard where some guys were playing volleyball. We both would have enjoyed playing but had to size up the rules of engagement. "Hey, Harry," she asked, "do they do pickup games, like back home. Where you say, *I got next?*" I just shrugged. But then I grabbed a ball and slapped a soft shot at her. She automatically dropped into a crouch for a bump, just like I knew she would. We did that for a while and then I set some shots for her to spike. Didn't take her long to realize I was showcasing our talent—an impromptu try-out with guys who weren't used to co-ed teams.

After a while one guy took off and they waved me in to replace him. Bryn just kept setting and bumping against the wall until I complained that I hurt my wrist and called to Bryn to take my place.

On the way home, sweaty and a bit grimy, Bryn remarked, "Did you see how all those guys looked at each other when you waved me in, like *what should we do?* And then the tall guy, Ramon, just shrugged, and everything was all right."

I fist-tapped Bryn on the shoulder. "They'll let you play anytime you want from now on."

That afternoon, I took Bryn by the bank to exchange her dollars to *Quetzales*. Then we dropped by the language school to arrange Spanish classes with the head teacher, Antonio. After he chatted with her in Spanish, checking her proficiency, they both decided she had a good grammatical base and so they would simply study vocabulary for the first hour and use it in conversation for the next. They got on well. He was perhaps a couple of years older than Bryn and an inch or two shorter. Built solid, but quick and smooth moving, he would make a good setter in our courtyard volleyball games. I decided I would invite him to join us soon if he didn't play already.

Chapter Eight; Harry

With Cobi off-site for a while, I invited Bryn to join me on my tours. It was as good a way as any to explore the region. One morning, crossing the lake to San Pedro, I had just finished my spiel on the history of the town and its distinctive clothing and language differences to my five clients when Bryn remarked, "You talked about Mayan culture. How it's the same but different from town to town. We're right in the heart of it here, aren't we? How do you know about it?"

"Books. Cobi has a great library. And the internet."

Bryn nodded to herself, like she was determining to do something. I stayed still. Let her process her thoughts. "That's really interesting," she remarked. "The thought that the women we saw weaving shawls and *huipils* in Santa Caterina yesterday are basically making their city's uniforms. Like school colors. Hmm." She pondered a while longer. "I want to find out more about all that." Then she surprised me with the leap of thought you can get with kids. "I'm part Mayan. I found that out from a test. And I mean, look at my mom's skin... like she's got a permanent tan. That's all from my grampa. Wouldn't it be cool if I could meet him?"

I raised my eyebrows. "That could involve a lot of people and their right to privacy. Some things are best left alone."

She squared at me in her seat, brows furrowed, jaw set. Then we docked and I led my party along the wobbly plank walkway to dry land.

For the next week, every time Bryn was not in class or helping clean she could be found pouring over books on Mayan culture. One day as I walked by her reading under a palm tree in the yard, she called out to me.

"Harry?"

"Yeah?"

"You taught history, right?"

"Uh-huh."

"Like what happened a long time ago. But what about recent history? Huh? What about a family's history? Like my history? Or are you only interested in dead people who can't come out and tell you that it didn't happen the way you think, the way you teach it? And anyway, when does history catch up to *now?* How long does it take for what happened to be history? I need your help to find my Mayan grandfather."

That stopped me cold, I can tell you. Hers was not a classic thesis but she knew how to get my attention and appeal to my professed love of historical truth and my weakness for helping youngsters. Thoughts scattered. How would Cobi react to resurrecting her long-ago lover? Okay, the kid wasn't necessarily planning to bring the guy around, make a scene. Or, maybe he wasn't even alive. Still. Would it be like meeting your ex after fifty years? And what about me? Would I suffer in the comparison? Would Cobi be sandwiched between two choices... even if he were still alive? A widower? Would she hate me for dragging up all the hurt and painful decisions from her past? "Bryn," I said, slowly collecting myself, "I understand your desire to know. But you have to consider other's..."

"This is my life."

"Of course it is. But you should get your grandmother's okay to push ahead. In fact, you need her help to even get started." She bobbed her head sharply—right, I will.

That evening, while preparing salad for supper, before I'd even had a chance to discuss this with Cobi, Bryn stuck her head in the door and announced, "Gramma texted. His name is Mateo Obregon. And she last saw him in Zaragoza, many years ago. It's fifty kilometers on the way to Guatemala City."

"I know where it is," I managed to squeeze in.

"I'm only allowed to find out if he is still alive and if his wife is still alive. Can we go tomorrow?"

Bryn and I rode in silence the next morning, she looking up facts, I believe, on her iPad while I negotiated the twisting, pock-mocked roads. "I think we should start with the local police station," she announced.

"Nah," I replied, "they might ask too many questions. The church would be better—the parish priest or his housekeeper. Or, we might just find some old farts hanging out downtown next to the fountain."

"Hey, watch how you talk about my grampa."

"Well, in case you haven't done the math he would be about the same age as your gramma, and me and you might want to get your imagination ready for what he would look like. Think old duffers on a bench."

After parking downtown, we wandered toward the central square. Before we could even begin to head toward the church, its bell tower visible several blocks ahead, I pulled Bryn's arm to study three old gentlemen parked on a bench. We hung back so as not to be rude while we stared. All three guys had on white cowboy hats, button down blue shirts and some very distinctive white pants, wide as cargo shorts, cut off below their knees and covered with swirling, brightly colored embroidery. Instead of a belt they used a sash that hung down between their legs. And the way they sat, presiding over the passing throng, you could tell they thought they were very cool indeed. To which I had to say, I would concur.

While Bryn snuck a picture with her phone, I mentioned that we could just ask those guys if they knew her *abuelo*. They sure looked like they could be on the same team.

"Si," the first guy replied, "Conozco Mateo. Está muy vicin."

Between the two of us and the three honor guards on the bench, we soon established that he was alive and well and was a widower and lived with his daughter in a blue house, third on a street leading off to the right. Having accomplished our mission, I was ready to turn around and head home, but Bryn had other ideas. Turns out she had only promised not to *meet* Mateo. But as long as we had come all that way, she was determined to at least get a look at him.

So, we took to strolling back and forth on the sidewalk across the street from his house for the next half hour. Eventually, a woman in her forties carrying a bag of groceries walked up to the door. Bryn gasped. "Whoa! That could be my half-aunt, my Mom's half-sister." Before I could stop her, she was across the street and sticking her foot in the door. She sputtered, "*Pardon. Senor Obregon esta aqui?*"

The woman studied her. "*Quien eres?*" she asked.

Bryn muttered and stumbled. I walked up and introduced myself, "*Soy* Harry Benson." Suspicion clouding her face, the woman's eyes cut from me to Bryn and back. "*Nosotros...*" I began, then stopped. "Do you happen to speak English, at all?"

"Jes," the woman replied. "I teach English."

"Good," I replied. "I am a teacher as well."

The woman opened her palms as if to say—and so?

Before I could answer, Bryn jumped in. "We are trying to find Mateo Obregon."

The woman rolled her open palm—and?

Bryn looked at me. I shrugged and extended my chin at her as if to say, you've come this far, finish it.

"I think Mateo may be my grandfather."

The woman held her hand to her forehead, fingers squeezing her temples.

"*Como puede...* how can this be?"

"I think Mateo may be my mother's father." The woman stared, befuddled. Bryn grinned broadly and wiggled with joy. "And that would mean that you are my mother's half-sister, my aunt," she enthused, barely holding herself back from an exuberant hug. "Hi, I'm Bryn," she finally said, sticking out her hand, to no response.

I nodded agreement to the woman's questioning expression. She finally, shook her head, as if to clear it, "So, who is your grandmother?"

"Her name is Cobi Evans. She worked in the Peace Corps in the early 70s. Here in Zaragoza with Mateo."

The woman held her hand to her mouth, "*Madre de dios...*" She looked around, not looking at anything. "If this is true... my father never told us. I will want to tell him... ask him."

"Take your time," I said and handed her a card for Posada del Sol. "Cobi runs it... when you think he... you're... ready."

Bryn bubbled, "So, what is your name? I'm Bryn. Bryn Mitchell."

The woman answered, half under her breath, "Ana Sofia Ruiz."

In the awkward pause, I could see a hundred questions racing behind Ana's eyes.

That's when Bryn looked through the doorway to a table in the corner of the living room. A glass votive candle flickered next to a statue of our Lady of Guadalupe and next to that was a picture of a man, perhaps in his sixties, next to a woman holding a bouquet. An anniversary celebration? Bryn pointed to the ornate silver frame with a black ribbon draped over the corners. "Is that my grandfather? *Es Mateo?*" she asked, "and your mother?"

Ana offered a sad nod as she stepped back, as if overwhelmed by our onslaught, to allow us into the house.

"I'm sorry... about her," Bryn said, studying the picture. "She was a kind-looking woman. I wish I had known her. And your father. When can I meet him?"

I took the moment to announce, "Well, we should be going." Bryn frowned, about to object. "Now!" I insisted, adding, "if we are to get back in time for supper."

"No," Ana cried. "*Papi! Venga.*"

I wanted to pull Bryn aside and remind her that Cobi really didn't want this whole business to go this far. But I couldn't really blame Bryn for pushing, pushing, pushing. We all want to know where we come from. Where we belong.

Chapter Nine; Cobi in Charleston

I was thrilled to be with my daughter. We were clumsy around each other at first. And not just, *Where do you keep the sugar?* sort of thing. We tiptoed around the past. Like with questions about her father. I finally decided to spill the whole story. Once I told her, Maya sat very still for a while. Then she huffed, slapped the table and said, "That's all I needed to know. All I want to know."

"But you bugged me constantly as a kid. And you held it against me when you left... that I never told you who your father was."

Maya cocked her head, thinking, crumbling her scone. Then in a flat, distant voice said, "I'm over that. The curiosity." She looked me in the eye, "Now it's just... facts. It would be like you found a picture of your long-lost uncle or somebody in a Civil War uniform. Would I want to hear his story? No. Not especially." Her eyes tightened into worn creases. "It was mostly that you kept it a secret. Wouldn't tell me."

I wanted to explain how I couldn't possibly have told a child adult secrets, but the set of her chin told me that we were beyond explanations and justifications, so I simply apologized. "I'm sorry."

Maya's face relaxed. "That works for me," she said and I knew we were good... for good. And just as surely, I knew I would not be going back to Guatemala anytime soon... if ever. Instead, I would pretend I was an astronaut returning to mother earth after fifty years in orbit. I was back where I started. Home, where I belonged.

It didn't take long to slide into the salty, languid coastal air. The syrupy, drawn out drawl of neighbors and shop keepers soothed like a mother's lullaby. I could feel myself slowing down, stretching out as I strolled through the historic district. The old houses, forced to maintain their antebellum condition because of extreme poverty after the

Civil War, now made for a living museum of pastel colors offset with jasmine vines trailing over wrought iron gates to tucked away gardens. I hadn't realized how much I had missed it all.

After the first few days, we developed a genteel routine of shopping and meals and afternoon rests and evening walks along Battery Street, nodding to the neighbors and the tourists. Our business was booming and we were busy cooking and cleaning in a way we had shared so many years ago in Pana.

And then, one Sunday in church, as I took in the congregation, some known from long ago, like my high school friend Corliss, others with unknown faces but familiar family names, my back stiffened. My chin firmed. I was feeling the starch of Charleston working its way back into the southern fabric of my being. The staunch defiance of all things *Yankee* for their *invasion* of the South 150 years ago. The distancing from African Americans. The social superiority and hierarchy based on ancestry. My jaws clenched with the same resolve that had driven me to join the Peace Corps in the first place—to get away to another way, to leave all this behind.

As the pastor droned, I drifted, floating images of Harry. Harry and me. I like that man. Am quite fond of him... more than that, actually... and feel bad about coaxing him down to Panajachel. Then leaving him there with Bryn. Poor guy.

A few days later, I sat on the front porch, my Campari and soda in hand. Nice drink that. Thanks to an Italian guest, way back. A white-haired couple, across the road, walked ahead of a teenage girl intently focused on her cell. Gramma looked back, said something. The girl shook her head, grimaced and kept poking at her phone. Could have been me and Bryn. How do you relate to adolescents? Apparently, Harry can. Thank God for that. How can you tell what's going on in their minds? Like Bryn asking me about Mateo. It's Maya all over again. Who is he? What happened? Can I meet him? I couldn't shut her down like I did with Maya. Look what happened then. I had to throw her a bone. Just his name. No contact.

"Hey, Cobi, what're you thinking?" Maya asked as she joined me.

"About how much I don't want to go back to Pana."

"Really? After all these years?"

I hesitated before repeating, "... after all these years... and a lot of unpacked baggage."

"Like what?" Sensing the reluctance in my pause, Maya continued, "Oh, I bet it's about my father... right? Has Bryn been taking up where I left off?"

I clenched my lips. My daughters... me. We get each other, think too much alike. "I just need some privacy. We don't all need to know everything about each other. People's feelings..."

Maya let that steep for the moment, along with her pot of tea. "So, I take it you're planning to stay here for the next while."

"Mmm," I murmured, then shrugged.

Chapter Ten; Bryn meets Mateo

I looked at Harry, biting my lips and hunching my shoulders. Oops. I hadn't expected things to go this far, but I was about to meet my grandfather, after all. We all stared at the doorway as a gray-haired man staggered into the room rubbing his eyes, as if he'd just woken from a nap. He was short. Shorter than Harry. But at least as big in the shoulders. His denim shirt was worn down at the cuffs. His elbows stuck out and his jeans were so shredded he would fit right in with my friends. He gave me a hard look. Then the same to Harry. He was my grandfather, all right. You could tell... forehead, cheekbones like mine and Mom's. I liked the way he tilted his head to look at me. It felt familiar, friendly. "*Abuelo*," I cried.

Confused, he darted a look at Ana. "They say she is your *nieta*. Your granddaughter," Ana told him. Turning to us, she added, "I taught him some English."

"My grandmother is Cobi," I said, nodding and smiling in anticipation of his enthusiastic response.

Instead he sank into a chair and stared at the floor for a long while. Finally, as if he just noticed us, he waved his hand for me and Harry to sit. Ana went to get drinks. Mateo studied me, doing his own genetic calculation. He reached his hand to his mouth, thumb on one corner, forefinger on the other. "*Tienes...* you have her mouth." Then lowering his fingers to caress his chin, added, "And her chin." I clutched my hands. He reached out his hand, palm up, asking to hold mine. His fingers were slightly curled as if he had held shovels and rakes all his life and they felt hard as the handles they had gripped year after year. I hunched forward in my chair and I could see his eyes soften as he lifted his left hand to my face and ran the back of his fingers along my cheek. He smelled like outside, and land, his clothes lived-in, warm and safe. I cried. He stood, touched my elbows raising me to my feet and swallowed me in an *abrazo*. It was like wrapping my arms around a pine tree, he was so solid.

Then we talked about Maya. He figured out how old she would be and I described the work we did at the guest house in Charleston. He didn't say anything when I explained about her divorce. He was surprised to hear about Cobi's *posada,* that it was so close to Zaragoza. He stopped to look out the window, his face frozen. "Cobi. So much time," he said, his voice stretched thin with the recollection. "We are young, like you." He looked to the side, sighed. "Then she is gone. I am sad."

We were all still for a while. Ana Sofia leaned in the doorway, her arms crossed. I caught a whiff of bread dough and hot spices. "You must stay to eat," she said. "I will make lunch."

"Can I help, *tia?*" I asked. Her face contorted like she was about to cry as she beckoned me into the kitchen. "We will make *pupusas*. Do you know what they are?" I shook my head. "My mother was from El Salvador. They are a traditional food. I can show you."

Chapter Eleven; Mateo

I liked this Harry. *Es muy hombre.* I could tell. We took our *cervesas* out to the porch to sit and watch the people going by. Between his stumbling Spanish and my broken English we established that neither of us knew Maya. *Mi hija.* My daughter. We both stopped talking for a while. I liked that in him. He knew things... how to give me time to think, a chance to sort out my feelings, mixed up as they are.

How is a man supposed to feel when a girl I never met before, never knew existed, shows up at my house and calls me *grampa?* And how about her mother? Never had a clue she existed. If I were rich I would worry if they were crooks, trying to fool me, to get money out of me. Ha! What money? Good thing I had this house and my daughter could move in when her bastard of a husband left her.

I glanced at Harry. He turned his head, an eyebrow raised. Waiting for me. My move. I liked this man more and more. Harry, the American, but not like the fish-belly-white tourists who come here. He blends in. More like us—a darker wave in a sea of brown. And not like the blacks from the islands down on the coast. No, he's a *gringo*, all right, but different. A good man. Now he's with Cobi, some way. I guess.

"How long you know Cobi?" I asked.

"About a year."

"Me, one years. Then she go." I thumped my heart. "Hurt." Harry took a deep breath. Looked at the sky. I gave him time to think. "Me, Cobi, we..." I stop, squeeze my eyes, trying to remember. "I don't remember how she look... from fifty years."

"I bet you don't..."

We stared at each other. He didn't look away. I could talk to this man. Tell him things I never told anybody else. I said, "I tell you... some things?" Harry ducks his chin slow then back up. He's not afraid to hear about sad things, about hurt, about loving. "We could have good life. Me and her. Long ago," I said, as if I had to convince my new friend. I stopped, closed my eyes, breathed deep. "I asked to my-self, is she ashamed of me? I am not good enough for her? I am a souvenir from her trip? Some nice thoughts for when she is old?" I turned in my chair to face Harry. "She make my loving be... *estupido*. Make me ask, she love me like I love her? And then, you tell me she don't go home, *al Norte,* like I think. She just go down the road with my child... our child... and never tell me. I never watch Maya grow up. Help her grow up. Well, I am... a part of her... her blood. And now, this girl. This Bryn. She is my blood. How can I not love her?"

"I hear you," Harry said with a sad face.

"Mira," I said, trying to help my new friend, "do you know this woman? This Cobi? I do not." I cupped my hands, my fingers touching together. "There is this hole between me knowing her and you knowing her. She run from me, long time ago."

Harry stared at his bottle, didn't say anything.

"She run from you?" I asked.

We finished our beers.

Chapter Twelve; Bryn, Maya and Cobi

I got tired of emailing and all that typing so I just called Maya and Cobi one afternoon.

"Hi Mom."

"Hi honey. Is everything all right?"

"Yeah, it's all good. Is Cobi there too?"

"Uh-huh."

"Can you put her on speaker phone? There's so much I want to tell you guys."

"Bryn, honey. How are you?"

"Hi Gramma. I miss you. So, let me tell all that's happening. You know Antonio, right? My Spanish teacher. Well, last week he took me on a language trip to Solola. We had to talk Spanish the whole time. First, we rode in the back of a pickup truck standing with other passengers hanging onto a chest-high rail, you know."

"Yes, I know, dear. I'd been living there for fifty years."

"Oh, yeah, right. But what I found most interesting was the tiny town and the big church with the small statues all wearing yellow button-down shirts and standing all in a row behind the high altar. And then there were two women that Antonio knew who squatted on a steep hillside planting sprouts for snap peas. They wore their *huipils* but in their local patterns... like the one Juanna left for us... with small birds and flowers. And Antonio spoke Mayan with them. That guy! He speaks English and Spanish plus both dialects of Mayan from his mother's and his father's side. And here's me barely knowing one extra language. But what was really cool was a big clinic for women right next to the church. I checked it out and they offer prenatal care and fertility planning, and postpartum counseling and well-baby care. I could really get into all that, you know?"

"That's important work, dear."

"Yeah, and Gramma you should see what happened next. So, we get back to town and the next day, after breakfast and the guests were gone for the day, a young man came up to us in tears. Juanna. Juanna, he pleaded, *Necesita, Juanna.*

"He needed the midwife."

"Yeah, Mom, it took me a minute to figure that out... Juanna the midwife. So, I went, *No hay. E muerto.* But when he turned away, all sad, I followed him, thinking maybe I could help... somehow. We went four blocks to a purple, stucco house on Calle Verde. Do you know it, Gramma?"

"Maybe."

"There was an old man sitting on a chair by the door, slumped, saying a rosary. From inside I could hear a tired groan that turned into a shriek of pain. I followed the husband into the house and stood in the doorway to the bedroom. There was a woman propped up on a bed, her belly all naked and huge and stretched. The man glanced at two women who had been talking soft and scared and shook his head and then went to the bed and patted his wife's leg.

The mother's legs were spread wide and she was breathing really fast. Her neck muscles were all tight and her eyes wide and staring. I don't know what made me realize it, but I just knew she was too tense to let that baby out. But then I thought of what I do for you Mom... when you get your migraines. You know. Dim the lights. Press on your temples and the back of your neck."

"Uh-huh. It really helps."

I must have made a noise because the women looked over at me and asked the husband who I was and what I was doing there. He mumbled something about Cobi and went out. While they looked at me, deciding if I was okay to be there, I asked if I could help. One of them, just held up her hands like *Whatever. I got nothin.*

"So, there was a glass-jar candle with a picture of a saint on it. They watched me light it with matches on the table. Then I got behind the headboard, reached my arms over and put my hands on the woman's shoulders. I started to rub her neck muscles. Then I started chanting the first thing that came into my head, slow and sing-song. "Baa Baa Black sheep, have you any wool? Yes sir, yes sir, three bags full." I repeated it over and over, rubbing her shoulders, stroking down her arms. She was starting to relax. But then she got another contraction and we had to start over. The women watched me, then looked at each other. They were like, it can't hurt, whatever she's doing. Then the mother seemed to get more energy as she focused on the candle. When the next contraction came her cry was different. The two women got around the foot of the bed and talked to her. I couldn't understand it all but they sounded like they were cheering her on. Then the child was out and crying. I cried too."

"It's a powerful, elemental experience, dear. Birthing."

"Yeah, Gramma, and like as primitive as you can get. Then I watched them tie and cut the cord. And after they cleaned the baby and laid him on the mother's chest to suck on her nipple. That's how all *that* gets going!"

"Yes dear."

"And then they massaged the woman's belly until she groaned and delivered a gooey mess that I later looked up... it's called the afterbirth."

"Uh-huh. It is."

"Okay. I guess I'm not telling you guys anything you don't know. But all that night I kept playing out the whole scene. It was terrific. So real And I was part of it. And I seemed to know how to help. And I liked how it felt to make it all be good."

"You did good. We're proud of you."

"Yeah, thanks, Mom. Well, that's the kind of work... that's what I want to do. Be a *partera,* a midwife in Guatemala."

"Well... that could happen."

"Yeah, so, let's see. Right? Oh, and something else I really, really wanted to tell you. I almost forgot. Really important. I met Grampa Mateo and Aunt Ana. She would be your half-sister, Mom. They are so cool. Isn't that great? You'd love to meet them. Both of you. Like when you come back, Gramma. Right?"

There was a long silence.

"Well, don't all shout at once. Uhm. So, okay bye. Love you guys."

Chapter Thirteen; Harry

Back in Pana, I had time to let Mateo's words sink in. He got me thinking. Had Cobi left me too? I bounced along in the back of a *tuk-tuk* to the nature preserve above town, then climbed and hiked, crossed the suspension bridge and climbed some more to work out feelings. When I was finally winded and sweating, I collapsed on the edge of a fragrant herb garden, sucking in the spicy smells while my breathing slowed and I allowed myself to vent. Well, damn. Had I been, what my high school kids would say, *dumped?* I finally decided to *give love a chance,* and now look. What the hell. Am I just some throwback-flower-child's fling with a *brother?* Hey, Cobi came down here, back in the day, didn't she? Why was that? Was she trying to prove she wasn't some class-conscious, racist magnolia blossom? Then she went and hooked up with a local *noble savage* and got knocked up. Weren't there enough *natives* to *go native with* back home... up north or down south or wherever the hell it is from here. Damn.

I picked up some pebbles, tossed them into the little pond, scattering the panicked goldfish. The sky is falling for you guys too, huh? I brooded. As they calmed and regrouped, so did I. Okay, I said to myself. I'm stuck in a backwater town, in the middle of nowhere, running a motel. But I'm not like some scruffy drunk at an isolated outpost on the Zambezi River, too lazy to move on. I can keep going. I could take off or I could settle down here. I got my teacher pension and social security and the rent from my D.C. apartment. I could go back to Washington or Lansing. Blah. So. What next? I've basically lived alone all my life. Getting here, to this place, has been fun. I know a little Spanish now, maybe I could keep going to Honduras, Nicaragua, Panama. Meantime, here's me, playing the classic drifter used to trotting into a woman's life then heading off to parts unknown. Except in this movie the lady leaves *me* behind. Damn.

Well, I said I would watch Bryn. Yeah, I'll be responsible for her till the end of August. It's nothing new for me. Been herding teens all my life. I'll decide on my next move after she goes home.

One morning, early July, restless in the quiet after the breakfast rush, I grabbed a ball and went to the volleyball court. Antonio was there with four of his buddies. They waved, remembering me. Two of them were doodling soccer moves, bouncing a ball from knee to head, flicking it over the shoulder, kicking it from behind—hackey-sack, show-off moves. Antonio set a ball to me. I slapped it back. He bumped. The other guys paired off. Soon we had a serious bump-set-strike drill going. When I stopped to correct one guy's technique, they all paused to watch and then practiced what I had shown. They were hurting for training, coaching, and I was glad to be doing something I enjoyed more than running a hotel. The next day I had two full squads working out.

Later that week, Bryn had me driving her for a quick visit to Mateo and Ana Sofia. Over beers on the porch, I told Mateo about my volleyball team. Turns out, he played a little as a young man and got pretty excited, suggested we join a league. Before I knew it, Bryn joined the discussion and Mateo was coming to stay with us in order to check out the team, which soon meant he was assistant coach and permanent live-in guest in room 4. I mean, why not?

Three afternoons a week, we guys ran the *Panajachel Panteras* through their drills. Me and Teo, that's what the squad called him. We made a good team. Between his Mayan dialect and Spanish slang from years on the job, he related to our guys in ways I never could. So, we played good cop/ bad cop. I would show technique and diagram strategy and Teo would do the pre-game hype and breaktime pump-em-up while singling out any slackers or fumblers.

One evening after practice, I trailed behind Mateo and Bryn as we walked home. Their body language was so telling—she leaning toward him, half turning to make eye contact when making a point; he half-shrugging in partial agreement, then reaching to touch her arm for his rejoinder. It was beautiful to see. Made me wish I had a child...

a grandchild to relate to. It struck me that I was like a hitch-hiker squeezing into this family's van... allowed along for a short ride. As they turned at the gate to our place, Bryn looked back to check on me. She smiled.

I guess I fit into this confused, extended family somehow. At least as far as Bryn was concerned I was uncle, coach, family friend... who knows what. But I couldn't help seeing her at that moment as an immigrant with a family and tradition, safety and acceptance, in two worlds. Maybe I could be the outsider support she needed as she chose one... or a blend of both families. Made for a good reason to stick around in my familiar role as Harry the counselor.

And so it went into late July. I was still troubled by Cobi's more than geographical distance. Was I just a combination manager for her B&B and camp counselor for her granddaughter? When my questions reached a peak, I called her.

"Hi, Cobi."

"Harry, is something wrong?"

"Does there have to be something wrong for us to talk?"

"Uh, no. It's nice to hear from you. How are things going down there?"

"Fine. Teo and I got the volleyball team beating everyone around the lake. Bryn fits right in doing the warm-ups with the guys. She's like mascot, cheerleader and trainer all wrapped up in one."

"Keep an eye on that girl. Don't let her get too interested in any one guy."

"Yes, ma'am. She's keeping busy making *pupusas* to sell from the souvenir stand."

"Making what? I never heard of those."

"They're a Salvadoran version of an *empanada*... pastie... calzone."

"Got it."

"She says she's saving for college."

"Oh, Harry, speaking of that, be sure to tell her... she got accepted at New Mexico. The letter came just this morning. She was so excited about their medical program."

"That's in Albuquerque, right?"

"Uh-huh. I'm looking forward to driving her there when she comes home next month."

"So... I gather you're not planning to come down here anytime soon."

"Uhm, no."

"I see."

"Anything else exciting going on?"

"Tomorrow Mateo is taking me and Bryn to a Mayan ritual site..."

"Ah, the *cueva sagrada* in San Jorge. Be careful it's pretty tricky making your way down to the cave... oh, there's a customer looking for me. I gotta run. Thanks for the call, Harry. Bye."

As I hung up, I thought... no juice, just polite business noise. Is Mateo right? Has she run away from me too?

The next morning, I was in a funk as the chicken bus rocked us through the curve looking down the rounded slopes to Panajachel and Lake Atitlan. Mateo, with a coil of rope over his shoulder, leaned against me as we swung through the bottom of the S curve. I wondered why we would need a rope. Bryn, on the far side of him grinned like a kid on a class trip to an historic site. Come to think of it, it sort of was that—a visit to her particular ancestral history.

Mateo tapped the driver on the shoulder and we lurched to a stop on a patch of gravel six feet from a sheer drop down to the lake. Easing along the stony path, our toes stubbed the insides of our hiking boots on the sharp descent into the hamlet of San Jorge.

Halfway down, an imp sprang from behind a pile of rubble. The boy looked Indian; short, not much taller than an average four-year old but to judge from his patter with Mateo must have been at least six or seven. *Jesus* was the scamp's name. He became a dangerous distraction, like a dog underfoot, as we inched down the rugged path across the face of the 45 degree slope. He scooted in front of Bryn, jostling her, before turning to offer his tiny hand as if he could offer any support should she stumble. Ten minutes of hop, slide, grab and lunge along a trail littered with the remains of sacrificial chickens brought us to a black gaping mouth of a cave and the fug of damp cavern mixed with wet ashes from burnt offerings. The ceiling, the walls, the floor were layered with the soot of generations of smoky sacrifices to the many gods, the *dioses,* of generation upon generation of highland Guatemalans. The floor of the cave had half a dozen randomly scattered stone pads—altars, I guess. On top of each a blanket of long green pine needles surrounded either a smoldering heap of a chicken carcass or a mound of grain or flower petals. Candles stood vigil next to carefully placed red apples—sacrifices, imprecations to the gods to ward off sickness and pain, to ensure good crops, healthy animals or many children.

I bumped my head against the low-slung ceiling. A touch to reset the hat turned my fingertips an oily black. As I tried to decide if I wanted to ruin a fresh laundered handkerchief to clean them, I sensed someone staring at me. I glanced back to see *Jesus* at eye level, standing on a rock. Mocking my distress over soiled fingers, he jabbed the ceiling, then drew a black strip straight down his forehead, between his eyes, to the tip of his nose. He grinned, then took a bite from an apple he apparently liberated from a sacrificial altar.

I didn't know why, but for some reason I suddenly wanted to apologize to the gods for this blasphemy. He's only a kid. Probably stunted from malnutrition. Hungry. He needs the food more than you do. And help me to get whole. Help me to either forget Cobi or figure out what's bothering her so we can get on together.

Where had that come from I wondered as I staggered away from the fetid smoke-filled air to the cave mouth and fresh breezes. I'm not religious, not even superstitious. No church. No religion. What was that all about?

Mateo took Bryn's hand to help her scale a rocky patch. We breached a rise to find *Jesus* kicking a half-inflated soccer ball with two other kids in a space the size of a bathroom that falls off hundreds of feet on both sides. As we neared, he beckoned, like a wood sprite, to follow him past a row of head-high boulders. When we caught up to him, he pointed to a hollow below.

A man faced a small smoldering fire, chanting, sprinkling water around the ashes causing tarry smoke to add a fresh coat to the blackened boulder behind it. Another man stood with his palms touching in the universal gesture for prayer. This was a purchased supplication or *oracion,* Mateo explained. The client talked to the shaman some time ago. Told him his troubles, problems, concerns and wishes. The shaman wrote them down on scraps of paper.

They drove three hours to reach this sacred site where the priest placed the bits of paper in a small clay pot in the middle of the smoking fire. After circling and chanting several more times, the shaman retrieved a red packet with a string hanging out. Mateo made eye contact with us and placed his hands over his ears. The shaman lit the string. The pot exploded with a stunning BANG! A cloud of confetti fluttered to the ground while the acrid tang of gun powder rose in a lazy cloud.

Something let go inside me. Whatever's going on with Cobi... with us... will either work its way out or it won't. I just had to be patient... at peace.

A child wailed to sounds of tumbling and crashing. Then silence.

"*Jesus.* He falls," Mateo cried, handing me one end of his rope as he skidded down the steep slope. I lost sight of him but could hear him talking to the boy. Then a giggle and *Jesus* came scrambling up the slope, two scratches on his cheek, soccer ball in hand. The scamp grinned at us and kept going.

It took both Bryn and me to haul Mateo up the slope. The rope snagged on bushes and we had to wait while he untangled and realigned himself before retying under his arms. When he finally got to us, his upper back and chest were chafed and raw from the rope. He sat, head between his knees breathing hard for a few minutes muttering words neither of us recognized but could assume were directed toward *Jesus* and his antics. I retrieved the rope and coiled it. Bryn offered her grandfather some water. After a bit, he slapped his knees and began to rise only to shout in pain and fall back down grabbing the small of his back.

What to do? There was no place to stretch out. It was all steep sided slopes, rocks and random footholds. Bryn and I tried to get him upright and walking but he screamed in pain. With no EMTs or park rangers to call, we finally resorted to helping Mateo crawl on all fours to the road 100 feet above. A woman came out of her house, laid out a mat and helped gently roll Mateo onto his back. I left Bryn with him and went to the highway to catch any ride I could.

Chapter Fourteen; Maya

As soon as I got off the phone with Bryn, I went to find Cobi on the porch.

"Ma, we got a problem. Mateo threw his back out, and is recovering at our place in Pana," I explained. She paused, tea cup in mid-air, then slowly set it down. "Bryn and Harry and Ana, when she can make it over, are looking after him. They got a chiropractor coming every day but Mateo is still in bad shape."

"Okaay..." she drawled, waiting for the rest.

"They gotta be stressed, between the customers and taking care of him. I'm thinking I should go down."

"Really? And what about up here. You'll be leaving me alone to run this place."

"Well, we can get Josh. Offer him more hours."

Cobi circled her tea cup in its saucer. She knew me well despite our living apart for so many years. She also knew I couldn't tolerate silence for very long. "Look," I finally said, "okay, I admit I wanted to know all about my father at first. Then I didn't. Now I do again. It's Bryn's fault. First, she hunts him up. Now she can't stop talking about him. I guess I would like to meet him, get to find out what he's like. What I missed." More silence from Cobi. "And besides, I could give a hand caring for him." Cobi looked at me, askance. "And I can get a chance to check out this *Harry* guy that is so important to my daughter and you."

"Do what you want," Cobi said, chin high, "you always do."

Two days later, above the clouds, I let my mind wander. Munching on my complimentary airline pretzels, I tried to picture the scene waiting for me. Harry would be there. I know what he looks like from Bryn and him in the shark picture. Cobi liked him enough to let him move in with her...

259

after all these years living alone, if you could call running a B&B living alone. So I guess he's okay. Bryn sure likes him.

Ana will be there, I presume. Ana Sofia... my half-sister. She sounds level headed and teaches English. That would be good; I don't know what my Spanish will be like after all these years. Will it feel good to meet her, to find I have a sib, the sister I never had?

And what about my father? Bryn couldn't shut up about him, telling us, "Mateo this," and "Mateo that," every time she called. I mean, what do you say to a man you've never met, who gave you half your genes? Let's think about it. What's the worst thing that could happen? He could take one look at me, wrinkle his nose and walk away. Well, I don't think he would shoot me or anything, but okay, rejection... maybe. Or he could just be, *Oh, you're my daughter. Okay, if you say so* and then walk away. Indifference. That I could take. Or he could drown me in tears... his long-lost daughter. I could stand that, I guess, but me, I'm not going all gooey over him. What I really couldn't stand would be him deciding I owed him my life story, telling him all the things I've done, all the things he missed while I was growing up. Nope. I don't do backstory. Like the way Cobi complains that I'm a messy cook—never putting things back, tidying as I go. I just charge ahead, full speed. That's how I do it. What's the good of chewing on grudges, replaying what happened, what could have been different? It's what's ahead, what's coming, that counts. And then watch, he'll want me to stay, like for the rest of the summer, so he can get to know me. No way. I'm the visiting nurse—in and out and *nice meeting you.* I'm totally over Panajachel.

As we taxi to the terminal, a wave of feelings comes over me. It's been thirty years since I was last here, excited to be leaving, glad to get away. And there will be all new people, strangers. I don't need them in my life. Don't want to go through all the hugs and kisses. I see enough people, a constant stream of new people in my business. Don't need more.

Chapter Fifteen; Harry

Bryn was excited, edgy, overpoured a cup of coffee for a guest. Maya was due in that afternoon, and we were going to pick her up at the airport right after the morning rush. Poking at my eggs, I wondered what Maya would look like as a late forties woman? Would she be short and fair like Cobi or tawny like Mateo? And remembering what Cobi had told me about Maya's impatience to leave Guatemala as soon as she could, would Panajachel and the language and the lake and markets evoke warm feelings of nostalgia and longing for her childhood, or the exact opposite? And would she connect with her sister? And what about her father? Mateo had never talked about Maya, how he felt about her. I wondered what my role was going to be, how it was all going to go down.

Chapter Sixteen; Cobi

I kept expecting a call from Maya that evening to hear how things had gone. Instead I got a quick email two days later.

Hi, Mom,

I'm not sure what I expected, or what I was afraid of, but Mateo is very cool. He's got these tough, hard hands and when I went to his bedside, he held my hand, looked at me with those big soft eyes and said, *"m'hija."* And it felt so good, you know, to have him call me his daughter. And then he told me that I did a good job raising Bryn. That she is a good girl. And the rest was easy... has been easy. Ana feels like the sister I would have liked to have all along. It's one big happy family. Wish you were here.

Oh, and do you remember Raul Jimenez that I was crazy about before I came north? Well, turns out his son Antonio is Bryn's Spanish teacher. And Carlos, Raul's brother, is the chiropractor who comes every day to work on dad. Let's just say, he's Raul, only better and more mature and separated at the moment. I might be staying here longer than I first figured.

One more thing, you know those *calzone* I make? Well, we added them to the menu for the *pupusa* stand. They're taking off. Bryn's summer-money project may be the beginning of a whole other business. Ana's even talking about quitting teaching and working at it full-time.

We'll get Bryn back to you in two weeks. Got her tickets: United 636 arr: 4:45, 4/18. I hope Josh can handle business while you settle her at school.

Thanks, Mom.

Maya

Chapter Seventeen; Mateo

One night after Bryn went back to her home to be with Cobi, Harry was driving me from volleyball practice. It's not so far to walk. But I can't walk good yet. I'm getting better. Carlos has really helped and I think he comes to see Maya as much as me. Anyway, I can tell that Harry is not very happy. When we stopped inside our gate, I said, "*Amigo,* you are sad."

He said, "Huh? Oh. Is it that obvious?"

I shrugged. I wondered if he missed Bryn. But no. Or maybe, with Maya running the *posada,* he felt useless. Maybe. But then I thought of Cobi. It was none of my business—him and her. Still, I wanted to tell him some things. "Harry," I said, "I think, you think about Cobi, *verdad?*" He made a face that said yes. So, I kept going. "I think many things. Long ago. When she go away." Harry just looked at the steering wheel. He didn't say anything. Then he shook his head and sighed. Maybe he worries how I feel. "*Amigo,* she is yours. Don't think about me. I forget her. I don't think about what happen so long ago. Me, I have three beautiful women take care of me. What more I want? *Hombre,* she is good. Go to her."

"Why should I chase her, if she doesn't know a good thing when she sees it?"

"*Bue,* I would have. I did not know where she go. You know where. Go to her, *amigo.*"

"Yeah, right."

Chapter Eighteen; Harry and Cobi

One night, a week later, I got a call from Cobi.

"Hi, Harry." There was a weighted pause. Then, "I miss you."

I'm tempted to quote Rhett Butler and say, *Frankly my dear, I don't give a damn.*

"Fair enough. I haven't... lately... Look, I've been doing a lot of thinking and stuff."

"Uh-huh. So have I."

"Let me explain, okay? I took Bryn to Albuquerque, right? And while she was in orientation, I drove up to Las Vegas... New Mexico, not Nevada. It's a cute, quiet town. I don't know how to say it without sounding... I don't know. There were a lot of Latinos there and jeans and cowboy hats and boots and... fewer Anglos..."

"... and that got you thinking about me. Is that it? That someone like me would feel more comfortable there. Wouldn't stand out so much. Less fear of harassment."

"Uhm... C'mon, Harry," she pleaded. I let up for a moment, gave her room to start over. "Anyhow, there was a real estate office with pictures of properties. And... to make a long story short. I bought this log cabin on a mountain. And it's so great! There are elk running through the five acres of pine trees and when I met the owners they were eating pancakes on the porch and hummingbirds kept dive bombing them. They smelled the syrup. Like nectar, I guess. And it is so quiet. No traffic. No noise. Just the wind and clean air."

What could I say? "Uh-huh. Sounds like you like it... there." Another long pause. We both felt it, like before you decide to dive off the high board.

"Harry. I want to share it with you. I miss you. I want you with me."

"I came to you once. Before. And you left me..."

Her voice was soft, soothing. "I'm sorry... it's my family..." In the ensuing pause, I could picture her tugging finger and thumb from the corners of her mouth. "Harry, I figured some things out," she began. A deep breath, then, "I love you."

Wow. That was strong. Still. "That's terrific. Nice to hear. But I've been a counselor too long to know when there is something... unsaid, that needs to be said. You're sitting on something, Cobi, and it needs to come out before I..."

"C'mon, okay? I'm trying to..." She hesitated, then with a puff of resolve, continued, "You know about me and Mateo... right?

"Of course. And he and I talked. He's not looking for some come-to-Jesus reconciliation moment. He's past all that. And he's happy to welcome Maya and Bryn into his life, no questions asked. I sense there's more you're not telling me." I made myself wait, like I waited for my students to spill, to name the Rumpelstiltskin in their lives.

In a soft, sibilant whisper Cobi finally spoke. "He was a guy in our Peace Corps program, from Indiana. Muncie, for chris' sake. It was after a going-home-party for him. We all got drunk and me and him... And he was blond and blue-eyed and I couldn't be sure if it was Mateo's or his. And what could I do Harry? If I told Mateo I was pregnant he would have wanted to do the honorable thing. And even if I wanted to be a Mayan *mamacita,* what if the baby had blue eyes? How would that sit with Mateo? And I for damn sure didn't want to live in Indiana in a Mennonite community with a permanently tanned, brown-eyed baby. And I couldn't go to Charleston to my uptight parents with a *piñata* belly and no wedding ring. I was going to be beat up no matter which way I turned. And when I finally saw that it was Mateo's child... how could I go back? I was just a kid. I didn't know what to do."

I could hear her breathing hard. A sob. I wanted to reach out and hug her. Instead I waited a count before I spoke. "What's your address?"

I heard a deep sigh.

Two weeks later, I made my way to Cobi's Las Vegas. She had described it as *cute and quiet.* Yeah, it was a cute little town, but not quiet. At the moment they were having some kind of fiesta in the plaza. Young women in parrot-colored Mexican dresses whirled to mariachi music. In between performances, a politician, I guessed, in jeans, cowboy hat and sport coat gave a speech in Spanish and English. Familiar smells from taco stands took me back to Pana. Hot dog and French fries felt like home. Interesting blend. I could see why Cobi felt comfortable here. I grabbed a taco and got back on the road.

I drove for what seemed a long time. Maybe half an hour. Cobi was really a ways out of town. I had to follow her directions carefully. Turn at the next left after the row of mailboxes. Drive through the creek. Low at this time of year. Pass the Turner place. A pinto and a bay mare in the corral.

I was climbing. The air thinning. The road steep and rocky... seriously rocky and full of ruts. I could have been in the Atitlan highlands. Then I crested the hill to a view of a log cabin snuggled within a circle of trees. I stopped in the middle of the road. Stepped out of the car into the vacuum of silence. It took a moment to feel the gentle breeze, to pick up the pine fragrance it brought. Then a loud bark and a blur of Australian Shepherd charging.

"Mandy! Stay!" I heard Cobi shout. Then she appeared on the porch, hunched to study me at the end of her drive. She straightened, and with a pleased, almost self-satisfied smile, opened her arms and slowly swung in a half circle to welcome me to herself and her kingdom—my princess in a wooden castle.

Vito's Tale

by

Joe Novara

Gypsy Shadow Publishing

Vito's Tale

by

Joe Novara

Gypsy Shadow Publishing, LLC.
Lockhart, TX
www.gypsyshadow.com

ISBN: 978-1-61950-618-0

Published in the United States of America

First eBook Edition: April 6, 2021

Chapter One; 1914, Tyrol

Hunkered under the artillery barrage bracketing no-man's land, Vito didn't hear the shell before it hit. The one that lifted his barrel-shaped body up, out of the trench and under an avalanche of cold wet soil. Before he had a chance to worry about suffocation, to determine which way led to air and release, another shell hurled him out of his temporary grave. He lay still, fifteen yards from what had been the frontline a few moments before. Stunned, unfeeling, was this the blessed moment of anesthesia before the pain of an injury registers? He tentatively wiggled arms, then legs, toes, neck. All good, thank God. He could see open mouths but couldn't hear screams, just yet, but he could feel the juddering shocks of artillery launched and landed. His body absorbed the penetrating jolts, but he was alive, still. He sobbed, lowered his head on wet, cold mud and cried.

How had he gotten to this place? Five months ago, he was in Sicily, pruning and tying grape vines in the glaring hot sun. He had a pregnant wife, two teenage daughters, a five-year old son. Life was hard with barely enough to eat. And now, in the Austrian Alps, he was still hungry, cold instead of warm, and people were trying to kill him. More tears.

When the draft notice came, he had no delusions. No high-flown thoughts of patriotism and glory. Not when he was thirty-seven with family responsibilities. He needed to make it out of here in one piece. His tears turned to cold anger and a fist slammed into the yielding earth. He needed to get away from the front line. A man groaned near him. Surprised and relieved that he could hear again, he spotted a soldier lying on his back, a red patch staining his ribs. *"Aiuta! Aiuta me!"* the man cried. He scuttled over, careful to keep his head below the ceiling of bullets whistling overhead. He grabbed the man's ankles and dragged him into a shell crater, its back edge sloping into a drop off. Once below ground level, Vito rolled the man onto his shoulder and hunched toward the hospital in the rear.

He didn't feel particularly noble when he handed off his burden for triage in the long line of stretchers. It was expected—what you did for each other. *"Morto,"* the medic said, after a quick check for pulse. *Well, I tried,* he thought, then looked around at the mayhem of a field hospital in the middle of an offensive. *Not all bad,* he thought. *At least I'm away from the worst of it. "E tu?"* the medic said, pointing to the blood on Vito's tunic—was he wounded? Vito shook his head and pointed to the dead soldier—his blood, then he bit his lip. Think fast, he told himself. Find some reason to stay longer, away from the front. *"Aqua!"* he called after the departing medic who jerked his head toward the large tent lined with bandaged men in cots.

Vito slowly made his way between rows of wounded. He had seen enough dead men to recognize one when he saw one... and the uneaten biscuit on his tray. He lifted three more biscuits on his leisurely stroll to the water bucket next to an empty cot in the back. After practically inhaling three ladles full of cool water, a wave of exhaustion toppled him onto the bed.

Sometime later he felt hands unbuttoning his bloody shirt. *"Niente,"* a medic snarled before shouting for the military police. It was time to leave. On his way out of the tent, Vito stopped, arrested by the almost forgotten aroma of boiling broth drifting under all the other smells of the bed-ridden, unwashed, wounded. He vowed he would return soon to this place of dry, warm sleep and hot food—injured or not.

It took a while to get back. Despite short rations and lack of cold-weather gear in the mountains, Vito's sturdy constitution wouldn't allow him to get sick. So, he tried to make himself ill by drinking boiled tobacco. No luck. Finally, one day he got a fever and was sent behind the lines. After a night's sleep in a warm bed and a couple of hot meals, he was good to go. Ever resourceful, when the nurse popped a thermometer in his mouth, he would wait till he turned his back and put his pipe in his armpit for a bit, then slide the thermometer there and watch the mercury rise to just above normal. So close, that checking by hand the nurse couldn't detect the difference. That worked for a couple more day's leave and offered a chance for reflection away from his moment-to-moment, live-or-die existence.

As he lay on his cot surrounded by soldiers from all over the country, he could hear different dialects. Strange. They were all Italians, wearing Italian military uniforms but some of the regional dialects were completely incomprehensible. If the doctors and nurses spoke in schoolbook Italian, they would generally be understood. But among themselves, around campfires, the soldiers might as well be speaking Swahili as far as Vito was concerned. In one way, it was interesting to find out that the only way he knew to speak Italian wasn't the only way. He found that guys from the south—Naples and Calabria and Sicily could make themselves understood. But folks from Venice or Bergamo or Tuscany, impossible. The crack Alpine corps had their own songs and stories and style. People from up north ate polenta and pesto and cheeses that he had never tasted before. The houses were different in the mountains. Springtime was dramatic and so very welcome after four months of ice and snow. And surprisingly to him, he enjoyed the differences in food and climate and language, not to mention his newfound ability to adapt to change, such as life in the army. If only he could use his wits to survive, *home* would never feel the same.

Chapter Two; 1914, Paceco, Sicily

Margherita sat at the kitchen table, her cup of ersatz coffee cooling to tepid. Chicory weeds. They were reduced to drinking boiled weeds. She pushed on the corner of the crude, scarred table with one short leg. Rock, rock. Her two teenage daughters were arguing in the bedroom they shared with their brother. The baby, Franco, slept with her. Lots of room in her bed now that Vito had marched off to play soldier somewhere, who knew where. No letters. Just her imagination to wonder and worry how he was... if he was... still. She had to tell him by letter that he had a second son. And then her milk dried up. Too much worry. Not enough to eat. Vito hadn't earned much as vineyard help, but if they were careful they could just squeak by. But then he got her pregnant, again, and left for the war. So now, she had to rely on food from her father, grow what she could, and pass her son around to other nursing mothers. And the only free food in abundance were prickly pears that got her constipated and cursing as she squatted in the bushes out back.

Yesterday, she sat at the kitchen table and cried for the longest time. She went to crack the one egg she found in the hen house and it was empty. Examining the shell, she found a tiny hole on one end. Rocco must have done it. He made the hole so he could suck out the egg. She almost laughed before she started crying. If he had just taken the egg, she wouldn't have known any better. But he thought he was being clever. She wanted to strangle him for being so stupid. Then she wanted to hug him because she, Vito, the war, this poor, sad place, all of it had gotten a kid so hungry he had to steal from his own mother. She cried all day.

Now, wondering what they would have for supper, she stood in the doorway peering past the sleepy village to the *saline* where windmills sucked ocean water into shallow ponds to evaporate into mountains of salt. Her youngest brother, Marco, worked there and came by her house on the way home from work every day. She spotted him and waved. *O dio,* what a handsome guy, she thought. My Vito was good looking too. But different. Craggy and thick like a big rock in a stream. Solid. While Marco was more tall and skinny, just a kid yet. He reached into a bag, pulled out a zucchini and waved it back and forth. She had to grin. Marco had that effect on her.

Zucchini. Reminded her of harvest time, the year she turned eighteen. That special, first time, she met Vito. They didn't have dances in those days, certainly no dating. The only time girls and guys could even see each other was at church or the market. But Vito, like all his *compare,* worked in the vineyards on market days and seldom went to church. So, when the call went out to all the surrounding villages, young people eagerly gathered to see and be seen while gently fondling bunches of sun-warmed muscatel and zinfandel before freeing them from sagging vines.

What an eye-treat for a young woman—strapping, bare-chested young men heaving loaded baskets to bronze shoulders. And there was Vito with his barrel chest and quiet black eyes snagging hers through the long sun-drenched days and all through the meals they shared at a long plank table. Seems the owners would boil up a huge pot of pasta and a heap of sautéed zucchini and mix it all together with olive oil and garlic. And everyone was so hungry and excited to be together they thought it was delicious and even kind of fun to eat out of bowls carved right into the table top. So, grapes and harvest and good times... so far away right now.

At least she had a zucchini in hand that she could fry up and mix with a handful of pasta. Vito loved his *pasta con zucchini.* Whenever she made that stupid meal, he would get that look on his face, the look he gave her at the first harvest, and she would know what to expect in bed that night. She was never crazy about that food, especially now. It was Vito who made it special.

Marco brushed through the door and over to the water pitcher. The THUNK of bag-on-table told her it was bread, day-old bread. Her mother never let her family eat baking right out of the oven. It smelled and tasted too good, tempting them to eat more than they absolutely needed while day-old met needs not wants. Margherita cuddled the half loaf while she told her brother about the hollow egg incident. He laughed like crazy. She finally did too.

They got to talking about their brother, Nino, who had gone to America to avoid the draft. She wished her Vito had done that. *He might yet... go to the States. After he comes home... knock on wood.* Then she'd be alone again until he saved enough money to bring them all over. *Madonna,* she prayed, can't we ever be a happy family together?

Chapter Three; 1916, Detroit

Antonino Maisano was among the many Sicilian men who sought their fortune in the Motor City in the early 1900s. There were not so many Sicilian women, however. And the few that were there, were in high demand. No American women could speak the language and cook the comfort food that those homesick men longed for. It was hard enough getting along in a strange country, with an unknown language, tough jobs and constant scorn from non-Italians. A man would want to come home to a bit of home away from home.

With marriageable Sicilian women in short supply, the fathers of these rare commodities were very protective of their treasures. Once a couple had secretly winked at each other a few times over the olive barrels in the local grocery, the boyfriend would tell the girl's father they had an *understanding*. And he and the girl would have to anxiously await permission to court.

And that's where Nino was, having caught the eye of a sweet girl from Erice, the next village up the mountain from his home town. He never knew her, or any of her thirteen brothers and sisters, in the old country. Eight miles on a donkey-cart road might as well have been a continent away. But once they saw each other in the Eastside of Detroit, they bonded like next-door sweethearts. Unfortunately, right after Nino and Eva made their intentions known, a *connected* guy from the old country put in his hand as well. Eva's father didn't like the *mafioso*. But he knew, and Nino knew, what could happen when a request to court a daughter was turned down. A rejected suitor might kidnap the woman, spend the night with her, and once irretrievably dishonored and unsuitable for anyone else, offer to save the day by marrying her.

Actually, Nino and Eva had first-hand experience of this practice. Eva and her sisters Pina and Caterina were walking to the grocery store alongside a railroad track. Just as they got to a crossing, a model T pulled up in front of them. Two guys jumped out and grabbed Caterina who screamed and wailed, arms flailing, as they raced across a railroad track just ahead of the deafening whoosh of a speeding train and its blaring steam whistle. The next day, Caterina was married in a civil ceremony and Eva had to see a doctor for an outbreak of eczema caused by the traumatic drama. The Rizzo sisters spent many long evenings comparing notes about their father's hesitation over the match, Caterina's moon-struck infatuation, her over-the-top performance in the abduction scene and possible complicity in the plot. They begrudgingly wished her well in her new life.

Wanting none of that, Nino wrote home asking his brother, Marco, to appeal to the *capo* in Trapani to call off his Detroit *soldier*. Nino knew the guy from the streets back home, knew he and Eva would want nothing to do with the hood. Nino could only hope that a fervent personal appeal would remind the *boss* that he had asked first and was a non-combatant in the mob structure.

Marco slammed his knuckles and his brother's letter on Margherita's table. *"Putanna diavolo,"* he swore. His older brother, Nino, always was a pain-in-the-ass, guy. Making a mess and leaving him and his sister to get him out of it. Older brothers were supposed to take care of things. But, no, not Nino. He bolted to America to avoid the draft. So, with no Nino around and his sister's husband up at the front and his dad ailing, he was in charge of keeping things going. And in case it wasn't hard enough to keep food on the table and look after the parents, now Nino wanted help with the *cosa nostra*. Margherita patted his hand while he fumed.

Marco knew all the local *mafiosi*. How could he not? Knew their families. Knew not to know too much. There was a strict line drawn. Yes or no. Belong or not. If you wanted to play it straight, no problem. Just look the other way and mind your own business. Still, it was hard not to crisscross once in a while over one thing or another. Like Nino did on the other side of the ocean.

While Marco fretted over the next few days, another letter arrived. This one came from Eva's oldest brother, Gennaro, himself a lieutenant in the Detroit *family.* There were two pages. The first was addressed to Marco telling him how to reach the *capo.* The second was to be presented to the Don himself. Under all the flowery, obsequious language, Gennaro's message was simple: *my sister is a nice kid, she's interested in a nice guy, Nino Maisano. You might know the family from Paceco. Our guy came a little late to the party after Nino already asked the father. Could you please ask him to back off?*

Marco didn't need a road map to find the local Don. He knew where he had coffee every morning. 'Nardo Batucci held court outside the only café in Piazza Garibaldi from 9 to 11 every day. Marco hung back in the doorway of a hardware store, cursing his brother one more time for putting him in this position. It never paid to draw attention to yourself when it came to the *black hand.* And worse yet, to be one-down—asking a favor and owing a favor in return. Muttering under his breath, he took his cap in hand and approached Batucci as he folded the morning paper.

'Nardo raised his chin—yeah, what do you want?

"Kind sir," Marco began. "I believe you know a certain, Gennaro Rizzo."

"What if I do?"

"He asked me to present this letter to you."

'Nardo rocked back in the chair, eyed Marco for a half minute. Marco stood his ground, unflinching, eyes respectfully down. *Damn Nino for making me go through this,* he fumed.

"Read it to me," 'Nardo demanded.

Nothing for it but to see it through, Marco decided. He carefully unfolded the letter, trembling from the surge of resentment at being made to simper and beg. That, plus a sense that a little show of spirit would be respected made him pull back a chair at the table. "May I?"

'Nardo responded with a cold stare. Marco stayed on his feet, resisting the urge to shrug—*no big deal, just asking*—before reading the letter. When he finished, the *capo* held out his hand. Marco very deliberately folded the letter and carefully put it back in the envelope before dropping it in the outstretched hand. After 'Nardo gave a dismissive wave, Marco put on his hat and briskly walked across the square keeping time with his racing heart rate. Replaying the scene, he decided, *I showed just the right amount of respect but I didn't grovel. And Nino, you owe me brother. If this war doesn't end soon, I'll be called up for the draft for sure. I'm counting on you to sponsor me, get me a job so I can come over there too.*

Chapter Four; 1918, Paceco, Sicily

The First World War finally came to an end. Vito and his buddy, Aldo Spezia, could feel the Mediterranean sun thawing their blood as the transport ship chugged down the Adriatic to Palermo. They used the time to decompress and ease back into the pace of simpler, slower, safer living. Aldo spoke of an invite from his cousin in New York to come live there and work in the thriving construction trades. The idea didn't register at first, as Vito anticipated the more immediate joy of seeing his wife and kids after a four-year absence.

A month later, after all the welcome home parties and luxurious sleep-ins disturbed by children's footsteps instead of reveille, Vito was back on the job in a local vineyard. He inched down a row between the vines. Lift. Tie. Cut the twine. He wondered why he felt restless. Out of sorts. He wasn't living in constant fear of being shot or bombed or, more commonly, dying from dysentery. He slept with his wife between clean sheets. Hugged his two girls and two sons. The little one, Franco, didn't even know him and resented his taking over the spot next to *mamma* in the bed.

Lift. Tie. Cut. He used to enjoy giving himself over to the rhythm of the work. Now it just seemed tedious after living in watchful tension for years. Bored, he listened this time when Aldo came by for wine one evening and repeated the invitation from his cousin in Brooklyn. If they went to New York, the cousin would set them up in a boarding house with other Italians and get him a job with his crew building tenements. They needed all the workers they could get. And they made a lot of money. Maybe he could go with Aldo, make a bundle and come back. Buy his own farm. Become a *padrone* and hire guys like himself. He had been away for four years already. What was a couple more doing basically the same thing he had been doing? Boarding house… barracks. Digging trenches… digging foundations.

Living away from home. He just had to convince Margherita, then take a deep breath and make it happen. It was a chance to do better than subsist in dirt-poor Paceco. He had to try something and being in the Army had shown him he could handle challenging and new.

At four and a half, Franco was intimidated by the man who filled up their tiny house, sucked up all the attention of his mother and sisters, gave him a swat on the butt for crying one time. And it made him nervous when his parents were in what used to be his bedroom and he could hear them talking. Not the words so much as the feelings. Not nice smooth talking—a deep man's voice and a sweet, mother's voice one at a time. This was different. His mother's voice seemed frightened, like she was begging, asking not to do something. His father sounded two ways. One was soft and low and slow. Like he was trying to be nice to his mother. But sometimes he would get loud and strong like a hand slapping a table hard. He just snuggled closer with his brother Rocco. But his sisters, Concetta and Angela, snuck out of the bedroom and listened right next to the parents' door. When the bed started to squeak, the sisters came back into the kid's room and began to talk.

Angela told me and Rocco, "Daddy thinks it best to go to America to make a lot of money and see what it's like over there. He might have to stay for two years or so. Then we'll decide if we should all move there."

Older sister, Concetta, said, "I don't want to go anywhere. I like it here. And besides, I like Luca and he likes me... and... and."

Then Angela said, "He wants to go to Brookolini with Aldo." Franco tried to imagine a place covered with tiny broccoli crowns. And he didn't even like broccoli. Who would want to go there? It was all very confusing and sad. The only good thing would be getting his place back in bed with *mamma*. Before they all nodded off, Angela said, "I think the idea of going to America is fun and exciting."

"Me too," Rocco chimed in. But Franco just wanted to be together with everyone, no matter where they were.

Chapter Five; 1919, Brooklyn

Crossing the ocean was no worse for Vito than riding troop trains and naval troop carriers—hurry up and wait, boring, bad food, snoring farting men jammed too close for comfort, boring and more boring. At least he had Aldo for company and pinochle. Finally, after two weeks of transit from Palermo to Naples to Ellis Island, Vito settled into his new, temporary home. Turns out it was a fifth floor flat in a tenement run by a couple from Calabria who lived in an adjoining flat and created a boarding house by squeezing six bunkbeds into the front room and bedroom next door. An oversized table clogged the tiny kitchen but was able to seat twelve men and huge bowls of pasta with beans, pasta with cauliflower and pasta with meat once a week for a belly-filling if not nutritional daily diet. The only running water was at the kitchen sink forcing a long line, morning and evening for the perpetually exhausted manual laborers. Another line formed at the outhouse in the backyard.

Luckily, Vito was not fussy and Army life had lowered his standards of comfortable living. After handing over the last of his ready cash for the first week's rent, Aldo's cousin came by on the next morning and escorted both of them to his worksite. Handed a shovel, they got to diminishing a huge pile of rubble on one corner of the project and wheeling it to another for five straight days.

At the end of the day, Friday, Vito scooped up his pay packet and tucked it into his vest, eager to hurry home and calculate what he had earned. He knew how much he was supposed to be earning per hour. But he wanted to count the bills and feel the change and most importantly figure how much a week's work in America would be worth in Sicily. A lot, he decided as he spread the money on a corner of his bunk and translated it into Lire. He would have to work for a month to make this much money in the vineyard. If he were careful, he could pay his room and board, save some, send some home and even have a little extra for cigarettes. They had these extra-long cigarettes in America, Pall Mall's in a red package. They were too good to smoke all at once so he cut them in half to make them last, even though he scorched his fingertips for the last drag. Another savings, a book of matches were two for a penny. He found that he could split a paper match by ripping it from the bottom and get two lights that way. He wasn't going to waste his hard-earned cash on himself and take food out of the mouth of his kids.

But some needs were hard to ignore, selfish as they were. His need for a woman, for one. It wasn't so bad in the war. Half the time he was scared out of his mind. The other half he was scrounging for food. But these days he was getting fed regularly and there were good looking women on every stoop. The longer he was away from home, the more women he saw and the better those ladies looked. And his fellow boarders in their bunks at night, would talk about a place above a bar where this Maria and that Giuseppina or Betta would do special things, besides the usual. Two months along, he finally asked, "What do they charge?"

One Saturday, washing out his socks and underwear in the basement sink next to his buddy, Aldo, Vito sighed deeply. Aldo stopped wringing his undershirt and said, "What?" Vito just shook his head. Aldo dropping his shirt in a willow basket for the trip to the clothesline strung from their dorm to the building next door, asked, "Miss the family?" Vito half-shrugged, intent on the scrub board and his soiled underpants. Basket on his hip, Aldo stopped at the foot of the stairs, "Look, my cousin invited me for dinner tomorrow. His wife's making couscous with fish." Vito looked up, eyebrows raised. "Let me ask him if you can come along." Vito nodded several times, eyes closed. He grabbed the underpants, wrung them with all his might, snapped them out and studied them. "Do you know a good doctor?"

Aldo frowned, brows pulled together, "Oh, *bedda madre!* Didn't you learn anything in the army, Vito. Use a condom." His friend rubbed the tip of his thumb against his first two fingers. "Yeah, they cost. But so does a doctor... *stupido.*" At the top of the stairs, he said, "I'll ask around... no names."

The next afternoon, at Piero's flat, three blocks away, Vito felt nervous as they climbed the stairs. He didn't know why. The tenement smelled just like theirs—stale grease, garlic, and general, never-cleaned grimy. But going to see a family was different. Like when he came home from the war—the shock of chairs and tables and clean clothes and curtains and couches and children after living rough for so long. This would be stepping into another world. But as much as he anticipated the invitation, he was unprepared for the flood of emotion when Piero opened the door to the aroma of familiar food and the welcoming smile of an aproned woman. His normally stoic face almost broke into tears from missing his family, from self-pity for the barren, hard life he had to endure. But when Gabriella kissed him on both cheeks, hands gently touching his shoulders, he was overcome with guilt and loosed two tears. She stepped back, nodded very slowly as if acknowledging and absorbing all that he was feeling. That's what he was missing. Then she pulled a boy, about the age of his Franco, from behind her skirt. "Mario," she said, "meet Mr. d'Angelo."

The next two hours were such a blur of marvelous food and easy conversation in a cocoon of family togetherness, that Vito could hardly pull himself back to the spartan existence in his boarding house. As he lay in his bunk bed that night, he tallied a list of pros and cons to bringing his family to the States. Italians were looked down on. People called them names. Gave them the worst, hardest jobs. But at least there were jobs. And a person, a family, could make a lot of money if they lived frugally and pooled their earnings. His family certainly knew how to live with next to nothing. The afternoon in Piero's apartment showed what it could be like. Nothing fancy. But it was a home with furniture and beds and space to relax and cook and afford a few extras. The only problem was, Gabriella had to work. But at least there was work for women in garment sweatshops. Nobody liked to have their wives work. But that was how it had to be. You had to adjust. The only alternative was continuing this bachelor existence, away from family, sending money and connecting every few years like sailors and soldiers and merchants. The visit with Piero and Gabriella showed another way it could be. And it looked good.

Before he fell asleep, he decided that he would work very hard to save as much as he could, send some to his wife every month and begin to look for apartments where he could set up his family like Piero did.

The following Sunday he and Aldo stopped into Morelli's who sold the smells of home as much as the handful of *ceci* beans they could barely afford. Wandering under the bunches of *oregano* that led to the cheese counter and the tongue tightening draw of *pecorino* and *parmigiano Reggiano*, Vito was lost in homesick reverie when he heard Morelli raise his voice. "But it was only two dollars last week."

After a long pause, a deep threatening voice said, "Now it's more."

Peeking around the five-foot banana bunch, Vito took in two *paisani*. The one talking was cleaning his finger nails with a longish pocket knife. The other, more muscular of the two, was half-sitting on the counter riffling the stack of paper bags. Aldo was by the door, head down, suddenly interested in the wicker basket full of snails. Morelli finally reached into the cash box and slapped the money on the counter. The two heavies left.

Outside Vito confronted Aldo. "*Porca miseria,*" he moaned. "Here too? Come all this way and the same damn shit."

"What do you think? You knew the mafia was here. Hell, you told me about your brother-in-law, Nino."

"I..." Vito stuttered, "I thought it would be different here. It gets me so mad. Look, those bastards just went into the bakery. Let's wait for them at the alley. Take care of them, like in the war. Huh? We were good—you and me. Give the money back to Morelli. What do you say?"

Aldo, lowered his brow, shook his head. "Let it go, Vito. You'd never win. They would jump on Morelli to make up the money and then come after you."

"But..."

"Go along to get along, *amico meo*. You didn't see nothing. Just be glad they haven't started at the worksite."

Feeling sorry for Morelli, Vito bought three *sanguine* for Piero and Gabriella as thanks for their hospitality a week ago. He had to keep from eating one of the blood-oranges himself on the way to their flat. He saw Mario bouncing a pink Spaldeen on the front steps of the tenement.

"Is your Dad home?" Vito asked.

"No, he went somewhere."

"Oh. Well, these are for you folks," he said, holding the bag toward the boy.

"Just give them to my mom."

After he considered the kid for a while, wondering why he didn't know the rules, Vito explained, "A man should never visit another man's wife when he's not in the house." Mario wrinkled his face, said, "Huh?" and went back to bouncing the ball.

Vito plopped the bag on the step and said, "You do it," and walked away muttering, "smart ass kid. No respect."

Back in his flat, a couple of the boarders were resting in bed, chatting... more like griping about a favorite theme— Damn America! The bread was soft. No crust. No taste. The cheese was soft. The lunch meat tasted terrible. And they had the nerve to call it Bologna... a great Italian city.

Vito quietly smoked his one half of a Pall Mall for the day and fought the urge to tell those guys to go back if they didn't like it here. But they soon left and he played back the afternoon. Italians brought a lot with them when they came to the States—the low-lifes, the food, the rules about men and women. Maybe the kid, Mario, had the answer—learn the language, play the games, forget the old rules, make new ones, adapt.

Chapter Six; 1920, Bound for America

Franco was excited to be finally going to America. Sort of. The people around him, the only people he had known his first eight years, were sad and crying. His mother kept hugging his sister Concetta who was staying with their grandparents and admonishing her fiancé Luca to take good care of her daughter. His sister, Angela, sniffled a little, too, but he could tell she really wanted to get going. She kept glancing at Carlo, the butcher apprentice, who showed up at the train station. He didn't look happy that she was leaving but at the last second, on the steps of the train, she shot him a smile. He dipped his chin in his quiet way. Big brother, Rocco, hefted the bag of buns and *biscotti* over his shoulder. "Just in case," his grandmother had said, "you never know what you might need on a ten-day crossing." Franco didn't feel like crying until his grandfather kissed him three times on each cheek, scratching him with two-day whiskers and hugging him so hard that two tears squeezed out. He might never see any of them again. But then the train whistle blew and he scampered up the stairs for the trip to Palermo and the overnight boat to Naples.

Franco had seen ships along the wharf in Trapani, so he wasn't particularly impressed with the Naples ferry. Still it was fun to be on one, exploring every stairwell, bathroom and lifeboat until dark. When Rocco finally led him down to the men's dorm and his place on the upper bunk, he couldn't sleep. It was first time in all his eight years he was sleeping outside his house, away from his mother, surrounded by strange, snoring men while gently rolling with waves. After a time, he snuck up the gangway to the open foredeck. The cool breeze felt good after the sounds and smells of the airless sleeping quarters.

Near the front of the ship, three men leaned against the rail smoking and talking softly. On a bench nearby a woman held a baby under her shawl, nursing the child. A soldier slept on another bench. His mother, arms crossed stood by another rail, facing the void of the cloud-covered, moonless night. His first impulse was to run up and hug her. Something stopped him. She looked like she wanted to be alone. Needed to be alone. Something else. Like maybe she was holding onto a long string tied to their front gate. And then, for the first time, he felt a distance from his mother. He was looking forward to... he didn't exactly know. But what was coming was exciting, not sad. He watched his mother for another long moment, sad but determined at suddenly feeling the responsibility to take point for the next part of their lives. He set his chin, marched down the gangway to his bunk but this time crawled in with his brother Rocco.

Margherita welcomed the enveloping darkness. Soothed by the waves purling along the hull, she let thoughts and feelings of the past months bubble up as they would. She missed Vito. Making love with him. His quiet, solid presence. Her rock. Two years was a long time. Would he be different? Would they be different? How could he do this... make them break up their family? She missed her daughter Connie already. And what about her wedding? Being there for her first baby? And now she would be living in a big city. What would that be like after living in the country? People. Noise. *It's supposed to snow there in the winter. Vito said the Italian wives he knows go to work. Cooking, cleaning, washing... that's work too. If I have to work all day, how does that get done? And what kind of work? Vito says they sew in a place full of Italian women. I can sew, but never like it was a job, like work. Will I be able to do it? And Angela, how do you raise a girl in New York? She's too old to go to their schools. Will she work too? Will she get tired of living there and want to go back to her ragazzo, Carlo. Might be just as well. We know what to expect back home, how things get done. And what's going to happen to my boys? Vito says he wants to save money and later on go back to Sicily, to what we know and love and are used to. I wonder if it will happen. We might change. The boys are young. They might change us. And who says Paceco will stay the same as we remember it.* "*O Dio,*" Margherita moaned, "what are we getting into?"

Two days into the Atlantic crossing, Margherita was moaning again. This time she was confined to her bunk in the pitching and rolling tangle of families and baggage amid the stink of diesel and vomit in steerage. Franco was the angel who flitted here and there bringing water, emptying pots and snatching crackers from the galley for any who could hold them down.

As far as he was concerned, he was on a mission, for the next ten days, to discover all there was to know about the tossing and creaking rust bucket. Since everyone else was laid up, he appointed himself to take care of things. He climbed ladders and stairs that led to doors which opened on engine room or wheelhouse, closet or head. The cook offered him treats and leftovers for the others who couldn't make it to the chow line. The crew liked it when he stopped by their quarters to watch them playing cards. He seemed to catch on to their games and they let him play a hand once in a while.

At the end of the trip, one day out of New York, Franco strolled around his ship inspecting the life boats, checking on the crew, looking into the pilot house. When he got to the galley the cook's helper motioned him into a corner. "You like chocolate?" he asked.

"*Ciocolatto?*" Franco answered. "*Si.*"

The man offered him a piece of brown, Fels-Naptha soap. Franco popped it into his mouth chewed once and swallowed before registering the taste. He gagged and spit while the man and his buddies laughed long and loud. Not long after, he got seriously ill from both ends.

Chapter Seven; 1920, Brooklyn

Of course, Margherita was delighted to see her husband waving outside the Ellis Island processing center. Aldo was there—a familiar face from home. She fussed with her hair, concerned that she looked gaunt and wan from ten days in steerage. But Vito didn't seem to mind. He hugged her so hard she could barely breathe. And when she finally inhaled, she drew in the familiar, welcome smells of her man, felt his smooth morning-shaved cheeks, his tight, strong muscled back and his hands in the small of her back sending an urgent message that would have to wait a little longer to be answered.

Frowning, flustered, "Where's Franco?" Vito asked.

Tumbling over each other with explanations, Angela, Rocco, and Margherita explained that the doctors decided that Franco needed to be quarantined in case he had a contagious disease. As Rocco described the cruel prank played on his brother, Vito's face tensed and hardened. "But don't worry," Angela hastened to add. "They told us we could check in two days."

"He'll be fine," Margherita reassured her glowering husband. "It's like he took a laxative."

Vito huffed quietly, wishing he could catch the sailor in a dark alley.

Meanwhile, confined to a hospital ward, Franco was bitterly disappointed that he couldn't enjoy the reunion with his father and family. The first day, he was as much sick with himself for being made a fool, as from the soap. The next day, he was back on his feet with nowhere to go and time to think. He scanned the surrounding land beyond the barred windows. No broccoli in Brookolini. How stupid could he be? *Okay, Franco,* he told himself, *time to wise up. Stop believing everything grownups tell you. Be careful. Not*

289

everyone is your friend. They might want to hurt you. You have to learn as much as you can about this new place, as fast as you can, for your sake and the family's.

Margherita was stunned and oppressed by the waves of people, the towering buildings, clanging trolley bells, cobblestone and cement on the way to their home. The cab stopped in front of a four-story brick building. Two men leaned on a light pole, smoking. Two women in aprons lounged on the five-stair stoop. One rocked an infant and winked at the one next to her before calling, "Hey, Vito, what's this one's name?"

Vito marched past them, muttering, "*Ignorante.*"

Margherita had other ideas. She stopped at the foot of the stairs, made eye contact with both women. Then she smiled and spoke in Sicilian, "I'm Mrs. d'Angelo. I just got off the boat from Naples and I could stand a good cup of coffee." Names, hugs, introductions to babies and kids in the street was followed by two strong cups of espresso and a homemade biscotto while Vito took Angela and Rocco to their apartment. A half-hour later, Mirella and Maria escorted Margherita to the second floor flat.

She wasn't sure what she was expecting, but the two-bedroom unit was dingy, drab and smelled of stale grease. There were a table and chairs in the kitchen, a stove, sink and running water. That much was good... better than home. There was a living room with a sofa and a wooden rocking chair. "They came with the apartment," Vito explained as she wrinkled her nose at the cotton bulging from the arm rests of the worn scarlet couch. "And the stuffed pheasant," he added, pointing to the only décor to be found in the spartan quarters. In their bedroom. Margherita paused to sit on the edge and pat the mattress. Smiling to herself, then up at Vito, *this much will be familiar,* she thought.

Angela was emptying the content of her suitcase on the bed in her tiny room, sorting the dirty clothes from two week's travel when Mirella's daughter, Tina, poked her head in and offered to show her the wash sink in the basement. "Wait, wait," Margherita called, "take all my things, too."

"Your nightgown won't dry by tonight," Angela reminded.

Margherita, tossed her chin and sucked her teeth loudly—so?

"Ma!" Angela called in shock.

Vito grinned and directed Margherita to the bathroom, explaining how he had searched to find a place with an indoor toilet and a tub with a circle curtain for a shower. She was impressed and couldn't wait for a long soak while Rocco squeezed in to show her how the knobs and plugs and pull-chain worked.

"But where will the boys sleep?" she finally asked as she lay out, exhausted, on the sofa. "Rocco here," Vito pointed to the couch. "Franco, on the floor with blankets."

"Uhm," she managed before falling deeply asleep. The smell of spaghetti sauce woke both her and her appetite now that she had been on solid ground for a few hours. Angela was setting the table with mismatched dishes and bent forks. "Mirella gave us some sauce and Pa had spaghetti. Let's eat." They all sat at the table, bowed their heads and thanked God to be all together again... almost all.

After dinner, Margherita ran her first-ever bath in a full-sized tub of hot water. After soaking for a half-hour, she called to Vito to wash her back. He let her know he would be waiting in bed. It was a marvelous reunion. He was so eager, but gentle and caring. He even cried after the second time. But it was strange that he used a condom. He never had before. But then, they really didn't want any more children, did they?

Vito stomped up the stairs to their flat, banged the door shut and yelled at Franco on his way to the bathroom, "Put water on." By the time he emerged, face washed, shaved and in a clean shirt, the pot on the stove was just beginning to bubble. Ravenous from a long day of humping hods of brick up sky scrapers, he grabbed a fistful of spaghetti from the cupboard and tossed it into the pot. He looked in the icebox and finally settled on a bowl of leftover beans. He flopped in a chair by the window, exhausted. Living in the boarding house, at least they had supper ready when he got home from work. Now, he beat his wife and daughter home by an hour and had to cook for himself... and wait for it to be ready. His wife working. What a disgrace that a man couldn't earn enough to let a woman do the woman's work in the home. So many changes. *And my daughter works too. The only consolation is that the other guys in the building and on the job face the same thing. The women need to work to just get by. And now Angela wants to go back home, to Carlo. I'll miss her and the extra money she used to bring home. But I had to tell her, if you want to go back, you have to earn the money. So, she's been putting most of it away for her ticket and her trousseau. One good thing, the boys can use her bedroom. Why is it always so hard? And Margherita comes home so exhausted and angry and it takes her all evening to calm down from the boss pushing her and all the ladies to sew faster and faster. I wish she didn't have to work and could have my supper ready.*

He jumped up to check on the pasta that had just barely softened enough to slide down the sides of the pot and under the water. "*Basta,*" he announced before draining the pasta in a colander and returning the noodles to the pot where he dumped yesterday's beans into the mix with a dollop of olive oil. He didn't bother to call Franco, ripped off a hunk of bread and ate straight out of the pot. Franco came into the kitchen and listened to the crunch of the *al dente* pasta as his father assuaged the worst pangs of his hunger. When his father paused to reach for the bottle of his homemade muscatel, the boy scooped a portion onto his plate. He knew not to engage his father in conversation at this point, at least not until he calmly spooned a second helping onto his plate. He chewed slowly, taking sips of water to continue the process of hydration of the crunchy pasta.

Rocco broke into the feeding frenzy, throwing his book bag into a corner and wincing at the sight of the *pasta fagiole.* He shrugged, grabbed a plate and sat at the table. He suddenly laughed. "You gotta hear this. At the barber shop, I had to stop right in the middle of sweeping up hair I was laughing so hard. This Calabrese guy was telling everyone about his neighbor who strained his back at work. So, he asked his wife to put some liniment into the bathtub. But she put too much in and went he went to sit down it scalded his balls. The guy in the chair said he could hear him scream for two floors away." Rocco paused to take another mouthful, chewed quickly, swallowed with difficulty and continued. "But here's the best part. Turns out his wife told the other women in the tenement that she had to whip up some egg white and pat it on his balls."

As stolid as Vito usually was, even he let out a snort of amusement at this extraordinary use of meringue. All three guys were laughing when Margherita came in the door.

"What's so funny?" she asked. The guys laughed all the harder.

"When I complain of sore muscles," Vito said, "let me be the one to put liniment in the bath water."

After supper, Margherita, Angela, Vito and Rocco dumped their pay packets on the kitchen table. It was understood that everyone shared in family expenses. Vito took a small amount out of Angela's earnings and shoved the rest back to her as savings for her return trip to Italy. He cut out a small amount for Rocco to cover trolley fare. Margherita set aside grocery money from her earnings. Vito portioned out rent. The rest went into savings. Even Franco, at nine, pitched in the spare change he got for delivering groceries for Morelli. The one time he objected, "But that's my money," the whole family glowered at him. "There's no *my money* in this family," Vito said. "If you want to keep *your money,* then you owe room and board like a boarding house. This is different. This is family."

Finally, the first day of school came. The towering brick building. Hundreds of kids running and shouting. But Franco wasn't nervous—just one more thing to get used to, to figure out. After all, he had crossed the ocean and when everyone else got sick, he was the one they counted on to work the system. By lunch time, he reevaluated the situation. School was going to be harder than he had anticipated. There was the language issue. He knew not a word of English. They put him in first grade with six-year olds—as if he didn't know how to read. He knew how to read, just not in English. And he could do the numbers. And the teacher didn't like him. Called him a name that made the other children snicker at him. What did *dago* mean, anyway? *Don't worry,* he told himself, *I'll catch up soon and get in a room with kids my own age.*

And then it was lunch. A big boy with red hair and brown little spots on his face snatched his bag. "Whatcha, got in here, punk?" he snarled. Some other kids in the playground gathered around. The boy opened the crumpled bag

"Pee... uw," he twisted his face, scrunching his nose and threw the bag into a puddle.

What's wrong with a crust of bread and a nice piece of cheese, Franco wondered, as he bent to retrieve the food. The boy kicked him in the butt and sent him splashing in the muddy water. The rest of the kids laughed while Franco retreated to a bench on the far side of the teeter-totter. The bread was soaked but the cheese was still good, he munched and pondered revenge.

"Hey," Rocco called as he jogged to Franco's side, "I heard some guys were messing with you."

"Good thing you're late. You couldn't have done anything. Too many of them."

"Still, look for me at lunch time. We'll eat together."

Franco looked at his wet socks, flicked some mud off and shook his head. He was small for his age, and skinny, and his butt still hurt. But he was sure he would think of something on his own.

That night his mother scolded him for getting his clothes muddy. He caught Rocco's eye and shook his head almost imperceptibly. "And besides," she added, "you need a haircut. Vito, the boy needs a haircut."

"Can't afford it," his father said.

"I know," Rocco chimed in. "I can cut it for him. I watch the barbers while I sweep. And yesterday, Mario dropped his scissors on the floor and the tip bent. Said I could have them. I can pound it straight with a hammer."

Franco shook his head. "Practice on someone else."

"Let him try," Vito said. "He's got to learn some time."

Before he could object further, Franco was on a stool with a towel around his neck and Rocco was snipping with his mangled scissors that snagged and pulled with every snip.

"*Aah! Managgia!*" Rocco shouted, jumping back. "*Verme,* he has lice. Head lice."

"No wonder... from that miserable boat," his mother said.

"Or the hospital," Angela added.

Rocco stood back, "Good thing we don't sleep together."

"Angela, take his sheets and pillow case and clothes to the basement. Boil them." To Rocco, she said, "Cut off all his hair. Vito shave his head and I'll sweep it up."

Franco itched and rubbed the ticklish hair clinging to his tears. He was already different enough at school, now he would be bald. He watched his father strop his straight razor then test the edge on his thumb while Rocco proudly whisked his father's shaving brush in the soap mug. Franco ducked, sneered and thoroughly resented his brother's pleasure in slathering his head in shaving cream.

He stared in the mirror when it was all done. How much more embarrassment could he suffer in one day? He bit his cheeks to keep from crying when his mother handed him the bag of hair to take out to the trash. On the way out, he automatically popped on his hat. *What if it has some lice, too,* he wondered. *It won't matter to me. I don't have any more hair. But someone else could get it, if they wore it.* Then he thought of the red-haired bully. He tucked the bag next to the steps inside the tenement front door.

The next morning, his hat drooped to his ears without the hair mass to buoy it up. *Just as well,* he thought. *Maybe no one will notice... but if they do.* He smiled to himself.

At lunch, the bully trudged over to him. "Whatcha got today? More stinkin' cheese?" He grabbed the bag and opened it. "What the hell!" he cried. Turning to the gang that followed him dropped the bag, shouting, "It's full of hair!"

Franco didn't know how to explain himself in English, so he snatched the bag back and said, "*Verme,*" while lifting his hat to show his bald head.

"What's that mean?" the boy roared.

"Aw, shit," an Italian boy said. "He's got cooties. And that's why his head is shaved."

Franco opened the sack and pushed it toward the Irish boy, thrusting it toward his head forcing him to walk backwards across the playground and up the school steps. Then he turned and waved it at all the followers who carefully retreated. He waited for a moment's emphasis before bobbing his chin as if to say, *so there, leave me alone.*

It wasn't perfect, but the rest of the kids left him alone for the rest of the semester and by the end of the year, he was double promoted into third grade where he progressed steadily.

Chapter Eight; 1922, Brooklyn

At home, Franco and Rocco quickly became the connection to the new world for their parents. They would read letters, bills, and newspaper aloud, translating as they went. "See, Ma," Rocco used to say, "you gotta learn to talk American so you can get your citizenship."

"I'm not American. I'm Italian," she would respond. "I don't want to be American. I want to go back to Italy. To my home."

Rocco and Franco would exchange glances. "Sure, Ma."

At fifteen, Rocco started announcing that he was about done with school and planned to drop out at the end of the year. He now knew English as well as any of the customers he served and with his knack for barbering, was on his way to a respectable profession. Angela, however, was not about to sink roots. She hated life in New York and sweatshop work. One night at the dinner table she held up a letter from Carlo and broke into tears. "I don't want to stay here. I want to go back home. Be with Carlo and Connie and Gramma."

Vito silently pounded his clenched fists on the table. "*Managgia la miseria,*" he rasped. "I'm working as hard as I can and nobody's happy. What more can I do?"

"I know, *caro,*" Margherita cried. "I'm trying too. But look at us in this smelly, crowded place. Cold in the winter. Hot in the summer."

"It was hot in Paceco, too," Rocco reminded. "And I was cold, most of the time, in winter."

"But it was different," Angela countered. "We were used to it, to the way things were. And I miss it."

Vito puffed out his cheeks, slowly exhaling, shaking his head.

"If you go back," Margherita whined, "we'll have half the family here, half there."

"Look," Vito reasoned. "Life goes on, no matter where we live. If we were home, our daughters would be marrying anyhow and be out of the house..."

"But not across the ocean."

"Yes, but what if their husbands were sailors or soldiers and had to be away much of the time?"

"They would still be near us," she cried. "I miss my daughters."

Angela came over to hug her mother. "I would miss you too, Mama."

"We can't afford it, just yet," Vito said. "She has to keep working a while longer."

Margherita firmed her chin and glanced at Angela who, knowing what was coming next, shook her head. "That's the problem, Vito," Margherita explained. "Angela may not be able to keep working at the shop much longer."

Vito shot a questioning look at Angela stiffly sitting across the table like a witness about to be cross-examined. After a pause to gather her thoughts and courage, Angela began. "Alfredo, our boss... he's from Trapani and calls me *paisana*. There's a lot of other Sicilian ladies sewing for him, but he calls <u>me</u> his neighbor. There's lots of young ladies in the shop, but he's always coming around me every chance he gets."

"But, what?" Vito's face set into a hard mask. "What is he doing?"

"Well..." Angela hesitated, looking to her mother to help explain.

"He comes over to her when she's working. Leans over her shoulder. Gets close to her at lunch. And the other women notice the special attention."

Vito waved his hand disgustedly, "But, does he touch her?"

"Well, no. Not yet," Angela said. "And besides he has onion breath."

"I'll have to talk to the bastard...behind the shop."

Margherita raised her chin and sucked her teeth for a loud, *tsk*. "The problem, both of you don't get, is that pretty soon he's going to want more. By force... or permission. Tell me Vito, do you want that *disgraziato* sitting at our table every Sunday dinner as your son-in-law just so we can work?"

"Aii!" Angela cringed at the thought.

"Somethings going to happen," Margherita continued, "and if we don't do it right, Angela will be out of a job and so will I. No more boat ticket. No more Sicily. And one more son-in-law. *Capisce?*"

Franco followed the discussion, calculating.

"I know," Rocco jumped in. "Why not get Carlo to send some money if he's so interested? She quits. Problem solved." Under the barrage of scornful looks, he muttered, "Well, I just thought..."

Everyone sat in silence for the longest time studying their dirty plates crusting with cold spaghetti sauce. Finally, when everyone retired to the front room, Franco edged close to Angela at the sink. "I got an idea," he said.

"You?" she said disdainfully.

"Okay, if that's the way you feel. You figure it out."

Later that evening she called to Franco on his way to the bathroom, "What're you thinking?"

"Just a minute," he said as he took his time doing his business and slowly washing his hands. Sometimes it was important to get respect. He came out and sat on her bed, ran his hand over his just starting to fuzz-over scalp. "Okay, here's the thing. People hate head lice. Right?" Angela flinched and inched away. "Okay," Franco continued, "the next time that creep gets too close and starts crowding you, just scratch your head and say, 'Man I hope I don't have my brother's cooties."

The next evening, after supper, Angela slipped Franco two *cannoli* she picked up on the way home. *You have to stay on your toes, all the time,* Franco reflected, savoring his solitary treat on the tenement rooftop.

Chapter Nine; 1924, Detroit

Nino and Eva were both exhausted. He from a long day on the line at the Ford Rouge plant. She from caring for their five girls under seven. After dinner, they sat at the table in no hurry to open the rare surprise of a letter. Tina had told them it was from Margherita. She could read now, after two years in school. Smart girl. Helpful, too. She stood on a step stool, elbow deep in the soapy water, washing dishes. As the eldest child, she was expected to help her mother more than her younger sisters. And in the case of dishes, it was a necessity, as her mother's eczema flared up in soapy hot water—the very rash triggered by Aunt Caterina's abduction. She wished she knew more of that story. Like if one of the Barettas would write a letter from California. It would sure be more exciting than boring Aunt Margherita with boring family nothings.

Instead, Tina had to use her imagination to fill in the blanks between her aunt's whispered snippets: "Pete Baretta got trapped inside a store he was supposed to burn because the owner wouldn't pay for protection..." *whatever that meant.* "He barely got away in time to throw Aunt Caterina and her kids into the back of his dump truck and head out West..." *where the cowboys and Indians are?* "They all almost died in the desert when they ran out of gas and water on the way to the coast. The boxes for her father's grapes had pretty pictures of California on the side." *big deal, her father fished in the ocean in Sicily and now he makes gin in the attic and has to give a cop $2 every week.* "Caterina made her bed now she has to lie in it..." *whatever that meant.*

Wrist deep in suds, Tina smiled to herself waiting to be asked to read the letters as she knew she would. "Pina," Nino ordered his third daughter, "go tell Zio Marco we have a letter from our sister and he should come over."

Learning to read had been a painful process. For five years she watched hordes of children shouting and screaming to each other in an incomprehensible language as they entered and left the grade school across the street. When it was her turn Tina eagerly trotted over to absorb all she could, starting with the English language. Total immersion was hard and made more difficult by Mrs. Murphy who made her sit in front of the class and lined up the other kids to spit in her hand when she couldn't answer a question. The playground was no easier. One day at recess, she and another timid girl, hovering near the fence, drew the attention of some rowdies who piled on top of them dislocating Tina's shoulder. Fearful that her mother would remove her from school if she knew the truth, she let her Uncle Tony, storyteller and amateur massage therapist, squeeze out a fib along with her laughing and groaning as his knowing hands worked muscle and joint under a layer of oil. Undaunted, she marched back to the schoolroom the next day, determined to learn. Before long she was up to grade level and tutoring her mother, who shared her drive to know.

Without being asked, Tina dried her hands and sat at the head of the table. Eva got up to make coffee and open a tin of homemade *biscotti*. Her father stayed in place fidgeting with the unopened letter while waiting for his brother and sister-in-law to arrive. As the eldest and first of the Maisano siblings to emigrate, he had paved the way for his brother, Marco, to find work and move next door with his wife Stella. Snug in an Italian enclave in Detroit's eastside, the brothers enjoyed a cushioned transition into American life. They had quickly felt at home with Eva and her large family of brothers and sisters scattered throughout the neighborhood. The Rizzo brothers were involved in transportation, some in trucking and excavating, others in freelance bootlegging of Canadian booze smuggled across the Detroit River. In all, they were a lively, loving bunch, mingling and crossing paths as often as possible. Nino and Marco felt bad that their sister, stuck in New York, missed out on the togetherness they enjoyed. Any news from her was welcome.

Five minutes later, Marco and his wife Stella, were seated at the kitchen table expectantly waiting for Tina to open the letter and begin reading. She began the laborious task of reading Italian cursive writing while barely proficient in printed English text. Syllable-by-syllable, she sounded out words her elders sometimes helped her complete.

"Good wishes and kisses to everyone. I hope you are all well. My son, Franco, who is now ten-years old is writing this letter for me and Vito." Looking at her father, Tina asked, "Will I meet him someday?"

"Someday. They will come here or we will go there. Someday. *Avanti!*"

"Everybody is healthy. Vito is working very hard. I sew ten hours a day but I make good money. I am sad because my daughter Angela went back to Sicily last week. My family is now in two parts. My daughters in Sicily. My sons in America. My daughter Connie had a baby boy, called Piero. And Angela plans to marry Carlo. I wish I was there."

"He's a good kid, that Carlo," Marco remarked. "I always liked him. They should be happy together."

"But the poor mother," Stella commiserated. "Imagine being separated from your kids."

"I thought you were just complaining about our two being on top of you all the time," Marco teased.

Stella swatted her husband while Tina continued with the closing remarks, good wishes and kisses for all.

"Do you ever wish you could go back?" Eva asked. Stella hugged Marco's arm, shaking her head. "Oh, I get homesick. Miss my mother and cousins. But I'm here. This is where I had my children. This is where I live."

Eva sighed deeply. "Yes. Me too, I guess."

Chapter Ten; 1929, Brooklyn

As soon as Angela left, Rocco and Franco abandoned their front-room sleeping arrangements and installed a bunkbed and dresser in her bedroom. At nineteen, Rocco was fully employed as the fourth chair in the neighborhood barber shop while fifteen-year old Franco, a sophomore in high school, would stop by Morelli's grocery after school, helping with the after-work rush. He knew all the customers' names, told jokes, teased, and to Morelli's delight often pushed sales by suggesting one or another item they hadn't realized they needed.

As an elective, Franco took voc-ed classes in automotive repair where the boys worked on city vehicles under the supervision of their teacher. One day he forgot his lunch at home and Rocco took advantage of a morning lull to run it by the school. Told that his brother was in the garage, he paused at the doorway to observe the class in progress. He was conscious of the contrast between his workplace and this. The smell of pomade and rose water, quiet conversation, and dancing fingers snapping shears and combs with clean hands versus the clang and bang, grease and oil on filthy hands and clothes.

It took a moment to spot his 110-pound brother in the middle of several burly types hoisting engine blocks and transmissions with chain pulleys or sliding from under cars. Franco was trying to remove a flat tire from a garbage truck. He had added a three-foot piece of pipe on the end of the tire wrench to provide the leverage he needed to crack the rusted nuts on the rim. Once loosed, he wedged a plank at an incline under the raised wheel. Then he carefully wiggled the heavy rim off the hub and rolled the tire down the ramp. Rocco took in the scene and pondered.

That night, as they lay in bed, he queried his brother. "Franky, I watched you working on the truck tire."

"Uh-huh."

"You shouldn't be doing that kind of work. You're too damn small."

"Up yours, Rocco," Franco said, offering a silent and unseen Italian salute from the upper bunk. "I'm getting the job done."

"Barely. But I like how you figured out to do it... with the pipe and the ramp. Makes me think you should work with your brain and not with muscles."

"What's it to you... one way or the other?"

"We all got to work around here. You may be the baby in the family but you got to pull your weight, too."

"Pa's not complaining."

"It's not about Pa. It's about you. You can't be serious about working in a garage all your life. Or squeezing tomatoes at Morelli's. C'mon you're better than that."

"Mind your own business, brother."

"In this family, we're all each other's business."

Sunday dinner was relaxed compared to weekday feeding frenzies. In the middle of a leisurely meal of roast chicken and potatoes *al forno,* Rocco said, "You know, I've been thinking about Franco."

Franco stopped mid-chew. "Why don't you think about something else, *frate meo.*"

Rocco shot him a determined look before continuing. "I watched my little brother trying to lift a heavy tire and use a heavy wrench. He's not a muscle man. But he used his head and figured out how to do it. I says to myself, *Bravo. The kid is smart. He can use his brains instead of his muscles.* Then in the barber shop, I get this customer. *Ingegnere* DiMarco. I asked him how he became an engineer. He said he went to a college here in Brooklyn. After four years he graduated. He got a job at this company. Works at a desk. Makes good money. I think Franco should do that."

Franco dropped his fork on the plate. His mother and father focused on him as if looking for something they had never seen before. He could hear the wheels in their brains turning: *Franco an engineer? Someone in our family going to college? We could say, 'our son the engineer.'*

"So, I asked Mr. Di Marco what it might cost for a year in college. He said, living at home, about $100, and maybe some more for books. We could do that. I could do that for my brother. Throw in $1 a week. You guys take care of the rest. And he could work during the summer."

"Hey!" Franco shouted, stood. "Who said I wanted any part of this plan? I'm just a kid in high school."

"Well, you got time to think about it," Rocco said, "talk to somebody at school, save some money, maybe take some classes you'll need instead of rupturing yourself lifting truck tires."

"You got it all figured out, huh? Who says I want to do that, huh?"

Vito folded his napkin, locked eyes with his youngest son and said, "I do." He turned to his wife, "That's why I came here. To give us a chance to do better." Tipping his head to Rocco, he added, "I just never thought of this. Good idea."

Franco grabbed his coat and shouted on his way out the door, "Did anyone think to ask what I think about the idea? As if it matters around here."

Chapter Eleven; 1929, Detroit

August, on a breathless, humid Sunday afternoon the grownups sat under the plum tree groaning with ripe purple fruit in Marco's backyard. When her brother Tony dropped by, Eva called out, "Tina make another pitcher of lemonade." Ten minutes later, as Tina carried the pitcher with two hands, walking carefully to avoid spilling, all the adults watched her negotiate the gate between the yards. As she filled his glass, her uncle Tony smiled, and said, "*Grazie.*" Then to his sister, "She's getting to be a big girl, now. What is she? Thirteen? I bet she's a big help to you with all your kids."

"She sure is. But in a couple weeks she goes back to school. It's hard without her."

"The oldest girl, that's her job... to help the mother," Stella said. "How much school does she need anymore?"

Tina stopped, squeezed the pitcher to her chest, as all the adults sized her up. Why did she feel that her future was about to be decided by this jury of elders? She held her breath as Uncle Marco asked, "How much education does a girl need? She can read and write. That's a lot for the women we know. Besides, her mother needs her more."

Tina didn't dare to look at her father, afraid he might agree with his brother. That's when Uncle Tony said, "Well, maybe she's got enough book learning. But why not have her learn to sew or something? Don't they have classes at that trade school? Burroughs is it? Over on Van Dyke?"

Eager to salvage at least a couple more years of schooling, Tina spoke up. "Yes, they do. My friend Teresa goes there." Registering the thoughtful frowns, she hurried to add, "And if I knew how to sew, I could make clothes for my sisters." Still picking up reluctance she improvised, "And who knows, I might even get a job. Like at your factory, right Pa?" She then remembered the pitcher in her hands and rushed to top off glasses all around.

Chapter Twelve; 1932, Brooklyn

Sixteen-year old Tina was part excited, part frightened and part infuriated that she was on a train to New York after the *uncles* decided not only that she was plenty old enough to leave school but needed to supplement her father's wages to help the family. She wished she were a man. They got to decide everything.

She had never met Aunt Margherita, Uncle Vito, cousins Rocco and Franco and now she was going to move in with them. In a tenement—whatever that was. And she would do sewing with her aunt in a sweatshop. Well at least all the workers would be Italian women and not the tough girls at Burroughs—although she was able to hold her own by the time she left.

Tina walked down the ramp into Grand Central Terminal. At the entryway to the monumental building she stopped to drink-in the moment. She may have been born in the United States but this was like getting off the boat in another country—crowds, noise, buildings on a scale she hadn't imagined. It took a moment before she registered a voice calling her name. A young man waved as he walked toward her. It had to be her cousin, Franco. She had seen a First Communion picture of him and appropriately aged him in her mind. She waved back.

Up close, he looked familiar, reminded her of her father around the nose and mouth. He stopped, suddenly shy, after running toward her so eagerly. He studied her a bit overlong, causing her to touch her hair and wonder if she needed fresh lipstick. Having satisfied his curiosity, he nodded briskly to himself. "So, Tina. Franco, here. I'm supposed to get you home," he announced, reaching for her valise.

"Oh, good. Thanks. Nice meeting you," she said to his departing back and followed him to a trolley stop. They nev-

er said another word between the noise and press of passengers. *Just as well,* Tina thought. *There's so much to take
in. Like I can't even see the tops of the buildings we're riding
by.*

Franco tugged her sleeve at a stop and they climbed
down. Walking next to her cousin, she began, "I've never
met your mother and father... or brother either. But I read
all the letters she wrote to my father. So, I think I kind of
know her."

"Actually, I wrote them. Ma can't write... or read either.
She tells me what to say. I write it down."

"Same for me... with my parents."

"Huh," Franco remarked as he set the valise down at
the foot of his stoop. "Dino," he called to a guy chatting up
a girl in a basement stairwell, "gimme a cigarette." While
he lit up, Tina scanned the block—four boys playing stick-
ball in the street, a mother dragging her crying son by the
ear while scolding him in Italian, a vendor selling green
beans from a pushcart by the curb, and a horse hitched
to a delivery wagon plopping manure in front of a grocery
store across the street. Busy. Fascinating. But she already
missed her white house on her quiet street where the only
noise came from school kids coming in the morning and
going in the afternoon. Absorbed as she was, Franco had to
call from the doorway, "Hey, cuz. Let's go."

She hurried up the dingy stairway trying not to notice
the trash and cat smell and the way her shoes stuck, just a
little, to each step.

"*Benvenuta, Tina,*" her Aunt Margherita crooned during
a long, strong hug. As they separated, the aunt kept one
hand on Tina's shoulder, nodding as if pleased with her
niece, then fingering a curl she uttered, "*bedda,*" and planted
a kiss on the girl's cheek. Her Uncle Vito rose from the rock-
er by the window to give Tina a beard-scratch, double kiss
on each cheek and a whiff of stale cigarette smoke. Rocco
emerged from the bedroom to give her a peck on the cheek.
"Hi. I'm Rocco. Make yourself at home," he said pointing
to a three-panel screen in a corner of the living room. Tina
could make out the head of a cot and pillow sticking out at
one end and a dresser at the other. "Thanks," she said and
after a moment's hesitation, grabbed her valise and began

unpacking. It wasn't much but at least it was her own bed and she wouldn't have to share it with her sisters.

Tina was sitting on the cot, eyes closed, collecting herself when she heard the sounds of chopping and the smell of onions coming from the kitchen. Sunday dinner. She rose, donned an apron and joined her aunt cutting up carrots for the roast. Margherita smiled warmly. "It's so nice to have a woman in the house. I miss my daughters."

"Thanks for having me," Tina replied. "I feel welcome."

Her cousin Franco sat at the kitchen table reading a textbook and making notes in a tablet. Unasked, her aunt brought a dish of grapes and a couple pieces of cheese to her son. Tina watched for a sign of thanks from the eighteen-year old. Nothing. She peeled potatoes, glancing occasionally at her cousin, nose in his book all the while wishing she had his opportunity to still be in school. At one point, her aunt out of the room, Franco held out his glass without looking up. "Get me some water, would you"

Tina closed her eyes; took a deep breath, deciding. *My dad, my uncles... yes, because that's the way it is. My mom, my aunt... yes, because I should. My cousin—nuh-uh.* "Get it yourself," she said. Franco looked up, locked eyes with her. She could read his thoughts: *So that's the way it's going to be? See if I help you anymore, cuz.*

Fine, she said back with her unblinking black eyes, *I'm not your servant.* Her aunt walked back in the room, noted her son's empty glass, filled it and set it next to him.

The next morning, Margherita took Tina to the sewing factory set up in a nearby tenement flat. On the way up the stairs, she counseled her niece, "Alfredo, the boss, can be a problem. He pays special attention to all the young girls. Don't encourage him. Just be polite and do your job." Tina nodded curtly. *Here goes,* she thought as they faced a long room with twenty sewing machines and women getting ready to start a long day at each one. A couple of the ladies waved to Margherita. One said, "Your niece from Detroit?"

Tina sat at a free machine and closed her eyes for a moment absorbing the stop-start clatter and whirr, so familiar from her sewing classes. A strong smell of onions at her shoulder brought those memories to an abrupt halt. Alfredo was over her shoulder explaining pay-by-the-piece and expected production rates and a fifteen-minute lunch and no more than two breaks. As soon as he left, she paused one more time, No, this was not school. And she sighed with the vision of the next two years on the job and the flat.

Chapter Thirteen; 1933, Brooklyn

Franco had just finished his first semester at Brooklyn Polytechnic. His stomach was in knots. It wasn't that the classes were so hard, although trigonometry was giving him fits. He liked shop class and the hands-on experiments and projects. English class, reading poems, was a joke. Why did engineers need that crap? He even made the wrestling team. At 112 pounds the coach was glad to get someone for the flyweight division which often meant a forfeit at their collegiate meets when challengers had no one in his weight class. Overall, college was going better than he had imagined. Except for fitting in. He fit in the classroom, but was out-classed everywhere else. He wore a suit and tie just like they did. But it was the same suit. His only suit. He could speak English correctly. But he didn't speak the language of his upper-class colleagues. How could he? Only he and his brother and his cousin Tina spoke English at home, if they thought about it. Many fellow students knew each other from their boarding schools or prep academies. There was no one from PS 106 joining him. He had nothing to say at lunch when they talked about their summer place on Long Island or dinner at *the club* or where they were going over break. And when the school hosted a holiday party he was depressed by the dazzling, stylish women he could never imagine dating, clinging to the arms of his classmates.

He sat at the table, staring at tickets to a neighborhood dance that his buddy Dino had given him. He didn't know any girl he could ask to the dance. Actually, he did know several girls that his mother wanted him to date. Nice Italian girls who were over-impressed by the fact he was such a hot prospect going to college and all. If he asked one of them out, it would be the talk of the neighborhood and he would be practically engaged.

Tina walked into the kitchen, picked the coffee pot off the stove and shook it. "There's enough for two cups," she said. "Want some?"

"Yeah. Okay." He watched her turn on the gas, reach on the shelf for two mismatched, chipped cups, then stand, arms crossed, lost in thought. *Tina,* he thought. *Tina's a girl. Hell yeah. I bet she would be glad to get out of the house for a change. And the best part is no complications. No expectations beyond having fun dancing. And I don't need to pretend I'm some 'swell' trying to impress her. She's seen me in my underwear and I her, more than once. We're even.*

By the end of spring semester, Margherita noticed that Franco was taking Tina out to dances most weekends with long walks in the evening and smiling eyes over the dinner table. This couldn't be happening... could it? First cousin romance wasn't typical in Sicilian culture. But it wasn't uncommon. No, this wouldn't do. She and Vito and Rocco hadn't struggled to put Franco through college just so he could marry his cousin. He could have done that without going to college. *Corsi, with his olive oil business, has a sweet daughter. And the Ambrosis with their bakery and delivery trucks have a daughter... what's her name? But no, he's getting interested in my niece. Damn, that Nino. Making trouble again. Sending his daughter to live with us and now look. Well, he sent her here and I can send her back... sooner rather than later. Besides, my son needs to focus on school, get his degree.*

In a discreet letter to her brother Marco, Margherita asked him to see if any factories in Detroit were hiring seamstresses. The word, two weeks later, was yes. Chrysler had started ramping up production on a new line of Plymouths and was paying top dollar. In no time, Tina was on the train. Back home, she was wedged in a crowded bed with three of her five sisters and turning over her paycheck to her father with a little kept out for carfare and lipstick. Something new, however, was the weekly, florid and sometimes torrid letter from her cousin Franco.

Chapter Fourteen; 1937, Detroit

Nino stood in front of the shoe store at Harper and Van Dyke longingly eyeing a pair of French-toe Florsheims tagged at $25. Three times the cost of clunky Thom McAnns in the store down the block. Scotch-buttery brown, delicately stitched, fine-grained leather, made for the kind of light, elegant footwear a shoe-proud Italian could admire. And now that Tina and Franco seemed closer to marriage, he should soon have an excuse to indulge his vanity. *After all, if a man can't get a new pair of shoes for his daughter's wedding, when can he? It would feel like a kind of blessing for what should prove a happy union.*

With the college degree his nephew would be earning in June, he should have a lot of job prospects, if not immediately because of the Depression, at least in the long run. There had to be jobs for an engineer in the Motor City. And if worse came to worst, there was no shame in driving a truck for a while like Eva's brothers. He chuckled to himself, thinking, *and I guess we know he comes from a good family, right? There's that.* But he would miss Tina's regular paychecks while she saved for her trousseau. Somebody had to. Franco sure wouldn't have any spare change, just now. *Come to think of it, she should probably hold onto her job till they get on their feet. I guess I better get used to my girls leaving. The next ones are all lined up for graduation, work and then marriage. Well at least I can look forward to getting a new pair of Florsheims every few years.*

313

Chapter Fifteen; 1937, Brooklyn

"Ma," Rocco called as he folded the paper. "I'm reading about this pension you can get with the new Social Security. Your boss has to pay some and you pay some but when you get sixty-five you can get money every month till you die."

"Pfft! Nobody gives you nothing."

"No, Margherita," Vito interrupted. "I been talking to Aldo and Piero. It's a good thing."

"So, I bring home less money. This is good?"

"But you get it back later when you retire," Rocco said. "The only thing is you have to be a citizen."

"I don't want to be American. Anyhow, I'm going back to Italy to be with my daughters." She paused, thinking, "... some time. And they will take care of me."

"We'll both go, *cara,* after we're sixty-five. And with both our pensions we can live comfortably and won't have to bother our children. Everything's cheaper in the old country and we know how to live simply."

"I don't even know how to talk English. You have to talk American to be an American citizen. Marta at work told me."

"Look, Ma. Think about it. In the meantime, let me work on it. Maybe I can sit in on some of the ceremonies and see how they test you for English speaking."

A week later, Rocco drilled his mother after dinner. "Okay, look. I sat in on the process. Turns out the judge asks the same three questions to see if you can understand and speak English. We're going to practice answering these questions every night for a week. 1. Who is the mayor of New York? You answer, La Guardia. 2. Who is the first president of the United States? George Washington. 3. Who is the president of the United States? Roosevelt."

"I can't remember all that," Margherita complained.

"You just have to remember three words—LaGuardia, Washington and Roosevelt. So, let's practice. The judge talks: blah, blah, blah: when he stops you say—La Guardia. When he talks again: blah, blah, blah and stops you say—Washington. Blah, blah, blah—Roosevelt. Again..."

Two weeks later, after filling out the naturalization form for his mother, Rocco took her for her scheduled interview. All the way to the USCIS office he grilled his mother on her three answers until she was perfect. Sure enough, she answered each question on cue. But when the examiner asked how many States made up the United States, Margherita could only stare blankly. The examiner addressed Rocco. "Your forms show your mother has lived and worked in this country as a productive member of society. Despite her language limitations, she has found a way to belong and contribute to our society. I see no reason to deny her request for citizenship."

"*Che cosa ha detto?*" Margherita asked her son.

"He says you're a citizen. Say thank you, Ma."

Chapter Sixteen; 1940, Detroit

A light breeze fluttered the sun-brightened plaid curtains Tina had sewn for their cozy starter apartment. She hummed to herself while frying chicken for their supper. Now that she was in her second trimester her appetite was returning with a vengeance. Franco was due home from Ford's soon and after supper she would take a nap before her midnight shift. She wouldn't be able to work too much longer but for the moment the double income was much appreciated.

She heard the front door slam and Franco's heavy steps pounding up the stairs. When he slumped in without looking at her, slammed his briefcase and drafting pencils on the kitchen table on the way to the front room and flopped on the couch, she felt her pulse quicken. She turned off the gas, deliberately made her way to the love chair opposite her husband and perched on the edge. "What?" she asked.

"I got canned."

"But you were set to get promoted to the lab. To run it. That's what you said."

"Well, I didn't want to go there."

"Why?"

"I don't know chemistry... not that much and I would have to manage a different department. Twenty people. There's twenty people there. And since they were eliminating my department, they let me go." He looked at his wife's stricken face and hurried to add, "But don't worry. I'll find something. I'll keep us going so you don't have to work. I'll do anything. I'm not afraid to work. Not ashamed."

Tina rose, turned her back, fists clenched. When she turned back her face was taut with anger. "Dammit, Franco. You got to push to get ahead. Take a chance. If you don't know... you learn."

"Easy for you to say. You think work is just doing production. Chugging out pieces. Sewing seat cushions and arm rests all day long. There are all kinds of people knowing people and knowing who to ask and how to brown-nose them. It's not just knowing what has to be done..."

"You're scared, aren't you? You don't have the guts to stand up for yourself."

Franco sat up. "You don't understand. I don't like to be told what to do. To be pussy-footing around going, *yes sir, whatever you say sir,* kissing ass, plotting to make a move, hob-knobbing on the golf-course, joining the country club."

"Excuses. If I had your education I wouldn't hold back."

Franco shook his head.

"So, I guess I have to keep working," Tina said as she cupped her hands around her belly, "and you'll stay at home."

"That's not going to happen. I'll find work. I'll take care of you... of us."

Tina half-looked away, corners of her mouth tensed.

"Look, maybe I'm not cut out for this kind of work, in big business..." Franco pleaded. "Did you ever think of that?"

"No, you're content to play pinochle with my dad and uncles. That's your speed. Maybe if you had to be the oldest child and take care of everyone else like I did... do what you were told whether you wanted to or not... you would be used to taking charge and doing what has to be done because someone had to do it instead of having mamma wipe your nose all the time."

Franco and Tina glared at each while their breathing slowed. Finally, Franco went to the door, said, "Later," and left to the sound of his wife's sob.

He never went to bars. But that evening he did. The ball game was on the radio. Tigers were playing the Indians. He didn't particularly like beer but he ordered a Goebles at the suggestion of a between-innings commercial. Chatter stopped at one point when the Tigers had a man on third, two outs. The manager called for a suicide bunt. The runner was tagged out at the plate. "See," a man at the bar said, "Cochrane shoulda never called for the bunt. If I was the manager, I woulda let Greenberg swing away."

"You sound like my wife," Franco lamented.

"She's a manager?"
"Wannabe."

Chapter Seventeen; 1950, Detroit

Vito and Margherita eased into Franco's new Ford Custom 4-door sedan outside the train station. They felt like rich people riding in the back with their own chauffeur at the wheel. That was nice. They never needed a car in New York but it certainly was convenient and worthy of their son, the *engineer* they had helped produce.

Nine-year old Roy sat in the front seat and would turn every-so-often to stare at his grandparents and smile. He chattered in English with Franco. Once he looked over the seat and announced, "I can talk Italian... *pane burro.*" Margherita smiled. *That's it?* she wondered. *Our Italian son married to an Italian woman and the only Italian their kid can say is bread and butter. Hold your tongue, Margherita, she told herself. You haven't seen your son or family... it's four now with one on the way, o Dio... in ten years. I've got to talk to that niece of mine. She can't keep making babies like this, confusing my son.*

They drove through a pleasant neighborhood of brick colonials facing a boulevard with trees, shrubs and flowers. "This is nice, Franco. Is this where you live?"

Franco's hands clutched the steering wheel. "No. Not here Ma." He could tell his son was looking at him. The kid felt his pain at the disappointment they both knew was coming when they drove into their working-class neighborhood.

Standing at the curb, Margherita took in the two-story frame house with gray asbestos siding snugged between two similar homes and their postage stamp lawns. *Well, at least there is grass in front of the houses... more than in Brooklyn,* she thought. *But this is it, huh? All that work to put him through college and this is the best he can do.*

Her first impressions were interrupted by Tina showing up on the porch in her seven-month pregnant self. Three other children crowded around her. Hugs and kisses pre-vailed for the next five minutes. A walk through the house did not change first impressions. Two tiny bedrooms down-stairs—one jammed full with a crib and two single beds. Then a small kitchen that led to a bathroom with stairs to the attic where, it turned out there was a bedroom. The grandparents would be sharing the loft room with Roy and would have to be conscious of rude noises, snoring and Vi-to's nighttime startles.

In bed that night, with the boy sleeping soundly near-by, Margherita unloaded. "Look at this, would you? Here I was thinking we might want to live with them for a few years instead of that nasty old tenement and they hardly have enough room for a cat, let alone us. The basement might do. But when I mentioned that, my niece wrinkled her nose and said she wouldn't keep a dog down there. What does she know? If she grew up in the old country, she wouldn't be so fussy. She doesn't know what we've been through and what we can get used to." Vito grunted assent.

"And look at Rocco. All right, he lives in a tiny flat like us and doesn't have room for us either. But, at least he has a lot of money with his barber shop in Greenwich Village and his house by Long Island."

"And his one son," Vito added. "Franco makes kids, not money."

"For this we sent him to college?"

"*Boh!* we each follow our own path."

During the night, Vito yelled loud and long. Once it was clear that nothing was wrong, Roy finally fell back asleep. The next morning, he reported to his dad. 'Yeah, he does that sometimes. If you ask him, he says he is getting hard of hearing and sometimes dreams he's deaf and ends up shouting to prove he can still hear."

"Oh."

"But I think he has nightmares from being in the war."

Two days later, Margherita watched Roy opening a can of Campbell's vegetable soup and emptying it into a pan. When he saw his grandmother watching, he put the pan on the stove, turned on the gas and made rolling gestures with his hands and mimed turning off the gas. Margherita started giggling at the thought of teaching a grandmother to boil soup. Soon Tina joined her and after an exchange in Italian they both laughed to the boy's consternation and puzzlement.

Chapter Eighteen; 1961, Harper Woods

Franco pulled into his driveway, station wagon packed solid, suitcases strapped to the roof and Vito in the passenger seat. Roy came out of the house to greet his recently widowed grandfather who quietly shook with grief as they embraced. Vito muttered something in Italian. The young man looked to his father for translation. Franco's brow gnarled in sorrow. "He said, grandma never made it back to Italy and their daughters."

To break the ensuing awkward pause, Roy patted his grandfather on the shoulder and offered to help unload. As he reached to untie the intricate web of ropes holding the rooftop baggage, he stopped to admire the handiwork. Franco explained that his father tied vines as a youth. The grandson tugged on one of the knots and shot a thumbs-up to his eighty-four year old grampa. Vito gently smiled acceptance of the compliment.

Just before the last trip into the house, Vito grabbed his son's arm and said. "*Bedda casa.* You've done good. Your mother would have been proud. Too bad she never saw it."

Vito, familiar with change over a long life of adaptation, soon made himself at home. He slept on a fold-out couch in the family room that had storage underneath for his limited wardrobe. The seven children, three more since the last visit, had plenty of room in the rambling ranch home and quickly adjusted to his presence.

The grandchildren were taken by surprise with some of his habits like the first morning he made toast from half a loaf of bread which they thought would be shared. Instead, Vito proceeded to fold and dunk each slice in an oversized bowl of coffee and milk. Tina, on the other hand, left alone with the old timer all day was less amused by his habits and had to ask Franco to talk to his dad about spitting in the sink, and smoking in the house, and sitting at the front room window mumbling when the mailman was a day late with his social security check.

One evening, six months later, Vito, apparently past the grieving process, announced over pinochle with his brother-in-law Nino, Franco and Tina that he wanted to return to Sicily, finally. And that he wanted to live apart from his daughters. And that he wanted to remarry. The game stopped cold and a heated discussion followed. Soon it became clear that Vito had thought it all through and was determined. A month later he was on his way. This time by plane instead of ship.

Chapter Nineteen; 1965, Paceco, Sicily

"Hey, Ma and Pa and the rest of you guys. Turns out cousin Peppe has a recorder and I thought I could do a live broadcast instead of writing a letter and all the folks here can say hello when I'm done. We just finished dinner at Aunt Angela's and they're all... well, the guys anyhow... watching soccer on TV. And I'm snugged in a corner with a microphone and none of them know what I'm saying.

"Oh, look, Pina just walked by with the pile of leftover boiled chicken and carrots and onions from the chicken soup. I gotta tell you about that. You know how boiled chicken looks all grey? Well, while we were eating I kept staring at the platter and I couldn't make out what I was seeing. Then, Grampa Vito grabs a chunk of breast and I suddenly recognize chicken feet sticking out. Not so bad. I guess they can add flavor too. Then I keep staring and there's the chicken's head... feathers, comb and eye lids closed. I guess every little bit counts around here.

"Your sister Connie just hugged me, Pa. She looks so much like your mother, Margherita. Reminds me of her. I overheard Connie and Angela chatting in Sicilian the other day. Man, that takes me back to gramma Eva and her sisters and brothers in Detroit. I could follow what they were saying. I guess I can recognize some words from when I was a kid. But I can't speak a lick. It's like smells, right? Language and words can beam you back to another time and place. And now they're giving me a slice of *tiramisu*. Great cake. I'll get to it soon as I'm done.

"Let's see. Where to start? The trip here. The flight was fine. I took the train from Rome to Naples. Then I got the overnight ferry to Sicily. The men's quarters—I remembered you talking about crossing the ocean as a kid, Dad—I bet it was like that. We were all jammed into this room—guys snoring in bunk beds, farting, smoking, tossing and turn-ing. Good thing it was a nice night on deck.

"Next morning, cousin Peppe met me at the dock. He's a year older than me. *Call me Joe,* he said. But turns out that's all the English he knows and that made the hour trip feel like forever. But as soon as I got to grampa's place, I got the usual face scrub with his three-day whiskers on both cheeks. He and Zia Teresa live in this small, stone-block walk-up. It's really tiny—one bedroom, kitchen, john and a hallway with a couch where I sleep.

"Your dad's happy, Pa. Much as you can tell by him. Every morning, he toddles off to church. I don't remember him being religious. Do you? Then he gets his grocery list... they buy food every day, for that day, around here. And you should hear Zia Teresa harp at him to buy good fish for supper not like the cheap crap he bought two days ago and gave them both a stomach ache. That lady... she's like a live-in housekeeper with a sense of humor. You know what she reminds me of... Ann Scarlatti next door. They're both serious, solid women you gotta like. She even had the good grace to laugh at herself when I stopped her from scrubbing my nylon golf shirt on a washboard when she has a perfect-ly good mini-washing machine. The shirt's a little stretched and pilled on one shoulder.

"So, yeah, *Nonno* Vito seems happy away from the noise and congestion of New York. He's mellow on his home turf. At last. And even though his daughters protest that he should have moved in with them... like it's their *dovere,* their duty, right?... I think they're glad that he's living on his own. No burden on them. More power to him, I say.

"But you should see the things they do to save money. Gramps cuts his cigarettes in half to get more tokes. I think you told me about that. And thanks for the tip. His eyes really lit up when I gave him the carton of Pall Malls. Oh, and here's another thing. Some nights, Zia goes to the bed-room to watch *her* 10 inch black and white TV, that she ap-parently brought to the marriage, while Gramps sits in the kitchen watching the electric meter spin. I love those two.

"Holy shit. I just saw Zia Teresa in the kitchen doorway giving me a Mona Lisa smile. Oh, man, I just remembered she lived in Detroit for ten years in the 50s. She and her husband ran a corner grocery store in Ma's old neighborhood. She told me they sold *Silvercuppa bread.* I think she understands enough English to know what I'm saying... oh, good she ducked back into the kitchen. I don't think I said anything to offend her.

"So, what else? Language. So far, I'm getting by with my college Italian and from watching *La Strada* ten times. Pina, Angela's oldest daughter is a teacher and she tutors me most nights. Uhm, you know, she's really very pretty. And besides that, I think she likes me. Or maybe, that's just how she treats relatives and guests. And I'm both. But she does hang all over me. Like she brings me a glass of water without my even asking and puts *biscotti* and coffee in front of me every time I sit down. Yesterday she shined my shoes. When I say, *No-no I can do it,* and try to help myself, she gets this hurt look on her face. Are all Italian women this way with men? Never mind, I know what you're going to say, Ma. But, don't worry I'm not going to marry my cousin even if she waits on me hand and foot.

"It feels so familiar around here even though it's so different. Like yesterday, we all went on a picnic but instead of watermelon and *salsiccia* at Chandler Park, we went to a deserted stretch of beach and ate sea urchins. Did you do that when you lived here, Pa? The women sit on chairs on the beach and the guys go snorkeling with a knife and net bag to pry the *ricci* off the rocks. Then we bring the catch to the ladies who cut them open with tiny sewing scissors. You take a piece of crusty bread and scoop out the bright orange roe inside. I can't say I was knocked out by it. Like I'd order it at a restaurant. But out there, after swimming in saltwater and with a squirt of lemon. Hmm.

"So, what I'm trying to say is, I feel like I'm with family... which I am. They're just talking in code. But all the rest is the same. Pina reminds me of Uncle Tony's Betty. And Aunt Angela could be Aunt Josie if she had stayed in the States all these years. The men don't play cards so much but there's the same kind of easy living feeling... that you don't live to work—you work to live. And the rest of the time can be spent in small talk and togetherness.

"And I get a kick out of the guys my age. They aren't into sports, so much. But boy do they love their cars. Peppe's buddy, Paolo, has a souped-up Fiat Cinquecento. He took me on the highway and pulled a U-turn at 50 miles an hour with that hot-rod go-cart. Turns out they do mountain acceleration races. Peppe rides tachometer for Paolo as they slam up the grades. But underneath all that, they are really hurting for a job. Paolo, for instance, has a fiancé and as soon as he can get a job they can get married. So, you can imagine the excitement when the government announced a civil service exam in Palermo for 300 Post Office jobs. Seven of us piled into three cars and raced up north. All those guys were hoping to get what they called, *sistemato…* to get settled with a job so they could get on with the rest of their lives.

"Well, nobody said it couldn't be fun to drive to Palermo. And you should have seen when they spotted a poor young woman driving alone. They took turns leap frogging around her, bracketing her front and back and making her slow down or speed up. She knew they were teasing and showing off and I guess she didn't mind the attention because I caught her smiling when we cut her off for the third time.

"So, anyhow this is a great place filled with beautiful people and they treat me like a king. You should come here Pop. Come back to your home for a visit. Well, I've talked long enough let me give your family a chance to say hello. *Zia Concetta, viene parlare con tuo fratello.*"

Chapter Twenty; 1970, Phone call between Brooklyn and Harper Woods

Franco: Angela sent word the old man is sick. Might be serious. I mean, he is ninety.

Rocco: Yeah. You think we should go see him... in case.

Franco: Mmm. What if he gets better?

Rocco: And we waste a trip...

Franco: Ah, what the hell. Let him get better. He doesn't need to die just to justify our trip.

Rocco: (laughs) Yeah. It might even do him good to see us. I wouldn't mind seeing my sisters. Haven't seen Connie since I was twelve, and Angela and her girls. It would be good to see them all.

Franco: And the places I vaguely remember... like our house in Paceco.

Rocco: Where would we stay? Do you know what his place is like?

Franco: My Roy went to see him five years ago. Remember?

Rocco: Yeah. Heard it was a good trip.

Franco: Pa lives with Teresa...

Rocco: The old dog. Just had to get married again, didn't he? Heard he put out the word to all the eligible women interested in a *paisano* with an American pension.

Franco: At least that way he didn't have to move in with our sisters. And Roy says Teresa is nice and he liked her a lot. But where they live now is real simple and small.

Rocco: Figures. The old man never splurged.

Franco: Always the same. Roy said he still splits matches in half. So, their place is tiny, up a flight of outside steps. We wouldn't be able to stay there. But I understand Pina and her husband have a big apartment in downtown Trapani. We could stay with them.

Rocco: Hmm, I guess. When you wanna go?

328

Franco: The sooner the better. How about next week?

Cagalupo Redux

by

Joe Novara

Gypsy Shadow Publishing

Cagalupo Redux

by

Joe Novara

Gypsy Shadow Publishing, LLC.
Lockhart, TX
www.gypsyshadow.com

ISBN: 978-1-61950-661-9

Published in the United States of America

First eBook Edition: May 10, 2021

Chapter One; Nick

I wonder if that's a woman coming toward me. Or is she going away? Coming toward me. If it is a woman, about now she's got to be getting concerned—alone on the beach, at the far end of Wilderness State Park, a man perhaps, gradually getting closer. I'm probably ruining her meditative stroll into the golden glitter edging over Lake Michigan.

Ha! If she only knew how old I am, how little threat I pose. Hell, if she's a young woman, maybe camping with her lover, she could easily outrun me back to safety. No need for her to imagine horrible things. She'd be the kind of interns we got at the newspapers. Fresh. Unblemished. So much promise and excitement in her eyes. Unless this girl's got tattoos or piercings. I hate that. Such a violation. Like graffiti on a church. But, this girl coming at me, if she had a minute, maybe we could talk about what she's doing these days—work, school, boyfriend. Maybe there's something troubling her. Something she'd want to have a real chat about. Not just texting. Talk. Imagine that. Fifty years ago that's where I would have started but not where I hoped to finish.

No. Now that's she closer, I can tell. She's not that young after all. Maybe a mother of teenagers, on a camping vacation, slouching through a moment of solitude before the rumpus begins. I wonder what her children are like. I bet she would be glad to talk about them. Imagine if there were a coffee bar out here and we could each order a mocha grande and just ease into the day talking about what her kids are doing in school. What sports they play. What worries her about this one or that one. That would be so cool. Women that age are old enough to look you in the eye. Sure enough of their bodies to offer a frank, breast-first hug. Not like young women who arch forward, limiting contact to their shoulders—as if I wouldn't know what breasts feel like in a hug. Yeah, a chat with this perfect stranger before continuing in opposite directions, that would be nice.

More talk. Maybe that's what you do when you get older... talk. Social intercourse instead of the other kind. A chat buddy. Ha!

Oh. Wait a sec. Now I can make out the lady. It is a lady. Graying-blond hair. Nice firm stride. Good posture. Actually, just a little bit roundy in her fuchsia tank suit. But nicely so. As we get closer she makes eye contact. Sizes me up. Quick friendly nod. And we walk past each other. A few steps on, I stop. Look back. She has stopped as well. She points south, back the way she has come. I nod and wait for her to join me. No talk. And as the sunrise shadow retreats across the beach, back over the pines standing guard along the dune ridge, we walk side by side into the sunlit beach. I like this kind of woman.

Chapter Two; Carol

There's a person way up the beach. I can't tell if it's a man or a woman. A guy wouldn't care, one way or the other. Well, that's not exactly true. A guy would hope it was a woman. Then he'd have a chance to size up and fantasize. But not us. We've got to worry, a little at least. Defenseless woman assaulted on the beach. Yeah, but no, the beach is different. It's not like a dark alley in the city. I mean, people are barefoot and practically naked, aren't they? If you can't feel safe here, where can you?

It is a man. He's older, head down looking for beach glass, or maybe Petoskey stones. Good luck with that. I don't think I've found four all summer. He's safe. And it's obvious that he's single. A wife would have disappeared that faded purple bathing suit ten years ago. And that shredded, sleeveless Michigan State tee shirt... But, I do like his foot-ball-player shoulders. And his legs are so heavy thighed and solid like he would be hard to knock over. But wait a minute, why do I feel like smiling? Why do I feel like I'm seeing someone I know but just can't remember who? It's around the eyes. It's a pleasant association. As we walk by, we both smile politely. Is it someone from the old neighbor-hood? Could that be why he's so familiar? I stop and turn for another look. He's looking at me, too. I was planning to head back home anyway, why not offer to walk with him?

On our way, I decide to let him start talking. But he doesn't. That's fine with me. I mean, this isn't exactly the time or place to swap e-match profiles, is it? So... he can be comfortable with silence. I like that.

I glance at him. He slides a look back. I know this guy, but I'm not going to play twenty questions with him. If he can be cool. I can be cool, too. I know, I'll surprise him and invite him up to the house. Eventually I'll figure it out.

Chapter Three; Nick

We walk for some time past the State Park beach. I'm quiet. I'm cool. This is nice. The woman suddenly starts heading away from the water. What's happening? She gestures with her head—c'mon. Is she mute? I look at the bluff rising up ahead of us. Fifty yards of knee-high beach grass stretch before me. Then a set of stairs. Four flights. Above that I see a glassed in, turret-like tower with a cedar shake roof—a widow's walk. That's what it is. I wonder if she's a widow. I notice a telescope on a tripod. From up there I bet she could see all the way past the State Park beach to the Mackinac Bridge. Could she have seen me coming? Scoped me out? Dream on, sucker.

As we climb the stairs, I see the rest of the roof—half a football field wide. More cedar shakes, brown, not yet weathered gray. It's a red brick mansion—third floor, second floor, plantation porch. What if she's just the caretaker and the owners are off somewhere for a month? Would you look at that? Finally, I'm on the lower deck as the woman slides open a door in the glass wall that fronts the lake. She walks in, leaving me to follow.

I feel a *Better Homes and Gardens* article coming on. Rosewood floors flow around islands of carpeting sprouting leather couches and bamboo lamps surrounded by jungles of paintings and crystal and burnished globes dangling and sparkling throughout. Behind me, a restless mural of the Great Lake is framed by a glass cinemascope screen, ten panels wide. Subtle tones of blue, gray and green bracketed between scudding clouds and tousled whitecaps are grounded by strands of beige sand and bearded saw grass...

"Coffee?" a voice echoes from the bowels of the cavern.

"Yeah, sure."

The first words we've spoken. I like her voice, mellow, slightly lazy, said with the kind of languor I associate with wealthy people. Well, she would be, wouldn't she? Be wealthy, I mean, to be living in this personal resort. Or... or maybe she's renting. Ha! Or house sitting for a friend. Could be. Does it matter? I glance down at a tabletop forested with framed photos. I begin to look for a husband, for kids. Instead I stop at the first one. It's a black and white picture of a round-faced girl sporting a black cowboy hat, studded vest and a mean looking six-gun while mounted on a black and white pony. I smile. Somewhere in my jumbled pile of family photos is a picture of me on the same horse. I'm sure it's the same one. Same costume. This lady and I probably wore the same props. Could we have grown up in the same neighborhood?

I smell the coffee, turn and watch the woman carrying a tray with a silver carafe and service. Surprisingly, in that short time she must have showered because her hair is still wet and I can see beads of moisture near the crook of her neck. She smiles. Wow. Stunning. She looks right at home in a peach cover-up that goes so well with the interior décor. Yeah, she lives here. This is her home.

We sit on the deck, savoring our coffee and the gentle SW breeze angling one-foot rollers along the shoreline. There are a lot of things I want to ask her starting with her current marital status. Not that it matters that much, really. It's not like I want to wedge my way into any part of this... this anchor. I like my life. My retired auto-parts van. It's a good thing we don't talk. It would only open up all kinds of contradictions, all kinds of differences. So, it's just as well we keep still; enjoy this bubble. If one of us tries to probe or poke it's going to burst. I'll just call this a *sometime thing* and be on my way. Got to be in Sault Ste. Marie around noon. The PR guy for LSSU—what's his name again? —needs to obsess over their annual report. Then over to Newberry. Gotta keep scufflin'. Me and my home on wheels. Still, that pony thing would be fun to explore, to find out if she lived in Detroit when I did, what neighborhoods, what schools.

Three days later, I'm back below the bridge. Hey, with an annual pass, it's cheaper at the State Park than a KOA. I'm taking a morning stroll on the beach. Up ahead is a figure. It takes a while to determine if the person is coming toward me or going away. Toward. Three minutes later I recognize the fuchsia bathing suit. Ha. I wonder if she spotted me with her scope, then ran down to the beach and, like in a B movie, where the characters bound toward each other in hair-floating slow motion to finally collapse in a tangled embrace. Marsha! John!

Or maybe I'm like this Paladin guy—Have Gun Will Travel. Only, my card would read, Have Pen Will Travel. Let me just kiss my horse, ma'am, before I ride off over the horizon. Or maybe she's this Rapunzel-like lady stuck in a castle pining for the foot-free, untrammeled rogue to come back into her life. In your dreams, hot shot.

We stand and look at each other. She grins. I love her soft helmet of heirloom-silver hair. She's got to be early sixties. Hard to tell. She certainly looks fit: upper arms defined but not buff, taut core, legs shaped and firm. Man, she's got it. Then she points my way back up the beach. She's probably thinking something like, I've shown you mine, now show me yours.

This whole game is going to blow up in a minute. There's never been any real money in freelance writing... not like her money, anyway. When she gets onto my situation, it's going to be all over... whatever this is between us. But for now, we walk. No talk. I can live with that. Apparently, she can too. That's not all bad.

Finally, I can see the trail to the campgrounds up ahead. This scene is about to dissolve to black. I decide I might as well break the grand silence since it's going to end soon anyhow. "My home is on wheels. I move around."

She faces me, raises her eyebrows and her hands in a *so what* gesture. Well, in for a nickel, in for a dime. "You know that picture of you in a cowboy outfit on a black and white pony? I got a picture of me riding the same pony."

She studies me for a long moment. "Really? We oughta talk."

Chapter Four; Carol

So, he finally makes the connection but not where I thought he would. He latched onto the pony. But I remember him from the potato chip factory. I was behind the counter and he would pop in three or four times a week after school, obviously interested in more than potato chips, I liked to think. I never did learn his name. He never asked for mine either. I wonder why? Considering how quiet he's been and how comfortable he seems with silence, maybe he's a non-talker. I had enough of that with Mario. He never spoke any more than he had to. Well, I take that back, he could babble on and on when he got excited about some hot deal. I guess what I'm starved for is conversation.

Chapter Five; Nick

So, we talk sitting on a piece of driftwood and then at my campsite over coffee and oatmeal, which is what I eat for breakfast. She doesn't seem to mind—even asks for seconds with raisins and a dash of brown sugar. We talk about the pony picture and how the whole gig wouldn't work today since there aren't enough stay-at-home moms. Over a second cup of coffee, we pause. We look at each other. Smile.

"So, where did you live, back then?" I ask.

"By the city airport."

"Geez, that's just up Gratiot a ways from where I lived. They had a nice strip of grass next to the hangars where we played football after school."

"Go figure."

"Yeah, So, that's where you grew up."

"Uh-huh."

There's an awkward silence. Where to, next? I want to know how she has come to live in such a magnificent house. But how? I could flat out ask. Or beat around the bush and hint a little. Instead, she holds my eye for a long moment, then says, "I suppose you're wondering how a kid from the East Side comes to live in such a fancy home."

"Yeah. The thought crossed my mind. Not that it's any of my business..."

She grins, rotates my chipped diner mug on the picnic table. "I married a local boy."

"What was his name? I knew everybody from Cagalupo."

"Cagalupo? Never heard of it."

"Well, you wouldn't have, if you weren't Italian. It's what us Sicilians living around Gratiot and Harper called our neighborhood. You know, like Hamtramck for the Poles or Cork Town for the Irish."

"I see," she says, eyes past my shoulder, a sip of coffee. "He never talked about it—his growing up." Back to me. "Mario. His name was Mario Galvano."

"What? No way. You were married to Mamo?"

"I never heard him called that before."

"We were in school together. That guy! He picked a fight with every kid in St. Joe's. Lord knows he had enough time. He was held back three times by the eighth grade."

Chapter Six; Carol

I look off at the white caps crenellating the Straits of Mackinac. That's not the Mario I knew. But then, he never did talk about those years. None of his daughters did either. Was he ashamed? Is that what drove him so hard? Lead to his heart problems? Mamo. That's all this guy remembers is a schoolyard bully with learning disabilities. And he's dying to know how he could afford a mansion on the Lake. How about a whole chain of hamburger joints followed by bagel outlets and a Tex-Mex fast food franchise? I watch his brow furrow. "People," I say. "Mario knew people and what they wanted to eat. Or rather, how they wanted to eat. And so, he made restaurants. He had the touch—the timing. Whatever you call it."

"How could he know all that? None of us ever ate out back then."

I break into a grin and a stifle a giggle.

"What?"

"I'm just remembering. One time after a game, or recital or... doesn't matter... anyhow my father decided to treat me to a burger and shake at a McDonald-type place. We walked in and sat down at a table. He kept looking around for a waitress to bring us a menu and take our order. After fifteen minutes he grabbed my hand and dragged me out of there grumbling about the bad service."

"Well, that's just what I'm saying. We weren't used to drive-through fast food. Now you're saying that somehow Mamo hooked into all that. But... he was so dumb in school."

I turn and pointedly look at his blue and yellow van as if to say, 'If you're so smart, why aren't you rich?'

He has the good grace to look abashed. "Okay, point taken. I just find it hard to believe."

"Believe. I admit, he may not have been school smart but he had a marvelous eye for the next trend. And timing. He knew when to buy and when to sell."

He nods in begrudging agreement. "I guess."

"So, to answer the question you never quite asked, he left me this beautiful house to live in. For as long as I want. But really it belongs to his daughters. And of course, I got some money. Insurance and all that. Oh, and a minor league hockey team. Have you ever heard of the K Wings?"

"Yeah. Yeah, I heard of them. I wrote some copy for their PR department. In Kalamazoo, right?"

I nod. "You're a writer?"

"Uh-huh. Journalism. PR. Corporate copy. Like that. I've been *downsized* just before—I don't know how many— newspapers and businesses folded in Michigan in the last ten years."

"Mario wasn't much for words... written or otherwise. But he knew his limitations." I pause. "He could have used a wordsmith like you."

Chapter Seven; Nick

I let that thought sink in. It didn't get very far—me working for Mamo. "You shared many quiet evenings, I take it. Is that you? At home with prolonged silences?"

She colors, looking at her hands. "Couples accommodate, absorb traits from each other."

"I wouldn't know."

"You never married?'

"Not long enough to rub onto each other—the way you're talking about."

She barks a laugh. I'm pleased to have reached her.

"But, I can get into good conversations," she says. "I've just been out of practice for a couple of years."

"But you don't natter," I add.

She gives me a look that I sometimes get from a client when I get a writing assignment just right. It's a look that says, *you get me.* But do I? I haven't connected this fast, this easily with a woman since... I can't remember if I ever did. I know it's my serve and I'm supposed to take the next step here. But what? I'd like to spend more time with this lady. But, hell, I don't even know her name. Well, I know her last name, Galvano. Without thinking I blurt out, "Nick. Nick Finazzo," and stick out my hand like I'm a real estate agent or something. What a strange social convention, shaking hands. But I had to do something.

The lady, like a kid deciding to go along with a make-believe game, offers her hand and with a childish grin says, "Carol Galvano. Pleased to meet you." We shake. Hold hands a little longer than necessary. Then silence again.

We have something going here. It's good. Solid. Should I make some excuse to hang around Cheboygan for a few days; see what develops? Should I get into dinner dates and a romantic cruise to Mackinac Island with a carriage ride to Arch Rock? I can't just let her drift away from me. We can't

344

keep pretending to meet by accident. I suddenly imagine her walking farther and farther away from me, way down the beach. I can't let that happen. What interest could she possibly have in me? It's my move. But what?

Chapter Eight; Carol

Well, well, well. This is turning out better and better by the minute. What an interesting man. How should I play this? I can hear my mother saying, 'No man likes a pushy woman. Let the man take the lead.' Yeah, well, mom is long gone and this guy is right here in front of me acting less than take-charge. He could just be shy. Or maybe gun-shy. Or maybe he's playing me, waiting for me to show my hand. Well, I've got nothing to hide. I've been married and I don't like to play games. So, let's get on with it, Mr. Nick. I'm going to ask for what I want. Sorry, mother. "Nick, could you give me a lift back to the house?"

Chapter Nine; Nick

Smooth. Nice save, Carol. "Sure," I reply. Let's take this one step at a time.

Did you ever invite someone over, then look around your place with their eyes? Fresh eyes? Evaluating, judging eyes? As Carol climbs into my van, I try to see what she sees: a ten-year old delivery van with two doors in the back that open on a mattress and a rumpled sleeping bag and last week's jeans and socks and briefs. Okay. I don't have to defend it. It's my man cave. I snatch a Ramen noodle wrapper from the dashboard and shove it in the plastic bag hanging from a radio knob. Welcome to my world, Ms. Carol.

We are comfortably quiet as we leave the campground except for the annoying question that keeps buzzing around in my mind. Finally, I ask, "Carol, how is it that you, you know, the first time we met... just invited me up to your house? I mean, I was some strange guy walking the beach."

"You seemed safe."

"Ouch. No man likes to be told he looks safe."

"But you were... you are."

"I suppose. I just don't like to hear it."

"I've been around long enough to make that call. Besides I recognized you from the Better Maid Potato Chip factory."

"Huh?"

"Yeah, you used to come in after school for a bag of hot potato chips just off the line."

"Oh, man those were delicious and only 10 cents. Wait a sec..." I could see the corner of her mouth turning up. She was waiting for me to make some kind of connection and she was enjoying it. A lot. "Whoa. You were the cute salesgirl with the blue eyes."

"Were? No woman likes to hear 'were cute.'"

Hitching around in her seat, she faces me full on, her eyes startling blue set in the gentle planes of her tanned face. "Your eyes. Those are your eyes!" I exclaim. "I lived in a world of brown-eyed women. You fascinated me."

"You could have said something."

"Teenaged boys aren't known for eloquence."

"Not like smooth-talking mature men saying, 'You used to be cute.'"

I duck my head—touché. Backfill, Nick. C'mon man. "Something just came to me. A couple days ago. On the beach. I recognized you, too. I just didn't realize it. It was your eyes." I cut a quick glance. Her face is coloring. She liked that. Whew. And now she's got a kind of self-satisfied grin working.

Can't let this get too heavy, too soon. As we come to a stop in her driveway, I stare at the lake for a moment. "Uhm, I just realized something else—you're why I get a warm feeling every time I smell French fries."

She gives me an arch look. A challenge, really, as if to say are you strong enough to face what you're feeling, mister? To embrace what's developing between us and not blow it off with a lame joke? Then, as I'm beginning to expect her to do, she provides the segue. "Have you ever been back there? In the neighborhood?"

"Naw. Just whizzing by on the freeway. That whole area was pretty sketchy even when we were kids. And I don't think it's been kept up since." She's cocking her head, eyebrow raised. She'd like to go down there, wouldn't she? With me? Ha! Let's see. "Uhm, you know, I've been thinking about a spec article for the Free Press, comparing open land in the UP to the vacant land in Detroit—the new frontier kind of thing. I'm heading there next."

Chapter Ten; Carol

There's my opening. Just have to ask to go along. I love it out here—the lake constantly changing colors and textures and moods. So open. Sometimes too open, too big. Makes me feel small and lonely... lately. Maybe when you've grown up in the city, you get used to limited horizons—jammed together houses, crisscrossed power lines. Like that time Maria brought a carload of her inner-city students out here for the day. They ran straight to the beach, sucked into the vacuum of no wind, no waves, total silence and miles of blue. Then like a flock of frightened birds, they flew back to the van and their iPods and cell phones, leaving the doors wide open but needing the car around them.

I study Nick. He's vaguely smiling, watching the cat paws swirl in the pre-storm ripples. "Could I come with you?"

He grins, "Sure. Get you an urban fix. There's too much space out here—the lake, the big empty house. You could get lost in it all."

Whoa! Are we tracking each other, or what? I open the van door and ask, "Want to come in and rattle around for a while or do you just want to snuggle in your cocoon?"

Chapter Eleven; Nick

Up in her third floor Widow Walk, I'm fascinated by a squall line charging out of the Southwest pushing a black line across the roiling gray waves and pewter clouds. Carol is next to me.

"Pretty spectacular," she murmurs.

"Nothing you'd see in East Side, Detroit."

"Not unless you went to Belle Isle. On hot muggy evenings, after a breathless day in our tiny house, my dad would pile us in the car and haul us out to the island and the Detroit River for a snatch of fresh air and a race into the chilly current coming down from Lake Huron."

"Huh. Us guys were more interested in taking girlfriends to Belle Isle after dark to watch the submarine races from the parking lot."

"I never got into that... good Catholic girl and all."

"Me neither, actually," I admit. "But it was good urban legend." We watch the rain sweep along the sand then pound against the glassed-in turret. I almost have to shout to be heard. "God that was a tense time—adolescence. So much posturing and self-consciousness."

I stare into the storm. Maybe it's the sky unloading, but I suddenly want to vent as well. "Lately, I find myself feeling like a second grader with a crush on a girl." I pause, grin to myself. "Angeline D'Angelo. God, I haven't thought of her in forever." Carol looks up, slightly amused, interested. "But I wasn't sure what to do with those feelings, what they should lead to. I guess what I'm trying to say is, now that I'm over... a little over... the hormone hump, I start to see women as something more than..."

Carol raises an eyebrow—yes, do go on.

I reach deep. I'm a writer. I can come up with words, appropriate words. "I'm starting to see women as more than

potential sex partners or, put more nobly, fellow collabora-
tors in the perpetuation of the human race."

Carol, howls with laughter.

"Well, I..."

Carol reaches for my hand, squeezes. "No, really, that
was a very sweet thought." Then she drops my hand, spins
away and guffaws once more. I look hurt, puzzled. She
puts her hand to her mouth and catches her breath. "I've
just never heard horniness, or rather, the lack thereof, described so clinically."

We stare at each other for another long moment. Is she
making fun of me? Did I sound that pretentious? She steps
closer and hugs me, tucking her head against my shoulder.
My, she fits nicely. We fit nicely. Then she pushes apart and
looks thoughtfully into my eyes. "And yes, I would really
like to go with you to haunt the old neighborhood and to
even watch submarine races on Belle Isle."

"It wouldn't be as exciting as back then."

"Not many things are. That doesn't mean it wouldn't be
enjoyable in its own way."

Why do I feel relieved and pumped at the same time?

Chapter Twelve; Carol

This guy! He's here and then he's there. Teasing... sort of. Acting sure of himself, then hesitant. This is exciting. There's so much to find out about Nick. What he's like when he gets mad; how he makes up. What he likes to eat. Does he like to cook? Is he Fox News or MSNBC? I like his sense of humor, especially when he's not trying to be funny. What does he need from me? What do I bring to the mix? God, I haven't done this in so long. What would Mario call it? Annual review. Yes, that was it. Every year we took stock and planned ahead for the business. But, we didn't do that with the marriage. I mean, who does, after a while? I almost forgot how much fun discovering one another could be. And if that isn't enough, we're going on a fun trip together. Perfect.

Chapter 13; Nick

We're cruising down Harper, just past Van Dyke in my van (The van was her idea. Maybe she didn't want to chance taking her BMW into this neighborhood). I know this is Harper because the street signs say so. But there are none of the landmarks: East Towne cinema, New York Carpet World, Thom McCann's, Federals. They're all gone. Missing teeth from a mile-long grin.

Crane. Our family street. No drug store on one corner. No Gulf gas station on the other. There are only six houses left on our block. My old house is gone. Uncle Roy's too. Just empty, overgrown lots. I park at the curb. After a bit, Carol says, "I wonder if this is what it's like to be really old—vivid memories with lots of spaces. Placeholders with no friends to fill them."

We go a couple more blocks and stop again. So strange. This is a corner that used to hold a thirty-five foot vacant lot. It used to be our *God's Little Half Acre* where we could hide in a forest of weeds, catch grasshoppers and study spider webs—green space between canyons of house fronts. Now, everything, as far as we can see, looks just like that lot. An occasional house dots the land like a *Little House on the Prairie*. But it's not really open land. It's gridded with streets and sewers and light poles. Overgrown shrubs, seemingly dropped out of nowhere, once defined parcel and plot. Equally strange, every so often, there's a brand-new home standing out like a volunteer sunflower in a cow pasture.

I point out a set of concrete steps, somehow left standing, on what used to be my Aunt Jenny's house. Carol and I climb the stairs and stand on the stoop. "I remember when they had these steps poured to the envy of all the neighbors." We turn in a circle surveying lots, fields, glimpses of a major intersection five blocks away that would never have been visible for all the structures in between. "You know what this feels like?" I ask.

"What?"

"Like I'm looking at a computer map. Streets with no houses or buildings and lots of green in between."

"I'm thinking something else," Carol remarks. "This feels like ground zero after Armageddon. Everybody left for the suburbs and now we can start all over again. This is a new frontier and we can either start farms or build more houses and businesses."

"So, which will it be?" I ask.

"Farms," she says, half-jokingly. "And we can spend the night in your covered wagon. If you pull it into one of these lots, it will look like it's just another abandoned junker."

"Hey!" I protest. But, I'm really quite pleased that we (or rather, she) worked out the tricky transition to our sleeping arrangements... for now and maybe later.

About the Author

A former corporate trainer and writing instructor, Joe Novara and his wife live in Kalamazoo, Michigan. Writings include novels, short stories, a memoir and various poems, anthologies and articles. He maintains a web/blog: Writing for Homeschooled Boys on his WordPress blog that includes his publication list.

WEBSITE: https://freefloatingstories.wordpress.com/
BLOG: http://joenovara.wordpress.com